序　言

　　首先，我們要感謝所有讀者對「學習出版有限公司」的支持與愛護，我們的「中高級英檢」系列，一直得到許多正面回應，讀者不斷問我們何時推出下一本全新的試題，他們想要在正式參加考試之前，多做一點練習，這樣的觀念非常正確，事前充分準備，就是成功之道。

　　英語是國際語言，所以通過「全民英語能力檢定」很重要，而取得「**中高級英檢證書**」的人，英語程度等同於「**大學非英語主修系所畢業**」。為了配合這項測驗，我們陸續推出了「中高級英檢 1000 字」、「中高級英語字彙 420 題」、「中高級英文法 480 題」、「中高級英語克漏字測驗」、「中高級英語閱讀測驗」、「中高級英語聽力檢定①②」，還有現在要出版的「中高級英語模擬試題①②」。每一本書各別針對不同的題型，都是很有練習價值的參考資料。

　　中高級英檢初試是在每年五月和十月舉辦，測驗內容分為兩部分，即聽力測驗和閱讀測驗。而「**中高級英語模擬試題 ②**」一共收錄四回完整的試題及詳解，每一回都分為聽力和閱讀兩部份，題型完全仿照全民英檢測驗，是準備報考中高級英檢者的必備書籍。

　　為了提供給讀者最正確的資料，書中所有試題都經專業外籍教師 Laura E. Stewart，及資深英語教師謝靜芳老師、陳威如老師，還有張碧紋老師審慎校對過，每一道題目都附有詳盡的解說及註釋，讓讀者能在最短的時間內，收事半功倍之效。另外，本書雖經審慎編校，但仍恐有疏漏之處，望各界先進不吝批評指教。

劉　毅

中高級英檢 高分秘訣

♠ Listening 聽力測驗

考聽力測驗最重要的秘訣就是「保持冷靜、保持清醒」，在考試時一定要聚精會神，把所有的注意力放在考卷上，愈專心、愈能聽懂題目內容。平心而論，英語畢竟不是母語，不常常練習聽，很容易就會聽不懂。建議考前至少要練習做四回完整的練習題，如果有多餘的準備時間，不妨多聽英語廣播節目，也會有所助益。

♥ Reading 閱讀能力測驗

閱讀測驗對一般的考生來說，應該是比較拿手的項目，全民英檢中心的網站上（http://www.gept.org.tw/）有公佈中高級參考字彙，除了做題目之外，把字彙弄懂也有助於增進閱讀能力。考試時，分秒必爭，看不懂的字可以先跳過去，因為只要了解整篇文章的大意，通常就足以作答了。

✦ Writing 寫作能力測驗

翻譯沒有什麼訣竅，就是考英文實力，要特別注意的是，翻完之後，要中英對照檢查一下，是否有把重要的名詞或連接詞翻譯出來，以免被扣分。至於作文部分，用字遣詞除了注意正確性之外，也要考慮到詞彙的難易度，寫中高級測驗的作文，當然不能像寫中級測驗一樣，如果從頭到尾都用簡單的字，恐怕較難拿到亮麗的分數。

♣ Speaking 口說能力測驗

口說測驗對所有人來說，恐怕都是最難的部分。根據作者觀察，要通過中高級口說能力測驗，其實並不難，只要你能儘量保持沉著，不必刻意用艱深的字彙回答，重點是流利與言之有物，還有不要因為緊張而停頓太久，記住，時間就是分數。

全民英語能力分級檢定測驗
GENERAL ENGLISH PROFICIENCY TEST
中高級聽力測驗
HIGH-INTERMEDIATE LISTENING COMPREHENSION TEST

This listening comprehension test will test your ability to understand spoken English. In this test, each conversation, short talk and question will be spoken JUST ONE TIME. They will not be written out for you. There are three parts to this test. Special instructions will be given to you at the beginning of each part.

Part A

In part A, you will hear 15 questions. After you hear a question, read the four choices in your test book and decide which one is the best answer to the question you have heard.

Example:

You will hear: Mary, can you tell me what time it is?

You will read: A. About two hours ago.
　　　　　　　　B. I used to be able to, but not now.
　　　　　　　　C. Sure, it's half past nine.
　　　　　　　　D. Today is October 22.

The best answer to the question "Mary, can you tell me what time it is?" is C: "Sure, it's half past nine." Therefore, you should choose answer C.

1. A. Before five.
   B. Two or three.
   C. Three hours.
   D. On the left.

2. A. Yes, I've seen it twice.
   B. I've heard about it.
   C. I saw it in a movie.
   D. Yes, many times.

3. A. I completely forgot.
   B. Nobody ever asked me.
   C. I had no idea.
   D. Yes, I don't think so.

4. A. He was too obese.
   B. He volunteered to.
   C. He wanted to join.
   D. He loves to read war novels.

5. A. I try my best to be there weekly.
   B. I do believe in God.
   C. They just renovated our church last month.
   D. I went on Christmas Eve last year.

6. A. That's OK. He doesn't mind.
   B. Nope, it's so boring.
   C. I fall asleep on the couch.
   D. You know, I really am.

7. A. We are out of toilet
      paper.
   B. The floor is all wet.
   C. Don't look at me.
   D. Maybe we need a pet.

8. A. Yes, I like Chinese New
      Year.
   B. It certainly is.
   C. I like the Moon Festival.
   D. The Dragon Boat races
      are pretty cool.

9. A. Noodles are delicious.
   B. Using chopsticks is
      great fun.
   C. Chinese history is
      thousands of years old.
   D. The Chinese invented
      paper.

10. A. Don't be late for
       class.
    B. The final exam is
       tomorrow.
    C. I think I can handle
       it.
    D. I have time to help
       you.

11. A. He graduated last
       spring.
    B. Here they come
       now.
    C. They argued and
       fought like dogs.
    D. They want to ask
       you a question.

Please turn to the next page. ⏩

12. A. We want more money.
    B. Our advisor says we go slowly.
    C. By the day after tomorrow, I hope.
    D. It's an exciting research project.

13. A. See Wall Street and the Statue of Liberty.
    B. Be careful, it's dangerous.
    C. Bring traveler's checks.
    D. I visited the "Big Apple" last year.

14. A. Fred paid his tuition.
    B. He cheated on an exam.
    C. He scored the winning goal.
    D Fred lost a wrestling match.

15. A. I'm going on vacation next week.
    B. It's really late.
    C. I'm leaving for sure.
    D. It's Friday, isn't it?

Part B

In part B, you will hear 15 conversations between a man and a woman. After each conversation, you will hear a question about the conversation. After you hear the question, read the four choices in your test book and choose the best answer to the question you have heard.

Example:

   You will hear: (Man)   May I see your driver's license?
                (Woman) Yes, officer. Here it is. Was I
                           speeding?
                (Man)   Yes, ma'am. You were doing sixty
                           in a forty-five-mile-an-hour zone.
                (Woman) No way! I don't believe you.
                (Man)   Well, it is true and here is your ticket.

                Question: Why does the man ask for the
                           woman's driver's license?

  You will read: A. She was going too fast.
                B. To check its limitations.
                C. To check her age.
                D. She entered a restricted zone.

The best answer to the question "Why does the man ask for the woman's driver's license?" is A: "She was going too fast." Therefore, you should choose answer A.

Please turn to the next page. ⟹

16. A. The man is punctual.
    B. She hates rush hours.
    C. The man exaggerates.
    D. The man is always late.

17. A. Excited and silly.
    B. Hot and sweaty.
    C. Funny and hungry.
    D. Romantic and shy.

18. A. In a prison.
    B. At an academic
       institution.
    C. At a foreign military
       base.
    D. At a government
       research center.

19. A. Never.
    B. She used to before.
    C. Not anymore.
    D. Not really.

20. A. Forgive everybody.
    B. Just forget about it.
    C. Don't be encouraged.
    D. Study and improve.

21. A. Not complete.
    B. Not satisfactory.
    C. Scary and
       unorganized.
    D. Unfinished.

22. A. To get noticed.
    B. To look like
       everyone else.
    C. To rebel and be
       different.
    D. To catch everyone's
       eye.

23. A. To walk with him.
    B. To go outside
       together.
    C. A question from
       him.
    D. A date with the man.

24. A. A thunderstorm.
    B. A hailstorm.
    C. A weather vane.
    D. A windstorm.

25. A. The works touch him deeply.
    B. The museum is touching.
    C. The paintings are so real.
    D. The sculptures seem alive.

26. A. Suicide is a disease.
    B. It's a benevolence.
    C. Committing suicide is terrible.
    D. Those people are mentally sick.

27. A. At a stationery shop.
    B. At the post office.
    C. At a bookstore.
    D. At a stamp exhibition.

28. A. He's keeping it a secret.
    B. He's 20 years old.
    C. He's one year old.
    D. He's 25 years old.

29. A. Not very well.
    B. Of course she can.
    C. She's scared of him.
    D. She's worried to death.

30. A. Shooting stars are mysterious.
    B. Shooting stars can teach you magic.
    C. If you see a shooting star, make a wish.
    D. Shooting stars bring daydreams.

Please turn to the next page. ⬛⟹

Part C

In part C, you will hear several short talks. After each talk, you will hear 2 to 3 questions about the talk. After you hear each question, read the four choices in your test book and choose the best answer to the question you have heard.

Example:

<u>You will hear:</u>

Thank you for coming to this, the first in a series of seminars on the use of computers in the classroom. As the brochure informed you, there will be a total of five seminars given in this room every Monday morning from 6:00 to 7:30. Our goal will be to show you, the teachers of our schoolchildren, how the changing technology of today can be applied to the unchanging lessons of yesterday to make your students' learning experience more interesting and relevant to the world they live in. By the end of the last seminar, you will not be computer literate, but you will be able to make sense of the hundreds of complex words and technical terms related to the field and be aware of the programs available for use in the classroom.

Question number 1: What is the subject of this seminar series?

You will read: A. Self-improvement.
B. Using computers to teach.
C. Technology.
D. Study habits of today's students.

The best answer to the question "What is the subject of this seminar series?" is B: "Using computers to teach." Therefore, you should choose answer B.

Now listen to another question based on the same talk.

You will hear:

Question number 2: What does the speaker say participants will be able to do after attending the seminars?

You will read: A. Understand today's students.
B. Understand computer terminology.
C. Motivate students.
D. Deal more confidently with people.

The best answer to the question "What does the speaker say participants will be able to do after attending the seminars?" is B: "Understand computer terminology." Therefore, you should choose answer B.

Please turn to the next page. ⟹

31. A. Leo.

    B. Horoscope.

    C. Aquarius.

    D. P's and Q's.

32. A. An exciting trip abroad.

    B. Diligence is required.

    C. Possible marriage plans.

    D. Great progress and good

    luck.

33. A. Chinese New Year.

    B. To improve cash flow.

    C. A new marketing

    campaign.

    D. There is no mention in

    this advertisement.

34. A. A free massage.

    B. A gourmet dinner.

    C. Free shopping

    coupons.

    D. A breakfast buffet.

35. A. The V.I.P. suite.

    B. A family

    dormitory.

    C. A deluxe twin

    bed.

    D. A business suite.

36. A. Eight percent.

    B. Eighty percent.

    C. Eighteen percent.

    D. Six to ten inches.

37. A. Morning showers only.

    B. Skies clearing up.

    C. Northeast winds coming.

    D. More wet weather.

38. A. It's informal and

       flexible.

    B. It's classical.

    C. It utilizes music.

    D. It follows tradition.

39. A. The teacher.

    B. Dancing manuals.

    C. The dancer.

    D. Imitating ballet.

40. A. The big studios.

    B. The front-runners.

    C. Nobody knows.

    D. A few big stars.

Please turn to the next page. ⏸⟹

41. A. Television shows.
    B. Movie entertainment.
    C. Theater revenues.
    D. Retiring actors.

42. A. A patient.
    B. A customer at a pharmacy.
    C. A chemist.
    D. A dermatologist.

43. A. Six.
    B. Two.
    C. Three.
    D. Twenty.

44. A. Find and clear minefields.
    B. Help dig up old weapons.
    C. Eliminate deadly chemicals.
    D. Help get rid of pollution.

45. A. It has a higher IQ.
    B. It's light.
    C. It has a keen sense of touch.
    D. It's extremely sensitive.

-The End-

中 高 級 閱 讀 測 驗

HIGH-INTERMEDIATE

READING COMPREHENSION TEST

This test has three parts, with 50 multiple-choice questions (each with four choices) in total. Special directions will be provided for each part. You will have 50 minutes to complete this test.

Part A: Sentence Completion

This part of the test has 15 incomplete sentences. Beneath each sentence, you will see four words or phrases, marked A, B, C and D. You are to choose the word or phrase that best completes the sentences. Then on your answer sheet, find the number of the question and mark your answer.

1. Sophia is a celebrated herbalist, who is proficient at
   _____.

   A. investigation
   B. acupuncture
   C. surgery
   D. operation

Please turn to the next page. ⟹

2. If the "morning-after pill" proves to be truly _____ and 100 percent effective as claimed, it will be placed on the market.
   A. notorious
   B. nonaligned
   C. nondairy
   D. nontoxic

3. The sanitation department of this company is very _____. No wonder the workmen there are well-paid.
   A. sufficient
   B. impatient
   C. efficient
   D. incompetent

4. Large factories pour tons of _____ into the air every day, which causes the serious air pollution.
   A. salary
   B. soot
   C. intense
   D. pore

5. Trash is not allowed to _____ in large amounts on the sidewalk for fear of making our environment dirty.
   A. translate
   B. circulate
   C. communicate
   D. accumulate

6. The couple quarreled a lot, and at last, they decided to
   get _____.
   A. divorced
   B. married
   C. single
   D. widowed

7. I tried to bake bread on my own yesterday. _____ speaking,
   I found it was not as difficult as most people believe.
   A. Frankly
   B. Amazingly
   C. Civilly
   D. Recklessly

8. We were sorry to see that Mr. Smith's eyes were bloodshot
   and teary, his hand shook when he lit a cigarette, and he
   coughed _____.
   A. bluffly
   B. gutlessly
   C. incessantly
   D. ordinarily

Please turn to the next page. ⫿⟹

9. Admit what you've done wrong. _____ like a man.
  A. Take your medicine
  B. Shave off your beard
  C. Put your foot down
  D. Pull your rank

10. When Father got my transcript with poor grades, he _____.
  A. lifted off
  B. came to life
  C. went on the rampage
  D. refreshed his memory

11. Grandfather is already 65 years old and he is going to _____ next month.
  A. be in my shoes
  B. be caught with his pants down
  C. turn his coat
  D. hang up his hat

12. This dam along with the four or five other dams along the river _____ part of the network of hydroelectric plants.
  A. form
  B. forms
  C. forming
  D. are formed

13. The doctor told me _____ private that the invalid will

    die in three weeks.

    A. with

    B. for

    C. of

    D. in

14. Peter was in a difficult situation. However, I couldn't help

    him, _____ I did pity him.

    A. for that

    B. not but that

    C. but that

    D. now that

15. Edward is such an reliable man. His conduct has always

    been _____ suspicion.

    A. below

    B. onto

    C. above

    D. into

Please turn to the next page. ⟹

Part B: Cloze

This part of the test has two passages. Each passage contains seven or eight missing words or phrases. There is a total of 15 missing words or phrases. Beneath each passage, you will see seven or eight items with four choices, marked A, B, C and D. You are to choose the best answer for each missing word or phrase in the two passages. Then, on your answer sheet, find the number of the question and mark your answer.

<u>Questions 16-22</u>

Nanotechnology is a field of research and innovation ___(16)___ building "things" — generally, materials and devices — on the scale of atoms and molecules. A nanometre is one-billionth of a metre: ten times the diameter of a hydrogen atom. The diameter of a human hair is, ___(17)___, 80,000 nanometres. At such scales, the ordinary rules of physics and chemistry no longer apply. For instance, materials' ___(18)___, such as their color, strength, conductivity and reactivity, can differ substantially between the nanoscale and the macro. Carbon "nanotubes" are ___(19)___ steel but six times lighter.

Nanotechnology is hailed ___(20)___ having the potential to increase the efficiency of energy consumption, help clean the environment, and solve major health problems. It is said to be able to massively increase manufacturing production ____(21)____

significantly reduced costs. Products of nanotechnology will be

smaller, cheaper, lighter ____(22)____ more functional and require

less energy and fewer raw materials to manufacture, claim

nanotech advocates.

16. A. cooperated with
    B. communicated with
    C. concerned with
    D. content with

20. A. to
    B. as
    C. for
    D. of

17. A. on all fours
    B. on average
    C. on an errand
    D. on credit

21. A. at
    B. for
    C. by
    D. off

18. A. citizens
    B. subconscious
    C. ghostwriters
    D. characteristics

22. A. very
    B. so
    C. instead
    D. yet

19. A. 100 times stronger than
    B. stronger than 100 times
    C. 100 times strong than
    D. strong than 100 times

Please turn to the next page. ▐⟹

Questions 23-30

An international brand of orange soda defended its image after reports claimed it contained a cancer-causing ___(23)___. The company that produces the drink acknowledged that trace amounts of the carcinogen benzene could be found in its product ___(24)___ it wasn't enough to harm people. Next time you take a sip of soda, take a look at the ingredients first. Some drinks contain the additives vitamin C and Sodium Benzoate, but when the two meet, they break down to form a ___(25)___. Benzene certainly causes cancer in humans, said a famous doctor. It can cause leukemia and other blood-related cancers in children. This fact ___(26)___ in a 1993 study.

Even more worrying is the fact that these two additives are often found together in fruit juices and jams. Children are especially ___(27)___ because their blood stream detoxification systems are not mature enough. And the amount of benzene in food increases when it reaches room temperature. In terms of the risk benzene poses, currently no amount is deemed ___(28)___. So the lower the exposure, the lower the risk. Usually it accumulates over time, so it might take 10 or 20 years to happen. So does the soda pose a risk? Coca Cola, which produces the drink, released a statement saying that the drink had recently pass tests by US and British health authorities ___(29)___ it adheres to Taiwanese health regulations. The company also said it was aware that benzene could be found in its product but that the amounts were so small, which posed no health threat.

As there is not enough evidence that such small amounts are harmful, stores in Taiwan say they will not take the product off their shelves. But they said they will ___(30)___ immediately if the Department of Health's food safety section confirms there is a risk.

23. A. persistence
    B. consequence
    C. instance
    D. substance

24. A. but that
    B. so that
    C. in order that
    D. in that

25. A. carbohydrate
    B. carcinogen
    C. DNA
    D. amylum

26. A. established
    B. establishing
    C. was established
    D. was to establish

27. A. at risk
    B. at peace
    C. at odds
    D. at the zenith

28. A. safety
    B. safely
    C. safe
    D. being safe

29. A. and
    B. that
    C. and that
    D. but

30. A. supply
    B. comply
    C. apply
    D. reply

Please turn to the next page. ▐⇨

Part C: Reading

In this part of the test, you will read several passages. Each passage is followed by several questions. There is a total of 20 questions. You are to choose the best answer, A, B, C or D, to each question on the basis of what is stated or implied in the passage. Then on your answer sheet, find the number of the question and mark your answer.

<u>Questions 31-35</u>

Treasure hunts have excited people's imagination for hundreds of years both in real life and in books such as Robert Louis Stevenson's *Treasure Island*. Kit Williams, a modern writer, had the idea of combining the real excitement of a treasure hunt with clues found in a book when he wrote a children's story, *Masquerade*, in 1979. The book was about a hare, and a month before it came out Williams buried a golden hare in a park in Bedfordshire. The book contained a large number of clues to help readers find the hare, but Williams put in a lot of "red herrings", or false clues, to mislead <u>them</u>.

Ken Roberts, the man who found the hare, had been looking for it for nearly two years. Although he had been searching in the wrong area for most of the time, he found it by logic, not by luck. His success came from the fact that he had gained an important clue at the start. He had realized that the words: "One of Six to Eight" under the first picture in the book connected the hare in some way to Katherine of Aragon, the first of Henry VIII's six wives. Even here, however, Williams had succeeded in misleading him. Ken knew that Katherine of Aragon had died at Kimbolton in Cambridgeshire in 1536 and thought that Williams had buried the hare there. He had been digging there for over a year before a new idea occurred to him. He found out that Kit Williams had spent his childhood near Ampthill, in Bedfordshire, and thought that he must have buried the hare in a place he knew well, but he still could not see the connection with Katherine of Aragon, until one day he came across two stone crosses in Ampthill Park and learnt that they had been built in her honor in 1773.

Even then his search had not come to an end. It was only after he had spent several nights digging around the cross that he decided to write to Kit Williams to find out if he was wasting his time there. Williams encouraged him to continue, and on February 24th 1982, he found the treasure. It was worth $3,000, but the excitement it had caused since its burial made it much more valuable.

31. The underlined word "them" in paragraph one refers to
    A. red herrings.   B. treasure hunts.
    C. Henry VIII's six wives.   D. readers of Masquerade.

Please turn to the next page. ▯⟹

32. What is the most important clue in the beginning to help Ken Roberts find the hare?
    A. Two stone crosses in Ampthill.
    B. Stevenson's Treasure Island.
    C. Katherine of Aragon.
    D. Williams' hometown.

33. The stone crosses in Ampthill were built
    A. to tell about what happened in 1773.
    B. to show respect for Henry VIII's first wife.
    C. to serve as a road sign in Ampthill Park.
    D. to inform people where the golden hare was.

34. Which of the following describes Roberts' logic in searching for the hare?
    a. Herny VIII's six wives.
    b. Katherine's burial place at Kimbolton.
    c. Williams' childhood in Ampthill.
    d. Katherine of Aragon.
    e. Stone crosses in Ampthill Park.
    A. a-b-c-e-d   B. d-b-c-e-a
    C. a-d-b-c-e   D. b-a-e-c-d

35. What is the subject discussed in the text?
    A. An exciting historical event.
    B. A modern treasure hunt.
    C. The attraction of Masquerade.
    D. The importance of logical thinking.

Questions 36-38

"American dream? What a lie!" this comment was made by a Cuban teenage girl. She was attending a huge protest in Havana, Cuba, against American immigration laws.

Tens of thousands of people, including Cuba's President, took part in the protest to remember 30 missing Cubans, including 13 children.

Their boat was lost in the Florida Straits after setting out from Cuba. It is one of the worst accidents involving Cubans being smuggled into the US. Fourteen people died in the sinking of a smuggler's boat in 1998, and about 40 people died in 1994 when a tugboat sank near Havana. People believe that the "Cuban Adjustment Act" is responsible for the 30 people disappearing.

This 1996 law gives special allowances to Cuban immigrants who reach the US by whatever means. It gives them resident's status and chances to work. It is very different from the US policy to immigrants from other countries. Because it encourages illegal immigration and these types of accidents, some called "the murderous law".

The US uses the so-called "dry foot" rule. Those found at sea are sent back to Cuba. But those who set foot on US soil are generally allowed to stay.

Please turn to the next page.

Castro said that the law encourages Cubans to undertake dangerous sea journeys with the hope of living in the US.

The immigration policy of the US has caused many problems between the US and Cuba. The two countries plan to meet to discuss immigration issues.

36. Why did so many people attend the protest?
   A. Because their children were missing.
   B. Because they were not allowed to enter the US.
   C. Because they wanted to come back to their homeland.
   D. Because they were against American immigration laws.

37. Why did so many people want to smuggle into the US?
   A. They wanted to live a better life there.
   B. They were treated well in their country.
   C. They had relatives in the US.
   D. The Americans were very friendly.

38. What is the result of "Cuban Adjustment Act"?
   A. The two countries never plan to meet.
   B. It is very quite the same as the US policy to immigrants from other countries.
   C. Those who set foot on the US soil or at sea are generally allowed to stay.
   D. It encourages Cubans to undertake dangerous sea journeys.

Questions 39-43

If you are ever lucky enough to be invited to a formal dinner party in Paris, remember that the French have their own way of doing things, and that even your finest manners may not be "correct" by French customs. For example, if you think showing up promptly at the time given on the invitation, armed with gifts of wine and roses, complimenting your hostess on her cooking, laughing heartily at the host's jokes and then leaping up to help the hostess will make you the perfect guest, think again.

Here Madame Nora Chabal, the marketing director of the Ritz Hotel in Paris, explained how it works.

The first duty of the guest is to respond to the invitation within 48 hours. Also, the guest may not ask to bring a guest because the hostess has chosen her own.

Flowers sent in advance are the preferred gift. They may also be sent afterwards with a thank-you note. It is considered a bad form to arrive with a gift of flowers in hand, which forces the hostess to find a vase when she is too busy to deal with it. See, that's the logic! The type of flowers sent has a code of its own, too.

Please turn to the next page. ⟹

One must never send chrysanthemums because they are considered too humble a flower for the occasion. Carnations are considered bad luck, and calla lilies are too reminiscent of funerals. A bouquet of red roses is a declaration of romantic intent. Don't send those unless you mean it — and never to a married hostess. Though the French love wine, you must never bring a bottle to a dinner party. It's as if you feared your hosts would not have enough wine on hand, and that's an insult. You may, however, offer a box of chocolates which the hostess will pass around after dinner with coffee.

If an invitation is for eight o'clock, the <u>considerate</u> guest arrives at 8:15. Guests who arrive exactly on time or early are merely thoughtless ones who are not giving the hostess those last few minutes she needs to deal with details and any crisis. The "correct" guest arrives between 15 to 20 minutes after the hour because dinner will be served exactly 30 minutes past the time on the invitation.

39. Which of the following statements is RIGHT according to the French custom?
　A. When you receive an invitation, reply to it within two days. You'd better send flowers in advance.
　B. Arrive exactly on time at the dinner party.
　C. Bring a bottle of good wine to the dinner party.
　D. Telephone to ask if you can bring a good friend to the party.

Please turn to the next page.

40. Which of the following is RIGHT about sending flowers?
    A. If someone is dead, send chrysanthemums or calla lilies.
    B. If someone is ill in hospital, send carnations.
    C. If you are invited to a dinner party, send red roses to the hostess.
    D. If you are in love with someone, send red roses.

41. If you are too busy to send flowers in advance, what should you do?
    A. Bring a bouquet of flowers when you go to the party.
    B. Send a bouquet of flowers afterwards with a thank-you note.
    C. Bring a bottle of wine instead of a bouquet of flowers.
    D. The hostess will never mind if you send flowers or not.

42. What does the word "<u>considerate</u>" in the last paragraph mean?
    A. 尊敬的　　　　　　　　B. 值得考慮的
    C. 考慮周到的　　　　　　D. 相當多的

43. What is the passage mainly about?
    A. How to hold a dinner party.
    B. How to send flowers.
    C. Good manners at a French dinner party.
    D. Different countries have different manners.

Please turn to the next page.

Questions 44-47

Easter, the principal festival of the Christian, celebrates the Resurrection of Jesus Christ on the third day after his Crucifixion. The origins of Easter date to the beginnings of Christianity, and it is probably the oldest Christian observance after the Sabbath (originally observed on Saturday, later on Sunday). Later, the Sabbath came to be regarded as the weekly celebration of the Resurrection. Meanwhile, many cultural historians find in the celebration of Easter a convergence of three traditions — Pagan, Hebrew and Christian.

According to St. Bede, an English historian of the early 8th century, Easter, derived from the name "Eostre", owes its origin to the old Teutonic mythology. Eostre was celebrated at the <u>vernal equinox</u>, when day and night get an equal share of the day. The English name "Easter" is much newer. When the early English Christians wanted others to accept Christianity, they decided to use the name Easter for this holiday so that it would match the name of the old spring celebration.

It was during Passover in 30 AD that Christ was crucified under the order of the Roman governor Pontius Pilate as the Jewish high priests accused Jesus of "blasphemy". The resurrection came three days later, on the Easter Sunday. Thus the early Christian Passover turned out to be a unitive celebration in memory of the passion-death-resurrection of Jesus. However,

R

by the 4th century, Good Friday came to be observed as a separate occasion. And the Pascha (Passover) Sunday had been devoted exclusively to the honor of the glorious resurrection.

Throughout Christendom the Sunday of Pascha had become a holiday to honor Christ. At the same time many pagan spring rites came to be a part of its celebration. Despite all the influence there was an important shift. No more glorification of the physical return of the Sun God. Instead, the emphasis was shifted to the Son of Righteousness who had won, banishing the horrors of death forever.

The Feast of Easter was well-established by the second century. But there had been dispute over the exact date of the Easter observance between the Eastern and Western Churches. The East wanted to have it on a weekday because early Christians observed Passover every year on the 14th of Nisan, the month based on the lunar calendar. But, the West wanted Easter to always be a Sunday regardless of the date.

To solve this problem the emperor Constantine called the Council of Nicaea in 325. The council decided that Easter should fall on Sunday following the first full moon after the vernal equinox. Fixing the date of the Equinox was still a

Please turn to the next page. ▢⟹

problem. The Alexandrians, noted for their rich knowledge in astronomical calculations were given the task. March 21 was made out to be the perfect date for spring equinox.

Accordingly, churches in the West observe it on the first day of the full moon that occurs on or following the Spring equinox on March 21. It became a movable feast between March 21 and April 25. Still some churches in the East observe Easter according to the date of the Passover festival. The preparation takes off as early as Ash Wednesday from which the period of penitence in the Lent begins. Lent and Holy Week end on Easter Sunday, the day of the resurrection.

44. This passage is mainly about
    A. a ritual held by a bishop.
    B. a regular service on Christmas.
    C. an admiration made by disciples.
    D. a principal festival for Christians.

45. The underlined words "vernal equinox" mean
    A. 滿月.　　B. 春分.　　C. 弦月.　　D. 秋分.

46. When did Good Friday come to be observed as a separate occasion?
    A. Early 8th century.　　B. 30 AD.
    C. By the 4th century.　　D. In 2006 AD.

47. What date on earth is Easter?

 A. On any Sunday.

 B. During the spring break.

 C. On the same day as April Fool's Day.

 D. Between March 21 and April 25.

Questions 48-50

A fish ladder provides a way for adult fish to go around dams or man-made barriers on their journey upstream to their spawning grounds.

The Corps first built a fish ladder at the locks in 1917. In 1976, the Corps of Engineers constructed a new, improved fish ladder using 21 steps (weirs) instead of just 10. The additional weirs reduce the distance that fish have to jump. Tunnels through each weir were also added. Both improvements make passage through the ladder easier for fish.

The Corps also increased the amount of water going through the fish ladder, called attraction water. Attraction water is swift-flowing water that moves in the opposite

Please turn to the next page.

direction that the fish climb. Because returning salmon instinctively know to swim upstream, the downstream movement of water attracts fish to the ladder, as does the "smell" of the water from the salmon's birthplace stream.

48. This passage is mainly about
    A. a tool invented by a fisherman.
    B. a device designed for salmon.
    C. a dam built in ancient times.
    D. a stream polluted seriously.

49. What are the two improvements for fish to pass through the ladder more easily?
    A. Extra baits and water.
    B. A large amount of capital and labor.
    C. Tunnels and additional weirs.
    D. An artificial ladder and a power plant.

50. What is NOT a feature of attraction water?
    A. Slowly-flowing.
    B. Rapidly-moving.
    C. Opposite-flowing.
    D. Swift-flowing.

-The End-

中高級聽力測驗詳解 ①

PART A

1. (**B**) How many more exits before we turn off?
    A. Before five.   B. Two or three.
    C. Three hours.   D. On the left.
    * exit〔'εksɪt〕*n.* 出口
    turn off 離開（某路）轉向另一條路

2. (**D**) Have you ever been to Disney World amusement park?
    A. Yes, I've seen it twice.
    B. I've heard about it.
    C. I saw it in a movie.
    D. Yes, many times.
    * amusement (ə'mjuzmənt) *n.* 娛樂
    Disney World amusement park 迪士尼樂園
    twice〔twaɪs〕*adv.* 兩次   ***hear about*** 聽說

3. (**C**) Didn't you know that our homeroom teacher was
    pregnant?
    A. I completely forgot.
    B. Nobody ever asked me.
    C. I had no idea.
    D. Yes, I don't think so.
    * ***homeroom teacher*** 導師
    pregnant〔'prεgnənt〕*adj.* 懷孕的
    completely (kəm'plitlɪ) *adv.* 完全地

4.(**A**) Why didn't your cousin serve in the military?

    A. He was too obese.

    B. He volunteered to.

    C. He wanted to join.

    D. He loves to read war novels.

    * cousin〔'kʌzn̩〕 *n.* 表（堂）兄弟姊妹

      serve〔sɜv〕 *v.* 服兵役   military〔'mɪlə,tɛrɪ〕 *n.* 軍隊

      serve in the military 服兵役

      obese〔o'bis〕 *adj.* 肥胖的

      volunteer〔,vɑlən'tɪr〕 *v.* 自願

5.(**A**) Do you attend church on a regular basis?

    A. I try my best to be there weekly.

    B. I do believe in God.

    C. They just renovated our church last month.

    D. I went on Christmas Eve last year.

    * attend〔ə'tɛnd〕 *v.* 上（學、教堂）

      attend church 做禮拜   regular〔'rɛgjələ〕 *adj.* 規律的

      basis〔'besɪs〕 *n.* 基礎；原則   ***on a~basis*** 以~的原則

      believe in 相信~的存在   renovate〔'rɛnə,vet〕 *v.* 翻新

6.(**D**) Aren't you tired of watching TV all day long?

    A. That's OK. He doesn't mind.

    B. Nope, it's so boring.

    C. I fall asleep on the couch.

    D. You know, I really am.

    * ***be tired of*** 厭倦   nope〔nop〕 *adv.* 不是

      fall asleep 睡著   couch〔kautʃ〕 *n.* 沙發

7. (**C**) Who made this awful mess in the bathroom?

    A. We are out of toilet paper.

    B. The floor is all wet.

    C. Don't look at me.

    D. Maybe we need a pet.

    * awful (ˈɔful) *adj.* 可怕的　　mess (mɛs) *n.* 亂七八糟
    be out of 沒有~　　toilet (ˈtɔɪlɪt) *n.* 廁所；浴室
    toilet paper 衛生紙

8. (**B**) Is Christmas your favorite western holiday?

    A. Yes, I like Chinese New Year.

    B. It certainly is.

    C. I like the Moon Festival.

    D. The Dragon Boat races are pretty cool.

    * western (ˈwɛstən) *adj.* 西方的
    certainly (ˈsɜtn̩lɪ) *adv.* 當然
    the Moon Festival 中秋節
    the Dragon Boat race 龍舟賽

9. (**B**) Which Chinese custom do foreigners enjoy most?

    A. Noodles are delicious.

    B. Using chopsticks is great fun.

    C. Chinese history is thousands of years old.

    D. The Chinese invented paper.

    * custom (ˈkʌstəm) *n.* 習俗
    foreigner (ˈfɔrɪnɚ) *n.* 外國人
    noodle (ˈnudl̩) *n.* 麵
    chopsticks (ˈtʃɑp‚stɪks) *n. pl.* 筷子
    invent (ɪnˈvɛnt) *v.* 發明

10. (**C**) Do you think you can afford their tuition rates?

  A. Don't be late for class.

  B. The final exam is tomorrow.

  C. I think I can handle it.

  D. I have time to help you.

  * afford (ə'fɔrd) v. 付得起

   tuition (tju'ɪʃən) n. 學費

   rate (ret) n. 費用　　*final exam* 期末考

   handle ('hændl̩) v. 處理；應付

11. (**C**) Please don't exaggerate. Just tell me what they did.

  A. He graduated last spring.

  B. Here they come now.

  C. They argued and fought like dogs.

  D. They want to ask you a question.

  * exaggerate (ɪg'zædʒə,ret) v. 誇張

   graduate ('grædʒu,et) v. 畢業　　argue ('argju) v. 爭執

   fight (faɪt) v. 打架 (三態變化是：fight-fought-fought)

12. (**C**) When will your project be completed?

  A. We want more money.

  B. Our advisor says we go slowly.

  C. By the day after tomorrow, I hope.

  D. It's an exciting research project.

  * project ('prɑdʒɛkt) n. 計畫

   complete (kəm'plit) v. 完成

   advisor (əd'vaɪzə) n. 顧問；導師

   research (rɪ'sɜtʃ) n. 研究

13. (**A**) What places should I visit in New York?

    A. See Wall Street and the Statue of Liberty.

    B. Be careful, it's dangerous.

    C. Bring traveler's checks.

    D. I visited the "Big Apple" last year.

    * *Wall Street* 華爾街 (位於紐約市，爲美國金融中心)

    statue (ˈstætʃʊ) *n.* 雕像   liberty (ˈlɪbɚtɪ) *n.* 自由

    the Statue of Liberty 自由女神像

    traveler's check 旅行支票

    the Big Apple 大蘋果 (指紐約市)

14. (**B**) Why was Fred thrown out of school?

    A. Fred paid his tuition.

    B. He cheated on an exam.

    C. He scored the winning goal.

    D. Fred lost a wrestling match.

    * *throw out* 撞出   cheat (tʃit) *v.* 作弊

    score (skor) *v.* 得分   goal (gol) *n.* 分數

    score a goal 得分   wrestling (ˈrɛslɪŋ) *n.* 摔角

    match (mætʃ) *n.* 比賽

15. (**C**) Are you working overtime or going home?

    A. I'm going on vacation next week.

    B. It's really late.

    C. I'm leaving for sure.

    D. It's Friday, isn't it?

    * overtime (ˈovɚˌtaɪm) *adv.* 超時地   *work overtime* 加班

    go on vacation 去渡假   *for sure* 一定

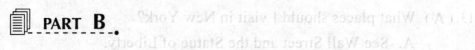

PART B

16. (**D**) M : Sorry I'm so late.

W : I'm used to it.

M : Hey, give me a break! I was caught in a traffic jam.

W : I'm getting tired of the same old excuse.

M : Believe it or not, it's the truth!

Question : Why is the woman a little upset?

A. The man is punctual.

B. She hates rush hours.

C. The man exaggerates.

D. The man is always late.

* **be used to** 習慣於～   **give me a break** 饒了我
be caught in 遇到   **traffic jam** 交通阻塞
get tired of 厭倦～   excuse (ɪk'skjus) n. 藉口
believe it or not 信不信由你
punctual ('pʌŋktʃuəl) adj. 準時的
rush hours 尖峰時間

17. (**A**) W : Could I please have a piece?

M : Go ahead. Be my guest.

W : Mmm! It's delicious! Chocolate drives me crazy!

M : They say it's an aphrodisiac.

W : Want to kiss and find out?

Question : How does the woman feel?

A. Excited and silly.   B. Hot and sweaty.

C. Funny and hungry.   D. Romantic and shy.

* piece〔pis〕n. (一) 片   **Go ahead.** 請便。

Be my guest. 我請客。；不要客氣。

drive sb. crazy 使某人發瘋

aphrodisiac〔,æfrə'dızı,æk〕n. 春藥；催情藥

silly〔'sılı〕adj. 愚蠢的

sweaty〔'swɛtı〕adj. 流汗的；費力的

romantic〔ro'mæntık〕adj. 浪漫的

shy〔ʃaı〕adj. 害羞的

18. (**B**) M：I can't believe it's almost over.

W：Me either. Four years of hard work.

M：Only two weeks to go and I'll get a diploma.

W：Yup. But we still have to get through our finals.

M：That'll be a piece of cake! No sweat!

Question：Where are they talking?

A. In a prison.

B. At an academic institution.

C. At a foreign military base.

D. At a government research center.

* **to go** 還有；剩下 (~時間、距離等)

diploma〔dı'plomə〕n. 文憑

yup〔jʌp〕adv. 是的   **get through** 通過考試

final〔'faınḷ〕n. 期末考   **a piece of cake** 容易的事

No sweat! 沒問題！   prison〔'prızn〕n. 監獄

academic〔,ækə'dɛmık〕adj. 學術的

institution〔,ınstə'tjuʃən〕n. 機構   base〔bes〕n. 基地

government〔'gʌvənmənt〕n. 政府

center〔'sɛntə〕n. 中心

19. (**D**) W: This Mongolian hot pot is bland.

M: Are you nuts? It's scrumptious!

W: I disagree. I feel it's missing something.

M: Beggars can't be choosers.

W: I'm not complaining; I'm just giving an opinion.

Question: Does the woman like it?

A. Never.

B. She used to before.

C. Not anymore.

D. Not really.

* Mongolian〔mɑŋˋgolɪən〕*adj.* 蒙古（人）的
  hot pot 火鍋　　bland〔blænd〕*adj.* 淡的
  nuts〔nʌts〕*adj.* 發瘋的
  scrumptious〔ˋskrʌmpʃəs〕*adj.* 極好的；很好吃的
  disagree〔͵dɪsəˋgri〕*v.* 不同意
  miss〔mɪs〕*v.* 漏掉　　beggar〔ˋbɛgɚ〕*n.* 乞丐
  chooser〔ˋtʃuzɚ〕*n.* 選擇者
  Beggars can't be choosers.【諺】乞丐沒有挑嘴的份。
  complain〔kəmˋplen〕*v.* 抱怨
  opinion〔əˋpɪnjən〕*n.* 意見　　***used to*** 以前常常

20. (**B**) M: My first day was a disaster.

W: Don't be so hard on yourself.

M: But it really was!

W: Put it behind you; it's water under the bridge.

M: You're right. Tomorrow is a brand new day.

Question: What is the woman's advice?

A. Forgive everybody.　　B. Just forget about it.

C. Don't be encouraged.　　D. Study and improve.

* disaster〔dız'æstə〕n. 災難；失敗

 be hard on 苛刻對待～

 put sth. **behind** sb. 把～置於腦後

 water under the bridge 不可改變的既成事實

 a brand new day 嶄新的一天

 forgive〔fə'gıv〕v. 原諒

 encourage〔ın'kɜıdȝ〕v. 鼓勵

 improve〔ım'pruv〕v. 改善

21. (**B**)　W: Hi, Professor. I'm here for our appointment.

　　　　M: Please have a seat. I have some comments on
　　　　　　your essay.

　　　　W: Did I pass?

　　　　M: Not yet. You need to rewrite it.

　　　　W: I was afraid of that.

　　　　Question: How was the essay?

　　　　A. Not complete.　　　B. Not satisfactory.

　　　　C. Scary and unorganized.　D. Unfinished.

* professor〔prə'fɛsə〕n. 教授

 appointment〔ə'pɔıntmənt〕n.（晤談的）約定

 comment〔'kɑmɛnt〕n. 評論　　essay〔'ɛse〕n. 短文

 rewrite〔ri'raıt〕v. 重寫

 complete〔kəm'plit〕adj. 完整的

 satisfactory〔,sætıs'fæktərı〕adj. 令人滿意的

 scary〔'skɛrı〕adj. 可怕的

 unorganized〔ʌn'ɔrgən,aızd〕adj. 沒有組織的

22. (**B**) M: Joe looks ridiculous!

W: Yes, doesn't he?

M: How could he dye his hair blue?

W: Maybe he just wants attention.

M: I think he's going through a rebellious phase.

Question: Which is NOT a reason for what Joe did?

A. To get noticed.

B. To look like everyone else.

C. To rebel and be different.

D. To catch everyone's eye.

* ridiculous (rɪ'dɪkjələs) *adj.* 可笑的　　dye (daɪ) *v.* 染色
attention (ə'tɛnʃən) *n.* 注意　***go through*** 經歷
rebellious (rɪ'bɛljəs) *adj.* 反抗的　　phase (fez) *n.* 階段
notice ('notɪs) *v.* 注意到　　rebel (rɪ'bɛl) *v.* 反抗
catch one's eye 引人注意

23. (**D**) M: They're very attractive. You look beautiful in them.

W: That's music to my ears.

M: I'm just telling the truth.

W: In that case, why don't you ask me out?

Question: What does the woman want?

A. To walk with him.

B. To go outside together.

C. A question from him.

D. A date with the man.

* attractive (ə'træktɪv) *adj.* 吸引人的
music to one's ears 中聽的話　***in that case*** 那樣的話
ask sb. out 邀請某人出去約會　　date (det) *n.* 約會

24. (**D**) M : That storm was something, wasn't it?

W : It sure was. It knocked down a lot of trees.

M : The wind blew our TV antenna off the roof!

W : Wow! We're lucky nobody got hurt.

M : Yeah, thank God we're all safe and sound.

Question : What type of storm hit their neighborhood?

A. A thunderstorm.

B. A hailstorm.

C. A weather vane.

D. A windstorm.

* storm〔stɔrm〕*n.* 暴風雨

something〔'sʌmθɪŋ〕*n.* 值得重視的東西 (人)

knock down 擊倒　　blow〔blo〕*v.* 吹

blow off 吹走　　roof〔ruf〕*n.* 屋頂

antenna〔æn'tɛnə〕*n.* 天線　　*get hurt* 受傷

thank God 謝天謝地　　*safe and sound* 安然無恙的

hit〔hɪt〕*v.* 侵襲

thunderstorm〔'θʌndə,stɔrm〕*n.* 雷雨

hailstorm〔'hel,stɔrm〕*n.* 夾帶冰雹的暴風雨

weather vane 風信計；風標

windstorm〔'wɪnd,stɔrm〕*n.* 暴風

25. (**A**) W : Why do you love the art museum so much?

M : The paintings and sculptures captivate me.

W : That sounds a little excessive to me.

M : No, I'm not, but some of the pieces touch my heart.

W : You're very sensitive.

Question：Why does the man love art?

A. The works touch him deeply.

B. The museum is touching.

C. The paintings are so real.

D. The sculptures seem alive.

* sculpture (ˈskʌlptʃɚ) n. 雕刻
   captivate (ˈkæptə,vet) v. 使著迷
   excessive (ɪkˈsɛsɪv) adj. 過度的
   touch (tʌtʃ) v. 感動　sensitive (ˈsɛnsətɪv) adj. 敏感的
   work (wɜk) n. 作品　deeply (ˈdiplɪ) adv. 深深地
   touching (ˈtʌtʃɪŋ) adj. 動人的
   alive (əˈlaɪv) adj. 有生氣的

26. (**C**) M：How do you feel about suicide?

W：I think it's awful, always wrong and never right!

M：I couldn't have said it any better.

Question：What do they agree on?

A. Suicide is a disease.

B. It's a benevolence.

C. Committing suicide is terrible.

D. Those people are mentally sick.

* suicide (ˈsuə,saɪd) n. 自殺　awful (ˈɔful) adj. 糟糕的
   disease (dɪˈziz) n. 疾病
   benevolence (bəˈnɛvələns) n. 善行
   commit suicide 自殺
   terrible (ˈtɛrəbl) adj. 可怕的；很糟的
   mentally (ˈmɛntlɪ) adv. 精神上地

27. (**B**) W: What are you mailing out?

M: My Christmas cards.

W: But it's not even Thanksgiving yet.

M: I know, but you can never be too early.

W: Boy, you really love to spread holiday joy!

Question: Where is this conversation taking place?

A. At a stationery shop.　B. At the post office.

C. At a bookstore.　D. At a stamp exhibition.

* mail〔mel〕v. 郵寄　*can never…too~* 再…也不爲過
spread〔sprɛd〕v. 散播　stationery〔'steʃənˌɛrɪ〕n. 文具
stamp〔stæmp〕n. 郵票
exhibition〔ˌɛksə'bɪʃən〕n. 展覽

28. (**D**) M: How come I'm 25 here in Taiwan and 24 in the USA?

W: The Chinese add a year when you're born.

M: Are you kidding me?

W: No. When you pop out of your mom, you're
already one year old.

M: What an interesting custom!

Question: How old is the man?

A. He's keeping it a secret.

B. He's 20 years old.

C. He's one year old.

D. He's 25 years old.

* add〔æd〕v. 加　*pop out* 跳出；蹦出
pop out of one's mom 從媽媽肚子裡跳出來；被媽媽生出來
custom〔'kʌstəm〕n. 習俗　*keep~a secret* 保守祕密

29. (**A**) W : Oh no, I've lost a contact lens!

M : Don't move. You might step on it.

W : Yes, you're right. It just fell out.

M : Come on! Get on your hands and knees and help me.

W : I'm afraid I'm as blind as a bat.

Question : Can the woman help?

A. Not very well.　　　B. Of course she can.

C. She's scared of him.　D. She's worried to death.

＊ *contact lens* 隱形眼鏡　　step〔stɛp〕*v.* 踩

fall out 掉出來　　*get on your hands and knees* 趴下來

as blind as a bat 視力很差

be worried to death 擔心得要死

30. (**C**) M : Hey look! A shooting star!

W : Cool! That was really neat.

M : We should make a wish.

W : What are you talking about?

M : Don't you know about that custom?

Question : What doesn't the woman know?

A. Shooting stars are mysterious.

B. Shooting stars can teach you magic.

C. If you see a shooting star, make a wish.

D. Shooting stars bring daydreams.

＊ *shooting star* 流星　　neat〔nit〕*adj.* 很棒的

make a wish 許願　　mysterious〔mɪs'tɪrɪəs〕*adj.* 神祕的

magic〔'mædʒɪk〕*n.* 魔法；巫術

daydream〔'de,drim〕*n.* 白日夢

PART C

Questions 31-32 refer to the following information.

Wednesday, February 2, 2005

If today is your birthday, here is your horoscope. Your zodiac sign is Aquarius and exciting and happy changes are in store for you in the year ahead. But your good fortune will not happen by chance. It will be the result of past diligence. Tremendous progress in many areas of your life will happen this year if you mind your P's and Q's. Don't take any shortcuts or dodge heavy assignments, because the rewards will depend on what you do.

Vocabulary

horoscope ('hɔrə,skop) *n.* 星座
zodiac ('zodɪ,æk) *n.* 黃道帶　　***zodiac sign*** 星座
Aquarius (ə'kwɛrɪəs) *n.* 水瓶座　　change (tʃendʒ) *n.* 改變
in store 可能發生　　ahead (ə'hɛd) *adv.* 在前方；在未來
fortune ('fɔrtʃən) *n.* 幸運　　***by chance*** 意外地
result (rɪ'zʌlt) *n.* 結果　　diligence ('dɪlədʒəns) *n.* 勤奮
tremendous (trɪ'mɛndəs) *adj.* 巨大的；驚人的
progress ('progrɛs) *n.* 進步　　area ('ɛrɪə) *n.* 領域

mind one's P's and Q's 謹慎行事

shortcut ('ʃɔrt,kʌt) *n.* 捷徑　　dodge (dadʒ) *v.* 閃避

assignment (ə'saɪnmənt) *n.* 任務

reward (rɪ'wɔrd) *n.* 獎賞　　*depend on* 視～而定

---

31. (**C**) What is your zodiac sign if today is your birthday?

     A. Leo.　　　　　　B. Horoscope.

     C. Aquarius.　　　　D. P's and Q's.

     * Leo ('lio) *n.* 獅子座

32. (**D**) What is the prediction for the year ahead?

     A. An exciting trip abroad.

     B. Diligence is required.

     C. Possible marriage plans.

     D. Great progress and good luck.

     * prediction (prɪ'dɪkʃən) *n.* 預測

      require (rɪ'kwaɪr) *v.* 需要

      marriage ('mærɪdʒ) *n.* 結婚

Questions 33-35 refer to the following advertisement.

Have a very happy holiday at the China World
Hotel. We have special discount rates for individuals,
business people, families and other groups. We offer
prices on weekend, short-term and long-term stays that
just can't be beat. Our single-day rate for a deluxe twin

bedroom is less than 79 U.S. dollars. This price includes a daily welcome drink, free Internet access and two free pieces of laundry done per day. It also includes a complimentary breakfast buffet in our lobby café. Enjoy free use of our swimming pool, gym and sauna, too. Last but not least we offer free parking, free mineral water and a free daily newspaper. What are you waiting for? Join us now for a great holiday experience.

Vocabulary

discount (ˈdɪskaʊnt) *n.* 折扣

individual (ˌɪndəˈvɪdʒʊəl) *n.* 個人

group (grup) *n.* 團體

short-term (ˈʃɔrtˈtɜm) *adj.* 短期的

long-term (ˈlɔŋˈtɜm) *adj.* 長期的

beat (bit) *v.* 擊敗；勝過　　deluxe (dɪˈlʌks) *adj.* 豪華的

twin bedroom 有兩張單人床的房間

include (ɪnˈklud) *v.* 包括　　*welcome drink* 迎賓酒

access (ˈæksɛs) *n.* 使用的權利

laundry (ˈlɔndrɪ) *n.* 送洗的衣物　　per (pɚ) *prep.* 每一

complimentary (ˌkɑmpləˈmɛntərɪ) *adj.* 免費的

buffet (buˈfe) *n.* 自助餐　　lobby (ˈlɑbɪ) *n.* 大廳

sauna (ˈsaʊnə, ˈsɔnə) *n.* 蒸汽浴；三溫暖

last but not least 最後一項要點　　*mineral water* 礦泉水

33. (**D**) Why are they offering special rates?

　　　A. Chinese New Year.

　　　B. To improve cash flow.

　　　C. A new marketing campaign.

　　　D. There is no mention in this advertisement.

　　　　 * *special rate* 特價　　improve (ɪmˋpruv) *v.* 改善

　　　　 cash flow 現金流轉　　marketing (ˋmɑrkɪtɪŋ) *n.* 行銷

　　　　 campaign (kæmˋpen) *n.* 活動

　　　　 mention (ˋmɛnʃən) *n.* 提到

34. (**D**) What does the room fee include?

　　　A. A free massage.

　　　B. A gourmet dinner.

　　　C. Free shopping coupons.

　　　D. A breakfast buffet.

　　　　 * fee (fi) *n.* 費用　　massage (məˋsɑʒ) *n.* 按摩

　　　　 gourmet (ˋgʊrme) *adj.* 出於美食家之手的

　　　　 gourmet dinner 美味晚餐

　　　　 coupon (ˋkupɑn) *n.* 折價券

35. (**C**) What type of room is only 79 dollars?

　　　A. The V.I.P. suite.

　　　B. A family dormitory.

　　　C. A deluxe twin bed.

　　　D. A business suite.

　　　　 * suite (swit) *n.* 套房

　　　　 dormitory (ˋdɔrmə͵torɪ) *n.* 宿舍

Questions 36-37 refer to the following weather forecast.

> Good morning, everybody! There's more wet weather! We have an 80 percent chance of rain showers today. There is a big storm front moving in from the northwest Great Lakes region. It will probably dump 6 to 10 inches on us by midnight tonight. The winds are also out of the northwest, coming in at about 5 miles per hour. Cloudy and overcast skies are expected for the next two days. It looks like lots more rain is in store for us. Keep those umbrellas and rain boots handy.

Vocabulary

forecast ('for,kæst) *n.* 預報   percent (pə'sɛnt) *n.* 百分比

chance (tʃæns) *n.* 機會   showers ('ʃauəz) *n. pl.* 陣雨

rain showers 陣雨   front (frʌnt) *n.* 【氣象】鋒面

region ('ridʒən) *n.* 區域   probably ('prɑbəblɪ) *adv.* 大概

dump (dʌmp) *v.* 落下 (在此指下雨)

inch (ɪntʃ) *n.* 英吋 (約 2.54 公分)

midnight ('mɪd,naɪt) *n.* 午夜十二時

mile (maɪl) *n.* 英哩 (約 1.6 公里)

cloudy ('klaudɪ) *adj.* 多雲的

overcast ('ovə,kæst) *adj.* 陰暗的

expect (ɪk'spɛkt) *v.* 預期   *rain boots* 雨鞋

handy ('hændɪ) *adj.* 就近的；在手邊的

36. (**B**) What is the chance of rain for the day?

    A. Eight percent.

    B. Eighty percent.

    C. Eighteen percent.

    D. Six to ten inches.

37. (**D**) What's the forecast for the next two days?

    A. Morning showers only.

    B. Skies clearing up.

    C. Northeast winds coming.

    D. More wet weather.

    * *clear up* 放晴

Questions 38-39 refer to the following article.

> Modern dance is a very individualistic art form. The primary source of each movement comes from inside each dancer. Modern dance is very expressionistic, meaning that it's emotional, personal and unique. Unlike ballet, which is a formal and classical style, modern dance does not recognize any conventional forms. It asserts that there are as many positions and movements as the dancer wants to create. Modern dance is revolutionary by definition. Modern dance is totally free, creative and innovative.

Vocabulary

modern dance 現代舞

individualistic〔ˏɪndəˏvɪdʒʊəl'ɪstɪk〕*adj.* 個人主義的

form〔fɔrm〕*n.* 形式　　primary〔'praɪˏmɛrɪ〕*adj.* 主要的

source〔sors〕*n.* 來源　　movement〔'muvmənt〕*n.* 動作

inside〔ɪn'saɪd〕*prep.* 在～之內

expressionistic〔ɪkˏsprɛʃən'ɪstɪk〕*adj.* 表現主義的

emotional〔ɪ'moʃənḷ〕*adj.* 情緒的

personal〔'pɝsnḷ〕*adj.* 個人的　　unique〔ju'nik〕*adj.* 獨特的

ballet〔bæ'le〕*n.* 芭蕾舞　　formal〔'fɔrmḷ〕*adj.* 正式的

classical〔'klæsɪkḷ〕*adj.* 古典的　　style〔staɪl〕*n.* 風格

recognize〔'rɛkəgˏnaɪz〕*v.* 認可

conventional〔kən'vɛnʃənḷ〕*adj.* 傳統的　　assert〔ə'sɝt〕*v.* 聲稱

position〔pə'zɪʃən〕*n.* 姿勢　　create〔krɪ'et〕*v.* 創造

revolutionary〔ˏrɛvə'luʃənˏɛrɪ〕*adj.* 完全創新的

by definition 當然；按照定義　　totally〔'totḷɪ〕*adv.* 完全地

creative〔krɪ'etɪv〕*adj.* 有創意的

innovative〔'ɪnəˏvetɪv〕*adj.* 創新的

38. (**A**) How is modern dance different from ballet?

　　A. It's informal and flexible.

　　B. It's classical.

　　C. It utilizes music.

　　D. It follows tradition.

　　* different〔'dɪfərənt〕*adj.* 不同的

　　 informal〔ɪn'fɔrmḷ〕*adj.* 非正式的

　　 flexible〔'flɛksəbḷ〕*adj.* 有彈性的

　　 utilize〔'jutḷˏaɪz〕*v.* 利用　　follow〔'falo〕*v.* 遵循

　　 tradition〔trə'dɪʃən〕*n.* 傳統

39. (**C**) Where do the movements of modern dance come from?

   A. The teacher.　　　B. Dancing manuals.
   C. The dancer.　　　D. Imitating ballet.

   * manual ('mænjuəl) n. 手冊；簡介
     imitate ('ɪmə,tet) v. 模仿

Questions 40-41 refer to the following article.

> This year's Golden Globe Awards are a real toss-up. All of Hollywood and the entertainment world are on the edge of their seats wondering who will win the coveted awards. This year's race is wide-open with no clear front-runners.
>
> This is in contrast to past years where the ceremony had a few big stars who received large majorities of votes. The big movie studios are enthusiastically promoting their films, directors and actors. It will be interesting to see who wins.

📖 Vocabulary

award (ə'wɔrd) n. 獎　　***Golden Globe Award*** 金球獎
toss-up ('tɔs,ʌp) n. 勝負難分；難以決定的事
Hollywood ('halɪ,wud) n. 好萊塢 (美國洛杉磯市的一區，為
   電影事業的中心)　　***entertainment world*** 娛樂界
be on the edge of one's seat 坐立難安

wonder (ˈwʌndɚ) v. 想知道

coveted (ˈkʌvɪtɪd) adj. 令人垂涎的；夢寐以求的

wide-open (ˈwaɪdˈopən) adj. 公開的

clear (klɪr) adj. 清楚的

front-runner (ˈfrʌntˈrʌnɚ) n. (比賽中的) 領先者

in contrast to 和～成對比

ceremony (ˈsɛrəˌmonɪ) n. 典禮　　receive (rɪˈsiv) v. 得到

majority (məˈdʒɔrətɪ) n. 大多數　　vote (vot) n. 投票；選票

studio (ˈstjudɪˌo) n. 攝影棚；電影公司

enthusiastically (ɪnˌθjuzɪˈæstɪklɪ) adj. 狂熱地；熱烈地

promote (prəˈmot) v. 宣傳；促銷　　film (fɪlm) n. 電影

director (dəˈrɛktɚ) n. 導演　　actor (ˈæktɚ) n. 演員

40. (**C**) Which actor or movie is favored to win this year?

　　A. The big studios.

　　B. The front-runners.

　　C. Nobody knows.

　　D. A few big stars.

　　* favor (ˈfevɚ) v. 偏愛；擁護；有希望

41. (**B**) What are the awards for?

　　A. Television shows.

　　B. Movie entertainment.

　　C. Theater revenues.

　　D. Retiring actors.

　　* entertainment (ˌɛntɚˈtenmənt) n. 娛樂

　　revenue (ˈrɛvəˌnju) n. 收入

　　retiring (rɪˈtaɪrɪŋ) adj. 退休的

Questions 42-43 are based on these instructions.

> For your skin rash, you must take two tablets, three times a day. Take them with water, after a meal, and on a full stomach. Do not take more than six per day and drink no alcoholic beverages whatsoever. You must also take a warm bath daily for about half an hour. After bathing, apply the ointment to the affected area. Rub it gently into the skin until it disappears. Drink lots of water and get a lot of rest.

📖 Vocabulary

instruction (ɪn'strʌkʃən) *n.* 指示；說明
rash (ræʃ) *n.* 發疹　　tablet ('tæblɪt) *n.* 藥片
full (fʊl) *adj.* 吃飽的　　stomach ('stʌmək) *n.* 胃
alcoholic (ˌælkə'hɔlɪk) *adj.* 含酒精的
beverage ('bɛvərɪdʒ) *n.* 飲料
whatsoever (ˌhwɑtso'ɛvɚ) *adj.* 無論什麼⋯也 (用於否定句)
bathe (beð) *v.* 沐浴　　apply (ə'plaɪ) *v.* 塗抹
ointment ('ɔɪntmənt) *n.* 藥膏
affected (ə'fɛktɪd) *adj.* 受感染的
area ('ɛrɪə) *n.* 區域　　rub (rʌb) *v.* 揉
gently ('dʒɛntlɪ) *adv.* 輕輕地
disappear (ˌdɪsə'pɪr) *v.* 消失

42. (**D**) Who is probably giving these instructions?
　　　A. A patient.　　　　B. A customer at a pharmacy.
　　　C. A chemist.　　　　D. A dermatologist.

　　* probably ('prɑbəblɪ) adv. 可能
　　　patient ('peʃənt) n. 病人　　customer ('kʌstəmə) n. 顧客
　　　pharmacy ('fɑrməsɪ) n. 藥房　　chemist ('kɛmɪst) n. 化學家
　　　dermatologist (,dɜmə'tɑlədʒɪst) n. 皮膚科醫生

43. (**A**) How many tablets must the patient take daily?
　　　A. Six.　B. Two.　　C. Three. D. Twenty.

　　* daily ('delɪ) adv. 每天

Questions 44-45 refer to the following recording.

　　　Did you know that rats are now being trained to detect land mines? In many war-torn areas of the world, rats are now helping demolition teams to find and eliminate these deadly explosives. The rat is light in weight, so it won't set off the bomb. It also has a keen sense of smell and can accurately find the scent of the explosives. After being trained, a rat finds the mine, scratches the earth above it, and for this service will receive a food reward. Pretty amazing, huh?

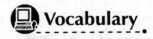 **Vocabulary**

- -

　　　rat (ræt) n. 老鼠　　train (tren) v. 訓練
　　　detect (dɪ'tɛkt) v. 偵測　　mine (maɪn) n. 地雷

land mine 地雷　　war-torn (ˈwɔrˌtɔrn) *adj.* 受戰爭破壞的

demolition (ˌdɛməˈlɪʃən) *n.* 拆毀

eliminate (ɪˈlɪməˌnet) *v.* 除去　　deadly (ˈdɛdlɪ) *adj.* 致命的

explosive (ɪkˈsplosɪv) *n.* 爆炸物　　*set off* 使爆炸

bomb (bɑm) *n.* 炸彈　　keen (kin) *adj.* 敏銳的

sense of smell 嗅覺　　accurately (ˈækjərɪtlɪ) *adj.* 準確地

scent (sɛnt) *n.* 氣味　　scratch (skrætʃ) *v.* 抓

earth (ɝθ) *n.* 泥土　　receive (rɪˈsiv) *v.* 得到

reward (rɪˈwɔrd) *n.* 獎賞　　pretty (ˈprɪtɪ) *adv.* 相當地

amazing (əˈmezɪŋ) *adj.* 驚人的

44. (**A**) What is the rat being trained to do?

    A. Find and clear minefields.

    B. Help dig up old weapons.

    C. Eliminate deadly chemicals.

    D. Help get rid of pollution.

    * minefield (ˈmaɪnˌfild) *n.* 佈雷區　　*dig up* 挖掘

      weapon (ˈwɛpən) *n.* 武器

      chemical (ˈkɛmɪkḷ) *n.* 化學物質

      get rid of 擺脫　　pollution (pəˈluʃən) *n.* 污染

45. (**B**) Why was the rat selected?

    A. It has a higher IQ.

    B. It's light.

    C. It has a keen sense of touch.

    D. It's extremely sensitive.

    * select (səˈlɛkt) *v.* 挑選

      IQ 智商 (= *Intelligence Quotient*)　　*sense of touch* 觸覺

      extremely (ɪkˈstrimlɪ) *adv.* 非常地

      sensitive (ˈsɛnsətɪv) *adj.* 敏感的

中高級閱讀測驗詳解 ①

PART A : Sentence Completion

1. (**B**) Sophia is a celebrated herbalist, who is proficient at <u>acupuncture</u>. 蘇菲亞是一位知名的中醫師，精通針灸。

    (A) investigation〔 ɪnˌvɛstə'geʃən〕 *n.* 調查

    (B) *acupuncture*〔'ækjuˌpʌŋktʃɚ〕 *n.* 針灸

    (C) surgery〔'sɝdʒərɪ〕 *n.* 外科手術

    (D) operation〔ˌɑpə'reʃən〕 *n.* 手術

    * celebrated〔'sɛləˌbretɪd〕 *adj.* 有名的

    herbalist〔'hɝblɪst〕 *n.* 中醫師

    proficient〔prə'fɪʃənt〕 *adj.* 精通的

    be proficient at 精通~

2. (**D**) If the "morning-after pill" proves to be truly <u>nontoxic</u> and 100 percent effective as claimed, it will be placed on the market.

    如果證實女用口服避孕藥真的<u>無毒</u>，且如聲稱的百分之百有效，它將會在市場上販售。

    (A) notorious〔no'torɪəs〕 *adj.* 惡名昭彰的

    (B) nonaligned〔ˌnɑnə'laɪnd〕 *adj.* 不結盟的

    (C) nondairy〔nɑn'dɛrɪ〕 *adj.* 不含乳製品的

    (D) *nontoxic*〔nɑn'tɑksɪk〕 *adj.* 無毒的

    * *morning-after pill* 女用口服避孕藥（房事後用）

    prove〔pruv〕 *v.* 證實　　effective〔ɪ'fɛktɪv〕 *adj.* 有效的

    claim〔klem〕 *v.* 聲稱

    place sth. on the market 將某物在市場上出售

3. (**C**) The sanitation department of this company is very
   <u>efficient</u>. No wonder the workmen there are well-paid.
   這家公司的衛生部門非常<u>有效率</u>。難怪那裡的工作人員待
   遇很優厚。

   (A) sufficient〔 səˋfɪʃənt〕 adj. 足夠的
   (B) impatient〔 ɪmˋpeʃənt〕 adj. 沒有耐心的
   (C) *efficient*〔 əˋfɪʃənt〕 adj. 有效率的
   (D) incompetent〔 ɪnˋkɑmpətənt〕 adj. 無能的

   * sanitation〔͵sænəˋteʃən〕 n. 衛生
     department〔 dɪˋpɑrtmənt〕 n. 部門
     no wonder 難怪
     workman〔ˋwɜkmən〕 n. 勞工
     well-paid〔ˋwɛlˋped〕 adj. 待遇優厚的

4. (**B**) Large factories pour tons of <u>soot</u> into the air every day,
   which causes the serious air pollution.
   大型工廠每天排放數噸的<u>油煙</u>進入空氣中，造成嚴重的空氣
   污染。

   (A) salary〔ˋsælərɪ〕 n. 薪水
   (B) *soot*〔 sut〕 n. 油煙
   (C) intense〔 ɪnˋtɛns〕 adj. 強烈的
   (D) pore〔 por〕 n. 毛孔

   * ton〔 tʌn〕 n. 噸（重量單位）　　cause〔 kɔz〕 v. 導致
     serious〔ˋsɪrɪəs〕 adj. 嚴重的　　*air pollution* 空氣污染

5. (**D**) Trash is not allowed to <u>accumulate</u> in large amounts on
   the sidewalk for fear of making our environment dirty.
   大量的垃圾不可以<u>堆積</u>在人行道上，以免把我們的環境弄髒。

(A) translate〔træns'let〕v. 翻譯

(B) circulate〔'sɝkjə,let〕v. 循環

(C) communicate〔kə'mjunə,ket〕v. 溝通

(D) *accumulate*〔ə'kjumjə,let〕v. 堆積；累積

* allow〔ə'laʊ〕v. 允許　　amount〔ə'maʊnt〕n. 數量
in large amount 大量地
sidewalk〔'saɪd,wɔk〕n. 人行道　　*for fear of* 以免
environment〔ɪn'vaɪrənmənt〕n. 環境

6. (**A**) The couple quarreled a lot, and at last, they decided to get <u>divorced</u>.

那對夫妻經常吵架，最後他們決定離婚。

(A) *divorce*〔də'vɔrs〕v. 離婚　　*get divorced* 離婚

(B) marry〔'mærɪ〕v. 結婚　　get married 結婚

(C) single〔'sɪŋgl̩〕adj. 單身的

(D) widowed〔'wɪdod〕adj. 鰥（寡）居的

* couple〔'kʌpl̩〕n. 夫妻　　quarrel〔'kwɔrəl〕v. 吵架
at last 最後　　decide〔dɪ'saɪd〕v. 決定

7. (**A**) I tried to bake bread on my own yesterday. <u>Frankly</u> speaking, I found it was not as difficult as most people believe.

我昨天試著要自己烤麵包。<u>坦白說</u>，我發現這不像大部分人所想那樣困難。

(A) *frankly*〔'fræŋklɪ〕adv. 坦白地

(B) amazingly〔ə'mezɪŋlɪ〕adv. 令人驚奇地

(C) civilly〔'sɪvl̩ɪ〕adv. 有禮貌地

(D) recklessly〔'rɛklɪslɪ〕adv. 魯莽地

8. (**C**) We were sorry to see that Mr. Smith's eyes were bloodshot and teary, his hand shook when he lit a cigarette, and he coughed <u>incessantly</u>.

我們很遺憾地看到，史密斯先生眼睛佈滿血絲，泛著淚光，當他點煙時，他的手會顫抖，而且他還<u>不斷地</u>咳嗽。

(A) bluffly (ˈblʌflɪ) adv. 率直地

(B) gutlessly (ˈgʌtlɪslɪ) adv. 無膽量地

(C) ***incessantly*** (ɪnˈsɛsn̩tlɪ) adv. 不斷地

(D) ordinarily (ˈɔrdn̩ˌɛrəlɪ) adv. 通常地

* bloodshot (ˈblʌdˌʃɑt) adj. 充血的

teary (ˈtɪrɪ) adj. 含淚的

shake (ʃek) v. 顫抖 (三態變化：shake-shook-shaken)

light (laɪt) v. 點燃 (三態變化：light-lit-lit)

cigarette (ˈsɪgəˌrɛt) n. 香煙

cough (kɔf) v. 咳嗽

9. (**A**) Admit what you've done wrong. <u>Take your medicine</u> like a man.

承認你所做錯的事。像個男子漢<u>接受處罰</u>吧。

(A) ***take one's medicine*** 某人接受處罰

(B) shave off one's beard 刮某人鬍子

beard (bɪrd) n. 鬍鬚

(C) put one's foot down 堅持己見

(D) pull one's rank 利用自己的階級而強迫別人接受命令

rank (ræŋk) n. 階級

* admit (ədˈmɪt) v. 承認

wrong (rɔŋ) adv. 錯誤地

10. (**C**) When Father got my transcript with poor grades, he <u>went on the rampage</u>.

當爸爸收到我那張成績很爛的成績單時，他<u>暴跳如雷</u>。

(A) lift off （飛機）升空；（火箭）發射

(B) come to life 甦醒

(C) **go on the rampage** 暴跳如雷

　　rampage〔'ræmpedʒ〕 n. 狂暴行為

(D) refresh *one's* memory 重新喚起某人的記憶

* transcript〔'træn,skrɪpt〕 n. 成績單

11. (**D**) Grandfather is already 65 years old and he is going to <u>hang up his hat</u> next month.

爺爺已經六十五歲了，他下個月將要<u>退休</u>。

(A) be in *one's* shoes 站在某人的立場設想

(B) be caught with *one's* pants down 被逮個正著

(C) turn *one's* coat 改變立場；變節

(D) **hang up** *one's* **hat** （到退休年齡）退休

12. (**B**) This dam along with the four or five other dams along the river <u>forms</u> part of the network of hydroelectric plants.

這座水壩連同沿著這條河的其他四、五座水壩，<u>形成</u>水力發電廠網路的一部份。

* A **along with** B「A 連同 B~」動詞須與 A 一致，故選 (B)

forms「形成」。

dam〔dæm〕 n. 水壩　　**along with** 連同

hydroelectric〔,haɪdroɪ'lɛktrɪk〕 adj. 水力發電的

plant〔plænt〕 n. 工廠

hydroelectric plant 水力發電廠

13. (**D**) The doctor told me <u>in</u> private that the invalid will die in three weeks.

醫生私底下告訴我，這位病人剩下三週壽命。

* ***in private*** 私底下（＝*privately*）

$$\left.\begin{array}{l} \text{in} \\ \text{with} \\ \text{by} \\ \text{on} \end{array}\right\} + （\text{great / much}）+ 抽象名詞 ＝（\text{very}）+ 副詞$$

例如：　with kindness ＝ kindly（親切地）

by accident ＝ accidentally（偶然地）

on purpose ＝ purposely（故意地）

invalid（ˈɪnvəlɪd）*n.* 病人

14. (**B**) Peter was in a difficult situation.　However, I couldn't help him, <u>not but that</u> I did pity him.

彼得的處境很困難。然而，我不能幫助他，<u>雖然</u>我真的同情他。

* 連接詞 ***not but that*** 表「雖然」，用法同 though。而 (A) for that「因為」，(C) but that「而不；若非」，(D) now that「因為；既然」，均不合句意。舉例如下：

For that he is honest, we all like him.

（因為他誠實，所以我們大家都喜歡他。）

I am not so old ***but that*** I may learn.

（我還沒老到不能學習的程度。）

She would have fallen ***but that*** I caught her.

（若非我拉住她，她就跌倒了。）

Now that you mention it, I do remember.

（因為你這麼一說，我就想起來了。）

situation（ˌsɪtʃʊˈeʃən）*n.* 情況　　pity（ˈpɪtɪ）*v.* 同情

15. (**C**) Edward is such an reliable man. His conduct has always been <u>above</u> suspicion.

艾德華是個這麼值得信賴的人。他的行為一直<u>不容置疑</u>。

* ***above suspicion*** 不容置疑

reliable〔rɪˋlaɪəbḷ〕*adj.* 值得信賴的

conduct〔ˋkɑndʌkt〕*n.* 行為

suspicion〔səˋspɪʃən〕*n.* 懷疑

PART B : **Cloze**

Questions 16-22

Nanotechnology is a field of research and innovation <u>concerned with</u> building "things" — generally, materials and

16
devices — on the scale of atoms and molecules.

奈米科技是一個研究和創新的領域，它和建構「東西」有關——通常是建構材料和裝置——而且是以原子和分子的規模來建構。

nanotechnology〔ˋnænəˌtɛkˋnɑlədʒɪ〕*n.* 奈米科技

research〔ˋrisɝtʃ〕*n.* 研究　　innovation〔ˌɪnəˋveʃən〕*n.* 創新

generally〔ˋdʒɛnərəlɪ〕*adv.* 通常

material〔məˋtɪrɪəl〕*n.* 材料；物質

device〔dɪˋvaɪs〕*n.* 裝置　　scale〔skel〕*n.* 規模

atom〔ˋætəm〕*n.* 原子　　molecule〔ˋmɑləˌkjul〕*n.* 分子

16. (**C**) (A) cooperate〔koˋɑpəˌret〕*v.* 合作

(B) communicate〔kəˋmjunəˌket〕*v.* 溝通

(C) ***concern***〔kənˋsɝn〕*v.* 與…有關

(D) content〔kənˋtɛnt〕*v.* 使滿足

A nanometre is one-billionth of a metre: ten times the diameter of a hydrogen atom. The diameter of a human hair is, <u>on average</u>, 17 80,000 nanometres. At such scales, the ordinary rules of physics and chemistry no longer apply.

奈米是十億分之一公尺：也是氫原子直徑大小的十倍。一般而言，人類頭髮的直徑是八萬奈米。在這樣的規模下，就不再適用一般的物理和化學法則。

> nanometre（'nænə,mitɚ）n. 奈米
> **one-billionth** 十億分之一
> metre（'mitɚ）n. 公尺（= *meter*）
> time（taɪm）n. 倍   diameter（daɪ'æmətɚ）n. 直徑
> hydrogen（'haɪdrəʒən）n. 氫
> ordinary（'ɔrdn,ɛrɪ）adj. 一般的   physics（'fɪzɪks）n. 物理學
> chemistry（'kɛmɪstrɪ）n. 化學   apply（ə'plaɪ）v. 適用

17. (**B**) (A) on all fours 完全一致
　　　 (B) *on average* 一般而言
　　　 (C) on an errand 跑腿   errand（'ɛrənd）n. 跑腿
　　　 (D) on credit 賒欠   credit（'krɛdɪt）n. 賒帳

For instance, materials' <u>characteristics</u>, such as their color, strength, 18 conductivity and reactivity, can differ substantially between the nanoscale and the macro. Carbon "nanotubes" are <u>100 times stronger than</u> steel but six times lighter.
19

例如，物質的特性，像是顏色、強度、傳導性和反應性，在奈米尺度和在大規模下，就會有很大的不同。奈米碳管比鋼管堅固一百倍，但是重量輕六倍。

strength〔strεŋθ〕n. 強度

conductivity〔,kɑndʌk'tɪvətɪ〕n. 傳導性

reactivity〔,riæk'tɪvətɪ〕n. 反應性　　differ〔'dɪfɚ〕v. 不同

substantially〔səb'stænʃəlɪ〕adv. 大大地

nanoscale〔'nænə,skel〕n. 奈米尺度

macro〔'mækro〕n. 大規模　　carbon〔'kɑrbən〕n. 碳

carbon nanotube 奈米碳管　　steel〔stil〕n. 鋼

18. (**D**)　(A) citizen〔'sɪtəzn̩〕n. 公民

　　　　　(B) subconscious〔sʌb'kɑnʃəs〕n. 潛意識

　　　　　(C) ghostwriter〔'gost,raɪtɚ〕n. 代筆人

　　　　　(D) *characteristic*〔,kærɪktə'rɪstɪk〕n. 特性

19. (**A**)　依句意，奈米碳管「比」鋼管「堅固一百倍」(A) *100 times*
　　　　　stronger than。

　　　　Nanotechnology is hailed <u>as</u> having the potential to increase
　　　　　　　　　　　　　　　　　　　　　　　　　20
the efficiency of energy consumption, help clean the environment,
and solve major health problems.

　　奈米科技被認定有潛力提高能源消耗的效率、協助清潔環境，並解
決重大健康問題。

hail〔hel〕v. 認定　　potential〔pə'tɛnʃəl〕n. 潛力

efficiency〔ə'fɪʃənsɪ〕n. 效率

consumption〔kən'sʌmpʃən〕n. 消耗

environment〔ɪn'vaɪrənmənt〕n. 環境

solve〔sɑlv〕v. 解決　　major〔'medʒɚ〕adj. 重要的

20. (**B**)　*be hailed as*… 被認定為…

It is said to be able to massively increase manufacturing production at significantly reduced costs.
21
據說它能夠在顯著減少成本的情況下，大量提高生產量。

> massively〔'mæsɪvlɪ〕*adv.* 大量地
>
> manufacturing〔ˌmænjə'fæktʃərɪŋ〕*adj.* 製造的
>
> ***manufacturing production*** 生產量
>
> significantly〔sɪg'nɪfəkəntlɪ〕*adv.* 顯著地
>
> reduced〔rɪ'djust〕*adj.* 減少的

21. (**A**) 表「價格、成本」，介系詞須用 *at*，故選 (A)。

Products of nanotechnology will be smaller, cheaper, lighter yet
22
more functional and require less energy and fewer raw materials

to manufacture, claim nanotech advocates.
奈米科技的產品會比較小、比較便宜、比較輕，但是卻更實用、能源需求較少，且製造原料也比較少，奈米科技的倡導者說。

> cheap〔tʃip〕*adj.* 便宜的
>
> functional〔'fʌŋkʃənḷ〕*adj.* 實用的
>
> require〔rɪ'kwaɪr〕*v.* 需要
>
> raw〔rɔ〕*adj.* 仍為原料的；未加工的
>
> ***raw material*** 原料
>
> manufacture〔ˌmænjə'fæktʃɚ〕*v.* 製造
>
> claim〔klem〕*v.* 宣稱
>
> nanotech〔'nænəˌtɛk〕*n.* 奈米科技
>
> advocate〔'ædvəkɪt〕*n.* 倡導者

22. (**D**) 依句意，選 (D) *yet*「但是」。

Questions 23-30

An international brand of orange soda defended its image after reports claimed it contained a cancer-causing <u>substance</u>.
23

有一個國際品牌的橘子汽水，在被報導說含有致癌物質之後，決心要捍衛它的形象。

brand〔brænd〕*n.* 品牌　　defend〔dɪˈfɛnd〕*v.* 捍衛
image〔ˈɪmɪdʒ〕*n.* 形象　　claim〔klem〕*v.* 宣稱
contain〔kənˈten〕*v.* 含有　　cancer〔ˈkænsɚ〕*n.* 癌症

23.(**D**) (A) persistence〔pɚˈzɪstəns〕*n.* 堅持

(B) consequence〔ˈkɑnsəˌkwɛns〕*n.* 結果

(C) instance〔ˈɪnstəns〕*n.* 例子

(D) *substance*〔ˈsʌbstəns〕*n.* 物質

The company that produces the drink acknowledged that trace amounts of the carcinogen benzene could be found in its product <u>but that</u> it wasn't enough to harm people.
24

生產那種飲料的公司承認，它的產品裡有微量的致癌苯，但是那並不足以對人體造成傷害。

acknowledge〔əkˈnɑlɪdʒ〕*v.* 承認　　trace〔tres〕*n.* 微量
carcinogen〔kɑrˈsɪnədʒən〕*n.* 致癌物質
benzene〔ˈbɛnzin〕*n.* 苯　　harm〔hɑrm〕*v.* 傷害

24.(**A**) 依句意，選 (A) *but that*「但是」，句中表反義的對等連接詞 but 連接前後兩個 that 所引導的名詞子句。而 (B) so that「以便於」，(C) in order that「爲了」，(D) in that「因爲」 (= *because*)，均不合句意。

Next time you take a sip of soda, take a look at the ingredients first.
Some drinks contain the additives vitamin C and Sodium Benzoate,
but when the two meet, they break down to form a <u>carcinogen</u>.
25

下次你要喝一口汽水時,要先看一下成分。有些飲料含有維他命 C 添加
物和苯甲酸鈉,但是當這兩樣東西碰在一起時,就會分解,然後形成致
癌物質。

sip〔 sɪp 〕*n.* 一口　　ingredient〔 ɪn'gridɪənt 〕*n.* 成分
additive〔'ædətɪv 〕*n.* 附加物
vitamin〔'vaɪtəmɪn 〕*n.* 維他命
sodium〔'sodɪəm 〕*n.* 鈉　　benzoate〔'bɛnzo,et 〕*n.* 苯酸鹽
Sodium Benzoate 苯甲酸鈉　　meet〔 mit 〕*v.* 碰到
break down 分解　　form〔 fɔrm 〕*v.* 形成

25. (**B**) (A) carbohydrate〔,kɑrbo'haɪdret 〕*n.* 碳水化合物
　　　　 (B) ***carcinogen***〔 kɑr'sɪnədʒən 〕*n.* 致癌物質
　　　　 (C) DNA 去氧核醣核酸
　　　　 (D) amylum〔'æmɪləm 〕*n.* 澱粉

Benzene certainly causes cancer in humans, said a famous doctor.
It can cause leukemia and other blood-related cancers in children.
This fact <u>was established</u> in a 1993 study.
26

苯一定會致癌,一位有名的醫生說。它會使兒童罹患血癌,或其他跟血
有關的癌症。這是一九九三年的研究所確立的事實。

certainly〔'sɝtn̩lɪ 〕*adv.* 一定　　leukemia〔 ljə'kimɪə 〕*n.* 血癌
related〔 rɪ'letɪd 〕*adj.* 有關的

26. (**C**) 依句意為被動語態,選 (C) ***was established***「被確立」。

Even more worrying is the fact that these two additives are often found together in fruit juices and jams. Children are especially <u>at risk</u> because their blood stream detoxification systems
27
are not mature enough.

更令人擔心的是，我們常常在果汁和果醬裡看到這兩種添加物。這對小孩子特別危險，因為他們的血流解毒系統的發育還不夠成熟。

worrying〔'wɝɪɪŋ〕*adj.* 令人擔心的　　jam〔dʒæm〕*n.* 果醬
especially〔ə'spɛʃəlɪ〕*adv.* 特別地　　***blood stream*** 血流
detoxification〔di,tɑksəfə'keʃən〕*n.* 解毒作用
mature〔mə'tʃur〕*adj.* 成熟的

27. (**A**) (A) ***at risk*** 在危險的狀態下
　　　　(B) at peace 和平地
　　　　(C) at odds 不一致
　　　　(D) at the zenith 位在最高峰　　zenith〔'zinɪθ〕*n.* 顛峰

And the amount of benzene in food increases when it reaches room temperature. In terms of the risk benzene poses, currently no amount is deemed <u>safe</u>. So the lower the exposure, the lower the
28
risk. Usually it accumulates over time, so it might take 10 or 20 years to happen.

而且當食物達到室溫時，苯含量就會提高。就苯所造成的風險而言，目前認爲不論含量高低都有危險。所以愈少接觸，風險就愈低。它通常會隨著時間而累積，所以可能要一、二十年才會發生影響。

temperature〔'tɛmpərətʃɚ〕*n.* 溫度
room temperature 室溫　　***in terms of*** 就…而言
risk〔rɪsk〕*n.* 風險　　pose〔poz〕*v.* 造成；帶來
accumulate〔ə'kjumjə,let〕*v.* 累積

28. (C) 「*be deemed* (*to be*) + 補語」表「被視爲…」，依句意，
選 (C) *safe*「安全的」。

So does the soda pose a risk? Coca Cola, which produces the
drink, released a statement saying that the drink had recently pass
tests by US and British health authorities <u>and that</u> it adheres to
                                              29
Taiwanese health regulations.

所以汽水會帶來風險嗎？生產這種飲料的可口可樂公司，發布了一項聲
明說，該飲料最近已經通過美國和英國衛生機關的測試，而且也有遵守
台灣的衛生條例。

> release〔rɪˈlis〕*v.* 發布
> statement〔ˈstetmənt〕*n.* 聲明
> recently〔ˈrisn̩tlɪ〕*adv.* 最近　　pass〔pæs〕*v.* 通過
> health〔hɛlθ〕*n.* 衛生
> authority〔əˈθɔrətɪ〕*n.* 公共事業機關；當局
> adhere〔ədˈhɪr〕*v.* 遵守
> regulation〔ˌrɛgjəˈleʃən〕*n.* 條例

29. (C) 依句意，選 (C) *and that*，句中對等連接詞 and 連接兩個由
that 所引導的名詞子句。

The company also said it was aware that benzene could be found
in its product but that the amounts were so small, which posed no
health threat.

這家公司還說，它們知道自己的產品裡面含有苯，但是量很少，不會對
健康造成威脅。

> aware〔əˈwɛr〕*adj.* 知道的　　threat〔θrɛt〕*n.* 威脅

As there is not enough evidence that such small amounts are harmful, stores in Taiwan say they will not take the product off their shelves. But they said they will <u>comply</u> immediately

30

if the Department of Health's food safety section confirms there is a risk.

因為沒有足夠的證據證明，苯含量這麼低也會有害，所以台灣的商店說，他們不會讓產品下架。但是如果衛生署的食品衛生課證實有風險存在，那麼他們會馬上遵守規定。

> evidence (ˈɛvədəns) *n.* 證據
> harmful (ˈhɑrmfəl) *adj.* 有害的
> ***take off*** 取下　　　shelf (ʃɛlf) *n.* 架子
> immediately (ɪˈmidɪɪtlɪ) *adv.* 立即
> ***Department of Health*** 衛生署　　　section (ˈsɛkʃən) *n.* 部；課
> ***food safety section*** 食品衛生課
> confirm (kənˈfɜm) *v.* 證實

30. (**B**) (A) supply (səˈplaɪ) *v.* 供應
    (B) ***comply*** (kəmˈplaɪ) *v.* 遵從
    (C) apply (əˈplaɪ) *v.* 適用；申請
    (D) reply (rɪˈplaɪ) *v.* 回答

PART C：Reading

Questions 31-35

Treasure hunts have excited people's imagination for hundreds of years both in real life and in books such as Robert Louis Stevenson's *Treasure Island*.

數百年來，不管是在現實生活中，還是在像羅伯特‧路易斯‧史蒂文生的「金銀島」這類書中，尋寶這件事，一直激發著人們的想像力。

> treasure〔ˈtrɛʒɚ〕n. 寶藏　　hunt〔hʌnt〕n. 追蹤；搜尋
> **treasure hunt** 尋寶
> excite〔ɪkˈsaɪt〕v. 引起；激發；喚起（興趣、感情、想像力等）
> imagination〔ɪ͵mædʒəˈneʃən〕n. 想像力
> **real life** 現實生活
> **Robert Louis Stevenson** 羅伯特‧路易斯‧史蒂文生【1850-1894，
> 　　是英國著名的散文作家、小說家。作品種類繁多，尤其愛好幻想和冒險
> 　　故事，「金銀島」（*Treasure Island*）即為他最受歡迎的小說之一。】

Kit Williams, a modern writer, had the idea of combining the real excitement of a treasure hunt with clues found in a book when he wrote a children's story, *Masquerade*, in 1979.

有位現代作家基特‧威廉斯，在 1979 年撰寫一本叫作「化裝舞會」的兒童故事書時，想到要將真正尋寶的刺激，與書中能找到的線索結合。

> combine〔kəmˈbaɪn〕v. 結合
> **combine** A **with** B 將 A 和 B 結合
> excitement〔ɪkˈsaɪtmənt〕n. 興奮；引起興奮的事物；刺激的事物
> clue〔klu〕n. 線索
> masquerade〔͵mæskəˈred〕n. 化裝舞會；偽裝；欺騙

The book was about a hare, and a month before it came out Williams buried a golden hare in a park in Bedfordshire. The book contained a large number of clues to help readers find the hare, but Williams put in a lot of "red herrings", or false clues, to mislead them.

這本書是關於一隻野兔，而在這本書問世前一個月，威廉斯將一隻金兔子，埋在貝德福郡的一座公園裡。書中有很多線索，可幫助讀者找到那隻兔子，但威廉斯也放入許多「假情報」，也就是假線索，要來誤導讀者。

hare〔hɛr〕 *n.* 野兔   ***come out*** （書籍）問世；出版

bury〔'bɛrɪ〕 *v.* 埋藏   golden〔'goldn̩〕 *adj.* 金的；金製的

Bedfordshire〔'bɛdfəd,ʃɪr , -ʃə〕 *n.* 貝德福郡【英國中部之一郡】

contain〔kən'ten〕 *v.* 包含；包括

a large number of 很多的   ***put in*** 放進；加進

herring〔'hɛrɪŋ〕 *n.* 鯡魚

red herring 用以引開他人注意之物；足以擾亂他人之情報

or〔ɔr〕 *conj.* 也就是   false〔fɔls〕 *adj.* 錯誤的；不實的

mislead〔mɪs'lid〕 *v.* 誤導

    Ken Roberts, the man who found the hare, had been looking for it for nearly two years. Although he had been searching in the wrong area for most of the time, he found it by logic, not by luck.

    肯‧羅勃茲，就是那位找到兔子的人，花了將近兩年的時間來找。雖然他大部份的時間，都在錯誤的地區尋找，但他找到那隻兔子，是靠邏輯，而非運氣。

nearly〔'nɪrlɪ〕 *adv.* 將近；幾乎   search〔sɝtʃ〕 *v.* 搜尋

logic〔'lɑdʒɪk〕 *n.* 邏輯   luck〔lʌk〕 *n.* 運氣

His success came from the fact that he had gained an important clue at the start. He had realized that the words: "One of Six to Eight" under the first picture in the book connected the hare in some way to Katherine of Aragon, the first of Henry VIII's six wives.

他的成功，是因爲一開始就掌握了一個重要的線索。他知道書上第一張圖底下的 "One of Six to Eight"（八的六個當中的第一個）是表示，那隻兔子和 Katherine of Aragon（阿拉貢的凱薩琳），也就是亨利八世六位妻子中的第一任，有某種程度的關聯。

fact〔fækt〕*n.* 事實　　gain〔gen〕*v.* 獲得

start〔stɑrt〕*n.* 開始　　***at the start*** 一開始

realize〔'riə,laɪz〕*v.* 了解　　connect〔kə'nɛkt〕*v.* 使有關聯

connect A ***to*** B 使 A 和 B 有關聯

way〔we〕*n.* 方面　　***in some way*** 在某方面

Henry VIII 亨利八世（唸成：Henry the Eighth）

Even here, however, Williams had succeeded in misleading him.
Ken knew that Katherine of Aragon had died at Kimbolton in
Cambridgeshire in 1536 and thought that Williams had buried the
hare there. He had been digging there for over a year before a
new idea occurred to him.

不過即使是在這一點上，威廉斯也成功地誤導了他。肯知道 Katherine
of Aragon 於 1536 年死於劍橋郡的 Kimbolton，所以就認為，威廉斯
把兔子埋在那裡。他在那裡挖了一年多，才想到一個新點子。

Cambridgeshire〔'kembrɪdʒ,ʃɪr , -ʃə〕*n.* 劍橋郡【英國東部之一郡】

dig〔dɪg〕*v.* 挖掘　　***sth. occurs to sb.*** 某人想到某事

He found out that Kit Williams had spent his childhood near
Ampthill, in Bedfordshire, and thought that he must have buried
the hare in a place he knew well, but he still could not see the
connection with Katherine of Aragon, until one day he came
across two stone crosses in Ampthill Park and learnt that they had
been built in her honor in 1773.

他發現基特・威廉斯童年時期都是在貝德福郡的 Ampthill 附近渡過，而
他認為基特・威廉斯一定是把那隻兔子，埋在自己熟悉的地方，但他仍
然不知道這個地方和 Katherine of Aragon 有何關聯，直到有一天，他
發現 Ampthill 公園裡有兩個石頭做的十字標誌，那就是在 1773 年，為
了紀念 Katherine of Aragon 而建造的。

find out 找出；發現　　spend〔spɛnd〕*v.* 渡過

childhood〔'tʃaɪld,hʊd〕*n.* 童年時期

know well 很了解；很熟悉

connection〔kə'nɛkʃən〕*n.* 關聯

come across 偶然遇見；偶然發現

cross〔krɔs〕*n.* 十字標記；十字架

learn〔lɝn〕*v.* 知道　　*in one's honor* 紀念某人

Even then his search had not come to an end. It was only after he had spent several nights digging around the cross that he decided to write to Kit Williams to find out if he was wasting his time there.

即使到了那時候，他的搜尋仍未結束。他只在十字標誌附近挖掘幾個晚上之後，就決定寫信給基特・威廉斯，好弄清楚他是不是在那裡浪費時間。

search〔sɝtʃ〕*n.* 搜尋　　*come to an end* 結束

around〔ə'raʊnd〕*prep.* 在…附近

Williams encouraged him to continue, and on February 24ᵗʰ 1982, he found the treasure. It was worth $3,000, but the excitement it had caused since its burial made it much more valuable.

威廉斯鼓勵他要繼續挖，而就在 1982 年 2 月 24 日，他發現了寶藏。這個寶藏價值三千英磅，但是自從它被掩埋以來，它所帶來的刺激，則是更有價值。

encourage〔ɪn'kɝɪdʒ〕*v.* 鼓勵

worth〔wɝθ〕*adj.* 有…價值的；值…的

cause〔kɔz〕*v.* 引起；帶來　　burial〔'bɛrɪəl〕*n.* 掩埋

valuable〔'væljuəbḷ〕*adj.* 有價值的

31. (**D**) 第一段中畫線的字 "them" 是指
    (A) 足以引開他人注意之物。　　(B) 尋寶。
    (C) 亨利八世的六位妻子。　　(D) 化裝舞會的讀者。
    * underlined〔͵ʌndə·'laɪnd〕*adj.* 畫線的
    refer〔rɪ'fɝ〕*v.* 是指

32. (**C**) 在故事的一開始，幫助 Ken Roberts 找到金兔子的最重要線索
    是什麼？
    (A) Ampthill 公園裡的兩個石頭做的十字標誌。
    (B) 史蒂文生的金銀島。
    (C) Katherine of Aragon。
    (D) 威廉斯的家鄉。
    * hometown〔'hom͵taʊn〕*n.* 家鄉

33. (**B**) 在 Ampthill 的兩個石頭做的十字標記是建造來
    (A) 告訴人們一七七三年發生的事。
    (B) 向亨利八世的第一任妻子致敬。
    (C) 當作 Ampthill 公園的路標。
    (D) 告訴人們金兔子的所在地。
    * respect〔rɪ'spɛkt〕*n.* 敬意　　***serve as*** 當作
    sign〔saɪn〕*n.* 標誌　　inform〔ɪn'fɔrm〕*v.* 告知

34. (**C**) 下列何者說明了 Roberts 尋找金兔子的邏輯推理？
    a. 亨利八世的六位妻子。
    b. Katherine 在 Kimbolton 的埋葬地點。
    c. 威廉斯在 Ampthill 公園所渡過的童年。
    d. Katherine of Aragon。
    e. Ampthill 公園裡，用兩顆石頭做的十字標記。
    (A) a-b-c-e-d　　　　　　(B) d-b-c-e-a
    (C) a-d-b-c-e　　　　　　(D) b-a-e-c-d

35. (**B**) 本文討論的主題是什麼？

(A) 好玩的歷史事件。　　(B) 現代的尋寶。

(C) 化裝舞會這本書的吸引力。

(D) 邏輯思考的重要性。

Questions 36-38

"American dream? What a lie!" this comment was made by a Cuban teenage girl. She was attending a huge protest in Havana, Cuba, against American immigration laws.

「美國夢？真是天大的謊言！」這是一名古巴少女的評論。她參加了位於古巴哈瓦那的大型抗議活動，反對美國移民法。

lie〔laɪ〕 *n.* 謊言　　comment〔'kɑmɛnt〕 *n.* 評論
Cuban〔'kjubən〕 *adj.* 古巴的
teenage〔'tin,edʒ〕 *adj.* 十幾歲的　　attend〔ə'tɛnd〕 *v.* 參加
huge〔hjudʒ〕 *adj.* 大型的　　protest〔'protɛst〕 *n.* 抗議
Havana〔hə'vænə〕 *n.* 哈瓦那【古巴共和國首都】
Cuba〔'kjubə〕 *n.* 古巴
against〔ə'gɛnst〕 *prep.* 反對
immigration〔,ɪmə'greʃən〕 *n.* 移民　　law〔lɔ〕 *n.* 法案

Tens of thousands of people, including Cuba's President, took part in the protest to remember 30 missing Cubans, including 13 children.

數十萬人參與了這個抗議活動，包括古巴總統，他們是為紀念三十名失蹤的古巴人，包括十三名孩童。

include〔ɪn'klud〕 *v.* 包括　　president〔'prɛzədənt〕 *n.* 總統
take part in 參與　　remember〔rɪ'mɛmbə〕 *v.* 紀念
missing〔'mɪsɪŋ〕 *adj.* 失蹤的　　Cuban〔'kjubən〕 *n.* 古巴人

Their boat was lost in the Florida Straits after setting out from Cuba. It is one of the worst accidents involving Cubans being smuggled into the US.

他們的船從古巴出發後，就消失在佛羅里達海峽。這是和古巴人偷渡到美國有關的事件中，最糟的一件。

Florida (ˈflɔrədə) n. 佛羅里達
strait (stret) n. 海峽　　**set out** 出發
involve (ɪnˈvɑlv) v. 使和…有關係
smuggle (ˈsmʌgl̩) v. 走私；偷渡

Fourteen people died in the sinking of a smuggler's boat in 1998, and about 40 people died in 1994 when a tugboat sank near Havana. People believe that the "Cuban Adjustment Act" is responsible for the 30 people disappearing.

在一九九八年時，有十四個人死在沉沒的偷渡船上，而一九九四年時，約有四十個人死於沉沒在哈瓦那附近的拖船上。人們認為「古巴調節法」要為這三十個人的消失負責。

sinking (ˈsɪŋkɪŋ) n. 沉沒
smuggler (ˈsmʌglɚ) n. 偷渡客
tugboat (ˈtʌgˌbot) n. 拖船
adjustment (əˈdʒʌstmənt) n. 調節
responsible (rɪˈspɑnsəbl̩) adj. 負責的
Act (ækt) n. 法令　　disappear (ˌdɪsəˈpɪr) v. 消失

This 1996 law gives special allowances to Cuban immigrants who reach the US by whatever means. It gives them resident's status and chances to work.

一九九六年的這個法案，給古巴移民特別的限額，而且不管這些移民是用什麼方法抵達美國的。該法案都會給他們居民身分以及工作機會。

> allowance〔ə'lauəns〕*n.* 限額
> immigrant〔'ɪməgrənt〕*n.* 移民
> mean〔min〕*n.* 手段　　resident〔'rɛzədənt〕*n.* 居民
> status〔'stetəs〕*n.* 身分　　chance〔tʃæns〕*n.* 機會

It is very different from the US policy to immigrants from other countries. Because it encourages illegal immigration and these types of accidents, some called "the murderous law".

這和美國對他國移民的態度是大不相同的。因為它鼓勵非法移民，並使這些意外發生，所以有些人稱之為「蓄意謀殺法案」。

> policy〔'pɑləsɪ〕*n.* 政策
> encourage〔ɪn'kɝɪdʒ〕*v.* 鼓勵；促進
> illegal〔ɪ'liɡl̩〕*adj.* 非法的
> immigration〔,ɪmə'greʃən〕*n.* 移民
> murderous〔'mɝdərəs〕*adj.* 蓄意謀殺的

The US uses the so-called "dry foot" rule. Those found at sea are sent back to Cuba. But those who set foot on US soil are generally allowed to stay.

美國採取所謂的「乾腳」規則。在海上被發現的偷渡客，會被遣返回古巴，但是已經踏上美國國土的人，通常都會被允許留下。

> so-called〔'so'kɔld〕*adj.* 所謂的
> dry〔draɪ〕*adj.* 乾的　　*set foot on* 腳踏入；到達
> soil〔sɔɪl〕*n.* 土地；國家
> generally〔'dʒɛnərəlɪ〕*adv.* 通常　　allow〔ə'lau〕*v.* 允許

Castro said that the law encourages Cubans to undertake dangerous sea journeys with the hope of living in the US.

The immigration policy of the US has caused many problems between the US and Cuba. The two countries plan to meet to discuss immigration issues.

卡斯楚說，這項法案鼓勵古巴人從事危險的海上旅程，因為他們希望能住在美國。

美國的移民政策導致美國和古巴之間產生許多問題。這兩個國家打算要會面，以商討移民問題。

Castro〔'kæstro〕n. 卡斯楚【1976 年開始擔任古巴總統】

undertake〔ˌʌndɚ'tek〕v. 從事

journey〔'dʒɝnɪ〕n. 旅程　　issue〔'ɪʃʊ〕n. 問題

36. (**D**) 為什麼有這麼多人參加抗議活動？

(A) 因為他們的孩子失蹤了。

(B) 因為他們不准進入美國。

(C) 因為他們要回到自己的祖國。

(D) 因為他們反對美國移民法。

* homeland〔'hom,lænd〕n. 祖國

37. (**A**) 為什麼有這麼多人要偷渡去美國？

(A) 他們想在那邊過更好的生活。

(B) 他們在自己的國家被善待。

(C) 他們在美國有親戚。

(D) 美國人非常友善。

* treat〔trit〕v. 對待

relative〔'rɛlətɪv〕n. 親戚

38. (**D**) 「古巴調節法」帶來什麼結果？

    (A) 兩國永遠不打算會面。

    (B) 古巴調節法所帶來的結果跟美國對他國的移民政策非常類似。

    (C) 已經踏上美國國土的人，或是在海上的人，通常會被允許留下。

    (D) 它鼓勵古巴人從事危險的海上旅程。

Questions 39-43

If you are ever lucky enough to be invited to a formal dinner party in Paris, remember that the French have their own way of doing things, and that even your finest manners may not be "correct" by French customs.

如果你在任何時候，幸運獲邀參加巴黎的正式晚宴，那麼你要記住法國人有自己的處事方法，而且根據法國習俗，即使你非常有禮貌，也有可能犯錯。

    invite〔ɪn'vaɪt〕v. 邀請   formal〔'fɔrml〕adj. 正式的

    dinner party 晚宴；宴會   ***have one's own way*** 照自己的方法

    fine〔faɪn〕adj. 無可挑剔的

    manners〔'mænɚz〕n. pl. 禮貌

    correct〔kə'rɛkt〕adj. 正確的   custom〔'kʌstəm〕n. 習俗

For example, if you think showing up promptly at the time given on the invitation, armed with gifts of wine and roses, complimenting your hostess on her cooking, laughing heartily at the host's jokes and then leaping up to help the hostess will make you the perfect guest, think again.

例如，如果你認爲根據邀請卡上的時間準時出現，手裡拿著酒和玫瑰當禮物，讚美女主人的廚藝，並聽主人說笑話而盡情歡笑，然後匆忙跑去幫女主人的忙，會讓你成爲完美的客人的話，你要再想一想。

> **show up** 出席　　promptly ('pramptlɪ) adv. 準時地
> invitation (,ɪnvə'teʃən) n. 邀請卡
> arm (ɑrm) v. 裝備；帶著　　gift (gɪft) n. 禮物
> wine (waɪn) n. 酒
> compliment ('kɑmplə,mɛnt) v. 讚美
> hostess ('hostɪs) n. 女主人
> heartily ('hɑrtɪlɪ) adv. 盡情地
> host (host) n. 主人　　leap (lip) v. 突然發生；倉促行事
> guest (gɛst) n. 客人

Here Madame Nora Chabal, the marketing director of the Ritz Hotel in Paris, explained how it works.

The first duty of the guest is to respond to the invitation within 48 hours. Also, the guest may not ask to bring a guest because the hostess has chosen her own.

以下是巴黎麗池飯店的行銷主管——諾拉・莎貝爾夫人，對於爲什麼會這樣的解釋。

客人的第一個責任，就是在四十八小時內回覆邀請。還有，客人不能要求帶其他的客人，因爲女主人已經選好自己的客人了。

> Madame ('mædəm) n. 夫人
> marketing ('mɑrkɪtɪŋ) n. 行銷
> director (də'rɛktə) n. 主管　　explain (ɪk'splen) v. 解釋
> work (wɜk) v. 起作用；發生影響
> duty ('djutɪ) n. 責任　　respond (rɪ'spɑnd) v. 回覆

Flowers sent in advance are the preferred gift. They may also be sent afterwards with a thank-you note. It is considered a bad form to arrive with a gift of flowers in hand, which forces the hostess to find a vase when she is too busy to deal with it. See, that's the logic! The type of flowers sent has a code of its own, too.

大家比較喜歡的禮物是事先送達的花。也可以事後送上附有感謝卡的花。在到達的時候,手上拿著花當禮物,被認為是不太好的方式,因為那將迫使女主人在很忙的時候,還要去找花瓶來處理花。看吧,道理就在那裡!要送哪一種花也有規矩。

in advance 事先　　preferred〔prɪ'fɜd〕*adj.* 被喜好的
afterwards〔'æftɚwɚdz〕*adv.* 之後
a thank-you note 感謝函
consider〔kən'sɪdɚ〕*v.* 認為　　form〔fɔrm〕*n.* 方式
force〔fɔrs〕*v.* 強迫　　*deal with* 處理
logic〔'lɑdʒɪk〕*n.* 道理　　code〔kod〕*n.* 規則

One must never send chrysanthemums because they are considered too humble a flower for the occasion. Carnations are considered bad luck, and calla lilies are too reminiscent of funerals.

一定不能送菊花,因為在這種場合,菊花被認為是很卑微的花。康乃馨被認為會招來厄運,而海芋太容易使人聯想到葬禮。

chrysanthemum〔krɪs'ænθəməm〕*n.* 菊花
humble〔'hʌmbl̩〕*adj.* 卑微的　　occasion〔ə'keʒən〕*n.* 場合
carnation〔kɑr'neʃən〕*n.* 康乃馨　　luck〔lʌk〕*n.* 運氣
calla lily〔'kælə'lɪlɪ〕*n.* 海芋
reminiscent〔ˌrɛmə'nɪsn̩t〕*adj.* 使人聯想的
funeral〔'fjunərəl〕*n.* 葬禮

A bouquet of red roses is a declaration of romantic intent. Don't send those unless you mean it — and never to a married hostess. Though the French love wine, you must never bring a bottle to a dinner party.

一束紅玫瑰是宣告一種浪漫的企圖。除非你要表達這個意思，否則不要送一束紅玫瑰——而且絕不能送給已婚的女主人。雖然法國人喜歡酒，但是你絕不能帶一瓶酒去參加晚宴。

> bouquet〔boˋke〕n. 花束　　declaration〔ˏdɛkləˋreʃən〕n. 宣告
> romantic〔roˋmæntɪk〕adj. 浪漫的
> intent〔ɪnˋtɛnt〕n. 意圖　　unless〔ənˋlɛs〕conj. 除非
> married〔ˋmærɪd〕adj. 已婚的　　bottle〔ˋbɑtl〕n. 瓶

It's as if you feared your hosts would not have enough wine on hand, and that's an insult. You may, however, offer a box of chocolates which the hostess will pass around after dinner with coffee.

這樣做好像你怕主人手邊沒有足夠的酒，而那是一種侮辱。但是你可以帶一盒巧克力，女主人可以在餐後喝咖啡時，讓大家傳著吃。

> as if 彷彿　　fear〔fɪr〕v. 害怕　　on hand 在手邊
> insult〔ˋɪnsʌlt〕n. 侮辱　　pass〔pæs〕v. 傳遞

If an invitation is for eight o'clock, the <u>considerate</u> guest arrives at 8:15. Guests who arrive exactly on time or early are merely thoughtless ones who are not giving the hostess those last few minutes she needs to deal with details and any crisis.

如果是邀請卡上寫八點到，體貼的客人會在八點十五分到。正好準時到達或提早到達的客人，只會被認為是不懂得替別人著想的人，因為他們沒給女主人最後那幾分鐘，女主人需要那幾分鐘來處理細節和任何危機。

considerate〔kən'sɪdərɪt〕adj. 體貼的
exactly〔ɪg'zæktlɪ〕adv. 精確地;正好
on time 準時　　merely〔'mɪrlɪ〕adv. 僅;只
thoughtless〔'θɔtlɪs〕adj. 不替他人著想的
detail〔'ditel〕n. 細節　　crisis〔'kraɪsɪs〕n. 危機

The "correct" guest arrives between 15 to 20 minutes after the hour because dinner will be served exactly 30 minutes past the time on the invitation.
「舉止得體的」客人,會在約定時間過後十五到二十分之間到達,因為晚餐會正好在邀請卡上的時間過三十分鐘後準備好。

correct〔kə'rɛkt〕adj. 舉止得體的
serve〔sɝv〕v. 將(食物、飲料)準備好

39. (**A**) 根據法國的習俗,下列哪一項敘述正確?
(A) 當你收到邀請,要在兩天之內回覆。你最好事先送花過去。
(B) 正好準時抵達宴會。
(C) 帶一瓶好酒去參加宴會。
(D) 打電話去問能不能帶一位好友去參加宴會。

* statement〔'stetmənt〕n. 敘述
receive〔rɪ'siv〕v. 收到　　reply〔rɪ'plaɪ〕v. 回覆
had better 最好

40. (**D**) 關於送花,下列何者正確?
(A) 如果有人死了,要送菊花或海芋過去。
(B) 如果有人生病躺在醫院裡,要送康乃馨。
(C) 如果你被邀請參加晚宴,要送紅玫瑰給女主人。
(D) 如果你愛著某人,要送紅玫瑰。

* dead〔dɛd〕adj. 死的　　**be in love with** 愛著

41. (**B**) 如果你忙到無法事先送花，你應該怎麼做？

    (A) 在去赴宴的時候，帶一束花。

    (B) 事後送一束花，附上一張感謝函。

    (C) 帶一瓶酒，而不是帶一束花。

    (D) 女主人絕不會介意你是否送花。

    * *instead of* 而不是　　mind〔maɪnd〕v. 介意

42. (**C**) 最後一段的 "considerate" 是什麼意思？

    (A) 尊敬的　　　　　　(B) 值得考慮的

    (C) 考慮周到的　　　　(D) 相當多的

43. (**C**) 本文主要是關於？

    (A) 如何舉辦晚宴。

    (B) 如何送花。

    (C) 在法國晚宴的良好禮儀。

    (D) 不同的國家有不同的禮儀。

    * mainly〔'menlɪ〕adv. 主要地　　hold〔hold〕v. 舉辦

Questions 44-47

Easter, the principal festival of the Christian, celebrates the Resurrection of Jesus Christ on the third day after his Crucifixion. The origins of Easter date to the beginnings of Christianity, and it is probably the oldest Christian observance after the Sabbath (originally observed on Saturday, later on Sunday).

復活節是基督徒的主要節慶，它是慶祝耶穌基督被釘死在十字架後的第三天復活。復活節的起源，要追溯到基督教的開端，而且它可能是安息日（原本是在星期六慶祝，後來改成星期天）之後，最古老的基督教慶典。

Easter (ˈistɚ) *n.* 復活節　　principal (ˈprɪnsəpḷ) *adj.* 主要的

festival (ˈfɛstəvḷ) *n.* 節慶

Christian (ˈkrɪstʃən) *n.* 基督徒　　*adj.* 基督教的

celebrate (ˈsɛlə‚bret) *v.* 慶祝

resurrection (‚rɛzəˈrɛkʃən) *n.* 復活

Jesus Christ (ˈdʒizəsˈkraɪst) *n.* 耶穌基督

crucifixion (‚krusəˈfɪkʃən) *n.* 釘死於十字架上

origin (ˈɔrədʒɪn) *n.* 起源　　***date (back) to*** 起源於

Christianity (‚krɪstʃɪˈænətɪ) *n.* 基督教

observance (əbˈzɝvəns) *n.* 慶典

Sabbath (ˈsæbəθ) *n.* 安息日

originally (əˈrɪdʒənḷɪ) *adv.* 原本

observe (əbˈzɝv) *v.* 慶祝

Later, the Sabbath came to be regarded as the weekly celebration of the Resurrection. Meanwhile, many cultural historians find in the celebration of Easter a convergence of three traditions — Pagan, Hebrew and Christian.

後來安息日被視為每個禮拜慶祝耶穌復活的日子。同時,許多文化歷史學家發現,復活節慶典結合了三個傳統——異教徒、希伯來人,以及基督徒。

regard (rɪˈgɑrd) *v.* 被視為

celebration (‚sɛləˈbreʃən) *n.* 慶祝

meanwhile (ˈmin‚hwaɪl) *adv.* 同時

historian (hɪsˈtɔrɪən) *n.* 歷史學家

convergence (kənˈvɝdʒəns) *n.* 會合

tradition (trəˈdɪʃən) *n.* 傳統　　pagan (ˈpegən) *n.* 異教徒

Hebrew (ˈhibru) *n.* 希伯來人

According to St. Bede, an English historian of the early 8th century, Easter, derived from the name "Eostre", owes its origin to the old Teutonic mythology. Eostre was celebrated at the <u>vernal equinox</u>, when day and night get an equal share of the day.

聖伯達是八世紀初的英國歷史學家，根據他的說法，Easter 是源自「春之女神 Eostre」的名字，而春之女神是日爾曼的神話。人們在春分那一天爲春之女神舉行慶典，也就是晝夜等長的那一天。

St. Bede〔'sent'bid〕n. 聖伯達【673-735 A.D.，英國僧侶、歷史學家及神學家，著有最早期的英國史】

derive〔də'raɪv〕v. 源自；得到

Eostre 春之女神【爲北歐盎格魯撒克遜人於春天祭拜的神祇】

owe one's origin to… 起源於…

Teutonic〔tu'tanɪk〕adj. 日爾曼的

mythology〔mɪ'θɑlədʒɪ〕n. 神話

vernal〔'vɜnl〕adj. 春天的

equinox〔'ikwə,nɑks〕n. 春秋分；晝夜平分時

the vernal equinox 春分   equal〔'ikwəl〕adj. 相同的

share〔ʃɛr〕n. 部份

The English name "Easter" is much newer. When the early English Christians wanted others to accept Christianity, they decided to use the name Easter for this holiday so that it would match the name of the old spring celebration.

英國人的「Easter」這個名稱是比較後來才有的。早期的英國基督徒想要其他人接受基督教，所以他們決定把復活節叫作 Easter，這樣會跟古老的春天慶典的名稱比較像。

match〔mætʃ〕v. 和…相似

It was during Passover in 30 AD that Christ was crucified under the order of the Roman governor Pontius Pilate as the Jewish high priests accused Jesus of "blasphemy".

在西元三十年的踰越節時，耶穌基督在羅馬總督本丟彼拉多的命令之下，被釘上十字架，當時耶穌基督被猶太高層神職人員控告「褻瀆罪」。

> Passover (ˈpæsˌovɚ) *n.* 踰越節
> crucify (ˈkrusəˌfaɪ) *v.* 釘死在十字架上
> order (ˈɔrdɚ) *n.* 命令　　Roman (ˈromən) *adj.* 羅馬的
> governor (ˈgʌvənɚ) *n.* 總督　　Jewish (ˈdʒuɪʃ) *adj.* 猶太的
> priest (prist) *n.* 神職人員　　accuse (əˈkjuz) *v.* 控告
> blasphemy (ˈblæsfɪmɪ) *n.* 褻瀆

The resurrection came three days later, on the Easter Sunday. Thus the early Christian Passover turned out to be a unitive celebration in memory of the passion-death-resurrection of Jesus.

三天後，耶穌基督在復活節星期日重生了。因此，爲了紀念耶穌受難——死亡——復活，早期的基督教踰越節變成聯合慶祝這兩個節日。

> ***turn out to be*** 成爲　　unitive (ˈjunətɪv) *adj.* 聯合的
> ***in memory of*** 爲了紀念
> passion (ˈpæʃən) *n.* 耶穌的受難
> death (dɛθ) *n.* 死亡

However, by the 4th century, Good Friday came to be observed as a separate occasion. And the Pascha (Passover) Sunday had been devoted exclusively to the honor of the glorious resurrection.

但是，到了四世紀時，耶穌受難日變成獨立慶祝的節日。而踰越節則專門只用來紀念光輝的重生。

Good Friday 耶穌受難日　　separate (ˈsɛpərɪt) *adj.* 獨立的

occasion (əˈkeʒən) *n.* 節日　　Pascha (ˈpæskə) *n.* 復活節

devote (dɪˈvot) *v.* 把…專用於 <*to*>

exclusively (ɪkˈsklusɪvlɪ) *adv.* 僅；專門地

honor (ˈɑnɚ) *n.* 尊敬　*v.* 致敬

glorious (ˈglorɪəs) *adj.* 光輝的

Throughout Christendom the Sunday of Pascha had become a holiday to honor Christ.　At the same time many pagan spring rites came to be a part of its celebration.　Despite all the influence there was an important shift.

在所有的基督教國家，復活節星期天已經變成紀念耶穌基督的節日。
同時，許多異教的春季慶典也變成這個慶祝活動的一部份。儘管基督教
造成了這些影響，但還有一個重要的轉變。

throughout (θruˈaut) *prep.* 遍及

Christendom (ˈkrɪsn̩dəm) *n.* 基督教國家

rite (raɪt) *n.* 慶典　　despite (dɪˈspaɪt) *prep.* 儘管

influence (ˈɪnfluəns) *n.* 影響　　shift (ʃɪft) *n.* 轉變

No more glorification of the physical return of the Sun God.
Instead, the emphasis was shifted to the Son of Righteousness who had won, banishing the horrors of death forever.

人們不再讚美太陽神的肉體復生。取而代之的是，人們變成強調獲勝的
正義之子，因為祂把死亡的恐懼永遠趕走了。

glorification (ˌglorəfəˈkeʃən) *n.* 稱讚

physical (ˈfɪzɪkl) *adj.* 肉體的　　***Sun God*** 太陽神

instead (ɪnˈstɛd) *adv.* 取而代之的是

emphasis (ˈɛmfəsɪs) *n.* 強調　　shift (ʃɪft) *v.* 轉變

righteousness (ˈraɪtʃəsnɪs) *n.* 正義

banish (ˈbænɪʃ) *v.* 趕走　　horror (ˈhɔrɚ) *n.* 恐怖

The Feast of Easter was well-established by the second century. But there had been dispute over the exact date of the Easter observance between the Eastern and Western Churches.

復活節是在西元二世紀時確立的。但是東西方教堂對於慶祝復活節的確切日子仍有爭論。

feast (fist) *n.* 節日
well-established (ˈwɛləˈstæblɪʃt) *adj.* 已確立的
dispute (dɪˈspjut) *n.* 爭論　　exact (ɪgˈzækt) *adj.* 確切的

The East wanted to have it on a weekday because early Christians observed Passover every year on the 14th of Nisan, the month based on the lunar calendar. But, the West wanted Easter to always be a Sunday regardless of the date.

東方教堂希望復活節是在平日，因為早期的基督教徒，每年都是在猶太曆的七月十四日慶祝復活節，而且是根據農曆的月份。可是西方教堂希望復活節不管幾月幾日，永遠都是在星期天。

weekday (ˈwikˌde) *n.* 平日
Nisan (ˈnaɪsæn) *n.* 猶太曆的第七個月
lunar (ˈlunɚ) *adj.* 陰曆的　　calendar (ˈkæləndɚ) *n.* 曆法
lunar calendar 陰曆　　*regardless of* 不管

To solve this problem the emperor Constantine called the Council of Nicaea in 325. The council decided that Easter should fall on Sunday following the first full moon after the vernal equinox.

為了解決這個問題，君士坦丁大帝在西元三二五年時，召開尼西亞會議。該會議決定，復活節應該要在春分過後，第一個滿月以後的星期日。

solve (salv) *v.* 解決　　emperor (ˈɛmpərɚ) *n.* 皇帝
call (kɔl) *v.* 召開　　council (ˈkaunsḷ) *n.* 會議

Fixing the date of the Equinox was still a problem. The Alexandrians, noted for their rich knowledge in astronomical calculations were given the task. March 21 was made out to be the perfect date for spring equinox.

但是要固定春分的日期仍舊是個問題。以天文計算知識豐富聞名的亞歷山大人，被賦予這個任務。他們推斷出三月二十一日最適合作爲春分的日期。

fix〔fɪks〕v. 固定
Alexandrian〔ˌælɪgˈzændrɪən〕n. 亞歷山大人
noted〔ˈnotɪd〕adj. 聞名的　　knowledge〔ˈnɑlɪdʒ〕n. 知識
astronomical〔ˌæstrəˈnɑmɪkl̩〕adj. 天文的
calculation〔ˌkælkjəˈleʃən〕n. 計算
task〔tæsk〕n. 任務　　**make out** 推斷出

Accordingly, churches in the West observe it on the first day of the full moon that occurs on or following the Spring equinox on March 21. It became a movable feast between March 21 and April 25.

因此，西方的教堂會在三月二十一日春分當天起的第一個滿月，來慶祝復活節。復活節變成不固定的節日，日期介於三月二十一日到四月二十五日之間。

accordingly〔əˈkɔrdɪŋlɪ〕adv. 因此　　occur〔əˈkɜ〕v. 發生
movable〔ˈmuvəbl̩〕adj. 不定的

Still some churches in the East observe Easter according to the date of the Passover festival. The preparation takes off as early as Ash Wednesday from which the period of penitence in the Lent begins. Lent and Holy Week end on Easter Sunday, the day of the resurrection.

仍然有些東方教堂會根據踰越節的日期，來慶祝復活節。他們早從聖灰星期三就開始準備，從這一天開始，就是懺悔的四旬期。四旬期和受難週都結束於復活節的星期日，也就是重生之日。

preparation〔͵prɛpəˋreʃən〕*n.* 準備　　***take off*** 開始

Ash Wednesday 聖灰星期三【在復活節前，基督教徒禁慾懺悔四十天（四旬期 Lent）的第一天，天主教在這一天，用灰在信徒頭上灑成十字架的形狀，象徵懺悔】

period〔ˋpɪrɪəd〕*n.* 時期　　penitence〔ˋpɛnətəns〕*n.* 懺悔

Lent〔lɛnt〕*n.* 四旬齋；受難節

Holy Week 受難週【復活節前一週】

44.(**D**) 本文主要是關於
(A) 一位主教所舉辦的儀式。　　(B) 聖誕節的固定儀式。
(C) 門徒的讚美。　　(D) 基督徒的主要節慶。

* ritual〔ˋrɪtʃʊəl〕*n.* 儀式　　bishop〔ˋbɪʃəp〕*n.* 主教
regular〔ˋrɛgjələ〕*adj.* 固定的
service〔ˋsɝvɪs〕*n.* 儀式
Christmas〔ˋkrɪsməs〕*n.* 聖誕節
admiration〔͵ædməˋreʃən〕*n.* 讚美
disciple〔dɪˋsaɪpḷ〕*n.* 門徒

45.(**B**) 畫底線的字 "vernal equinox" 是什麼意思？
(A) 滿月。　　(B) 春分。
(C) 弦月。　　(D) 秋分。

* underlined〔͵ʌndəˋlaɪnd〕*adj.* 畫底線的

46.(**C**) 耶穌受難日什麼時候變成單獨慶祝的節日？
(A) 八世紀初。　　(B) 西元三十年。
(C) 四世紀。　　(D) 西元二○○六年。

47. (**D**)　復活節究竟是哪一天？

　　(A) 任何一個星期天。

　　(B) 在春假期間。

　　(C) 跟四月的愚人節同一天。

　　(D) 在三月二十一日和四月二十五日之間。

　　* **on earth** 究竟　　break〔brek〕n. 休假

Questions 48-50

A fish ladder provides a way for adult fish to go around dams or man-made barriers on their journey upstream to their spawning grounds.

　　魚梯提供成魚一條在水壩附近游動的道路，同時魚梯也是魚逆流游回產卵地時，途中的人造障礙物。

> ladder〔'lædə〕n. 梯子
>
> **fish ladder** 魚階【為使魚逆流游上瀑布或水壩，而做成的一系列階梯式水道】
>
> provide〔prə'vaid〕v. 提供　　adult〔ə'dʌlt〕adj. 發育成熟的
>
> dam〔dæm〕n. 水壩　　man-made〔'mæn'med〕adj. 人造的
>
> barrier〔'bærɪə〕n. 障礙物　　journey〔'dʒɝnɪ〕n. 旅程
>
> upstream〔'ʌp'strim〕adv. 逆流地　　spawn〔spɔn〕v. 產卵
>
> ground〔graund〕n. 場地

The Corps first built a fish ladder at the locks in 1917. In 1976, the Corps of Engineers constructed a new, improved fish ladder using 21 steps (weirs) instead of just 10.

　　美國軍團首先於一九一七年時，在水閘建了一座魚梯。一九七六年時，工程師團又建了一座改良過的新魚梯，有二十一階（魚梁），取代原本只有十階的魚梯。

Corps〔kɔr〕*n.* 軍團　　lock〔lɑk〕*n.* 水閘
engineer〔͵ɛndʒə'nɪr〕*n.* 工程師
construct〔kən'strʌkt〕*v.* 建造
improved〔ɪm'pruvd〕*adj.* 改良的　　step〔stɛp〕*n.* 階
weir〔wɪr〕*n.* 魚梁　　*instead of* 取代

The additional weirs reduce the distance that fish have to jump.
Tunnels through each weir were also added. Both improvements
make passage through the ladder easier for fish.

增加的魚梁減少了魚必須跳躍的距離。而且通過每一級魚梁的隧道也增
加了。這兩項進步使得魚兒更容易通過魚梯。

additional〔ə'dɪʃənḷ〕*adj.* 增加的　　tunnel〔'tʌnḷ〕*n.* 隧道
improvement〔ɪm'pruvmənt〕*n.* 進步
passage〔'pæsɪdʒ〕*n.* 通過；道路

The Corps also increased the amount of water going through
the fish ladder, called attraction water. Attraction water is swift-
flowing water that moves in the opposite direction that the fish
climb.

工程師團還增加了魚梯的流水量，這道流水叫作吸引式水流。吸引式
水流是一道快速流動的水流，其方向和魚類爬行方向相反。

attraction〔ə'trækʃən〕*n.* 吸引力
swift〔swɪft〕*adv.* 快速地　　flowing〔'floɪŋ〕*adj.* 流動的
opposite〔'ɑpəzɪt〕*adj.* 相反的　　direction〔də'rɛkʃən〕*n.* 方向
climb〔klaɪm〕*v.* 爬行；攀登

Because returning salmon instinctively know to swim upstream,
the downstream movement of water attracts fish to the ladder, as
does the "smell" of the water from the salmon's birthplace stream.

因為要返回產卵地的鮭魚，有逆流上游的本能，所以向下流動的水，會吸
引鮭魚來到魚梯，那些水流就像是有鮭魚出生地的水流「味道」一樣。

> salmon ('sæmən) *n.* 鮭魚
>
> instinctively (ɪn'stɪŋktɪvlɪ) *adv.* 本能地
>
> downstream ('daʊn'strim) *adv.* 順流地
>
> movement ('muvmənt) *n.* 移動　　attract (ə'trækt) *v.* 吸引
>
> as (əz) *conj.* 如…　　smell (smɛl) *n.* 氣味
>
> birthplace ('bɝθ,ples) *n.* 出生地　　stream (strim) *n.* 水流

48. (**B**) 本文主要是關於

    (A) 一位漁夫發明的工具。

    (B) 為鮭魚所設計的裝置。

    (C) 古代建造的水壩。

    (D) 受到嚴重污染的水流。

    * invent (ɪn'vɛnt) *v.* 發明　　device (dɪ'vaɪs) *n.* 裝置
    design (dɪ'zaɪn) *v.* 設計　　ancient ('enʃənt) *adj.* 古代的
    pollute (pə'lut) *v.* 污染　　seriously ('sɪrɪəslɪ) *adv.* 嚴重地

49. (**C**) 讓魚類更容易通過魚梯的兩項進步是什麼？

    (A) 額外的魚餌和水。　　　(B) 大量的資金和勞工。

    (C) 隧道和增加的魚梁。　　(D) 人造階梯和發電廠。

    * bait (bet) *n.* 魚餌　　capital ('kæpətl) *n.* 資金
    labor ('lebɚ) *n.* 勞工　　artificial (,ɑrtə'fɪʃəl) *adj.* 人造的
    power plant 發電廠

50. (**A**) 下列何者不是吸引式水流的特色？

    (A) 流速緩慢。　　　　　(B) 快速流動。

    (C) 流動方向相反。　　　(D) 快速流動。

    * rapidly ('ræpɪdlɪ) *adv.* 快速地

全民英語能力分級檢定測驗
GENERAL ENGLISH PROFICIENCY TEST
中 高 級 聽 力 測 驗
HIGH-INTERMEDIATE LISTENING COMPREHENSION TEST

This listening comprehension test will test your ability to understand spoken English. In this test, each conversation, short talk and question will be spoken JUST ONE TIME. They will not be written out for you. There are three parts to this test. Special instructions will be given to you at the beginning of each part.

Part A

In part A, you will hear 15 questions. After you hear a question, read the four choices in your test book and decide which one is the best answer to the question you have heard.

Example:

You will hear: Mary, can you tell me what time it is?

You will read: A. About two hours ago.
              B. I used to be able to, but not now.
              C. Sure, it's half past nine.
              D. Today is October 22.

The best answer to the question "Mary, can you tell me what time it is?" is C: "Sure, it's half past nine." Therefore, you should choose answer C.

1. A. The ring shrunk.
   B. I love jewelry.
   C. It's pure gold.
   D. It makes my finger itch.

2. A. The police use radar guns.
   B. The weather is fine for driving.
   C. A speeding ticket is fifty bucks.
   D. It costs one hundred dollars to see the race.

3. A. It's at 8 a.m.
   B. It's over by noon.
   C. French class starts after lunch.
   D. Class ends at nine fifteen.

4. A. It takes two minutes.
   B. You have to use quarters.
   C. It costs two dollars.
   D. It's automatic.

5. A. I want a top ten school.
   B. Accounting or business.
   C. I plan to attend graduate school.
   D. I'm ready for the challenge.

6. A. He sure is.
   B. He hopes to someday.
   C. Mom wants to retire next year.
   D. Search me, not him.

7. A. A piece on the outside broke.
   B. It was late returning.
   C. Space is a big mystery.
   D. The astronauts all had PhDs.

8. A. He's fluent in Japanese already.
   B. He wants to be a teacher.
   C. The tuition is expensive.
   D. Yes, he has already made up his mind.

9. A. My family is very healthy.
   B. Luckily, no I haven't.
   C. I broke a window once.
   D. I'm always breaking my glasses.

10. A. The teacher never pays attention.
    B. I never miss a single class.
    C. I'm just too shy.
    D. I'd like to help teach.

11. A. I'm very nervous about it.
    B. I don't know what to say.
    C. I'd appreciate your help, yes.
    D. It's next Monday at 9 a.m.

Please turn to the next page.

12. A. I like Shakespeare.
    B. The Bible is interesting.
    C. I have a weak singing voice.
    D. I love "We Are The World."

13. A. You need a blood test.
    B. Register one week ahead.
    C. They let you take your time.
    D. It lasts about three hours.

14. A. I have a thin skin.
    B. I have a weak immune system.
    C. That's a good answer. I don't know!
    D. I've never had the flu before.

15. A. I love ice cream.
    B. I drink water like a fish.
    C. Only when the weather is hot.
    D. I like coffee sometimes.

Part B

In part B, you will hear 15 conversations between a man and a woman. After each conversation, you will hear a question about the conversation. After you hear the question, read the four choices in your test book and choose the best answer to the question you have heard.

Example:

<u>You will hear</u>: (Man)   May I see your driver's license?
(Woman) Yes, officer. Here it is. Was I speeding?
(Man)   Yes, ma'am. You were doing sixty in a forty-five-mile-an-hour zone.
(Woman) No way! I don't believe you.
(Man)   Well, it is true and here is your ticket.

Question: Why does the man ask for the woman's driver's license?

<u>You will read</u>: A. She was going too fast.
B. To check its limitations.
C. To check her age.
D. She entered a restricted zone.

The best answer to the question "Why does the man ask for the woman's driver's license?" is A: "She was going too fast." Therefore, you should choose answer A.

Please turn to the next page. ⟹

16. A. No, it isn't.
    B. Yes, he is.
    C. No, it is.
    D. Yes, it is.

17. A. They are passionately in love.
    B. They're new friends and they like each other.
    C. They're planning to make up.
    D. They are hoping to get engaged.

18. A. Seeing Uncle Bert with a beauty.
    B. Seeing Uncle Bert alone.
    C. That his friend got divorced.
    D. That they were kissing at the mall.

19. A. It's going to be a super day.
    B. Cold and snowy.
    C. A shower will arrive.
    D. A cold front is moving in.

20. A. Giving him a flu shot.
    B. Examining his throat.
    C. Trying to repair the tooth.
    D. Injecting the man with a painkiller.

21. A. He's ten years old.
    B. He is ten months old.
    C. He's almost two.
    D. He's eleven years old.

22. A. $ 1.25.
    B. $ 1.35.
    C. 25 cents.
    D. 25 bucks.

23. A. She's allergic to it.
    B. She feels it's too pricey.
    C. She has an upset stomach.
    D. She dislikes it.

24. A. What the longest building
    is.
    B. What the largest
    man-made object is.
    C. What the oldest temple is.
    D. What the tallest structure is.

25. A. He's a manic depressive.
    B. He lost his girlfriend.
    C. He is losing his hair.
    D. He lost millions in a big
    deal.

26. A. Her braces were removed.
    B. She got new false teeth.
    C. She had a great dental
    exam.
    D. She hurt her arm and leg.

27. A. They both got ripped off.
    B. Student theft is on the rise.
    C. Student fees will be twice
    as expensive.
    D. The school is cutting
    student programs.

28. A. At a beauty salon.
    B. At a massage
    parlor.
    C. At a tailor shop.
    D. At a barber shop.

29. A. Hiking is a little
    dangerous.
    B. Five a.m. is way
    too early.
    C. He pulled a leg
    muscle.
    D. He also collects
    insects.

30. A. Go to a hospital.
    B. Call the E.R.
    hotline.
    C. Get some medicine
    ASAP.
    D. Get to a pharmacy
    fast.

Please turn to the next page. ⟹

Part C

In part C, you will hear several short talks. After each talk, you will hear 2 to 3 questions about the talk. After you hear each question, read the four choices in your test book and choose the best answer to the question you have heard.

Example:

<u>You will hear</u>:

Thank you for coming to this, the first in a series of seminars on the use of computers in the classroom. As the brochure informed you, there will be a total of five seminars given in this room every Monday morning from 6:00 to 7:30. Our goal will be to show you, the teachers of our schoolchildren, how the changing technology of today can be applied to the unchanging lessons of yesterday to make your students' learning experience more interesting and relevant to the world they live in. By the end of the last seminar, you will not be computer literate, but you will be able to make sense of the hundreds of complex words and technical terms related to the field and be aware of the programs available for use in the classroom.

Question number 1: What is the subject of this seminar series?

You will read: A. Self-improvement.
                B. Using computers to teach.
                C. Technology.
                D. Study habits of today's students.

The best answer to the question "What is the subject of this seminar series?" is B: "Using computers to teach." Therefore, you should choose answer B.

Now listen to another question based on the same talk.

You will hear:

    Question number 2: What does the speaker say participants will be able to do after attending the seminars?

You will read: A. Understand today's students.
                B. Understand computer terminology.
                C. Motivate students.
                D. Deal more confidently with people.

The best answer to the question "What does the speaker say participants will be able to do after attending the seminars?" is B: "Understand computer terminology." Therefore, you should choose answer B.

Please turn to the next page. ⏘⟹

31. A. In the Republic of
   Congo.
   B. On an ocean cruise.
   C. At an amusement
   park.
   D. At a boat race.

32. A. To keep their
   cameras dry.
   B. So they won't fall
   out.
   C. They might drown.
   D. The boat might tip
   over.

33. A. India.
   B. Egypt, Nile River.
   C. South America,
   Amazon River.
   D. Africa, the Congo.

34. A. Soccer.
   B. Rugby.
   C. American football.
   D. Basketball.

35. A. Both teams are from
   Miami.
   B. Both teams are
   undefeated.
   C. All the players are
   healthy.
   D. Both have excellent
   offenses and defenses.

36. A. Summer school
   applicants.
   B. Spring term students.
   C. Fall semester
   registrants.
   D. All graduate students.

37. A. A credit card.
    B. An instructor's approval.
    C. A paid tuition receipt.
    D. A number two lead pencil.

38. A. A car smashed the gate.
    B. A gun battle broke out.
    C. A vote was announced.
    D. Terrorists exploded a bomb.

39. A. They imposed a curfew.
    B. They captured suspects.
    C. They interrogated terrorists.
    D. They're going to evacuate.

40. A. Run For Your Life.
    B. Body For Life.
    C. Burn Fat.
    D. Exercise to Lose and Win.

41. A. Just 30 minutes a day.
    B. Five times a day.
    C. Just 12 weeks.
    D. Just 12 days a month.

Please turn to the next page. ▯⟹

42. A. Two.
    B. Several.
    C. One.
    D. None.

43. A. BBC international news.
    B. Soft stereo music.
    C. Two feature films.
    D. A duty free seminar.

44. A. Athletes are playing lazily.
    B. Team owners are selfish.
    C. Pros are behaving terribly.
    D. The fans are disgraceful.

45. A. Being good role models.
    B. Taking illegal drugs.
    C. Breaking the law.
    D. Acting like nasty kids.

-The End-

中高級閱讀測驗

HIGH-INTERMEDIATE

READING COMPREHENSION TEST

This test has three parts, with 50 multiple-choice questions (each with four choices) in total. Special directions will be provided for each part. You will have 50 minutes to complete this test.

Part A: Sentence Completion

This part of the test has 15 incomplete sentences. Beneath each sentence, you will see four words or phrases, marked A, B, C and D. You are to choose the word or phrase that best completes the sentences. Then on your answer sheet, find the number of the question and mark your answer.

1. When your _____ gets three drops of alcohol to every drop of your blood, you pass out.
   A. bloodstream
   B. brainstorm
   C. heartbeat
   D. vision

Please turn to the next page. ⟹

2. In the United States, 30 percent of the adult _____ has a "weight problem."
   A. circulation
   B. population
   C. congratulation
   D. regulation

3. Walking _____ no special equipment, and it can give you many of the same benefits as jogging or running.
   A. suffers
   B. differs
   C. requires
   D. acquires

4. Milk, cheese and tuna are all rich in an amino acid that helps produce a neurotransmitter in the brain that _____ sleep.
   A. induces
   B. supposes
   C. intends
   D. quivers

5. Happiness and unhappiness are not really flip sides of the same emotion. They are two _____ feelings.
   A. instant
   B. consistent
   C. distinct
   D. instinctive

6. Most people have a car or want to have one. The _____ automobile seems to represent the ultimate level in freedom and convenience.
   A. private
   B. constructive
   C. breathless
   D. emphatic

7. Because of the energy crisis, scientists in the major oil-consuming nations have become _____ interested in the potential of solar energy.
   A. sufficiently
   B. increasingly
   C. colloquially
   D. collectively

8. The Greenhouse Effect is caused by the action of the sun on gases that are released when we burn coal, oil, or other fuels _____.
   A. warmly
   B. boisterously
   C. delicately
   D. casually

Please turn to the next page. ⟹

9. Pardon me, and feel free to tell me what I can do to _____ the damage I caused.
   A. be blessed with
   B. fetch up
   C. make up for
   D. get the best of

10. Never _____ others' affairs. It's not your business.
   A. adapt yourself to
   B. poke your nose into
   C. meet your Maker for
   D. give a stimulus to

11. A special present, _____, was given to him by his mother for his birthday.
   A. which a chameleon
   B. a chameleon
   C. that is a chameleon
   D. chameleon

12. He works hard _____ he should fail.
   A. lest
   B. for fear of
   C. in case of
   D. X

Please turn to the next page.

13. He never comes without bringing me a bunch of flowers.

It means

    A. he scarcely brings me a bunch of flowers when comes

        to see me.

    B. he brings me a bunch of flowers at times when he calls

        on me.

    C. he never comes to visit me with a bunch of flowers.

    D. he carries a bunch of flowers to see me all the time.

14. Choose the WRONG sentence.

    A. The house the windows of which are broken is

        unoccupied.

    B. The house of which the windows are broken is

        unoccupied.

    C. The house's windows are broken is unoccupied.

    D. The house whose windows are broken is unoccupied.

15. No two men are of a mind. The word "a" in the sentence

means

    A. different.

    B. the same.

    C. high.

    D. low.

Please turn to the next page. ⇨

Part B: Cloze

This part of the test has two passages. Each passage contains seven or eight missing words or phrases. There is a total of 15 missing words or phrases. Beneath each passage, you will see seven or eight items with four choices, marked A, B, C and D. You are to choose the best answer for each missing word or phrase in the two passages. Then, on your answer sheet, find the number of the question and mark your answer.

Questions 16-23

The police in Taipei County are testing a new electronic system that shows the addresses of people ___(16)___ the police. Because many streets in the cities and towns of Taipei County have the same street names, the police are often unsure ___(17)___ exactly where they are supposed to go in the event of an emergency. If the system works well, there are plans to introduce it in other parts of the country. The Police Duty Center often needs over a minute just to ___(18)___ the precise address of a report. Taipei County's Yonghe has a Jhonghe Road while Jhonghe has a Yonghe Road. And there are Jhongshan Roads all over the place. Even local residents are often unable ___(19)___ correct directions, so the police sometimes have an impossible job. Many reports do not ___(20)___ , said Taipei County Police Duty Center Director. In the future, any call to 110 from a fixed line telephone in the county will immediately have its address ___(21)___ . Every second counts with emergency calls and the

Taipei County Police Duty Center's use of technology is probably overdue. Every call to the emergency line will have its address shown on a map, greatly ___(22)___ the police. They also hope the system will help cut down ___(23)___ prank calls. If the system proves to be effective, the police are looking to implement it all over the country.

16. A. who calls
    B. who call
    C. which calls
    D. which call

17. A. that
    B. with
    C. in
    D. of

18. A. leave out
    B. stand out
    C. work out
    D. hollow out

19. A. to giving
    B. for giving
    C. that give
    D. to give

20. A. be with child
    B. have the influence
    C. go into detail
    D. sit tight

21. A. appear
    B. appearing
    C. be appeared
    D. to appear

22. A. to assist
    B. assisting
    C. assisted
    D. assist

23. A. on
    B. for
    C. in
    D. by

Please turn to the next page. ⇨

Questions 24-30

What is intelligence anyway? When I was in the army, I took an intelligence test that all soldiers took, and, against ____(24)____ of 100, scored 160. I had an auto repairman once, who, on these intelligence tests, could not possibly have scored more than 80. ____(25)____, when anything went wrong with my car I hurried to him — and he always fixed it.

Suppose my auto repairman designed questions for some intelligence tests. On every one of them I'd prove myself a fool. In a world where I have to work with my hands, I'd do poorly. Consider my auto repairman ____(26)____. He had a habit of telling jokes. One time he said, "Doc, a deaf-and-dumb man needed some nails. Having entered a store, he put two fingers together on the counter and made ____(27)____ movements with the other hand. The clerk brought him a hammer. He ____(28)____ his head and pointed to the two fingers he was hammering. The clerk brought him some nails. He picked out the right size and left. Well, Doc, the next man who came in was blind. He wanted scissors. ____(29)____ do you suppose he asked for?" I lifted my right hand and made scissoring movements with two fingers. He burst out laughing and said, "Why, you fool, he used his voice and asked for them. I've been practicing that on all my customers today, but I knew ____(30)____ I'd catch you."

"Why is that?" I asked. "Because you are so goddamned educated, Doc. I knew you couldn't be very smart." And I have an uneasy feeling he had something there.

24. A. an average
    B. a total
    C. an exam
    D. a number

25. A. Then
    B. Thus
    C. Therefore
    D. Yet

26. A. again
    B. as usual
    C. too
    D. as well

27. A. cutting
    B. hammering
    C. waving
    D. circling

28. A. nodded
    B. raised
    C. shook
    D. turned

29. A. What
    B. How
    C. Who
    D. Which

30. A. for sure
    B. at once
    C. in fact
    D. right now

Please turn to the next page. ⟹

Part C: Reading

In this part of the test, you will read several passages. Each passage is followed by several questions. There is a total of 20 questions. You are to choose the best answer, A, B, C or D, to each question on the basis of what is stated or implied in the passage. Then on your answer sheet, find the number of the question and mark your answer.

Questions 31-34

In 1901, H. G. Wells, an English writer, wrote a book describing a trip to the moon. When the explorers landed on the moon, they discovered that the moon was full of underground cities. They expressed their surprise to the "moon people" they met. In turn, the "moon people" expressed their surprise. "Why," they asked, "are you traveling to outer space when you don't even use your inner space?"

H.G. Wells could only imagine traveling to the moon. In 1969, human beings really did land on the moon. People today know that there are no underground cities on the moon. However, the question that the "moon people" asked is still an interesting one. A growing number of scientists are seriously thinking about it.

Underground systems are already in place. Many cities have underground car parks. In some cities, such as Tokyo, Seoul and Montreal, there are large underground shopping areas. The "Chunnel", a tunnel connecting England and France, is now complete.

But what about underground cities? Japan's Taisei Corporation is now designing a network of underground systems, called "Alice Cities." The designers imagine using surface space for public parks and using underground space for flats, offices, shopping, and so on. A solar dome would cover the whole city.

Supporters of underground development say that building down rather than building up is a good way to use the earth's space. The surface, they say, can be used for farms, parks, gardens, and wilderness. H.G. Wells' "moon people" would agree. Would you?

31. The explorers in H. G. Wells' story were surprised to find that the "moon people"
    A. knew so little about the earth.
    B. understood their language.
    C. lived in so many underground cities.
    D. were ahead of them in space technology.

Please turn to the next page. ▭⇒

32. What does the underlined word "it" in paragraph 2 refer to?
    A. Discovering the moon's inner space.
    B. Using the earth's inner space.
    C. Meeting the "moon people" again.
    D. Traveling to outer space.

33. What sorts of underground systems are already here with us?
    A. Offices, shopping areas, power stations.
    B. Tunnels, car parks, shopping areas.
    C. Gardens, car parks, power stations.
    D. Tunnels, gardens, offices.

34. What would be the best title for the text?
    A. Alice Cities —— Cities of the Future
    B. Space Travel with H. G. Wells
    C. Enjoy Living Underground
    D. Building Up, Not Down

Questions 35-37

```
---------------------------| THEATRE |-------------------
                           ------------

                         City Varieties

                              The Headrow, Leeds.  Tel. 430808

        Oct. 10-11  only A Night at the Varieties.  All the fun of an
   old music hall with Barry Cwer, Duggle Brown, 6 dancers,
   Mystina, Jon Barker, Anne Duval and the Tony Harrison Trio.
   Laugh again at the old jokes and listen to your favourite songs.
   Performances: 8 pm nightly

   Admission: £5;  under 16 or over 60  £4.
```

York Theatre Royal

St. Leonard's Place, York. Tel. 223568

Sep. 23 —— Oct. 17 *Groping for Words* —— a comedy by Sue Townsend. Best known for her Adrian Mole Diaries, Townsend now writes about an evening class which two men and a woman attend. A gentle comedy.

Admission: First night, Mon. £2; Tue. —— Fri. £3.25-5.50; Sat. £3.50-5.75.

Halifax Playhouse

King's Cross Street, Halifax. Tel. 365998

Oct. 10-17 *On Golden Pond* by Ernest Thompson. This is a magical comedy about real people. A beautifully produced, well-acted play for everyone. Don't miss it.

Performances: 7:30 pm
Admission: £2. Mon. 2 seats for the price of one.

Grand Theatre

Oxford Street, Leeds. Tel. 502116
Restaurant and Cafe.

Oct 1-17 *The Secret Diary of Adrian Mole, aged 13*. Sue Townsend's musical play, based on her best-selling book.

Performances: Evenings 7:45; October 10-17, at 2:30 pm.
No Monday performances.
Admission: Tues. —— Thurs. £2-5; Fri & Sat: £2-6.

Please turn to the next page. ⟹

35. Which theatre offers the cheapest seat?
    A. Halifax Playhouse.
    B. City Varieties.
    C. Grand Theatre.
    D. York Theatre Royal.

36. If you want to see a play with old jokes and songs, which phone number will you ring to book a seat?
    A. 502116
    B. 223568
    C. 365998
    D. 430808

37. We may learn from the text that Sue Townsend is
    A. a writer.
    B. an actress.
    C. a musician.
    D. a director.

Questions 38-41

A thief, who dropped a winning lottery ticket at the scene of his crime, has been given a lesson in honesty. His victim, who picked up the ticket, then claimed the $25,000 prize, managed to trace him and handed over the cash. The robbery happened when a math professor named Vinicio Sabbatucci, 58, was changing a tyre on an Italian motorway. Another motorist, who stopped "to help," stole a suitcase from his car and drove off. The professor found the dropped ticket and put it in his pocket before driving home to Ascoli in eastern Italy.

Next day, he saw the lottery results on TV and, taking out the ticket, realized it was a winner. He claimed the 60 million lira prize. Then he began a battle with his conscience. Finally, he decided he could not keep the money despite having been robbed. He advertised in newspapers and on radio, saying: "I'm trying to find the man who robbed me. I have 60 million lira for him —— a lottery win. Please meet me, anonymity guaranteed."

Professor Sabbatucci received hundreds of calls from people hoping to trick him into handing them the cash. But there was one voice he recognized, and he arranged to meet the man in a park. The robber, a 35-year-old unemployed father of two, gave back the suitcase and burst into tears. He could not believe what was happening. "Why didn't you keep the money?" he asked. The professor replied: " I couldn't because it's not mine." Then he walked off, <u>spurning</u> the thief's offer of a reward.

Please turn to the next page. ⟹

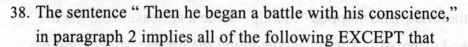
38. The sentence " Then he began a battle with his conscience,"
   in paragraph 2 implies all of the following EXCEPT that
   A. he knew what he should do as soon as he saw the lottery
      results.
   B. he hesitated about keeping the money for himself.
   C. he thought for a moment of avenging himself on the
      robber.
   D. he came to realize that honesty is more important than
      money.

39. Hundreds of people phoned professor Sabbatucci because
   they
   A. wanted to make fun of him.
   B. hoped to get the money.
   C. knew who the robber was.
   D. lost the lottery ticket.

40. The word "spurning" in the last paragraph can be replaced by
   A. accepting.
   B. claiming.
   C. rejecting.
   D. canceling.

41. If the story appears in a newspaper, the best title might be
   A. "A Thief's Lucky Day."
   B. "A Popular Math Professor."
   C. "A Magic Lottery."
   D. "A Reward of Dishonesty."

Questions 42-45

This is a page from a college information handbook. It tells you where you can find various college services and facilities.

Where To Find Help In The College

Here is the location of some important college services and facilities. Rooms numbered 100-130 are on the first floor and those numbered 200-230 on the second floor of the main college block.

Student Services Centre
Careers (Room 127)
The staff members are available to advise on career choice and applications for higher education.

Accommodation office (Room 207)
Mrs. J Mardle is available each afternoon from 1:30 to 4:30 to assist students with problems relating to housing.

Medical Room (Room 113)
Mrs. J Wright, the college nurse, is available each morning from 9:30 to 12:00 am. The college doctor is in attendance on Wednesday mornings.

Sports Office (Room 195)
Mrs. B Murie can provide information about sports and keep-fit activities.

Student Union Office (Room 230)
A range of services and advice (travel etc.) is provided.

Food Service (Room 200)
Mr. G Nunn is the manager and will do his best to help if you require a special diet.

Library (Room 114)
Besides books, this also has photocopying, video, audio-visual and computing facilities.

Self Access Language Learning Center (Room 224)
Students can attend on a drop-in basis from 9:00 am to 4:15 pm.

Please turn to the next page. ⟹

42. Where should you go for help if you fail to find a place to live?
    A. Room 200.
    B. Room 207.
    C. Room 113.
    D. Room 224.

43. Where should you go for help if you want to apply for a scholarship?
    A. Room 113.
    B. Room 200.
    C. Room 195.
    D. We don't know.

44. As a foreign student, you may go to Room 230 to
    A. book a plane ticket back to your motherland.
    B. ask for supply of some special food.
    C. inquire about educational fees.
    D. obtain a copy of certificate.

45. Which of the following statements is NOT true?
    A. You need a reservation in the Language Learning Centre.
    B. You are able to watch video programs in the library.
    C. The college nurse is available for some time before noon.
    D. Student Services Centre can help students apply for higher education.

Questions 46-50

_____ Scientists say people living in areas where bird flu has been found in poultry or wild birds should keep their cats indoors. They believe the potential role of felines in spreading the virus is being overlooked. Cats have been known to become infected with the H5N1 virus and lab experiments show they can give it to other cats, although nobody knows whether they can transmit it to people or poultry. A virologist and vegetarian warned that as well as passing H5N1 to other species, cats may help the virus to adapt into a more highly infectious strain in humans, which could spark a pandemic. We have to take a number of precautionary measures. We need to keep in mind that in principle mammals can be infected and that they can spread the disease.

Animals such as dogs, foxes, ferrets and seals may also be vulnerable to infection. In areas where H5N1 has been found in poultry or wild birds, cats should be kept away from infected birds or their droppings, and cats suspected of such contacts or showing symptoms of infection should be quarantined and tested. If animals or other carnivores show signs of illness, they should be tested for H5N1. When wild birds are infected we have seen that cats are quite effective in catching them and catching the disease. In this way they could be sentinels.

Please turn to the next page. ⟹

Deaths from H5N1, which has infected 191 people and killed 108, have been reported in cats in countries like Asia, Iraq and Germany. Tigers and leopards in zoos in Thailand have also died after eating fresh chicken carcasses. The potential role of cats should be considered in official guidelines for controlling the spread of H5N1 virus. Studies at a university have shown that cats can be infected through the respiratory tract, in a similar way to humans, but that the more likely route is through the gut by eating infected birds. The animals develop serious or fatal disease and can transmit the virus to other cats. We know that cat-to-cat transmission is possible. That is important because it would predispose the virus to adapt to mammals. We cannot exclude that.

It has also been shown that the amount of virus excreted by cats through the respiratory tract or in feces is lower than the levels from chickens. The scientists do not know how long cats can excrete the virus, the minimal amount of virus needed to cause infection in cats or whether virus transmission from cats to poultry, humans and other species is possible. But given the potential contribution of these carnivore hosts to both virus transmission and its adaptation to mammals, we believe the time for increased surveillance and precaution is here. Scientists need to learn more about what role, if any, cats have in spreading H5N1 before making such blanket recommendations.

46. H5N1 virus will lead to
    A. AIDS.   B. SARS.
    C. bird flu.   D. diabetes.

47. If animals or other carnivores show signs of illness, they
    should be _____ H5N1.
    A. referred to   B. examined for
    C. regarded as   D. kept away from

48. The rate of deaths from H5N1 is about
    A. 47.5%.   B. 38.5%.
    C. 56.5%.   D. 60.5%.

49. According to the passage, which of the following is
    CORRECT?
    A. Cat-to-cat transmission is almost impossible in this world.
    B. Cats have been known to become infected with the
       H5N1 virus.
    C. Cats may help the bacterium to adapt into a more highly
       infectious strain in humans.
    D. It is out of the question that cats can be infected through
       the respiratory tract.

50. Which of the following could be the topic sentence for this
    passage?
    A. Keeping away from the wild animals is necessary.
    B. Cats may play a role in bird flu spread.
    C. There are a lot of differences between cats and human
       beings.
    D. What's the potential for cats to spread a fatal disease?

中高級聽力測驗詳解 ②

PART A

1. (**D**) Why aren't you wearing your wedding ring?
   A. The ring shrunk.　　　B. I love jewelry.
   C. It's pure gold.　　　D. It makes my finger itch.

   * wedding ('wɛdɪŋ) n. 婚禮
   shrink (ʃrɪŋk) v. 縮水 (三態變化為 : shrink-shrank-shrunk)
   jewelry ('dʒuəlrɪ) n. 珠寶　　pure (pjʊr) adj. 純粹的
   pure gold 純金　　itch (ɪtʃ) v. 發癢

2. (**C**) What's the fine for speeding on the highway?
   A. The police use radar guns.
   B. The weather is fine for driving.
   C. A speeding ticket is fifty bucks.
   D. It costs one hundred dollars to see the race.

   * fine (faɪn) n. 罰金　　speeding ('spidɪŋ) n. 超速
   highway ('haɪ,we) n. 公路　　radar ('redɑr) n. 雷達
   gun (gʌn) n. 槍　　ticket ('tɪkɪt) n. 罰單
   buck (bʌk) n. 美元　　race (res) n. 比賽

3. (**A**) What time does your final exam start?
   A. It's at 8 a.m.　　　B. It's over by noon.
   C. French class starts after lunch.
   D. Class ends at nine fifteen.

   * ***final exam*** 期末考　　***by noon*** 在中午之前
   French (frɛntʃ) n. 法語

4. (**C**) How much does the automatic car wash cost?

    A. It takes two minutes.

    B. You have to use quarters.

    C. It costs two dollars.

    D. It's automatic.

    * automatic〔͵ɔtə'mætɪk〕*adj.* 自動的
    automatic car wash 電動洗車
    quarter〔'kwɔrtɚ〕*n.* (美國、加拿大) 二角五分銀幣

5. (**B**) What are you going to major in in college?

    A. I want a top ten school.

    B. Accounting or business.

    C. I plan to attend graduate school.

    D. I'm ready for the challenge.

    * major〔'medʒɚ〕*v.* 主修
    college〔'kɑlɪdʒ〕*n.* 大學   top〔tɑp〕*adj.* 頂尖的
    accounting〔ə'kauntɪŋ〕*n.* 會計學
    business〔'bɪznɪs〕*n.* 商業
    attend〔ə'tɛnd〕*v.* 上 (學)   *graduate school* 研究所
    challenge〔'tʃælɪndʒ〕*n.* 挑戰

6. (**A**) Is your father really retiring?

    A. He sure is.

    B. He hopes to someday.

    C. Mom wants to retire next year.

    D. Search me, not him.

    * retiring〔rɪ'taɪrɪŋ〕*adj.* 退休的   retire〔rɪ'taɪr〕*v.* 退休

7. (**A**) Why did the Space Shuttle explode?

    A. A piece on the outside broke.

    B. It was late returning.

    C. Space is a big mystery.

    D. The astronauts all had PhDs.

    * *space shuttle* 太空梭　　explode〔ɪk'splod〕*v.* 爆炸

    break〔brek〕*v.* 破掉　　space〔spes〕*n.* 太空

    mystery〔'mɪstərɪ〕*n.* 祕密

    astronaut〔'æstrə,nɔt〕*n.* 太空人

    PhD 博士學位（= *doctor of philosophy*，此處指的是高深

    的學問）

8. (**D**) Is your brother really going to study in Japan?

    A. He's fluent in Japanese already.

    B. He wants to be a teacher.

    C. The tuition is expensive.

    D. Yes, he has already made up his mind.

    * fluent〔'fluənt〕*adj.* 流利的　　tuition〔tju'ɪʃən〕*n.* 學費

    make up one's mind 某人下定決心

9. (**B**) Have you ever broken a bone?

    A. My family is very healthy.

    B. Luckily, no I haven't.

    C. I broke a window once.

    D. I'm always breaking my glasses.

    * break〔brek〕*v.* 折斷；打破

    bone〔bon〕*n.* 骨頭

10. (**C**) Why don't you ever participate in class?

    A. The teacher never pays attention.

    B. I never miss a single class.

    C. I'm just too shy.

    D. I'd like to help teach.

    * participate (pɑr'tɪsə‚pet) *v.* 參加

    pay attention 注意   miss (mɪs) *v.* 錯過

    single ('sɪŋgl̩) *adj.* 單一的   shy (ʃaɪ) *adj.* 害羞的

11. (**C**) Would you like to practice for your job interview?

    A. I'm very nervous about it.

    B. I don't know what to say.

    C. I'd appreciate your help, yes.

    D. It's next Monday at 9 a.m.

    * practice ('præktɪs) *v.* 練習   interview ('ɪntə‚vju) *n.* 面談

    nervous ('nɝvəs) *adj.* 緊張的

    appreciate (ə'priʃɪ‚et) *v.* 感激

12. (**D**) What's one of your favorite songs?

    A. I like Shakespeare.

    B. The Bible is interesting.

    C. I have a weak singing voice.

    D. I love "We Are The World."

    * favorite ('fevərɪt) *adj.* 最喜愛的

    Shakespeare ('ʃek‚spɪr) *n.* 莎士比亞 (英國的劇作家和

      詩人，1564-1616)

    the Bible 聖經   weak (wik) *adj.* 差的

13. (**D**) How long will a full medical exam take?

    A.　You need a blood test.

    B.　Register one week ahead.

    C.　They let you take your time.

    D.　It lasts about three hours.

    * full〔fʊl〕*adj.* 完全的　　*medical exam* 健康檢查

    blood〔blʌd〕*n.* 血液　　register〔'rɛdʒɪstɚ〕*v.* 登記

    take one's time 慢慢來　　last〔læst〕*v.* 持續

14. (**B**) How come you're always catching a cold?

    A.　I have a thin skin.

    B.　I have a weak immune system.

    C.　That's a good answer.　I don't know!

    D.　I've never had the flu before.

    * *How come⋯?* 爲什麼～？（接直說法）

    catch a cold 得到感冒

    have a thin skin 臉皮薄

    immune〔ɪ'mjun〕*adj.* 免疫的

    system〔'sɪstəm〕*n.* 系統　　flu〔flu〕*n.* 流行性感冒

15. (**C**) Do you like to drink cold beverages?

    A.　I love ice cream.

    B.　I drink water like a fish.

    C.　Only when the weather is hot.

    D.　I like coffee sometimes.

    * beverage〔'bɛvərɪdʒ〕*n.* 飲料

    drink like a fish 牛飲

PART B .

16. (**D**) M : You speak great Chinese!

W : You must be kidding. My pronunciation is
atrocious!

M : No, it isn't. Don't be so hard on yourself.

W : My tones are all mixed up. The four tones really
confuse me.

M : I understand you perfectly.

Question : Is the man's praise sincere?

A. No, it isn't.

B. Yes, he is.

C. No, it is.

D. Yes, it is.

* pronunciation〔prə͵nʌnsɪ'eʃən〕*n.* 發音
atrocious〔ə'troʃəs〕*adj.* 糟透的
be hard on 苛刻對待　　tone〔ton〕*n.* 音的高低
mix up 混淆　　*the four tones* （中國話的）四聲
confuse〔kən'fjuz〕*v.* 使困惑
praise〔prez〕*n.* 讚美　　sincere〔sɪn'sɪr〕*adj.* 真誠的

17. (**B**) W : Here's my name card. Please drop me a line.

M : I'll keep in touch for sure.

W : I'd appreciate that.

M : Here's my e-mail address. I'll be waiting to hear
from you.

W : Here's mine, too. Adios, amigo.

Question: How do they feel about each other?

A. They are passionately in love.

B. They're new friends and they like each other.

C. They're planning to make up.

D. They are hoping to get engaged.

* ***name card*** 名片　　***drop sb. a line*** 寄短信給某人
keep in touch 保持聯絡　　***hear from*** 得知某人的音信
adios〔‚ɑdɪ'os〕*interj.* 再見　　amigo〔ə'migo〕*n.* 朋友
passionately〔'pæʃənɪtlɪ〕*adv.* 熱情地
make up 和好　　***get engaged*** 訂婚

18. (**A**) M: I ran into your Uncle Bert at the mall.

W: Really? Was he with anyone?

M: Yes, he was arm in arm with a beautiful blonde.

W: That must be his new wife.

M: I didn't even know he and your aunt got divorced!

Question: What surprised the man?

A. Seeing Uncle Bert with a beauty.

B. Seeing Uncle Bert alone.

C. That his friend got divorced.

D. That they were kissing at the mall.

* ***run into*** 巧遇　　mall〔mɔl〕*n.* 購物中心
arm in arm 臂挽著臂
blonde〔blɑnd〕*n.* 金髮的女人
divorce〔də'vɔrs〕*v.* 與～離婚
beauty〔'bjutɪ〕*n.* 美女

19. (**B**) W: What's the forecast for tomorrow?

M: It's supposed to snow 12 inches.

W: Oh, darn it. Another snowstorm! Winter is depressing!

M: It's super cold, too.

W: Ain't that the truth?

Question: How will tomorrow be?

A. It's going to be a super day.

B. Cold and snowy.

C. A shower will arrive.

D. A cold front is moving in.

* forecast ('for,kæst) n. 預報

   be supposed to 應該   snow (sno) v. 下雪

   inch (ɪntʃ) n. 英吋 (約 2.54 公分)

   darn it 該死 (= *damn it*)

   snowstorm ('sno,storm) n. 暴風雪

   depressing (dɪ'prɛsɪŋ) adj. 鬱悶的

   ain't (ent) is not 的縮寫

   snowy ('snoɪ) adj. 下雪的

   shower ('ʃauɚ) n. 陣雨   *cold front* 冷鋒

20. (**D**) M: Doc, I chipped my tooth on an ice cube.

W: How does it feel?

M: The pain is horrendous, almost unbearable!

W: Here's a painkiller. Please try to relax.

M: That needle is longer than my finger!

Question: What is the dentist doing?

A. Giving him a flu shot.

B. Examining his throat.

C. Trying to repair the tooth.

D. Injecting the man with a painkiller.

* doc〔dɑk〕*n.* 醫生（用於稱呼）

  chip〔tʃɪp〕*v.* 弄缺（東西的邊緣）

  ice cube 冰塊　　pain〔pen〕*n.* 疼痛

  horrendous〔hɔ'rɛndəs〕*adj.* 可怕的

  unbearable〔ʌn'bɛrəbḷ〕*adj.* 難以忍受的

  painkiller〔'pen,kɪlɚ〕*n.* 止痛藥

  relax〔rɪ'læks〕*v.* 放鬆　　needle〔'nidḷ〕*n.*（注射的）針

  dentist〔'dɛntɪst〕*n.* 牙醫　　*give sb. a shot* 替某人打針

  examine〔ɪg'zæmɪn〕*v.* 檢查　　throat〔θrot〕*n.* 喉嚨

  repair〔rɪ'pɛr〕*v.* 修補　　inject〔ɪn'dʒɛkt〕*v.* 注射

21. (**B**) W: Congratulations on your new child.

M: Thank you, we're very excited.

W: Where's he from and how old is he?

M: He's from Korea and he's ten months old.

W: God bless you. Good luck.

Question: How old is their new adopted child?

A. He's ten years old. B. He is ten months old.

C. He's almost two. D. He's eleven years old.

* congratulations〔kən,grætʃə'leʃənz〕*n. pl.* 恭喜

  Korea〔ko'riə〕*n.* 韓國

  adopted〔ə'dɑptɪd〕*adj.* 收養的

22. (**A**) M: Excuse me, where's the Metro from here?

W: Go down this street three blocks and take a right. You'll see the entrance there.

M: Thanks and how much is the fare?

W: You have to buy a token which costs a dollar twenty-five.

M: You're a big help. Thanks a bunch.

Question: How much does a subway ride cost?

A. $ 1.25.   B. $ 1.35.   C. 25 cents.   D. 25 bucks.

* Metro〔'mɛtro〕*n.* 地下鐵   ***take a right*** 右轉
  entrance〔'ɛntrəns〕*n.* 入口   fare〔fɛr〕*n.* 車資
  token〔'tokən〕*n.* 代幣   ***Thanks a bunch***. 非常謝謝。
  subway〔'sʌb‚we〕*n.* 地下鐵   cent〔sɛnt〕*n.* 一分錢

23. (**D**) W: Where do you feel like eating?

M: I'm in the mood for Japanese!

W: Great, let's have sushi and seafood.

M: That sounds great. Let's also order some raw fish.

W: Yuck. No way, Jose!

Question: How does the woman feel about sashimi?

A. She's allergic to it.   B. She feels it's too pricey.

C. She has an upset stomach.

D. She dislikes it.

* ***feel like*** 想要   mood〔mud〕*n.* 意向
  sushi〔'susɪ〕*n.* 壽司   ***raw fish*** 生魚片 (= *sashimi*)
  yuck〔jʌk〕*interj.* 表示厭惡的聲音
  allergic〔ə'lɝdʒɪk〕*adj.* 過敏的   pricey〔'praɪsɪ〕*adj.* 昂貴的
  upset〔ʌp'sɛt〕*adj.* 不舒服的   stomach〔'stʌmək〕*n.* 胃

24. (**B**) M：What is the largest man-made object in the world?

W：How about the pyramids in Egypt?

M：Nope, but good guess.

W：Oh, I know.　The Great Wall of China.

M：Bingo, you got it.　You're right on the money!

Question：What does the man want to know?

A.　What the longest building is.

B.　What the largest man-made object is.

C.　What the oldest temple is.

D.　What the tallest structure is.

＊ man-made（'mæn'med）*adj.* 人造的

　　object（'abdʒɪkt）*n.* 物體

　　pyramid（'pɪrəmɪd）*n.* 金字塔

　　Egypt（'idʒɪpt）*n.* 埃及

　　nope（nop）*adv.* 不是　　***good guess*** 猜得好

　　the Great Wall 萬里長城

　　bingo（'bɪŋgo）*interj.* 好（表示意外的歡喜）

　　You're right on the money! 你說得非常正確！

　　temple（'tɛmpḷ）*n.* 廟

　　structure（'strʌktʃə）*n.* 建築物

25. (**C**) W：Hey, you're getting a bald spot.

M：Please, don't remind me.

W：Don't be so gloomy.　It's no big deal.

M：I don't want to look older; besides, I like my hair.

W：I can think of worse things to lose.　Cheer up!

Question : Why is the man a little sad?

A. He's a manic depressive.

B. He lost his girlfriend.

C. He is losing his hair.

D. He lost millions in a big deal.

* bald〔bɔld〕 *adj.* 禿頭的　　　spot〔spɑt〕 *n.* 部位

remind〔rɪ'maɪnd〕 *v.* 提醒

gloomy〔'glumɪ〕 *adj.* 悶悶不樂的

It's no big deal. 沒什麼大不了的。

besides〔bɪ'saɪdz〕 *adv.* 此外

I can think of worse things to lose. 我可以想到更糟的事。

　　（表示還有其他的事更糟，用來安慰別人）

Cheer up! 振作！

manic〔'mænɪk〕 *adj.*【醫學】狂躁症的

depressive〔dɪ'prɛsɪv〕 *n.* 憂鬱症患者

million〔'mɪljən〕 *n.* 百萬　　　deal〔dil〕 *n.* 交易

26. (**A**) M : You got your braces off. Your teeth look great.

W : Yeah, I'm very pleased with the results.

M : Wow, your teeth are so pearly white, too.

W : I just had them bleached.

M : I bet that cost an arm and a leg.

Question : What happened to the woman?

A. Her braces were removed.

B. She got new false teeth.

C. She had a great dental exam.

D. She hurt her arm and leg.

* brace〔bres〕n. (牙齒)矯正器；牙套
  pleased〔plizd〕adj. 高興的
  result〔rɪ'zʌlt〕n. 結果
  pearly〔'pɝlɪ〕adj. 似珍珠的
  bleach〔blitʃ〕v. 漂白　　bet〔bɛt〕v. 打賭
  an arm and a leg 過高的代價
  remove〔rɪ'muv〕v. 去除　　**false teeth** 假牙
  dental〔'dɛntl̩〕adj. 牙齒的
  exam〔ɪg'zæm〕n. 檢查 (= *examination*)
  hurt〔hɝt〕v. 使受傷

27. (**C**) W: I heard our tuition is going to double!

　　M: That's right. It's highway robbery.

　　W: I'm going to form a student protest march.

　　Question: Why are the two students angry?

　　A. They both got ripped off.

　　B. Student theft is on the rise.

　　C. Student fees will be twice as expensive.

　　D. The school is cutting student programs.

* tuition〔tju'ɪʃən〕n. 學費
  double〔'dʌbl̩〕v. 加倍　　highway〔'haɪˌwe〕n. 公路
  robbery〔'rɑbərɪ〕n. 搶劫
  highway robbery 過高的價格
  form〔fɔrm〕v. 組成　　protest〔'protɛst〕n. 抗議
  march〔mɑrtʃ〕n. 遊行　　**rip off** 偷竊
  theft〔θɛft〕n. 偷竊　　**on the rise** 增加中
  fee〔fi〕n. 學費　　cut〔kʌt〕v. 削減

28. (**D**) M: I'd like a trim, please.

　　　　W: How much off the back and sides?

　　　　M: Oh, about an inch or so.　Please don't cut too much.

　　　　W: OK, I understand, not too short.

　　　　M: Please shave my sideburns, too.

　　　　Question: Where are they?

　　　　A.　At a beauty salon.

　　　　B.　At a massage parlor.

　　　　C.　At a tailor shop.

　　　　D.　At a barber shop.

　　　* trim〔trɪm〕*n.* 理髮
　　　　How much off the back and sides? 後面和旁邊要剪去多少？
　　　　or so 大約　　　shave〔ʃev〕*v.* 刮（鬍子）
　　　　sideburns〔'saɪd,bɜnz〕*n.* 鬢角
　　　　beauty salon 美容院　　***massage parlor*** 按摩院
　　　　tailor shop 服裝店　　***barber shop*** 理髮院

29. (**B**) W: Want to go for a hike with me tomorrow morning?

　　　　M: That sounds great.　What time?

　　　　W: We meet at 5 a.m.

　　　　M: You're pulling my leg, right?

　　　　W: No, the early bird catches the worm, and a beautiful
　　　　　　 sunrise to boot!

　　　　Question: How does the man feel?

　　　　A.　Hiking is a little dangerous.

　　　　B.　Five a.m. is way too early.

C. He pulled a leg muscle.

D. He also collects insects.

* ***pull one's leg*** 嘲弄（某人）

The early bird catches the worm. 【諺】早起的鳥兒有蟲吃。

to boot 而且　　muscle（'mʌsḷ）n. 肌肉

collect（kə'lɛkt）v. 收集　　insect（'ɪnsɛkt）n. 昆蟲

30. (**A**) M：Ouch! Something just bit me! It really stings.

W：It was probably a bee or a hornet.

M：God, I hope not. I'm allergic to bee stings.

W：Let's get to an E.R. It's better to be safe than sorry.

M：That would put my mind at ease, thanks.

Question：What are they going to do?

A. Go to a hospital.

B. Call the E.R. hotline.

C. Get some medicine ASAP.

D. Get to a pharmacy fast.

* bite（baɪt）v. 咬（三態變化為：bite-bit-bitten）

sting（stɪŋ）v. 刺痛　n. 螫傷

hornet（'hɔrnɪt）n. 大黃蜂

allergic（ə'lɝdʒɪk）adj. 過敏的

E.R. 急診室（= emergency room）

It's better to be safe than sorry. 安全總比遺憾好。

at ease 輕鬆地　　hotline（'hɑt,laɪn）n. 熱線電話

ASAP 儘快（= as soon as possible）

pharmacy（'fɑrməsɪ）n. 藥房

PART C.

Questions 31-33 refer to the following announcement.

Good morning, brave adventurers, and welcome aboard the African Queen. We are about to embark on a dangerous journey down the Congo River. We'll see wild elephants, hungry crocodiles, ferocious hippopotamuses and huge python snakes. Everyone should be careful to keep your arms and legs inside the boat at all times. Don't worry. I have a rifle in case we are attacked by the local savages. These headhunters would just love to have us for dinner! Be prepared to get wet as we approach a giant waterfall around the next bend. You are all free to take pictures, but don't get your cameras wet. Now, have fun and good luck on Disneyland's famous Wild Jungle Cruise!

Vocabulary

brave (brev) *adj.* 勇敢的   adventurer (əd'vɛntʃərə) *n.* 冒險者
aboard (ə'bord) *prep.* 登上 (船、車、飛機)   *be about to* 即將
embark (ɪm'bark) *v.* 從事   journey ('dʒɝnɪ) *n.* 旅程
the Congo River 剛果河   wild (waɪld) *adj.* 野生的
crocodile ('krakə,daɪl) *n.* 鱷魚   ferocious (fə'roʃəs) *adj.* 凶猛的
hippopotamus (,hɪpə'patəməs) *n.* 河馬
python ('paɪθan) *n.* 蟒蛇   *at all times* 時常

rifle〔ˈraɪfḷ〕n. 步槍　　*in case* 以防　　attack〔əˈtæk〕v. 攻擊

local〔ˈlokḷ〕adj. 當地的　　savage〔ˈsævɪdʒ〕n. 野蠻人

headhunter〔ˈhɛd͵hʌntɚ〕n.（原始部落的）獵頭族

approach〔əˈprotʃ〕v. 接近　　giant〔ˈdʒaɪənt〕adj. 巨大的

waterfall〔ˈwɔtɚ͵fɔl〕n. 瀑布　　bend〔bɛnd〕n. 轉彎處

free〔fri〕adj. 自由的　　camera〔ˈkæmərə〕n. 相機

jungle〔ˈdʒʌŋgḷ〕n. 叢林　　cruise〔kruz〕n.（坐船）旅行

31. (**C**) Where are these passengers really at?

　　　A. In the Republic of Congo.

　　　B. On an ocean cruise.　　C. At an amusement park.

　　　D. At a boat race.

　　　* passenger〔ˈpæsṇdʒɚ〕n. 乘客

　　　　the Republic of Congo 剛果民主共和國

　　　　amusement park 遊樂園　　race〔res〕n. 比賽

32. (**A**) Why does the guide warn them about the waterfall?

　　　A. To keep their cameras dry.

　　　B. So they won't fall out.

　　　C. They might drown.　　D. The boat might tip over.

　　　* guide〔gaɪd〕n. 導遊　　warn〔wɔrn〕v. 警告

　　　　fall out 掉出去　　drown〔draʊn〕v. 溺死　　*tip over* 翻覆

33. (**D**) What fictional place are they in?

　　　A. India.　　　　　　B. Egypt, Nile River.

　　　C. South America, Amazon River.

　　　D. Africa, the Congo.

　　　* fictional〔ˈfɪkʃənḷ〕adj. 虛構的　　India〔ˈɪndɪə〕n. 印度

　　　　Nile River 尼羅河　　*Amazon River* 亞馬遜河

Questions 34-35 refer to this following introduction.

Welcome to Rich Stadium, citizens of the world, for the 2006 National Football League's Super Bowl Championship Game. Tonight, the Dallas Cowboys will be fighting the Miami Dolphins for bragging rights to claim they're the best team in the world! This matchup proves to be extra exciting as both teams are undefeated, solid on defense, and both have explosive offensive potential. Both teams lead the league in most statistical categories. Both coaching staffs are experienced, all the players are healthy, and now it's time to introduce tonight's starting lineups.

Vocabulary

stadium ('stediəm) *n.* 運動場；球場

citizen ('sɪtəzn̩) *n.* 公民　　national ('næʃənḷ) *adj.* 國家的

league (lig) *n.* 聯盟　　***Super Bowl*** 超級盃

championship ('tʃæmpiən͵ʃɪp) *n.* 冠軍 (頭銜)

Dallas ('dæləs) *n.* 達拉斯 (美國德州的城市)

cowboy ('kau͵bɔɪ) *n.* 牛仔　　fight (faɪt) *v.* 對抗

Miami (maɪ'æmɪ) *n.* 邁阿密 (美國佛羅里達州東南海岸都市)

dolphin ('dɑlfɪn) *n.* 海豚　　brag (bræg) *v.* 誇耀

right (raɪt) *n.* 權利　　claim (klem) *v.* 宣稱

matchup ('mætʃ͵ʌp) *n.* 比賽

prove (pruv) *v.* 證實　　extra ('ɛkstrə) *adv.* 特別地

exciting〔ɪkˋsaɪtɪŋ〕*adj.* 刺激的

undefeated〔͵ʌndɪˋfitɪd〕*adj.* 未曾被擊敗的

solid〔ˋsɑlɪd〕*adj.* 團結的；堅固的

defense〔dɪˋfɛns〕*n.* 防禦

explosive〔ɪkˋsplosɪv〕*adj.* 爆炸性的

offensive〔əˋfɛnsɪv〕*adj.* 攻擊的

potential〔pəˋtɛnʃəl〕*n.* 潛能　　lead〔lid〕*v.* 在…中佔首位

statistical〔stəˋtɪstɪk!〕*adj.* 統計上的

category〔ˋkætə͵gorɪ〕*n.* 範疇；類別

coaching staff 教練團

experienced〔ɪkˋspɪrɪənst〕*adj.* 有經驗的

introduce〔͵ɪntrəˋdjus〕*v.* 介紹　　lineup〔ˋlaɪn͵ʌp〕*n.* 成員

34. (**C**) What sport is being played?

    A. Soccer.　　　　　　B. Rugby.

    C. American football.　D. Basketball.

    * soccer〔ˋsɑkɚ〕*n.* 足球　　rugby〔ˋrʌgbɪ〕*n.* 橄欖球

      football〔ˋfʊt͵bɔl〕*n.* 美式足球

35. (**A**) Which statement is NOT true?

    A. Both teams are from Miami.

    B. Both teams are undefeated.

    C. All the players are healthy.

    D. Both have excellent offenses and defenses.

    * statement〔ˋstetmənt〕*n.* 敘述

      excellent〔ˋɛks!ənt〕*adj.* 優秀的

      offense〔əˋfɛns〕*n.* 攻擊；攻方

Questions 36-37 are based on the following instructions.

> To register for spring semester classes, you must report to the auditorium of the Classroom Building. Don't forget to bring the spring course schedule and syllabus. Also, you'll need a number two lead pencil, your student I.D. card, and your advisor's permission-consent form. Wait in line, receive a registration form, fill it out carefully and then submit your forms into the proper slots marked on the wall. If a certain course is full, you will be promptly notified.

💻 Vocabulary

instructions (ɪn'strʌkʃənz) *n. pl.* 指示

register ('rɛdʒɪstɚ) *v.* 報名　　spring (sprɪŋ) *adj.* 春季的

semester (sə'mɛstɚ) *n.* 學期　　report (rɪ'port) *v.* 報到

auditorium (,ɔdə'torɪəm) *n.* 禮堂

course (kors) *n.* 課程　　schedule ('skɛdʒʊl) *n.* 時間表

syllabus ('sɪləbəs) *n.* 教學大綱　　lead (lɛd) *n.* 鉛

student I.D. card 學生證　　advisor (əd'vaɪzɚ) *n.* 指導教授

permission (pɚ'mɪʃən) *n.* 准許

consent (kən'sɛnt) *n.* 同意　　form (fɔrm) *n.* 表格

in line 排隊　　receive (rɪ'siv) *v.* 收到

registration (,rɛdʒɪ'streʃən) *n.* 登記；註冊

registration form 報名表　　***fill out*** 填寫

submit〔sʌbˋmɪt〕v. 提交　　proper〔ˋprɑpɚ〕adj. 適當的

slot〔slɑt〕n. 狹長的孔　　mark〔mɑrk〕v. 標示

certain〔ˋsɝtn̩〕adj. 某一個的

promptly〔ˋprɑmptlɪ〕adv. 立即地　　notify〔ˋnotəˏfaɪ〕v. 通知

36.（ **B** ）Who are these instructions for?

　A. Summer school applicants.

　B. Spring term students.

　C. Fall semester registrants.

　D. All graduate students.

　＊ summer〔ˋsʌmɚ〕adj. 夏季的

　　applicant〔ˋæpləkənt〕n. 申請人

　　term〔tɝm〕n. 學期　　*spring term* 春季班

　　fall〔fɔl〕adj. 秋季的

　　registrant〔ˋrɛdʒɪstrənt〕n. 登記者

　　graduate〔ˋgrædʒuɪt〕adj.（大學）畢業生的；研究生的

　　a graduate student 研究生

37.（ **D** ）What do you need to register?

　A. A credit card.

　B. An instructor's approval.

　C. A paid tuition receipt.

　D. A number two lead pencil.

　＊ instructor〔ɪnˋstrʌktɚ〕n. 指導老師

　　approval〔əˋpruvl̩〕n. 同意；肯定

　　receipt〔rɪˋsit〕n. 收據

Questions 38-39 refer to the following news report.

A car bomb exploded outside a police station in downtown Baghdad, Iraq, yesterday killing more than ten and injuring scores of people. Authorities are calling this a "terrorist act" and several revolutionary groups are claiming responsibility. American military forces have secured the area and are imposing a strict curfew from 9 p.m. to 9 a.m. on the whole city. Meanwhile, the mayor of Baghdad announced that another vote will be held next week to decide on an exit plan to withdraw coalition forces and replace them with new Iraqi Army personnel.

Vocabulary

bomb〔bɑm〕*n.* 炸彈　　explode〔ɪk'splod〕*v.* 爆炸

Baghdad〔'bægdæd〕*n.* 巴格達（伊拉克首都）

Iraq〔ɪ'rɑk〕*n.* 伊拉克（亞洲西南部的共和國）

injure〔'ɪndʒɚ〕*v.* 使受傷　　*scores of* 很多的

authorities〔ə'θɔrətɪz〕*n. pl.* 當局

terrorist〔'tɛrərɪst〕*n.* 恐怖份子　　act〔ækt〕*n.* 行動

revolutionary〔ˌrɛvə'luʃənˌɛrɪ〕*adj.* 革命的

responsibility〔rɪˌspɑnsə'bɪlətɪ〕*n.* 責任

military〔'mɪləˌtɛrɪ〕*adj.* 軍事的

military force 軍隊　　secure〔sɪ'kjur〕*v.* 保護

impose〔ɪm'poz〕*v.* 把～強加於

strict〔strɪkt〕adj. 嚴格的　curfew〔'kɝfju〕n. 宵禁

meanwhile〔'min,hwaɪl〕adv. 在這期間

mayor〔'meɚ〕n. 市長　announce〔ə'naʊns〕v. 宣布

vote〔vot〕n. 投票　exit〔'ɛgzɪt〕n. 離去

withdraw〔wɪð'drɔ〕v. 撤退　coalition〔,koə'lɪʃən〕n. 聯盟

replace〔rɪ'ples〕v. 取代　Iraqi〔i'rɑkɪ〕adj. 伊拉克的

army〔'ɑrmɪ〕n. 軍隊　personnel〔,pɝsn̩'ɛl〕n. 人員

38. (**D**) What happened at the police station?

　　A. A car smashed the gate.

　　B. A gun battle broke out.

　　C. A vote was announced.

　　D. Terrorists exploded a bomb.

　　* smash〔smæʃ〕v. (猛力) 打破；打碎

　　　gate〔get〕n. 大門

　　　gun battle 槍戰　***break out*** 發生

39. (**A**) How did the military respond to the violence?

　　A. They imposed a curfew.

　　B. They captured suspects.

　　C. They interrogated terrorists.

　　D. They're going to evacuate.

　　* respond〔rɪ'spɑnd〕v. 回應

　　　violence〔'vaɪələns〕n. 暴力行為

　　　capture〔'kæptʃɚ〕v. 逮捕

　　　suspect〔'sʌspɛkt〕n. 嫌疑犯

　　　interrogate〔ɪn'tɛrə,get〕v. 質問

　　　evacuate〔ɪ'vækju,et〕v. 撤退

Questions 40-41 refer to the following advertisement.

Change your mind, change your body, change your life! Imagine, just 12 weeks from now, having the lean, healthy body you've always wanted. You don't have to turn your life upside down to get it, just follow the *Body for Life Program.* You have to exercise every day for 30 minutes, either lifting weights or jogging on a machine. In addition, you must eat five light meals every day, excluding all fat, sugar and oily foods. It sounds so simple but it really works. Thousands are doing it now and proving it's true. Join now and succeed.

Vocabulary

advertisement〔͵ædvɚ'taɪzmənt〕 *n.* 廣告
imagine〔ɪ'mædʒɪn〕 *v.* 想像　　lean〔lin〕 *adj.* 瘦的
upside down 顛倒地　　program〔'progræm〕 *n.* 計畫
either A *or* B 不是 A，就是 B　　*lift weights* 舉重
jog〔dʒɑg〕 *v.* 慢跑　　*in addition* 此外
light〔laɪt〕 *adj.* 清淡的　　*light meal* 便餐
exclude〔ɪk'sklud〕 *v.* 排除在外
fat〔fæt〕 *n.* 脂肪　　oily〔'ɔɪlɪ〕 *adj.* 油膩的
work〔wɝk〕 *v.* 有效　　prove〔pruv〕 *v.* 證明
true〔tru〕 *adj.* 眞的　　join〔dʒɔɪn〕 *v.* 加入
succeed〔sək'sid〕 *v.* 成功

40. (**B**) What's the name of the program?

    A.　Run For Your Life.

    B.　Body For Life.

    C.　Burn Fat.

    D.　Exercise to Lose and Win.

41. (**C**) How long is the program?

    A.　Just 30 minutes a day.

    B.　Five times a day.

    C.　Just 12 weeks.

    D.　Just 12 days a month.

    * time〔taɪm〕*n.* 次數

Questions 42-43 are based on the following announcement.

About an hour after take-off, dinner will be served. You'll have a choice of two dishes. Please take a look at the menu on the back of the seat in front of you. Drinks will be served twice and are always available upon request. We have two movies available for your viewing pleasure tonight. We'll also have several BBC news reports and continuous stereo music for your listening pleasure. Please sit back, relax and enjoy your flight on We Never Crash Airlines. We promise to get you there in one piece!

Vocabulary

announcement〔ə'naʊnsmənt〕*n.* 宣布；聲明
take-off〔'tek'ɔf〕*n.*（飛機）起飛
serve〔sɜv〕*v.* 供應　　choice〔tʃɔɪs〕*n.* 選擇
dish〔dɪʃ〕*n.* 菜餚　　menu〔'mɛnju〕*n.* 菜單
available〔ə'veləbḷ〕*adj.* 可獲得的
request〔rɪ'kwɛst〕*n.* 要求　　*upon request* 一經請求
pleasure〔'plɛʒɚ〕*n.* 樂趣　　report〔rɪ'pɔrt〕*n.* 報導
continuous〔kən'tɪnjʊəs〕*adj.* 不中斷的
stereo〔'stɛrɪo〕*adj.* 立體音響的
sit back 放鬆休息　　flight〔flaɪt〕*n.* 飛行
crash〔kræʃ〕*v.*（飛機）墜毀
promise〔'prɑmɪs〕*v.* 承諾　　*in one piece* 無恙地

42.（ **C** ）How many meals will be served?
　　　A. Two.　　　　　B. Several.
　　　C. One.　　　　　D. None.

43.（ **D** ）Which is NOT part of the entertainment program?
　　　A. BBC international news.
　　　B. Soft stereo music.
　　　C. Two feature films.
　　　D. A duty free seminar.

　　* entertainment〔͵ɛntɚ'tenmənt〕*n.* 娛樂
　　　international〔͵ɪntɚ'næʃənḷ〕*adj.* 國際的
　　　soft〔sɔft〕*adj.* 輕柔的　　*feature film* 電影長片
　　　duty free 免稅的　　seminar〔'sɛmə͵nɑr〕*n.* 研討會

Questions 44-45 refer to the follow editorial.

We at the New York Times, would like to comment on the sorry state of professional athletes in our country today. The poor conduct and disgraceful behavior of many athletes are embarrassing to every sports fan, adults and youth alike! What happened to sports in America? Where did those selfless, dedicated, hard working athletes of yesteryear disappear to? Where are the role models? Today's millionaire superstars are more like spoiled brats or selfish babies! Taking illegal drugs, brawling on the court, carrying weapons, and being accused of rape and tax evasion! Yes, it's a national and cultural disgrace. We demand change, or we will boycott professional sports.

Vocabulary

comment〔'kɑmɛnt〕*v.* 評論　　sorry〔'sɑrɪ〕*adj.* 可悲的
state〔stet〕*n.* 狀況　　professional〔prə'fɛʃənl〕*adj.* 職業的
athlete〔'æθlit〕*n.* 運動員　　conduct〔'kɑndʌkt〕*n.* 品行；行為
disgraceful〔dɪs'gresfəl〕*adj.* 可恥的
behavior〔bɪ'hevjɚ〕*n.* 行為
embarrassing〔ɪm'bærəsɪŋ〕*adj.* 令人尷尬的
adult〔ə'dʌlt〕*n.* 成年人　　selfless〔'sɛlflɪs〕*adj.* 無私的
dedicated〔'dɛdə,ketɪd〕*adj.* 專注的
yesteryear〔'jɛstɚ'jɪr〕*n.* 去年

disappear〔,dɪsə'pɪr〕v. 消失　　***role model*** 模範

millionaire〔,mɪljən'ɛr〕n. 百萬富翁

spoiled〔spɔɪld〕adj. 寵壞的　　　brat〔bræt〕n. 頑童

spoiled brat 寵壞了的孩子　　selfish〔'sɛlfɪʃ〕adj. 自私的

illegal〔ɪ'ligḷ〕adj. 違法的　　drug〔drʌg〕n. 毒品

brawl〔brɔl〕v. 打架　　court〔kort〕n. 球場

weapon〔'wɛpən〕n. 武器　　accuse〔ə'kjuz〕v. 指控

rape〔rep〕n. 強姦　　tax〔tæks〕n. 稅

evasion〔ɪ'veʒən〕n. 逃避　　national〔'næʃənḷ〕adj. 全國的

cultural〔'kʌltʃərəl〕adj. 文化的

disgrace〔dɪs'gres〕n. 恥辱　　demand〔dɪ'mænd〕v. 要求

boycott〔'bɔɪ,kat〕v. 聯合抵制

44. (**C**) Why are the writers so upset?

A. Athletes are playing lazily.

B. Team owners are selfish.

C. Pros are behaving terribly.

D. The fans are disgraceful.

* lazily〔'lezɪlɪ〕adv. 懶散地　　owner〔'onɚ〕n. 老闆

pro〔pro〕n. 職業選手　　behave〔bɪ'hev〕v. 表現

45. (**A**) The superstars are not doing what?

A. Being good role models.

B. Taking illegal drugs.

C. Breaking the law.

D. Acting like nasty kids.

* break〔brek〕v. 違反　　act〔ækt〕v. 行為

nasty〔'næstɪ〕adj. 討厭的

中高級閱讀測驗詳解 ②

PART A : Sentence Completion

1. (**A**) When your <u>bloodstream</u> gets three drops of alcohol to every drop of your blood, you pass out.

當你每一滴流動的<u>血液</u>中，含有三滴酒精時，你就會不省人事。

(A) ***bloodstream*** (′blʌd͵strim) *n.* (體內循環的) 血流

(B) brainstorm (′bren͵stɔrm) *n.* 靈機一動

brainstorming 腦力激盪 (每人自由提供意見，一起討論的會議方法)

(C) heartbeat (′hɑrt͵bit) *n.* 心跳；心搏

(D) vision (′vɪʒən) *n.* 視力；洞察力

* drop (drɑp) *n.* (一) 滴　　alcohol (′ælkə͵hɔl) *n.* 酒精

blood (blʌd) *n.* 血液　　***pass out*** 昏倒

2. (**B**) In the United States, 30 percent of the adult <u>population</u> has a "weight problem."

在美國，百分之三十的成年<u>人口</u>都有體重問題。

(A) circulation (͵sɝkjə′leʃən) *n.* (氣體、液體、血液) 循環

(B) ***population*** (͵pɑpjə′leʃən) *n.* 人口

a large/small population 人口多/少

(C) congratulation (kən͵grætʃə′leʃən) *n.* 恭喜 (常用複數)

(D) regulation (͵rɛgjə′leʃən) *n.* 規則

* percent (pə′sɛnt) *n.* 百分比

adult (ə′dʌlt) *adj.* 成年的

3. (**C**) Walking <u>requires</u> no special equipment, and it can give
you many of the same benefits as jogging or running.

走路不<u>需要</u>任何特殊的裝備，卻能夠帶給你和慢跑或跑步
一樣的好處。

(A) suffer (ˈsʌfɚ) v. 受苦；遭受（痛苦、損害）

(B) differ (ˈdɪfɚ) v. （與）～不同

(C) *require* (rɪˈkwaɪr) v. 需要

(D) acquire (əˈkwaɪr) v. 學得；養成（習慣、行為）；獲得

* equipment (ɪˈkwɪpmənt) n. 設備
  benefit (ˈbɛnəfɪt) n. 好處

4. (**A**) Milk, cheese and tuna are all rich in an amino acid that
helps produce a neurotransmitter in the brain that <u>induces</u>
sleep.

牛奶、乳酪和鮪魚都含有一種豐富的氨基酸，有助於在大腦中
製造一種<u>引發</u>睡眠的神經傳導素。

(A) *induce* (ɪnˈdjus) v. 引發

(B) suppose (səˈpoz) v. 認為

(C) intend (ɪnˈtɛnd) v. 打算

(D) quiver (ˈkwɪvɚ) v. 顫抖

* cheese (tʃiz) n. 乳酪
  tuna (ˈtunə) n. 鮪魚   *be rich in* 富含有～
  amino (ˈæmɪno) adj. 氨基的
  amino acid 氨基酸
  produce (prəˈdjus) v. 製造
  neurotransmitter (ˌnjurəˈtrænsmɪtɚ) n. 神經傳導素
  brain (bren) n. 大腦

5. (**C**) Happiness and unhappiness are not really flip sides of the same emotion. They are two <u>distinct</u> feelings.

快樂與不快樂並非眞的是同一個情感的兩面。他們是完全<u>不同</u>的兩種情感。

(A) instant (ˈɪnstənt) adj. 立即的；速食的

(B) consistent (kənˈsɪstənt) adj. 一致的

(C) *distinct* (dɪˈstɪŋkt) adj. 有區別的

(D) instinctive (ɪnˈstɪŋktɪv) adj. 本能的

* *flip side* 反面；（唱片的）B 面

emotion (ɪˈmoʃən) n. 情緒

6. (**A**) Most people have a car or want to have one. The <u>private</u> automobile seems to represent the ultimate level in freedom and convenience.

大部分的人都有車子，或想要擁有一輛車。<u>自用</u>汽車似乎代表著極度的自由與方便。

(A) *private* (ˈpraɪvɪt) adj. 私有的

(B) constructive (kənˈstrʌktɪv) adj. 建設性的

(↔ *destructive*)

(C) breathless (ˈbrɛθlɪs) adj. 呼吸困難的

(D) emphatic (ɪmˈfætɪk) adj. 語句被強調的；有力的

* automobile (ˈɔtəməˌbil) n. 汽車

represent (ˌrɛprɪˈzɛnt) v. 代表

ultimate (ˈʌltəmɪt) adj. 極度的

level (ˈlɛvl̩) n. 程度

freedom (ˈfridəm) n. 自由

convenience (kənˈvinjəns) n. 方便

7. (**B**) Because of the energy crisis, scientists in the major oil-consuming nations have become <u>increasingly</u> interested in the potential of solar energy.

因為能源危機，主要的石油消費國家的科學家已經<u>逐漸地</u>對太陽能的潛力產生興趣。

(A) sufficiently〔 sə'fɪʃəntlɪ 〕adv. 足夠地

(B) *increasingly*〔 ɪn'krisɪŋlɪ 〕adv. 增加地

(C) colloquially〔 kə'lokwəlɪ 〕adv. 用口語地

(D) collectively〔 kə'lɛktɪvlɪ 〕adj. 共同地

* energy〔'ɛnədʒɪ 〕n. 能源　　crisis〔'kraɪsɪs 〕n. 危機

major〔'medʒə 〕adj. 主要的

consume〔 kən'sjum 〕v. 消耗

potential〔 pə'tɛnʃəl 〕n. 潛力　　solar〔'solə 〕adj. 太陽的

8. (**D**) The Greenhouse Effect is caused by the action of the sun on gases that are released when we burn coal, oil, or other fuels <u>casually</u>.

溫室效應是由於我們<u>任意地</u>燃燒煤、石油或其他燃料時，所產生的氣體受到太陽照射而導致的。

(A) warmly〔'wɔrmlɪ 〕adv. 溫暖地

(B) boisterously〔'bɔɪstərəslɪ 〕adv. 喧鬧地

(C) delicately〔'dɛlə,ketlɪ 〕adv. 優雅地

(D) *casually*〔'kæʒuəlɪ 〕adv. 隨便地

* *Greenhouse Effect* 溫室效應　　cause〔 kɔz 〕v. 導致

action〔'ækʃən 〕n. 活動；作用　　gas〔 gæs 〕n. 氣體

release〔 rɪ'liz 〕v. 釋放　　coal〔 kol 〕n. 煤

fuel〔'fjuəl 〕n. 燃料

9. (**C**) Pardon me, and feel free to tell me what I can do to <u>make up for</u> the damage I caused.

原諒我。儘管告訴我可以做什麼，來<u>彌補</u>我所造成的損失。

(A) be blessed with 幸好有

(B) fetch up 達到

(C) *make up for* 彌補

(D) get the best of （在交易中）獲得最大的利益

* pardon〔'pɑrdn〕 *v.* 原諒　　*feel free* 儘管（覺得自在）
damage〔'dæmɪdʒ〕 *n.* 損失

10. (**B**) Never <u>poke your nose into</u> others' affairs. It's not your business. 不要<u>多管閒事</u>。這不關你的事。

(A) adapt *oneself* to 適應　　adapt〔ə'dæpt〕 *v.* 使適應

(B) *poke one's nose into* 管閒事

poke〔pok〕 *v.* 把鼻子伸出

(C) meet *one's* Maker 死　　Maker〔'mekɚ〕 *n.* 造物主

(D) give a stimulus to 刺激

stimulus〔'stɪmjələs〕 *n.* 刺激

* affair〔ə'fɛr〕 *n.* 事情

11. (**B**) A special present, <u>a chameleon</u>, was given to him by his mother for his birthday.

一個特殊的禮物，<u>一隻變色龍</u>，是他媽媽送給他的生日禮物。

* a chameleon 做為 A special present 的同位語，故選 (B)。
其位置還可以放句尾，改寫成 A special present was given
to him by his mother for his birthday, *a chameleon*.。
chameleon〔kə'milɪən〕 *n.* 變色龍

12. (**A**) He works hard <u>lest</u> he should fail.

他努力工作，<u>以免失敗</u>。

* 連接詞 *lest*「以免~」連接前後兩個句子，而由 *lest* 所引導表示「否定目的」的副詞子句中，助動詞 should 不因主要子句的時式而改變，選 (A)。而 (B) for fear of「以免」，(C) in case of「倘若」，均為介系詞片語，用法不合。

13. (**D**) He never comes without bringing me a bunch of flowers. It means <u>he carries a bunch of flowers to see me all the time</u>.

他從來沒有來看我，不帶一束花的。這句話的意思是

(A) 當他來看我時，他很少帶一束花。

(B) 當他來看我時，他有時候會帶一束花。

(C) 他從來沒有帶過一束花來看我。

(D) <u>他總是帶著一束花來看我。</u>

* *never…without~* 沒有…不~　　*a bunch of flowers* 一束花

scarcely ('skɛrslɪ) *adv.* 很少　　*at times* 有時候

call on 拜訪（人）　　*all the time* 總是

14. (**C**) 窗子破了的那棟房子沒有人住。

(C) The house's windows *are broken is unoccupied.* (誤)

* 兩動詞 are broken 和 is unoccupied 之間須有連接詞。

broken ('brokən) *adj.* 破掉的

unoccupied (ʌn'ɑkjə‚paɪd) *adj.* 沒有人住的

15. (**B**) No two men are of a mind. The word "a" in the sentence means <u>the same</u>. 沒有兩個人的想法是相同的。句中的 "a" 意思是<u>相同的</u>。

* *a(n)* 相當於 the same，例如：Birds of a feather flock together. 【諺】物以類聚。　　mind (maɪnd) *n.* 想法

PART B：Cloze

Questions 16-23

The police in Taipei County are testing a new electronic system that shows the addresses of people <u>who call</u> the police.
16

台北縣的警察正在測試一個新的電子系統，那個系統可以顯示報警民眾的地址。

> police〔pə'lis〕*n.* 警察
> county〔'kaʊntɪ〕*n.* 縣　　test〔tɛst〕*v.* 測試
> electronic〔ɪ,lɛk'trɑnɪk〕*adj.* 電子的
> address〔'ædrɛs〕*n.* 地址

16.(**B**) 先行詞是人，故關代須用 who，又 people 是複數名詞，故動詞用 call，選 (B)。

Because many streets in the cities and towns of Taipei County have the same street names, the police are often unsure <u>of</u> exactly
17
where they are supposed to go in the event of an emergency.

因為台北縣有許多城鎮的街道名稱相同，所以如果發生緊急事件，警方常不確定究竟要到哪邊去。

> *be supposed to* 應該　　*in the event of* 如果發生
> emergency〔ɪ'mɝdʒənsɪ〕*n.* 緊急事件　*adj.* 緊急的

17.(**D**) 因空格後的 exactly where…of an emergency 是名詞子句，故空格應填介系詞，選 (D) *of*。
　　　be unsure of 不確定

If the system works well, there are plans to introduce it in other parts of the country. The Police Duty Center often needs over a minute just to <u>work out</u> the precise address of a report.
18

如果這個系統很有效，他們就打算要在國內其他地方引進這個系統。警察勤務中心常常要花一分多鐘，才能確定報警的確切地址。

work〔wɜk〕v. 運作　　introduce〔͵ɪntrə'djus〕v. 引進
duty center 勤務中心　　precise〔prɪ'saɪs〕adj. 確切的
report〔rɪ'port〕n. 報告

18. (**C**) (A) leave out 省略　　(B) stand out 突出
　　　　　(C) ***work out*** 確定　　(D) hollow out 挖出

Taipei County's Yonghe has a Jhonghe Road while Jhonghe has a Yonghe Road. And there are Jhongshan Roads all over the place. Even local residents are often unable <u>to give</u> correct directions, so
19
the police sometimes have an impossible job.

台北縣的永和有一條中和路，中和也有一條永和路。而且到處都有中山路。即使是當地的居民，也常常無法表達正確的方向，所以警方有時候會接到不可能的任務。

local〔'lokḷ〕adj. 當地的　　resident〔'rɛzədənt〕n. 居民
correct〔kə'rɛkt〕adj. 正確的　　direction〔də'rɛkʃən〕n. 方向

19. (**D**) ***be unable to V***.「無法⋯」，選 (D) ***to give***。

Many reports do not <u>go into detail</u>, said Taipei County Police Duty
20
Center Director. In the future, any call to 110 from a fixed line telephone in the county will immediately have its address <u>appear</u>.
21

台北縣警察勤務中心的主任說，許多報案電話都沒有講得很詳細。未來，任何人用市話在台北縣撥打一一〇，這個電子系統都可以立即顯現地址。

director〔dəˋrɛktɚ〕n. 主任　　fixed〔fɪkst〕adj. 固定的
fixed line telephone 固網有線電話；市話
immediately〔ɪˋmidɪɪtlɪ〕adv. 立即

20. (**C**) (A) be with child 懷孕
(B) influence〔ˋɪnfluəns〕n. 影響
(C) **go into detail** 詳細說明　　detail〔ˋditel〕n. 細節
(D) sit tight 坐穩；靜止不動

21. (**A**) 使役動詞 have 接受詞之後，須接原形動詞表「主動」，故選
(A) **appear**「出現」。

Every second counts with emergency calls and the Taipei County Police Duty Center's use of technology is probably overdue. Every call to the emergency line will have its address shown on a map, greatly <u>assisting</u> the police.
　　　　　　　　　　　　22
對緊急電話來說，每一秒都很重要，所以也許台北警察勤務中心早該運用這項科技了。電子系統會在電子地圖上，把每一通打到緊急專線的地址顯示出來。這對警方有很大的幫助。

count〔kaʊnt〕v. 有重要意義
technology〔tɛkˋnɑlədʒɪ〕n. 科技
overdue〔ˋovɚˋdju〕adj. 早該實現的　　map〔mæp〕n. 地圖

22. (**B**) 兩動詞之間沒有連接詞，第二個動詞須改為現在分詞，故選 (B)
assisting。本句是由…, and it greatly assists…簡化而來。
assist〔əˋsɪst〕v. 協助

They also hope the system will help cut down <u>on</u> prank calls. If
the system proves to be effective, the police are looking to
implement it all over the country.

23

他們同時也希望這套系統有助於減少惡作劇電話。如果這套系統有用，
警方期待全國都能使用該系統。

> prank〔præŋk〕*n.* 惡作劇　　prove〔pruv〕*v.* 證實
> effective〔ə'fɛktɪv〕*adj.* 有效的
> implement〔'ɪmplə,mɛnt〕*v.* 實施

23. (**A**) ***cut down on~***　減少～

Questions 24-30

    What is intelligence anyway? When I was in the army, I took
an intelligence test that all soldiers took, and, against <u>an average</u>

24

of 100, scored 160.

    智慧究竟是什麼？當我在陸軍服役時，我參加了所有軍人都要考的
智力測驗，對照平均分數一百分，我得了一百六十分。

> intelligence〔ɪn'tɛlədʒəns〕*n.* 智力；智慧
> anyway〔'ɛnɪ,we〕*adv.* 無論如何
> army〔'ɑrmɪ〕*n.* 陸軍　　***be in the army*** 在陸軍服役中
> soldier〔'soldʒɚ〕*n.* 軍人　　against〔ə'gɛnst〕*prep.* 對照
> score〔skor〕*v.* 得分

24. (**A**) 依句意，選 (A) ***an average***「平均」。而 (B) a total「總數；
　　　　總分」，(C) 考試，(D) 數目，均不合句意。

I had an auto repairman once, who, on these intelligence tests, could not possibly have scored more than 80. <u>Yet</u>, when anything
₂₅
went wrong with my car I hurried to him — and he always fixed it.

我以前有一位修理工，他在那些智力測驗中，絕不可能拿到超過八十分的成績。但是，當我的車子有任何問題時，我都會趕快去找他——而他總是能把它修好。

auto〔ˋɔto〕n. 汽車　repairman〔rɪˋpɛrmən〕n. 修理工
go wrong 出毛病；故障　hurry〔ˋhɝɪ〕v. 趕往
fix〔fɪks〕v. 修理

25.(**D**) 依句意，選 (D) *Yet*「但是」。而 (A) 然後，(B) 因此，(C) 因此，
均不合句意。

Suppose my auto repairman designed questions for some intelligence tests. On every one of them I'd prove myself a fool. In a world where I have to work with my hands, I'd do poorly.

假設我的汽車修理工來設計一些智力測驗的題目。我想每一題都可以證明我是個傻瓜。我在必須用手來做事的世界，我會表現得很差勁。

suppose〔səˋpoz〕v. 假設　design〔dɪˋzaɪn〕v. 設計
prove〔pruv〕v. 證明　fool〔ful〕n. 呆子；傻瓜
poorly〔ˋpʊrlɪ〕adv. 差勁的

Consider my auto repairman <u>again</u>. He had a habit of telling jokes.
₂₆
One time he said, "Doc, a deaf-and-dumb man needed some nails. Having entered a store, he put two fingers together on the counter and made <u>hammering</u> movements with the other hand.
₂₇

再想想我的汽車修理工。他的嗜好是說笑話。有一次他說:「博士,一個又聾又啞的人需要一些釘子。所以他走進店裡,把兩隻手指頭放在櫃檯上,然後用另外一隻手做搥打的動作。

consider〔kən'sɪdə〕v. 考慮;細想　　habit〔'hæbɪt〕n. 嗜好
joke〔dʒok〕n. 笑話　　deaf〔dɛf〕adj. 聾的
dumb〔dʌm〕adj. 啞的　　nail〔nel〕n. 釘子
finger〔'fɪŋɚ〕n. 手指　　counter〔'kaʊntɚ〕n. 櫃檯
movement〔'muvmənt〕n. 動作

26. (**A**) 依句意,選 (A) *again*「再一次」。而 (B) as usual「一如往常」,
　　　　(C) too「也」,(D) as well「也」,均不合句意。

27. (**B**) (A) cut〔kʌt〕v. 切斷　　(B) *hammer*〔'hæmɚ〕v. 搥打
　　　　(C) wave〔wev〕v. 揮手　　(D) circle〔'sɝkḷ〕v. 畫圈圈

The clerk brought him a hammer. He <u>shook</u> his head and pointed
　　　　　　　　　　　　　　　　　　　　　　28
to the two fingers he was hammering. The clerk brought him
some nails. He picked out the right size and left.
店員拿給他一支鎚子。他搖搖頭,然後指著他正在搥的兩隻手指頭。於
是店員拿給他一些釘子。他選了正確的尺寸之後就離開了。

clerk〔klɝk〕n. 店員　　*pick out* 挑選

28. (**C**) (A) nod〔nɑd〕v. 點頭　　(B) raise〔rez〕v. 舉起
　　　　(C) *shake*〔ʃek〕v. 搖動　　(D) turn〔tɝn〕v. 翻轉

Well, Doc, the next man who came in was blind. He wanted
scissors. <u>What</u> do you suppose he asked for?" I lifted my right
　　　　　29
hand and made scissoring movements with two fingers.

嗯，博士，下一個走進來的人是個瞎子。他要買剪刀。你認為他會問什麼？」我舉起我的右手，然後用兩隻手指頭做出剪刀的動作。

> blind〔blaɪnd〕*adj.* 瞎的　　scissors〔'sɪzɚz〕*n. pl.* 剪刀
> lift〔lɪft〕*v.* 舉起　　scissor〔'sɪzɚ〕*v.* 用剪刀剪下

29. (**A**) 依句意，你認為他會問「什麼」，選 (A) ***What***。

He burst out laughing and said, "Why, you fool, he used his voice
and asked for them. I've been practicing that on all my customers
today, but I knew <u>for sure</u> I'd catch you."
30

他忽然大笑起來，然後說：「為什麼要這樣，呆子，他可以開口說他要
買剪刀啊。我今天已經問過我所有的顧客，但是我確定你會被騙。」

> burst〔bɝst〕*v.* 突然　　practice〔'præktɪs〕*v.* 做；實施
> customer〔'kʌstəmɚ〕*n.* 顧客　　catch〔kætʃ〕*v.* 欺騙

30. (**A**) (A) ***for sure*** 確定地　　(B) at once 立刻

(C) in fact 事實上　　(D) right now 馬上

"Why is that?" I asked. "Because you are so goddamned educated,
Doc. I knew you couldn't be very smart." And I have an uneasy
feeling he had something there.

「為什麼？」我問。「因為你受了這麼多教育，博士。我知道你不會太
聰明。」他說的有道理，所以我覺得很不自在。

> goddamned〔'gɑd'dæmd〕*adv.* 極其；非常
> educated〔'ɛdʒʊ,ketɪd〕*adj.* 受過教育的
> uneasy〔ʌn'izɪ〕*adj.* 不自在的
> ***He had something there***. 他說的有道理。

📁 PART C：Reading

Questions 31-34

In 1901, H. G. Wells, an English writer, wrote a book describing a trip to the moon. When the explorers landed on the moon, they discovered that the moon was full of underground cities.

在一九○一年時，英國作家威爾斯寫了一本描述月球之旅的書。當探險家登陸月球時，他們發現月球充滿地下城市。

describe〔dɪ'skraɪb〕v. 描述　　explorer〔ɪk'splorɚ〕n. 探險家
land〔lænd〕v. 登陸　　discover〔dɪ'skʌvɚ〕v. 發現
be full of 充滿　　underground〔'ʌndɚ'graʊnd〕adj. 地下的

They expressed their surprise to the "moon people" they met. In turn, the "moon people" expressed their surprise. "Why," they asked, "are you traveling to outer space when you don't even use your inner space?"

他們對遇到的「月球人」表達自己的驚訝。接著，「月球人」也表達他們的驚訝。他們問道：「你們為什麼要在還沒有利用內部空間之前，就到外太空去旅行呢？」

express〔ɪk'sprɛs〕v. 表達　　**in turn** 接著
outer space 外太空　　**inner space** 內層空間【地球深處】

H.G. Wells could only imagine traveling to the moon. In 1969, human beings really did land on the moon. People today know that there are no underground cities on the moon.

威爾斯只能想像到月球旅行。在一九六九年，人類真的登陸月球了。現在人們知道月球上沒有地下城市。

imagine〔ɪ'mædʒɪn〕v. 想像　　**human beings** 人類

However, the question that the "moon people" asked is still an interesting one. A growing number of scientists are seriously thinking about <u>it</u>.

但是，「月球人」所問的問題仍然很令人感興趣。有愈來愈多的科學家認真思考<u>利用內層空間這件事</u>。

> growing〔'groɪŋ〕adj. 增加的　　　***a number of*** 許多
> seriously〔'sɪrɪəslɪ〕adv. 認真地

Underground systems are already in place. Many cities have underground car parks. In some cities, such as Tokyo, Seoul and Montreal, there are large underground shopping areas. The "Chunnel", a tunnel connecting England and France, is now complete.

地下系統已經安排就緒了。許多城市都有地下停車場。在某些城市，像是東京、首爾和蒙特婁，它們都有大型的地下購物區。連接英法的「英法海底隧道」，現在也完工了。

> ***in place*** 準備就緒　　***car park*** 汽車停車場
> Tokyo〔'tokɪ,o〕n. 東京　　Seoul〔sol〕n. 首爾【韓國首都】
> Montreal〔,mɑntrɪ'ɔl〕n. 蒙特婁【位於加拿大的城市】
> Chunnel〔'tʃʌnəl〕n. 英法海底隧道　　tunnel〔'tʌnḷ〕n. 隧道
> connect〔kə'nɛkt〕v. 連接　　complete〔kəm'plit〕v. 完成

But what about underground cities? Japan's Taisei Corporation is now designing a network of underground systems, called "Alice Cities." The designers imagine using surface space for public parks and using underground space for flats, offices, shopping, and so on. A solar dome would cover the whole city.

　　但是地下城市呢？日本大成公司正在設計的地下系統網絡叫作「艾莉絲城」。設計師想像要利用表面空間來蓋公園，然後用地下空間來蓋公寓、辦公室、購物中心等。整個城市會用太陽能屋頂覆蓋住。

> corporation〔͵kɔrpə'reʃən〕n. 有限股份公司
> design〔dɪ'zaɪn〕v. 設計　　network〔'nɛt͵wɝk〕n. 網絡
> designer〔dɪ'zaɪnɚ〕n. 設計師　　surface〔'sɝfɪs〕n. 表面
> flat〔flæt〕n. 公寓　　*and so on* 等等
> solar〔'solɚ〕adj. 利用太陽能的　　dome〔dom〕n. 圓屋頂
> cover〔'kʌvɚ〕v. 覆蓋　　whole〔hol〕adj. 整個的

　　Supporters of underground development say that building down rather than building up is a good way to use the earth's space. The surface, they say, can be used for farms, parks, gardens, and wilderness. H.G. Wells' "moon people" would agree. Would you?

　　支持往地下發展的人說，對運用地球空間而言，往地下蓋會比往地上蓋有利。他們說，表面空間可以用來當農地、公園、花園和荒野。威爾斯的「月球人」也會同意。那麼你呢？

> supporter〔sə'portɚ〕n. 支持者　　*rather than* 而不是
> wilderness〔'wɪldənɪs〕n. 荒野

31. (**C**) 在威爾斯的故事裡的探險家，很驚訝地發現「月球人」
    (A) 對於地球的了解很少。
    (B) 聽得懂他們的語言。
    (C) <u>住在這麼多地下城市裡。</u>
    (D) 在太空科技方面超前他們。

    * ahead〔ə'hɛd〕adv. 超前
    　technology〔tɛk'nɑlədʒɪ〕n. 科技

32. (**B**) 第二段中畫線的字 "it" 指的是？

  (A) 發現月球的內層空間。 (B) 利用地球的內層空間。

  (C) 再度遇到「月球人」。 (D) 到外太空去旅行。

  * underlined〔͵ʌndəˋlaɪnd〕*adj.* 畫底線的
   refer〔rɪˋfɝ〕*v.* 是指

33. (**B**) 我們已經有哪幾種地下系統了？

  (A) 辦公室、購物區、發電廠。

  (B) 隧道、停車場、購物區。

  (C) 花園、停車場、發電廠。 (D) 隧道、花園、辦公室。

  * *power station* 發電廠

34. (**A**) 最適合本文的標題是？

  (A) 艾莉絲城──未來之城 (B) 和威爾斯一起從事太空旅行

  (C) 享受地下生活 (D) 往上建，不是往下

Questions 35-37

THEATRE

City Varieties

The Headrow, Leeds. Tel. 430808

  Oct. 10-11 only *A Night at the Varieties*. All the fun of an old music hall with Barry Cwer, Duggle Brown, 6 dancers, Mystina, Jon Barker, Anne Duval and the Tony Harrison Trio. Laugh again at the old jokes and listen to your favourite songs.

Performances: 8 pm nightly

Admission: £5; under 16 or over 60 £4.

York Theatre Royal

St. Leonard's Place, York. Tel. 223568

Sep. 23 —— Oct. 17 *Groping for Words* —— a comedy by Sue Townsend. Best known for her Adrian Mole Diaries, Townsend now writes about an evening class which two men and a woman attend. A gentle comedy.

Admission: First night, Mon. £2; Tue. —— Fri. £3.25-5.50; Sat. £3.50-5.75.

Halifax Playhouse

King's Cross Street, Halifax. Tel. 365998

Oct. 10-17 *On Golden Pond* by Ernest Thompson. This is a magical comedy about real people. A beautifully produced, well-acted play for everyone. Don't miss it.

Performances: 7:30 pm
Admission: £2. Mon. 2 seats for the price of one.

Grand Theatre

Oxford Street, Leeds. Tel. 502116
Restaurant and Cafe.

Oct 1-17 *The Secret Diary of Adrian Mole, aged 13*. Sue Townsend's musical play, based on her best-selling book.

Performances: Evenings 7:45; October 10-17, at 2:30 pm. No Monday performances.
Admission: Tues. —— Thurs. £2-5; Fri & Sat: £2-6.

劇　場

城市綜藝秀

里茲，Headrow 路。電話：430808

十月十日到十一日，只有**綜藝之夜**。一場歌舞表演的所有樂趣，由 Barry Cwer、Duggle Brown，六名舞者，以及 Mystina、Jon Barker、Anne Duval 和 Tony Harrison Trio。聽著老笑話再笑一次，聽著你最喜歡的歌。

表演：每晚八點

入場費：五英鎊；十六歲以下或六十歲以上，四英鎊。

約克皇家戲院

約克，聖李奧納多區。電話：223568

九月二十三日到十月十七日，**言語的摸索**——Sue Townsend 所寫的喜劇。她最有名的作品是阿默日記，這部喜劇是關於在夜校上課的二男一女。是一部溫馨的喜劇。

入場費：首場，星期一，兩英鎊；星期二到星期五，三點二五英鎊到五點五英鎊；星期六，三點五英鎊到五點七五英鎊。

Halifax 戲院

Halifax，國王的十字街。電話：365998

十月十日到十七日，推出 Ernest Thompson 所寫的**金池塘**。這是由真人真事改編的迷人喜劇。是一部製作精美、表演精湛的戲劇，適合每人觀賞。千萬不要錯過。

演出：晚上七點半

入場費：星期一，二英鎊。一人付費兩人同行。

豪華大戲院

里茲，Oxford 街。電話：502116
餐廳和咖啡廳。

十月一日到十七日，**十三歲阿默的秘密日記**。那是 Sue Townsend 的音樂劇，是根據她最暢銷的書改編的。

演出：晚上七點四十五分，十月十日到十七日是下午兩點三十分。星期一沒有演出。

入場費：星期二到星期四，二到五英鎊；星期五和星期六：二到六英鎊。

theatre〔'θiətə〕*n.* 戲院（= *theater*）
variety〔və'raɪətɪ〕*n.* 綜藝秀；聯合演出（= *variety show*）
Leeds〔lidz〕*n.* 里茲【英格蘭北部城市】
music hall 歌舞雜耍表演
favourite〔'fevərɪt〕*adj.* 最喜歡的（= *favorite*）
performance〔pə'fɔrməns〕*n.* 演出　　nightly〔'naɪtlɪ〕*adv.* 每晚
admission〔əd'mɪʃən〕*n.* 入場費　　£ 英鎊（= *libra*〔'laɪbrə〕）
York〔jɔrk〕*n.* 約克【英格蘭北約克郡首府】
royal〔'rɔɪəl〕*adj.* 皇家的　　place〔ples〕*n.* 區域
grope〔grop〕*v.* 摸索　　comedy〔'kamədɪ〕*n.* 喜劇
known〔non〕*adj.* 有名的　　diary〔'daɪərɪ〕*n.* 日記
evening class 夜校上課　　attend〔ə'tɛnd〕*v.* 上（學）
gentle〔'dʒɛntḷ〕*adj.* 溫和的　　***first night*** 首演
Halifax〔'hælə,fæks〕*n.* 哈利法克斯【英格蘭北部城市】
playhouse〔'ple,haʊs〕*n.* 戲院　　cross〔krɔs〕*n.* 十字型
golden〔'goldṇ〕*adj.* 金色的　　pond〔pand〕*n.* 池塘
magical〔'mædʒɪkḷ〕*adj.* 迷人的　　real〔'rɪəl〕*adj.* 真的
produce〔prə'djus〕*v.* 製作　　act〔ækt〕*v.* 演出
play〔ple〕*n.* 戲劇　　miss〔mɪs〕*v.* 錯過
grand〔grænd〕*adj.* 豪華的　　secret〔'sikrɪt〕*adj.* 秘密的
best-selling〔'bɛst'sɛlɪŋ〕*adj.* 最暢銷的

35. (**A**) 哪一家戲院開出的票價最便宜？

    (A) <u>Halifax 戲院。</u>   (B) 城市綜藝秀。

    (C) 豪華大戲院。   (D) 約克皇家戲院。

36. (**D**) 如果你想看有老笑話和老歌的演出，你會打哪一支電話訂位？

    (A) 502116   (B) 223568   (C) 365998   (D) <u>430808</u>

    * book〔bʊk〕*v.* 預訂

37. (**A**) 我們可以從本文得知 Sue Townsend 是

    (A) <u>一位作家。</u>   (B) 一位女演員。

    (C) 一位音樂家。   (D) 一位導演。

    * actress〔'æktrɪs〕*n.* 女演員

      musician〔mju'zɪʃən〕*n.* 音樂家

      director〔də'rɛktɚ〕*n.* 導演

Questions 38-41

    A thief, who dropped a winning lottery ticket at the scene of his crime, has been given a lesson in honesty. His victim, who picked up the ticket, then claimed the $25,000 prize, managed to trace him and handed over the cash.

    有個小偷在犯罪現場掉了一張中獎的彩券，這件事給他上了誠實的一課。偷竊事件的受害者撿到這張彩券，並獲得了兩萬五千元的獎金，那個人還設法要找到他，然後把現金還給他。

    winning〔'wɪnɪŋ〕*adj.* 獲勝的；贏的   lottery〔'latərɪ〕*n.* 彩票

    a winning lottery ticket 中獎彩票   scene〔sin〕*n.* 現場

    crime〔kraɪm〕*n.* 犯罪   victim〔'vɪktɪm〕*n.* 受害者

    claim〔klem〕*v.* 索取；獲得   prize〔praɪz〕*n.* 獎金

    manage〔'mænɪdʒ〕*v.* 設法   trace〔tres〕*v.* 找到

    hand over 交給

The robbery happened when a math professor named Vinicio Sabbatucci, 58, was changing a tyre on an Italian motorway. Another motorist, who stopped "to help," stole a suitcase from his car and drove off. The professor found the dropped ticket and put it in his pocket before driving home to Ascoli in eastern Italy.

這起竊案是發生在義大利的高速公路上，當時一位五十八歲的數學教授，名叫 Vinicio Sabbatucci，正在換輪胎。另一個汽車駕駛人停下來「幫忙」，但卻從教授的車裡偷走了一個手提箱，然後開車離去。在教授開車回到位於義大利東部的阿斯科利的家之前，他發現了這張被遺落的彩券，並且把它放進口袋裡。

robbery ('rabərɪ) n. 竊盜案　　professor (prə'fɛsə) n. 教授
tyre (taɪr) n. 輪胎 (= tire)　　Italian (ɪ'tæljən) adj. 義大利的
motorway ('motə,we) n. 高速公路
motorist ('motərɪst) n. 汽車駕駛人
suitcase ('sut,kes) n. 手提箱　　drive off 開車離去
pocket ('pakɪt) n. 口袋　　eastern ('istɚn) adj. 東部的

Next day, he saw the lottery results on TV and, taking out the ticket, realized it was a winner. He claimed the 60 million lira prize. Then he began a battle with his conscience. Finally, he decided he could not keep the money despite having been robbed.

隔天，他看到電視上的彩券開獎結果，他拿出那張彩券，意識到那是一張中獎的彩券。他去領了六千萬里拉的獎金。然後他開始和良心交戰。最後，他決定儘管自己被搶，還是不能把這些錢留下來。

realize ('riə,laɪz) v. 了解；意識到
winner ('wɪnɚ) n. 獲勝的事物
lira ('lɪrə) n. 里拉【義大利的貨幣單位】
battle ('bætl) n. 戰爭　　conscience ('kanʃəns) n. 良心
despite (dɪ'spaɪt) prep. 儘管　　rob (rab) v. 竊盜

He advertised in newspapers and on radio, saying: "I'm trying to find the man who robbed me. I have 60 million lira for him —— a lottery win. Please meet me, anonymity guaranteed."

他在報紙上和廣播刊登廣告，說：「我正在找偷我東西的人。我要給他六千萬里拉——那是一張彩券所贏得的獎金。請和我見個面，我保證你的姓名會保密。」

> advertise (ˈædvɚˌtaɪz) v. 登廣告
> anonymity (ˌænəˈnɪmətɪ) n. 匿名
> guarantee (ˌgærənˈti) v. 保證

Professor Sabbatucci received hundreds of calls from people hoping to trick him into handing them the cash. But there was one voice he recognized, and he arranged to meet the man in a park. The robber, a 35-year-old unemployed father of two, gave back the suitcase and burst into tears.

Sabbatucci 教授接到了幾百通電話，那些人希望能騙他把現金交出來。但是他認出了一個聲音，他安排在公園和那個人見面。那個小偷是個三十五歲，有著兩個孩子的失業父親，他交還了那個手提箱，而且突然嚎啕大哭。

> receive (rɪˈsiv) v. 接到　　trick (trɪk) v. 欺騙
> hand (hænd) v. 交給　　recognize (ˈrɛkəgˌnaɪz) v. 認出
> arrange (əˈrendʒ) v. 安排　　robber (ˈrabɚ) n. 盜賊；搶匪
> unemployed (ˌʌnɪmˈplɔɪd) adj. 失業的
> *burst into tears* 突然嚎啕大哭

He could not believe what was happening. "Why didn't you keep the money?" he asked. The professor replied: " I couldn't because it's not mine." Then he walked off, spurning the thief's offer of a reward.

他不敢相信會發生這樣的事。「你爲什麼不把錢留著？」他問。教授回答：「我不能，因爲那不是我的錢。」然後就走開了，拒絕小偷所提供的酬金。

      reply〔rɪˋplaɪ〕v. 回答　　***walk off*** 離去
      spurn〔spɝn〕v. 拒絕　　reward〔rɪˋwɔrd〕n. 酬金；獎賞

38. (**A**) 第二段中「然後他開始和良心交戰」這句話暗示下列各項敘述，除了
    (A) 他一看到彩券開獎結果，就知道該怎麼做了。
    (B) 他猶豫要不要把錢留給自己。
    (C) 他考慮了一下要不要向搶匪報仇。
    (D) 他了解誠實比錢重要。

    * imply〔ɪmˋplaɪ〕v. 暗示　　***as soon as*** 一…就…
      hesitate〔ˋhɛzə͵tet〕v. 猶豫
      avenge〔əˋvɛndʒ〕v. 報仇　　***come to*** 成爲

39. (**B**) 數百人打電話給 Sabbatucci 教授，因爲他們
    (A) 想要取笑他。　　　　(B) 希望拿到那筆錢。
    (C) 知道誰是搶匪。　　　(D) 遺失了那張彩券。

    * phone〔fon〕v. 打電話　　***make fun of*** 取笑

40. (**C**) 最後一段的 "spurning" 可以換成
    (A) accept〔əkˋsɛpt〕v. 接受　(B) claim〔klem〕v. 認領
    (C) ***reject***〔rɪˋdʒɛkt〕v. 拒絕　(D) cancel〔ˋkænsl〕v. 取消

    * replace〔rɪˋples〕v. 替換

41. (**A**) 如果這則故事出現在報紙上，最好的標題可能是
    (A) 「小偷幸運的一天」。　(B) 「受歡迎的數學教授」。
    (C) 「神奇的彩券」。　　　(D) 「不誠實的獎賞」。

    * appear〔əˋpɪr〕v. 出現　　title〔ˋtaɪtl〕n. 標題
      popular〔ˋpɑpjələ〕adj. 受歡迎的

Questions 42-45

This is a page from a college information handbook. It tells you where you can find various college services and facilities.

Where To Find Help In The College

Here is the location of some important college services and facilities. Rooms numbered 100-130 are on the first floor and those numbered 200-230 on the second floor of the main college block.

Student Services Centre

Careers (Room 127)
The staff members are available to advise on career choice and applications for higher education.

Accommodation office (Room 207)
Mrs. J Mardle is available each afternoon from 1:30 to 4:30 to assist students with problems relating to housing.

Medical Room (Room 113)
Mrs. J Wright, the college nurse, is available each morning from 9:30 to 12:00 am. The college doctor is in attendance on Wednesday mornings.

Sports Office (Room 195)
Mrs. B Murie can provide information about sports and keep-fit activities.

Student Union Office (Room 230)
A range of services and advice (travel etc.) is provided.

Food Service (Room 200)
Mr. G Nunn is the manager and will do his best to help if you require a special diet.

Library (Room 114)
Besides books, this also has photocopying, video, audio-visual and computing facilities.

Self Access Language Learning Center (Room 224)
Students can attend on a drop-in basis from 9:00 am to 4:15 pm.

這是大學資訊手冊中的一頁。它告訴你可以在哪裡找到各種大學服務和設施。

在大學裡，要到哪裡尋求協助

以下是一些重要的大學服務和設施的位置。房間號碼從 100 到 130 是在本部大樓一樓，而房間號碼 200 到 230 則是在二樓。

學生服務中心

生涯規劃（127 室）

你可以和工作人員會面，並從他們那裡得到關於選擇職業，以及申請高等教育學校的資訊。

住宿辦公室（207 室）

每天下午一點半到四點半，你都可以去見 J Mardle 女士，她會協助學生解決關於住宿的問題。

醫務室（113 室）

J Wright 是校護人員，每天早上九點半到十二點，你都可以見到她。校醫星期三早上會在醫務室。

體育辦公室（195 室）

B Murie 女士可以提供你有關運動和保持健康的活動資訊。

學生會辦公室（230 室）

提供一系列的服務與建議（旅遊等）。

飲食服務（200 室）

負責人是 G Nunn 先生，如果你需要特殊飲食，他會盡力協助你。

圖書館（114 室）

除了書本之外，這裡還有提供影印服務、電視、視聽設備，以及電腦設施。

外語自學中心（224 室）

學生們可以偶爾來上一次課，從早上九點開始到下午四點十五分。

handbook〔'hænd,bʊk〕n. 手冊

various〔'vɛrɪəs〕adj. 各種不同的

facility〔fə'sɪlətɪ〕n. 設施

location〔lo'keʃən〕n. 位置　　number〔'nʌmbə〕v. 編號

floor〔flor〕n. 樓層　　main〔men〕adj. 主要的

block〔blɑk〕n. 大樓　　centre〔'sɛntə〕n. 中心（= center）

career〔kə'rɪr〕n. 生涯；職業　　staff〔stæf〕n. 工作人員

member〔'mɛmbə〕n.（組織的）一員

available〔ə'veləbḷ〕adj. 可會見的

advise〔əd'vaɪz〕v. 建議

application〔,æplə'keʃən〕n. 申請

higher education 高等教育

accommodation〔ə,kɑmə'deʃən〕n. 住宿

assist〔ə'sɪst〕v. 協助　　relate〔rɪ'let〕v. 有關

housing〔'haʊzɪŋ〕n. 住宿　　medical〔'mɛdɪkḷ〕adj. 醫療的

attendance〔ə'tɛndəns〕n. 出席

keep-fit〔'kip'fɪt〕adj. 保持健康的　　*student union* 學生會

range〔rendʒ〕n. 一系列　　advice〔əd'vaɪs〕n. 建議

manager〔'mænɪdʒə〕n. 負責人　　*do one's best* 盡力

require〔rɪ'kwaɪr〕v. 需要　　diet〔'daɪət〕n. 飲食

besides〔bɪ'saɪdz〕prep. 除⋯之外

photocopying〔'fotə,kɑpɪɪŋ〕n. 影印服務

video〔'vɪdɪ,o〕n. 電視

audio-visual〔'ɔdɪə'vɪʒuəl〕adj. 視聽的

computing〔kəm'pjutɪŋ〕n. 使用電腦

access〔'æksɛs〕n. 取得；使用

attend〔ə'tɛnd〕v. 參加；上（學）

drop-in〔'drɑp'ɪn〕adj. 偶爾一次的

basis〔'besɪs〕n. 基礎

42. (**B**) 如果你找不到地方住，應該到哪裡尋求協助？

(A) 200 室。 　　　　(B) <u>207 室。</u>

(C) 113 室。 　　　　(D) 224 室。

* **go for** 尋求

43. (**D**) 如果你想要申請獎學金，應該到哪裡尋求協助？

(A) 113 室。 　　　　(B) 200 室。

(C) 195 室。 　　　　(D) <u>我們不知道。</u>

* scholarship〔'skɑlɚ‚ʃɪp〕*n.* 獎學金

44. (**A**) 如果你是外國學生，你會去 230 室

(A) <u>訂回國的機票。</u> 　　(B) 請求供應一些特別的食物。

(C) 詢問有關學費的事。 　　(D) 拿到證書的影印本。

* foreign〔'fɔrɪn〕*adj.* 外國的
  motherland〔'mʌðɚ‚lænd〕*n.* 祖國
  supply〔sə'plaɪ〕*n.* 供應 　　inquire〔ɪn'kwaɪr〕*v.* 詢問
  educational〔‚ɛdʒʊ'keʃənḷ〕*adj.* 教育的 　　fee〔fi〕*n.* 學費
  obtain〔əb'ten〕*v.* 得到 　　copy〔'kɑpɪ〕*n.* 影印本
  certificate〔sə'tɪfəkɪt〕*n.* 證明書

45. (**A**) 下列敘述何者不正確？

(A) <u>在語言學習中心必須要預約。</u>

(B) 你可以在圖書館看電視節目。

(C) 你可以在中午以前的任何時間見到校護人員。

(D) 學生服務中心可以協助學生申請高等教育學校。

* statement〔'stetmənt〕*n.* 敘述
  reservation〔‚rɛzɚ'veʃən〕*n.* 預訂
  program〔'progræm〕*n.* 節目

Questions 46-50

_____ Scientists say people living in areas where bird flu has been found in poultry or wild birds should keep their cats indoors. They believe the potential role of felines in spreading the virus is being overlooked.

_____ 科學家說，住在家禽或野鳥被發現有禽流感的區域的人，應該把貓留在室內。他們認為，貓科動物在傳播病毒上的潛在作用被忽略了。

> flu〔flu〕*n.* 流行性感冒　　***bird flu*** 禽流感
> poultry〔'poltrɪ〕*n.* 家禽　　wild〔waɪld〕*adj.* 野生的
> indoors〔'ɪn'dorz〕*adv.* 在室內
> potential〔pə'tɛnʃəl〕*adj.* 潛在的　　role〔rol〕*n.* 作用
> feline〔'filaɪn〕*n.* 貓科動物　　spread〔sprɛd〕*v.* 傳播
> virus〔'vaɪrəs〕*n.* 病毒　　overlook〔,ovə'luk〕*v.* 忽略

Cats have been known to become infected with the H5N1 virus and lab experiments show they can give it to other cats, although nobody knows whether they can transmit it to people or poultry.

人們已經知道，貓會感染 H5N1 病毒，而且實驗證實牠們會將病毒傳給其他小貓，雖然沒有人知道牠們會不會把病毒傳給人類或家禽。

> infect〔ɪn'fɛkt〕*v.* 感染　　lab〔læb〕*adj.* 實驗室的
> experiment〔ɪk'spɛrəmənt〕*n.* 實驗
> show〔ʃo〕*v.* 證明　　transmit〔træns'mɪt〕*v.* 傳染

A virologist and vegetarian warned that as well as passing H5N1 to other species, cats may help the virus to adapt into a more highly infectious strain in humans, which could spark a pandemic.

一位病毒學家兼獸醫警告大家，貓不但會把H5N1病毒傳給其他物種，
牠們還會將病毒改造成更容易傳染給人類的品種，然後引發全國流行病。

  virologist〔vaɪˈrɑlədʒɪst〕*n.* 病毒學家
  veterinarian〔ˌvɛtrəˈnɛrɪən〕*n.* 獸醫
  warn〔wɔrn〕*v.* 警告 *as well as* 以及
  pass〔pæs〕*v.* 傳遞；傳播 species〔ˈspiʃɪz〕*n.* 物種
  adapt〔əˈdæpt〕*v.* 改造；適應
  infectious〔ɪnˈfɛkʃəs〕*adj.* 傳染性的
  strain〔stren〕*n.* 品系 spark〔spɑrk〕*v.* 引起
  pandemic〔pænˈdɛmɪk〕*n.* 全國流行病

We have to take a number of precautionary measures. We need to
keep in mind that in principle mammals can be infected and that
they can spread the disease.

我們必須採取許多預防措施。我們要記住原則上，哺乳類動物都會被感
染，而且也會傳播疾病。

  a number of 許多
  precautionary〔prɪˈkɔʃənˌɛrɪ〕*adj.* 預防的
  measure〔ˈmɛʒɚ〕*n.* 措施 *keep in mind* 記住
  principle〔ˈprɪnsəpḷ〕*n.* 原則 *in principle* 原則上
  mammal〔ˈmæmḷ〕*n.* 哺乳類動物 spread〔sprɛd〕*v. n.* 傳播

  Animals such as dogs, foxes, ferrets and seals may also be
vulnerable to infection. In areas where H5N1 has been found in
poultry or wild birds, cats should be kept away from infected
birds or their droppings, and cats suspected of such contacts or
showing symptoms of infection should be quarantined and tested.

　　像是狗、狐狸、雪貂、和海豹,也是很容易被感染的動物。在家禽和野鳥身上有發現 H5N1 病毒的地方,應該讓貓遠離被感染的鳥兒,或其糞便,疑似和那些鳥接觸的貓,或是出現感染症狀的貓,都應該要隔離並接受檢查。

ferret〔ˋfɛrɪt〕n. 雪貂　　seal〔sil〕n. 海豹
vulnerable〔ˋvʌlnərəbḷ〕adj. 易受傷的;易受攻擊的
infection〔ɪnˋfɛkʃən〕n. 感染　　**keep away** 遠離;避開
droppings〔ˋdrɑpɪŋs〕n. pl. (鳥獸的) 糞
suspect〔səˋspɛkt〕v. 懷疑　　contact〔ˋkɑntækt〕n. 接觸
symptom〔ˋsɪmptəm〕n. 症狀
quarantine〔ˋkwɔrənˌtin〕v. 隔離
test〔tɛst〕v. 檢查;測試

If animals or other carnivores show signs of illness, they should be tested for H5N1. When wild birds are infected we have seen that cats are quite effective in catching them and catching the disease. In this way they could be sentinels.

如果有動物或其他食肉動物出現生病的跡象,就要接受 H5N1 病毒的檢測。當野鳥被感染時,我們會看到小貓很有效率地抓住那些鳥,並因此感染疾病。這樣一來,小貓就可以作為疾病的哨兵。

carnivore〔ˋkɑnəˌvor〕n. 食肉動物　　sign〔saɪn〕n. 跡象
illness〔ˋɪlnɪs〕n. 疾病　　effective〔əˋfɛktɪv〕adj. 有效率的
catch〔kætʃ〕v. 捕捉;感染　　disease〔dɪˋziz〕n. 疾病
in this way 這樣一來　　sentinel〔ˋsɛntənḷ〕n. 哨兵

Deaths from H5N1, which has infected 191 people and killed 108, have been reported in cats in countries like Asia, Iraq and Germany.

已經有191人感染 H5N1 病毒，然後有108人因此死亡，根據報導，有些國家的貓也感染了 H5N1 病毒，像是亞洲國家、伊拉克，以及德國。

> report〔rɪˋport〕v. 報導　　Asia〔ˋeʃə〕n. 亞洲
> Iraq〔ɪˋrɑk〕n. 伊拉克　　Germany〔ˋdʒɝmənɪ〕n. 德國

Tigers and leopards in zoos in Thailand have also died after eating fresh chicken carcasses. The potential role of cats should be considered in official guidelines for controlling the spread of H5N1 virus.

泰國動物園裡的老虎和美洲豹，也在吃了新鮮的小雞屍體之後死亡。在擬定控制 H5N1 病毒傳播的官方指導方針時，應該要考慮到貓的潛在作用。

> leopard〔ˋlɛpəd〕n. 美洲豹　　Thailand〔ˋtaɪlənd〕n. 泰國
> carcass〔ˋkɑrkəs〕n.（動物的）屍體
> consider〔kənˋsɪdə〕v. 考慮　　official〔əˋfɪʃəl〕adj. 官方的
> guideline〔ˋgaɪd͵laɪn〕n. 指導方針
> control〔kənˋtrol〕v. 控制

Studies at a university have shown that cats can be infected through the respiratory tract, in a similar way to humans, but that the more likely route is through the gut by eating infected birds.

有所大學的研究顯示，小貓會經由呼吸道被感染，跟人很類似，但是小貓比較有可能被感染的途徑，是透過吃了感染病毒的鳥，而使內臟受到感染。

> university〔͵junəˋvɝsətɪ〕n. 大學
> respiratory〔rɪˋspaɪrə͵torɪ〕adj. 呼吸的
> tract〔trækt〕n. 管；道　　similar〔ˋsɪmələ〕adj. 相似的
> route〔rut〕n. 途徑　　gut〔gʌt〕n. 內臟

The animals develop serious or fatal disease and can transmit the virus to other cats. We know that cat-to-cat transmission is possible. That is important because it would predispose the virus to adapt to mammals. We cannot exclude that.

這些動物罹患了嚴重而致命的疾病，牠們還會把病毒傳染給其他小貓。我們知道小貓之間可能會互相傳染。那很重要，因為那會使病毒先適應哺乳動物。所以我們不能排除把那件事考量進去。

develop〔dɪ'vɛləp〕v. 患（病）　　serious〔'sɪrɪəs〕adj. 嚴重的
fatal〔'fetḷ〕adj. 致命的　　transmit〔træns'mɪt〕v. 傳染
transmission〔træns'mɪʃən〕n. 傳染
predispose〔ˌpridɪs'poz〕v. 使…先傾向於
exclude〔ɪk'sklud〕v. 排除

It has also been shown that the amount of virus excreted by cats through the respiratory tract or in feces is lower than the levels from chickens.

由小貓透過呼吸道或排泄物所排放出來的病毒量顯示，小貓排出來的病毒量還比雞少。

excrete〔ɪk'skrit〕v. 排泄　　feces〔'fisiz〕n. pl. 糞便

The scientists do not know how long cats can excrete the virus, the minimal amount of virus needed to cause infection in cats or whether virus transmission from cats to poultry, humans and other species is possible.

科學家不知道小貓要過多久才會把病毒排出來，也不知道要讓小貓感染，最少要多少病毒，他們也不曉得病毒有沒有可能從小貓傳給家禽、人類，以及其他動物。

minimal〔'mɪnɪmḷ〕adj. 最少的

But given the potential contribution of these carnivore hosts to both virus transmission and its adaptation to mammals, we believe the time for increased surveillance and precaution is here.

但是如果這些動物宿主對病毒的傳播，以及適應哺乳動物這兩方面，都有潛在的貢獻，那麼我們相信，現在就要開始加強檢查和預防。

given (ˈɡɪvən) prep. 如果有
contribution (ˌkɑntrəˈbjuʃən) n. 貢獻
host (host) n. 宿主
adaptation (ˌædəpˈteʃən) n. 適應
increased (ɪnˈkrist) adj. 增強的
surveillance (səˈveləns) n. 檢查
precaution (prɪˈkɔʃən) n. 預防

Scientists need to learn more about what role, if any, cats have in spreading H5N1 before making such blanket recommendations.

如果小貓真的有傳播 H5N1 病毒的作用，那麼科學家們應該在做出非常全面性的建議之前，多去了解這件事。

if any 如果有的話　　such (sʌtʃ) adv. 非常
blanket (ˈblæŋkɪt) adj. 全面性的
recommendation (ˌrɛkəmɛnˈdeʃən) n. 建議

46. (C) H5N1 病毒會導致

(A) 愛滋病。　　　　(B) 嚴重急性呼吸道綜合症。
(C) 禽流感。　　　　(D) 糖尿病。

* lead to 導致
SARS 嚴重急性呼吸道綜合症。
(= Severe Acute Respiratory Syndrome)
diabetes (ˌdaɪəˈbitɪs) n. 糖尿病

47. (**B**) 如果有動物或其他食肉動物出現生病的跡象，牠們應該要接受
　　　　　　＿＿＿＿＿＿＿＿ H5N1。

　　(A) 是指　　(B) 檢查　　(C) 視爲　　(D) 遠離

　　＊ refer〔rɪˋfɝ〕v. 是指　　examine〔ɪgˋzæmɪn〕v. 檢查
　　　　regard〔rɪˋgɑrd〕v. 視爲　　*keep away from* 遠離

48. (**C**) 因爲 H5N1 而死亡的比率約爲

　　(A) 百分之四十七點五。

　　(B) 百分之三十八點五。

　　(C) 百分之五十六點五。

　　(D) 百分之六十點五。

　　＊ rate〔ret〕n. 比率

49. (**B**) 根據本文，下列何者正確？

　　(A) 在這個世界上幾乎不可能發生小貓之間互相傳染。

　　(B) 人們已經知道小貓會感染 H5N1 病毒。

　　(C) 小貓會將細菌改造成更容易傳染給人類的品種。

　　(D) 小貓是不可能經由呼吸道被感染的。

　　＊ bacterium〔bækˋtɪrɪəm〕n. pl. 細菌
　　　　out of the question 完全不可能的

50. (**B**) 下列哪一句可以當作本文的主題句？

　　(A) 遠離野生動物是有必要的。

　　(B) 小貓可能在禽流感的傳播上，扮演了一個角色。

　　(C) 小貓和人類之間有很大的差異。

　　(D) 小貓傳播致命疾病的可能性有多高。

　　＊ necessary〔ˋnɛsə͵sɛrɪ〕adj. 必要的
　　　　potential〔pəˋtɛnʃəl〕n. 可能性

全民英語能力分級檢定測驗
GENERAL ENGLISH PROFICIENCY TEST
中高級聽力測驗
HIGH-INTERMEDIATE LISTENING COMPREHENSION TEST

This listening comprehension test will test your ability to understand spoken English. In this test, each conversation, short talk and question will be spoken JUST ONE TIME. They will not be written out for you. There are three parts to this test. Special instructions will be given to you at the beginning of each part.

Part A

In part A, you will hear 15 questions. After you hear a question, read the four choices in your test book and decide which one is the best answer to the question you have heard.

Example:

<u>You will hear</u>: Mary, can you tell me what time it is?

<u>You will read</u>: A. About two hours ago.
               B. I used to be able to, but not now.
               C. Sure, it's half past nine.
               D. Today is October 22.

The best answer to the question "Mary, can you tell me what time it is?" is C: "Sure, it's half past nine." Therefore, you should choose answer C.

1. A. No, it doesn't.

   B. I don't have anything to throw out.

   C. It stops here at 10 p.m.

   D. It stops on Center Street.

2. A. It's the "red eye" leaving at 2 a.m.

   B. It departs from the old terminal.

   C. It's a two-hour flight.

   D. It's always on time.

3. A. It's one dimensional.

   B. It's multi-functional.

   C. It's outdated.

   D. It's also a laptop.

4. A. Turn left at the first intersection and go down two blocks.

   B. It's located near the harbor.

   C. Today is Sunday. Don't worry.

   D. They relocated to another area.

5. A. Is that a promise?

   B. I love to sprint along the beach.

   C. Let's all go by ourselves.

   D. No, thanks. Not tonight.

6. A. Yes, I'd like some socks.

   B. Do they have software?

   C. Could you buy some electrical tape for me?

   D. They have fresh groceries.

7. A. Until next September.

   B. For 18 months.

   C. My dentist put them on.

   D. I had gaps in my teeth.

8. A. It's a temporary skyscraper.

   B. It is for now.

   C. It towers over the skyline.

   D. It is definitely a monumental structure.

9. A. Yes, I was here once before.

   B. You look familiar, too.

   C. Yes, how did you know?

   D. I'm sorry I forgot your name.

10. A. It's right on schedule.

    B. I plan to do a survey.

    C. Someone gathers and collects data.

    D. I bring it with me at times.

Please turn to the next page. ⏸⇨

11. A. I love the New York
      Yankees.
    B. The Dallas Cowboys
      had an awful year.
    C. Pro athletes have
      changed in recent years.
    D. The salaries are
      exorbitant.

12. A. Fill out an application
      for employment.
    B. Just fill out an employee
      request form.
    C. It's possible to apply.
    D. Everyone is entitled to
      personal time.

13. A. Nothing else, thanks.
    B. No, I really don't care
      what you think.
    C. Yes, I ordered this dish.
    D. No, we're fine. Thank
      you.

14. A. I wish we could
      have some rainfall.
    B. I think it will be
      dry soon.
    C. The temperatures
      are rising and
      falling.
    D. The forecast will
      come out soon.

15. A. I'll look and see.
    B. I'll be right back
      with it.
    C. Security is not
      here right now.
    D. I'll check on the
      situation.

Part B

In part B, you will hear 15 conversations between a man and a woman. After each conversation, you will hear a question about the conversation. After you hear the question, read the four choices in your test book and choose the best answer to the question you have heard.

Example:

> <u>You will hear</u>: (Man)　May I see your driver's license?
> (Woman) Yes, officer. Here it is. Was I speeding?
> (Man)　Yes, ma'am. You were doing sixty in a forty-five-mile-an-hour zone.
> (Woman) No way! I don't believe you.
> (Man)　Well, it is true and here is your ticket.
>
> Question: Why does the man ask for the woman's driver's license?

> <u>You will read</u>: A. She was going too fast.
> B. To check its limitations.
> C. To check her age.
> D. She entered a restricted zone.

The best answer to the question "Why does the man ask for the woman's driver's license?" is A: "She was going too fast." Therefore, you should choose answer A.

Please turn to the next page. ▯⟹

16. A. In a bookstore.
    B. In a campus study hall.
    C. At a library.
    D. In a private lounge.

17. A. He misunderstood her.
    B. He didn't clean his ears.
    C. He bought her a cake.
    D. He mispronounced a
       word.

18. A. A big discount.
    B. To mail some packages.
    C. To apply for a position.
    D. A quick price estimate.

19. A. Don't be clumsy.
    B. Don't drink and surf.
    C. Never have liquids near
       a computer.
    D. Electricity shouldn't get
       into water.

20. A. It stinks.
    B. It's very dirty.
    C. It's a toilet.
    D. It's too small.

21. A. They both do.
    B. He does.
    C. He doesn't.
    D. She might be
       persuaded.

22. A. Play the bongos.
    B. Do martial arts.
    C. Play snooker.
    D. Play table tennis.

23. A. One week.
    B. Fifteen days.
    C. Five straight days.
    D. Twenty four hours.

24. A. She failed miserably.
    B. She almost passed.
    C. She destroyed the car.
    D. She lost her license.

25. A. A weather balloon.
    B. Storm clouds.
    C. A commercial airliner.
    D. A military aircraft.

26. A. Asking her for a date.
    B. Joining the club.
    C. Starting to lose weight.
    D. Learning how to dance.

27. A. Fill up the gas tank.
    B. Find a restroom first.
    C. Get some wiper fluid.
    D. Check the oil pressure.

28. A. Saying silly things.
    B. Arguing ferociously.
    C. Talking about animals.
    D. Practicing English pronunciation.

29. A. He got lucky.
    B. He almost died.
    C. He changed his opinion fast!
    D. He wants to find that girl.

30. A. At a bus terminal.
    B. At the circus.
    C. In a school cafeteria.
    D. At a funeral.

Please turn to the next page. ▯⟩

Part C

In part C, you will hear several short talks. After each talk, you will hear 2 to 3 questions about the talk. After you hear each question, read the four choices in your test book and choose the best answer to the question you have heard.

Example:

<u>You will hear:</u>

Thank you for coming to this, the first in a series of seminars on the use of computers in the classroom. As the brochure informed you, there will be a total of five seminars given in this room every Monday morning from 6:00 to 7:30. Our goal will be to show you, the teachers of our schoolchildren, how the changing technology of today can be applied to the unchanging lessons of yesterday to make your students' learning experience more interesting and relevant to the world they live in. By the end of the last seminar, you will not be computer literate, but you will be able to make sense of the hundreds of complex words and technical terms related to the field and be aware of the programs available for use in the classroom.

Question number 1: What is the subject of this seminar series?

Please turn to the next page.

You will read: A. Self-improvement.
B. Using computers to teach.
C. Technology.
D. Study habits of today's students.

The best answer to the question "What is the subject of this seminar series?" is B: "Using computers to teach." Therefore, you should choose answer B.

Now listen to another question based on the same talk.

You will hear:

Question number 2: What does the speaker say participants will be able to do after attending the seminars?

You will read: A. Understand today's students.
B. Understand computer terminology.
C. Motivate students.
D. Deal more confidently with people.

The best answer to the question "What does the speaker say participants will be able to do after attending the seminars?" is B: "Understand computer terminology." Therefore, you should choose answer B.

Please turn to the next page. ▯⟹

31. A. The top fire official.
    B. The city safety inspector.
    C. The commissionaire.
    D. The police chief.

32. A. Poor training program.
    B. Flawed equipment.
    C. Defective vehicles.
    D. Low morale.

33. A. Find and fix the problem.
    B. Initiate new programs.
    C. Purchase safety devices.
    D. Donate time and money.

34. A. Jog after breakfast.
    B. "Pump iron" every afternoon.
    C. Exercise before breakfast.
    D. Practice for a marathon.

35. A. Increased heart rate.
    B. Lower blood pressure.
    C. A dark complexion.
    D. Increased feeling of energy.

36. A. To all senior citizens.
    B. To the government officials.
    C. The citizens of Tampa.
    D. To the Health Administration.

37. A. Insects are a threat.
    B. Parks will be sprayed, so avoid the danger.
    C. Mosquitoes spread disease.
    D. Pitch in and help us out.

38. A. At dusk.
    B. Around midday.
    C. From dawn to dusk.
    D. From 5 a.m. to 7 a.m.

39. A. A meeting is starting soon.
    B. Their boss is waiting for them.
    C. They want to miss a client.
    D. Their girlfriends are waiting.

40. A. Sprint fast to the meeting.
    B. Buy a few things.
    C. Chat with a girl.
    D. "Hustle" some clients.

Please turn to the next page.

41. A. All day, every day.

    B. From noon till midnight.

    C. 24 days a month, 7 hours a day.

    D. Every day from 9 a.m. to 7 p.m.

42. A. Shirts and pants.

    B. Hats and gloves.

    C. Blankets and pillows.

    D. Put quarters in only.

43. A. Put in some lint.

    B. Flatten out your dollar bills.

    C. Put in powder detergent.

    D. Put quarters in only.

44. A. The Tigers.

    B. The Eagles.

    C. Basketball team.

    D. The championship team.

45. A. A sports reporter.

    B. A team parent.

    C. The referee.

    D. The team coach.

-The End-

中高級閱讀測驗

HIGH-INTERMEDIATE
READING COMPREHENSION TEST

This test has three parts, with 50 multiple-choice questions (each with four choices) in total. Special directions will be provided for each part. You will have 50 minutes to complete this test.

Part A: Sentence Completion

This part of the test has 15 incomplete sentences. Beneath each sentence, you will see four words or phrases, marked A, B, C and D. You are to choose the word or phrase that best completes the sentences. Then on your answer sheet, find the number of the question and mark your answer.

1. The most _____ explanation for the recession would seem to be that people had lost confidence in the economy.
   A. pictorial
   B. productive
   C. prescriptive
   D. plausible

Please turn to the next page. ⟹

2. He was an _____ by nature; he preferred reading a book at home alone to going out with friends.
   A. introvert
   B. egoist
   C. adversary
   D. exhibition

3. Some children display an _____ curiosity about every new thing they encounter.
   A. inherent
   B. unquenchable
   C. insensitive
   D. uninvited

4. As the plane descended gradually, we were able to enjoy the _____ view of the city.
   A. paralyzed
   B. panoramic
   C. patronizing
   D. paralleled

5. Students learning about how life began on Earth may be presented with the _____ question, "Which came first, the chicken or the egg?"
   A. pressing
   B. perplexing
   C. peripheral
   D. penetrating

6. Although research has shown that asparagus does contain many important nutrients, it is not, as it was once regarded, a(n) _____.

A. delicacy

B. organism

C. resonance

D. panacea

7. If there is smoke in a room, you should _____ out of the room slowly. Don't panic.

A. crawl

B. crutch

C. cruise

D. cringe

8. The children in the neighborhood have an exclusive club that _____ everyone over eight.

A. roots out

B. sneers at

C. leaves out

D. hangs around

Please turn to the next page. ⇨

9. Most people believed that Mr. Smith committed the crime but _____ with a plea of insanity.
   A. came down
   B. put up
   C. got away
   D. passed away

10. The man who was seen hanging around the area _____ the shooting was considered to be the prime suspect in the murder case.
   A. beforehand
   B. other than
   C. no sooner than
   D. prior to

11. "Are you coming to Dr. Kennedy's lecture tonight?"
   "No, I'm sorry I _____ able to attend."
   A. will not have been
   B. can't be
   C. am not to
   D. won't be

12. _____, this shabby eatery provides excellent food.
   A. Very to my surprise
   B. Much to my surprise
   C. Very to my disappointment
   D. Much to my disappointment

13. He didn't care _____ his schoolwork so he flunked
    again.
    A. for
    B. in
    C. of
    D. about

14. Come _____ may, we will never give up our project.
    A. what
    B. whatever
    C. as
    D. it

15. We don't think she is as attractive as her younger sister,
    _____?
    A. isn't she
    B. do we
    C. is she
    D. don't we

Please turn to the next page. ⟹

Part B: Cloze

This part of the test has two passages. Each passage contains seven or eight missing words or phrases. There is a total of 15 missing words or phrases. Beneath each passage, you will see seven or eight items with four choices, marked A, B, C and D. You are to choose the best answer for each missing word or phrase in the two passages. Then, on your answer sheet, find the number of the question and mark your answer.

Questions 16-23

Ancient science, or natural philosophy, as it was called, saw ____(16)____ conflict between scientific knowledge and religious ____(17)____. However, conflict between scientists and religious leaders ____(18)____ in the medieval age, the age of theological inquiry.

The relationship between Christianity and science became ____(19)____ adversarial as scientific researchers developed new ways of seeing the natural world — ways that ____(20)____ Christian teachings. Such beliefs as creation and geocentrism (the theory that the earth is the center of the universe) were increasingly ____(21)____ rational doubt, which in turn threatened to ____(22)____ the authority and power of the Church leaders.

Galileo, the Italian scientist who advanced the notion of a
heliocentric (sun-centered) universe, __(23)__ as the traditional
symbol of the conflict of this age.

16. A. any
    B. no
    C. every
    D. some

17. A. believe
    B. trust
    C. faith
    D. thought

18. A. has arisen
    B. have arisen
    C. arose
    D. arising

19. A. increasingly
    B. additionally
    C. absolutely
    D. relatively

20. A. commemorated
    B. contradicted
    C. apologized
    D. prevailed

21. A. committed to
    B. prone to
    C. open to
    D. inclined to

22. A. underlie
    B. understand
    C. undersell
    D. undermine

23. A. sits
    B. stands
    C. lies
    D. crouches

Please turn to the next page. ⬛⟹

Questions 24-30

____(24)____ all one can say about it, however, the nature and value of art are still not widely understood by the general public. In a society preoccupied with material success, ____(25)____, art does not appear to be very useful, since it does not produce such obvious benefits as those of medicine or engineering. Even those artists (including performers) who are widely known and accepted are usually admired more for their commercial success than for their artistic talents, ____(26)____ that they can compete in the business world. Generally, careers in the arts are considered highly risky because they seldom offer financial security. Such attitudes about art have led to a situation in which children are systematically (although not necessarily intentionally) discouraged from developing their talents. By the time adulthood is reached, the average American has suppressed all artistic inclinations. ____(27)____ adults are thus cut off from or are only partly aware of one of man's primary ways of knowing his world and understanding himself.

Still, it is difficult to defend art on the basis of ____(28)____. Art ultimately must be valued because of its capacity to improve the quality of life: by increasing our sensitivity to

___(29)___ , by sharpening our perceptions, by reshaping our

values or by instilling the idea that moral and societal concerns

___(30)___ material well-being.

24. A. Regard
    B. Despite
    C. In spite
    D. In regard

25. A. as our society
    B. like the one we are in
    C. as ours has been
    D. like our society has
       been with

26. A. being shown
    B. having shown
    C. having been shown
    D. show

27. A. Many more
    B. Far many
    C. Far more
    D. Far too many

28. A. its immediate utility
    B. being utilized
    C. its utilitarian
       immediacy
    D. some immediate usage

29. A. other's surrounding
    B. other's and ours
       surroundings
    C. other's and our
       surrounding
    D. others and our
       surroundings

30. A. take precedence over
    B. are precedent with
    C. have preceded
    D. precede over

Please turn to the next page. ▮⟹

Part C: Reading

In this part of the test, you will read several passages. Each passage is followed by several questions. There is a total of 20 questions. You are to choose the best answer, A, B, C or D, to each question on the basis of what is stated or implied in the passage. Then on your answer sheet, find the number of the question and mark your answer.

Questions 31-34

Data collection aids the smooth functioning of government, business, and research. Personal data is used for tax assessment, job selection, credit rating, and many other purposes. Aggregate data is useful for planning and formulating social policies. The general availability of data supports freedom of speech and freedom of the press.

Conversely, the gathering of data can erode personal privacy. Data can be used for blackmail, especially large-scale political blackmail by governments or police with too much power. Harassment of individuals by law enforcement agencies and monopolistic corporations (including utility companies) can also occur. Errors in data collection can lead to many unfair practices, such as denial of employment or denial of credit. Outdated or incomplete data can lead to personal trauma. Retention of information for long periods can result in excessive punishment of a person for a misdemeanor long since atoned for.

31. According to the passage, the author is
   A. favorable to data collection.
   B. unfavorable to data collection.
   C. fearful of the possible uses of the data collected.
   D. resigned to the inevitability of intrusions on privacy.

32. The reason that data supports freedom of speech and
   freedom of the press is that
   A. people need to discuss data freely.
   B. the more data we have, the freer people are to discuss it.
   C. it fits into a free enterprise system.
   D. it makes data available to the general public.

33. The passage implies that
   A. some governments would blackmail their citizens.
   B. people with credit problems are victims of unfair data
      collection practices.
   C. data collection should be abolished.
   D. personal trauma victims should be compensated.

34. When information is retained too long, it may result in
   A. press censorship.
   B. punishment more than one deserves.
   C. government interference.
   D. unemployment.

Please turn to the next page.

Questions 35-39

The process of perceiving other people is rarely translated (to ourselves or others) into cold, objective terms. "She was 5 feet 8 inches tall, had fair hair, and wore a colored skirt." More often, we try to get inside the other person to <u>pinpoint</u> his or her attitudes, emotions, motivations, abilities, ideas and characters. Furthermore, we sometimes behave as if we can accomplish this difficult job very quickly — perhaps with a two-second glance.

We try to obtain information about others in many ways. Experts suggest several methods for reducing uncertainties about others: watching, without being noticed, a person interacting with others, particularly with others who are known to you so you can compare the observed person's behavior with the known others' behavior. Try to observe a person in a situation where social behavior is relatively unrestrained or where a wide variety of behavioral responses are called for. Deliberately structure the physical or social environment so as to observe the person's responses to specific stimuli. Ask people who have had or have frequent contact with the person about him or her. And use various strategies in face-to-face interaction to uncover information about another person — questions, self-disclosures, and so on.

Getting to know someone is a never-ending task, largely because people are constantly changing and the methods we use to obtain information are often imprecise. You may have known someone for ten years and still know very little about him. If we accept the idea that we won't ever fully know another person, it enables us to deal more easily with those things that get in the way of accurate knowledge such as secrets and deceptions. It will also keep us from being too surprised or shocked by seemingly inconsistent behavior. Ironically, those things that keep us from knowing another person too well, (e.g. secrets and deceptions) may be just as important to the development of a satisfying relationship as those things that enable us to obtain accurate knowledge about a person (e.g. disclosures and truthful statements).

35. The word "pinpoint" in paragraph one basically means
    A. appreciate.   B. obtain.
    C. interpret.   D. identify.

36. What do we learn from the first paragraph?
    A. People are better described in cold, objective terms.
    B. The difficulty of getting to know a person is usually underestimated.
    C. One should not judge people by their appearances.
    D. One is usually objective when assessing other people's personality.

Please turn to the next page. ⇨

37. It can be inferred from the suggestions of the experts that

    A. people do not reveal their true self on every occasion.

    B. in most cases we should avoid contacting the observed person directly.

    C. the best way to know a person is by making comparisons.

    D. face-to-face interaction is the best strategy to uncover information about a person.

38. In developing personal relationships, secrets and deceptions, in the author's opinion, are

    A. personal matters that should be seriously dealt with.

    B. barriers that should be done away with.

    C. as significant as disclosures and truthful statements.

    D. things people should guard against.

39. The author's purpose in writing the passage is

    A. to give advice on appropriate conduct for social occasions.

    B. to provide ways of how to obtain information about people.

    C. to call the reader's attention to the negative side of people's characters.

    D. to discuss the various aspects of getting to know people.

Questions 40-43

A revolution in our understanding of Earth is reaching its climax as evidence accumulates that the continents of today are not venerable landmasses but amalgams of other lands repeatedly broken up, juggled, rotated, scattered far and wide, then crunched together into new configurations like ice <u>swept</u> along the shore of a swift-flowing stream.

After considerable modification this became the now largely accepted concept of "plate tectonics," explaining much of what is observed regarding our dynamic planet. Some oceans, such as the Atlantic, are being split apart, their opposing coasts carried away from one another at one or two inches per year as lava wells up along the line of separation to form new seafloor. Other oceans, such as the Pacific, are shrinking as seafloor descends under their fringing coastlines or offshore arcs of islands.

The earth's crust, in this view, is divided into several immense plates that make up the continents and seafloors, and all float on a hot, plastic, subterranean "mantle." What causes these plates to jostle each other, splitting apart or sliding under one another at their edges, is still a mystery to geologists: it may be friction from circulating rock in the earth's mantle, or it may be an effect produced by gravity.

Please turn to the next page. ▮⟹

40. What is the author's main purpose in the passage?
    A. To dispel misconceptions about the rotation of the earth.
    B. To praise geologists for their explorations and discoveries.
    C. To compare and contrast the Atlantic and Pacific oceans.
    D. To explain the theory of plate tectonics.

41. The author implies that people used to believe the continents were
    A. frozen chunks of rock.
    B. rotating masses of rock.
    C. hardened crusts of lava.
    D. immobile bodies of land.

42. The word "swept" as used in the first paragraph could be replaced by
    A. won.   B. cleaned.
    C. carried.   D. removed.

43. According to the passage, the Pacific Ocean is changing in which of the following ways?
    A. It is growing warmer.
    B. It is getting smaller.
    C. It is being split apart.
    D. It is filling up with lava.

Questions 44-47

Most of us are taught to think linearly; that is, our thinking goes in straight lines. A causes B causes C causes D; we are taught to look for cause and effect. The natural world is not so simple; it is a huge system of systems. A fundamental principle of environmental thinking is that biospheric elements circulate in systems. For example, environmental scientists talk about the carbon cycle or the nitrogen cycle or the water cycle as they admonish us to think systematically. Systematic thinkers focus on wholes rather than on parts. Within wholes they concern themselves with relationships more than objects, with processes more than structures.

For example, a gallon of gasoline contains a lot of carbon. When it's burned in your car, the carbon combines with oxygen to form CO_2. The carbon in oil does not come from plants living now but from plants that lived millions of years ago. So burning millions of gallons of gasoline today quickly releases extraordinary amounts of CO_2 that nature had not figured into the current carbon balance between plants and animals. But now that there aren't enough growing plants to take up the extra CO_2, it's accumulating rapidly.

Please turn to the next page. ⟹

In fact, we humans further insult the system by cutting down forests to get timber or by clearing land for farming or ranching. Environmentalists, most atmospheric scientists, and some political leaders are warning us that the extra carbon dioxide is adding to the greenhouse effect that warms the planet and probably will change the climate system.

The point (of this article) is that different parts of a system are so interconnected that we can never do merely one thing. We should always ask, "And then what?"

44. What is a fundamental principle of environmental thinking?
　　A. Biospheric elements circulate in systems.
　　B. Biospheric elements circulate in parts.
　　C. Biospheric elements focus on the environment.
　　D. Biospheric elements focus on the natural world.

45. What do systematic thinkers focus on?
　　A. Parts rather than wholes.
　　B. Wholes rather than parts.
　　C. Objects rather than relationships.
　　D. Structures rather than processes.

46. How do humans further insult the system?
　　A. By cutting down forests.
　　B. By taking up more CO_2.
　　C. By allowing the growth of plants.
　　D. By burning millions of gallons of gasoline.

47. What is the point of this article?
    A. Environmental protection is most essential for all of us.
    B. The extra carbon dioxide is adding to the greenhouse effect that warms the planets.
    C. Different parts of a system are so interconnected that we can never do merely one thing.
    D. Humans should be taught to think linearly.

Questions 48-50

Memorandum to: Department Managers, Research Division
From : Akira Inoue, Sr. V.P. for Research

The federal government has just announced for the next fiscal year it will accept applications from small unaffiliated businesses for grants to conduct research and initial product development in several frontier technologies, including semiconductors, robotics and micro-robotics, and laser application. Both U.S.-based and non-U.S. firms are eligible for these grants, except that for non-U.S. firms all government-funded activities must be carried out in the U.S. See the attached circular for other restrictions.

We plan to apply for funding for some of our on-going projects. As a non-U.S. firm, we will have to submit documentation on what work we are carrying out, where it is being carried out, and by whom.

Please turn to the next page. ▯⟹

> As a first step, could you please review your activities and submit to Ms. Lee by April 10 a list of projects. We will then decide which projects stand the best chance of being funded and proceed accordingly.

48. What is the subject of this memorandum?
    A. National security
    B. Accounting practices
    C. Government regulations
    D. A source for project funding

49. What does the company hope to obtain?
    A. Investment
    B. Government support
    C. Bank credit
    D. Import concessions

50. What does Mr. Inoue want from department managers?
    A. Ideas for new projects
    B. Cost reductions
    C. Staffing changes
    D. Recommendations

中高級聽力測驗詳解 ③

PART A

1. (**C**) Do you know when the garbage truck comes at night?
   A. No, it doesn't.
   B. I don't have anything to throw out.
   C. It stops here at 10 p.m.
   D. It stops on Center Street.

   * ***garbage truck*** 垃圾車　　***throw out*** 丟出去
     stop ﹝ stɑp ﹞ *v.* 停留

2. (**A**) What time does your flight leave for Hong Kong?
   A. It's the "red eye" leaving at 2 a.m.
   B. It departs from the old terminal.
   C. It's a two-hour flight.
   D. It's always on time.

   * ***leave for*** 前往　　***red eye*** 夜航航班（尤指深夜從西海岸
     起飛，清晨到達東海岸的）
     depart ﹝ dɪˈpɑrt ﹞ *v.* 離開
     terminal ﹝ ˈtɝmənḷ ﹞ *n.* 航空站　　***on time*** 準時

3. (**B**) This cell phone has a radio, a television, a camera, and
   a pager all in one.
   A. It's one dimensional.
   B. It's multi-functional.

C. It's outdated.

D. It's also a laptop.

* ***cell phone*** 行動電話　　radio (ˈredɪˌo) *n.* 收音機

pager (ˈpedʒɚ) *n.* 呼叫器

dimensional (dəˈmɛnʃənḷ) *adj.* ～次元的

multi-functional (ˈmʌltəˌfʌŋkʃənḷ) *adj.* 多功能的

outdated (autˈdetɪd) *adj.* 舊式的

laptop (ˈlæpˌtɑp) *n.* 筆記型電腦

4. (**A**) How do I get to the tax office from here?

A. Turn left at the first intersection and go down two blocks.

B. It's located near the harbor.

C. Today is Sunday. Don't worry.

D. They relocated to another area.

* ***tax office*** 國稅局

intersection (ˌɪntɚˈsɛkʃən) *n.* 十字路口

be located 位於～　　harbor (ˈharbɚ) *n.* 港口

relocate (riˈloket) *v.* 使遷移　　area (ˈɛrɪə) *n.* 地區

5. (**D**) Are you joining us for an evening jog?

A. Is that a promise?

B. I love to sprint along the beach.

C. Let's all go by ourselves.

D. No, thanks. Not tonight.

* jog (dʒɑg) *v.* 慢跑　　promise (ˈprɑmɪs) *n.* 承諾

sprint (sprɪnt) *v.* 奮力而跑

6. (**C**) Do you need any supplies from the hardware store?

    A. Yes, I'd like some socks.

    B. Do they have software?

    C. Could you buy some electrical tape for me?

    D. They have fresh groceries.

    * supplies (sə'plaɪz) *n. pl.* 日用品

      hardware ('hɑrd,wɛr) *n.* 五金

      socks (sɑks) *n. pl.* 襪子

      software ('sɔft,wɛr) *n.* 軟體

      electrical tape 電工膠帶   grocery ('grosərɪ) *n.* 雜貨

7. (**B**) How long have you been wearing braces on your teeth?

    A. Until next September.

    B. For 18 months.

    C. My dentist put them on.

    D. I had gaps in my teeth.

    * brace (bres) *n.* (牙齒) 的支架；牙套

      dentist ('dɛntɪst) *n.* 牙醫   gap (gæp) *n.* 縫

8. (**B**) Is Taipei 101 the tallest building in the world?

    A. It's a temporary skyscraper.

    B. It is for now.

    C. It towers over the skyline.

    D. It is definitely a monumental structure.

* temporary ('tɛmpə,rɛrɪ) adj. 暫時的
  skyscraper ('skaɪ,skrepɚ) n. 摩天大樓
  tower ('tauɚ) v. 高聳
  skyline ('skaɪ,laɪn) n. 天際
  definitely ('dɛfənɪtlɪ) adv. 明確地
  monumental (,manjə'mɛntḷ) adj. 紀念性的
  structure ('strʌktʃɚ) n. 建築物

9. (C) Is this your first time here?
   A. Yes, I was here once before.
   B. You look familiar, too.
   C. Yes, how did you know?
   D. I'm sorry I forgot your name.

   * familiar (fə'mɪljɚ) adj. 熟悉的

10. (A) How's your research report coming along?
    A. It's right on schedule.
    B. I plan to do a survey.
    C. Someone gathers and collects data.
    D. I bring it with me at times.

    * research (rɪ'sɝtʃ) n. 研究
      come along 進展   *on schedule* 按照進度
      survey (sɚ've) n. 調查
      gather ('gæðɚ) v. 收集
      collect (kə'lɛkt) v. 收集
      data ('detə) n. pl. 資料   *at times* 有時候

11. (**A**) Which professional team do you root for?

    A. I love the New York Yankees.

    B. The Dallas Cowboys had an awful year.

    C. Pro athletes have changed in recent years.

    D. The salaries are exorbitant.

    * professional〔prəˈfɛʃən!〕 *adj.* 職業的

    root for 為~加油　　awful〔ˈɔfʊl〕 *adj.* 糟糕的

    pro〔pro〕 *adj.* 職業的

    athlete〔ˈæθlɪt〕 *n.* 運動員

    salary〔ˈsælərɪ〕 *n.* 薪水

    exorbitant〔ɪgˈzɔrbətənt〕 *adj.* 過高的

12. (**B**) How do I apply for a leave of absence?

    A. Fill out an application for employment.

    B. Just fill out an employee request form.

    C. It's possible to apply.

    D. Everyone is entitled to personal time.

    * *apply for* 申請

    a leave of absence 請假　　*fill out* 填寫

    application〔ˌæpləˈkeʃən〕 *n.* 申請書

    employment〔ɪmˈplɔɪmənt〕 *n.* 職業；工作

    employee〔ˌɛmplɔɪˈi〕 *n.* 員工

    request〔rɪˈkwɛst〕 *n.* 要求

    form〔fɔrm〕 *n.* 表格

    entitle〔ɪnˈtaɪt!〕 *v.* 給予（某人）~的權利

13. (**D**) Would you like to order another dish?

    A. Nothing else, thanks.

    B. No, I really don't care what you think.

    C. Yes, I ordered this dish.

    D. No, we're fine. Thank you.

    * order〔'ɔrdɚ〕*v.* 點餐　　dish〔dɪʃ〕*n.* 菜餚

      care〔kɛr〕*v.* 在乎

14. (**A**) What do you think of this dry spell?

    A. I wish we could have some rainfall.

    B. I think it will be dry soon.

    C. The temperatures are rising and falling.

    D. The forecast will come out soon.

    * *think of* 認為　　*dry spell* 乾旱期

      rainfall〔'ren͵fɔl〕*n.* 降雨

      temperature〔'tɛmpərətʃɚ〕*n.* 溫度

      rise〔raɪz〕*v.* 上升　　fall〔fɔl〕*v.* 下降

      forecast〔'for͵kæst〕*n.* 預報　　*come out* 出來；報導

15. (**B**) We're ready for the check.

    A. I'll look and see.

    B. I'll be right back with it.

    C. Security is not here right now.

    D. I'll check on the situation.

    * check〔tʃɛk〕*n.* 帳單

      security〔sɪ'kjurətɪ〕*n.* 保證人　　*check on* 調查

      situation〔͵sɪtʃu'eʃən〕*n.* 情況

PART B.

16. (**C**) M : Excuse me, I've lost three books. What's your policy?

W : You'll have to pay for them.

M : I was afraid of that. What's the total? How much do I owe?

W : Let me see your card, please.

M : I've lost that, too!

Question : Where are they?

A. In a bookstore.

B. In a campus study hall.

C. At a library.

D. In a private lounge.

* policy ('pɑləsɪ) *n.* 策略　*pay for* 付~的費用
   total ('totḷ) *n.* 總額　owe (o) *v.* 欠
   campus ('kæmpəs) *adj.* 校內的　*study hall* 自修教室
   library ('laɪˌbrɛrɪ) *n.* 圖書館
   private ('praɪvɪt) *adj.* 私人的
   lounge (laʊndʒ) *n.* 休憩室

17. (**A**) W : Sorry, I definitely didn't order cake.

M : Are you sure?

W : Yes, I ordered steak, not cake!

M : My goodness! I misheard you. They do sound alike, though!

W : Maybe the problem was my pronunciation.

Question: What did the waiter do?

A. He misunderstood her.

B. He didn't clean his ears.

C. He bought her a cake.

D. He mispronounced a word.

* definitely〔'dɛfənɪtlɪ〕adv. 確定地
  My goodness! 我的天！
  mishear〔mɪs'hɪr〕v. 聽錯　　alike〔ə'laɪk〕adj. 相似的
  pronunciation〔prə͵nʌnsɪ'eʃən〕n. 發音
  misunderstand〔͵mɪsʌndə'stænd〕v. 誤會
  mispronounce〔͵mɪsprə'naʊns〕v. 發錯～的發音

18. (**D**) M: Global Movers.　May I help you?

W: Yes, I'm being sent overseas next year.　What are your rates?

M: We'll send a company rep over to give an estimate.

W: Can't you tell me over the phone?

M: Sorry, ma'am, we have to evaluate your household items in person.

Question: What does the customer want?

A. A big discount.

B. To mail some packages.

C. To apply for a position.

D. A quick price estimate.

* global〔'globl̩〕adj. 全球的
  mover〔'muvɚ〕n. 搬家業者　　send〔sɛnd〕v. 派遣
  overseas〔'ovɚ'siz〕adv. 到海外

rate〔ret〕*n.* 費用   company〔'kʌmpənɪ〕*n.* 公司

rep.〔rɛp〕*n.* 代表（ = *representative* ）

estimate〔'ɛstə,met〕*n.* 估價單；估價

ma'am〔mæm〕*n.* 女士

evaluate〔ɪ'vælju,et〕*v.* 評估

household〔'haʊs,hold〕*adj.* 家庭的

item〔'aɪtəm〕*n.* 物品   ***in person*** 親自

customer〔'kʌstəmɚ〕*n.* 顧客

discount〔'dɪskaʊnt〕*n.* 折扣

package〔'pækɪdʒ〕*n.* 包裹

position〔pə'zɪʃən〕*n.* 職位

19. (**C**) W: Oh no! I spilt juice on my keyboard.

    M: Quickly, turn it over. Turn it upside down. Turn everything off.

    W: I hope I didn't ruin it!

    Question: What should the woman have known?

    A. Don't be clumsy.

    B. Don't drink and surf.

    C. Never have liquids near a computer.

    D. Electricity shouldn't get into water.

    * spill〔spɪl〕*v.* 使溢出（三態變化爲：spill-spilt-spilt ）

    keyboard〔'ki,bord〕*n.* 鍵盤

    turn over 翻轉   ***upside down*** 顚倒

    turn off 關掉（電器）   ruin〔'ruɪn〕*v.* 破壞

    clumsy〔'klʌmzɪ〕*adj.* 笨拙的

    surf〔sɝf〕*v.* 在電腦網路上瀏覽

    liquid〔'lɪkwɪd〕*n.* 液體   electricity〔ɪ,lɛk'trɪsətɪ〕*n.* 電

20. (**B**) M：Pardon me for saying this, but your fish tank is filthy!

W：The fish don't care.　Give me a break!

M：Yes, they do!　You're being cruel to animals.

W：What are you going to do about it?

M：I'm going to report you to the Society for the Prevention of Cruelty to Animals!

Question：What is the problem with the aquarium?

A. It stinks.　　　　B. It's very dirty.

C. It's a toilet.　　　D. It's too small.

* pardon (ˈpɑrdn̩) v. 原諒　　　***fish tank*** 魚缸

filthy (ˈfɪlθɪ) adj. 骯髒的

Give me a break! 饒了我吧！

cruel (ˈkruəl) adj. 殘忍的　　　report (rɪˈport) v. 告發

society (səˈsaɪətɪ) n. 協會

prevention (prɪˈvɛnʃən) n. 防止

cruelty (ˈkruəltɪ) n. 殘忍

the society for the Prevention of Cruelty to Animals

愛護動物協會

aquarium (əˈkwɛrɪəm) n. 水族館

stink (stɪŋk) v. 發惡臭　　　toilet (ˈtɔɪlɪt) n. 廁所

21. (**A**) W：Seattle is simply gorgeous in autumn!

M：Yes, the leaves are so colorful.

W：I love the cool temperatures, too.

M：We should move there.

W：That's not a bad idea.

Question : Who wants to live in Seattle?

A. They both do.

B. He does.

C. He doesn't.

D. She might be persuaded.

* Seattle〔si'ætḷ〕*n.* 西雅圖（位於美國華盛頓州）
simply〔'sɪmplɪ〕*adv.* 非常地
gorgeous〔'gɔrdʒəs〕*adj.* 極好的
autumn〔'ɔtəm〕*n.* 秋天
colorful〔'kʌləfəl〕*adj.* 多彩的
persuade〔pə'swed〕*v.* 說服

22. (**D**) M : Congratulations on your victory.

W : Thanks so much, but it was nothing.

M : Are you kidding? You won the whole tournament.

W : I got lucky, I guess.

M : No, you're the best ping pong player in the county.

Question : What does the woman do well?

A. Play the bongos.   B. Do martial arts.

C. Play snooker.   D. Play table tennis.

* congratulations〔kən,grætʃə'leʃənz〕*n. pl.* 恭喜
victory〔'vɪktərɪ〕*n.* 勝利
tournament〔'tɜnəmənt〕*n.* 錦標賽
ping pong〔'pɪŋ,pɑŋ〕*n.* 乒乓球
county〔'kaʊntɪ〕*n.* 郡；縣
bongos〔'bɑŋgoz〕*n. pl.* 拉丁小鼓   *martial arts* 武術
snooker〔'snukə〕*n.* 撞球   *table tennis* 桌球

23. (**C**) W：How about this weather? Isn't it awful?

M：It's so gray and gloomy! It's very depressing.

W：This is the fifth day of continuous rain.

M：Don't remind me. I miss the sunshine.

W：Let's hop on a plane and fly south.

Question：How long has it been raining?

A.　One week.

B.　Fifteen days.

C.　Five straight days.

D.　Twenty four hours.

* gray〔gre〕*adj.* 陰暗的

gloomy〔'glumɪ〕*adj.* 陰暗的

depressing〔dɪ'prɛsɪŋ〕*adj.* 令人沮喪的

continuous〔kən'tɪnjuəs〕*adj.* 連續的

remind〔rɪ'maɪnd〕*v.* 提醒

sunshine〔'sʌn,ʃaɪn〕*n.* 陽光

hop〔hɑp〕*v.* 上（車、飛機、船）

south〔sauθ〕*adv.* 向南邊

straight〔stret〕*adj.* 連續的

24. (**A**) M：Did you pass your driver's test?

W：No, I flunked it. I messed up bad.

M：What happened?

W：I ran a red light and killed a dog.

M：You're lucky you weren't arrested! Better luck next time.

Question: How did she do?

A. She failed miserably.

B. She almost passed.

C. She destroyed the car.

D. She lost her license.

* flunk〔flʌŋk〕v.（考試）不及格

    mess up 搞砸　　**run a red light** 闖紅燈

    arrest〔ə'rɛst〕v. 逮捕

    fail〔fel〕v. 失敗

    miserably〔'mɪzərəblɪ〕adv. 悲慘地

    destroy〔dɪ'strɔɪ〕v. 破壞

    license〔'laɪsn̩s〕n. 駕照

25. (**D**) W: I think I saw a UFO last night.

    M: That's impossible! Where were you?

    W: I was driving down North Mountain Road.

    M: Oh, that's right next to the Air Force Base.
    You just saw a Harrier jet hovering!

    W: I bet you're right. It looked just like a spaceship!

    Question: What did the woman probably see?

    A. A weather balloon.

    B. Storm clouds.

    C. A commercial airliner.

    D. A military aircraft.

* **UFO** 不明飛行物體（= *Unidentified Flying Object*）

Air Force Base 空軍基地　　**Harrier jet** 獵兔犬噴射機

hover（'hʌvɚ）v.（飛機）盤旋在空中

spaceship（'spes,ʃɪp）n. 太空船

weather balloon 氣象氣球（尤指用於天氣預報的）

storm clouds （危險的）前兆

commercial（kə'mɝʃəl）adj. 商業的

airliner（'ɛr,laɪnɚ）n. 班機

military（'mɪlə,tɛrɪ）adj. 軍事的

aircraft（'ɛr,kræft）n. 飛機

26. (**B**) M : How often do you exercise?

W : I do aerobic dancing three times a week.

M : Do you do it by yourself?

W : No, I joined a fitness club. Aerobics is one of the many classes.

M : How much is the membership?

Question : What is the man thinking about?

A. Asking her for a date.

B. Joining the club.

C. Starting to lose weight.

D. Learning how to dance.

* **aerobic dancing** 有氧舞蹈　　**fitness club** 健身俱樂部

aerobics（,eə'robɪks）n. 有氧運動

membership（'mɛmbɚ,ʃɪp）n. 會員資格

lose weight 減輕體重

27. (**A**) W: We're almost on empty.

M: You're right! We're riding on fumes.

W: Help me find a gas station.

M: There's a mini-mart self-service station!

W: Do you know how to pump gas?

Question: What do they need to do?

A. Fill up the gas tank.

B. Find a restroom first.

C. Get some wiper fluid.

D. Check the oil pressure.

* *We're almost on empty.* 我們幾乎快沒油了。

fumes〔fjumz〕*n. pl.* 煙霧

We're riding on fumes. 字面意思是「我們正靠著煙霧來開車。」是誇飾法，引申為「我們快沒油了。」

gas station 加油站

self-service〔'sɛlf's˞vɪs〕*adj.* 自助的

pump〔pʌmp〕*v.* 抽（水）　　*pump gas* 加油

fill up 裝滿　　*gas tank* 油箱

wiper fluid 雨刷精　　*oil pressure* 油壓

28. (**A**) M: I'm so hungry that I could eat a horse.

W: You're so fat that you look like a pig!

M: You're so scary that you look like a witch!

W: You're so ugly that the doctor slapped your mother when you were born!

M：OK, let's cool it.　Enough is enough.　We're being too silly.

Question：What are they doing?

A.　Saying silly things.

B.　Arguing ferociously.

C.　Talking about animals.

D.　Practicing English pronunciation.

＊ scary〔'skɛrɪ〕*adj.* 可怕的

witch〔wɪtʃ〕*n.* 巫婆　　ugly〔'ʌglɪ〕*adj.* 醜陋的

slap〔slæp〕*v.* 摑～耳光

cool〔kul〕*v.* 使～平靜下來

Enough is enough. 要適可而止。

silly〔'sɪlɪ〕*adj.* 愚蠢的

argue〔'ɑrgju〕*v.* 爭執

ferociously〔fə'roʃəslɪ〕*adv.* 十分強烈地

pronunciation〔prə,nʌnsɪ'eʃən〕*n.* 發音

29. (**C**) W：Her husband died of a heart attack.

M：Poor thing.　What a shame!

W：He was 95.　She's only 29.　He left her with millions!

M：Oh man, what a lucky lady!

Question：What did the man do?

A.　He got lucky.

B.　He almost died.

C. He changed his opinion fast!

D. He wants to find that girl.

* ***die of*** 死於～   ***heart attack*** 心臟病發作

  Poor thing. 好可憐的人。

  What a shame! 眞可惜！

  opinion〔əˈpɪnjən〕*n.* 意見

30. (**B**) M：I'd like a box of popcorn, two candy bars and a coke.

W：What size drink do you want?

M：Large, please.

W：Want any butter, salt or cheese on the popcorn?

M：All three would be great. Thanks.

Question：Where might the speakers be?

A. At a bus terminal.

B. At the circus.

C. In a school cafeteria.

D. At a funeral.

* popcorn〔ˈpɑpˌkɔrn〕*n.* 爆米花

  candy bar 單獨包裝的塊狀糖

  butter〔ˈbʌtɚ〕*n.* 奶油   salt〔sɔlt〕*n.* 鹽

  cheese〔tʃiz〕*n.* 乳酪

  terminal〔ˈtɜmənḷ〕*n.* (公車) 總站

  circus〔ˈsɜkəs〕*n.* 馬戲團

  cafeteria〔ˌkæfəˈtɪrɪə〕*n.* 自助餐廳

  funeral〔ˈfjunərəl〕*n.* 葬禮

📁 PART C.

Questions 31-33 refer to the following information.

As Fire Chief of this city, I promise to mount a comprehensive investigation as to why we've had so many incidences of equipment malfunction lately. Our training and maintenance program is second to none. We put our lives on the line at every fire, so we take any equipment breakdowns or technical glitches very seriously. Faulty or defective equipment can cost precious lives and cause serious injury. I promise once again to get to the bottom of the oxygen tank problems.

🖥 Vocabulary

chief〔tʃif〕*n.* 長官　　promise〔'pramɪs〕*v.* 承諾

mount〔maʊnt〕*v.* 進行；展開

comprehensive〔ˌkamprɪ'hɛnsɪv〕*adj.* 廣泛的

investigation〔ɪnˌvɛstə'geʃən〕*n.* 調查

as to 關於　　incidence〔'ɪnsədəns〕*n.* 發生率

equipment〔ɪ'kwɪpmənt〕*n.* 設備；裝備

malfunction〔mæl'fʌŋkʃən〕*n.* 故障

training〔'trenɪŋ〕*n.* 訓練

maintenance〔'mentənəns〕*n.* 維修

program〔'progræm〕*n.* 計畫　　*second to none* 首屈一指的

on the line 瀕於危險中　　take〔tek〕v. 認為；對待

breakdown〔'brek,daʊn〕n. 故障

technical〔'tɛknɪkl̩〕adj. 技術的

glitch〔glɪtʃ〕n. 小故障　　seriously〔'sɪrɪəslɪ〕adv. 認真地

faulty〔'fɔltɪ〕adj. 有缺點的

defective〔dɪ'fɛktɪv〕adj. 有缺陷的

cost〔kɔst〕v. 付出（代價）　　precious〔'prɛʃəs〕adj. 寶貴的

cause〔kɔz〕v. 導致　　serious〔'sɪrɪəs〕adj. 嚴重的

injury〔'ɪndʒərɪ〕n. 受傷　　*once again* 再一次

get to the bottom of 徹底查明　　*oxygen tank* 氧氣筒

31. (**A**) Who is talking?

　　A. The top fire official.

　　B. The city safety inspector.

　　C. The commissionaire.

　　D. The police chief.

　　* top〔tɑp〕adj. 最高的　　official〔ə'fɪʃəl〕n. 官員
　　　safety〔'seftɪ〕n. 安全　　inspector〔ɪn'spɛktɚ〕n. 督察員
　　　commissionaire〔kə,mɪʃən'ɛr〕n.（旅館）接待員

32. (**B**) What seems to be the problem?

　　A. Poor training program.

　　B. Flawed equipment.

　　C. Defective vehicles.

　　D. Low morale.

　　* flawed〔flɔd〕adj. 有缺點的
　　　vehicle〔'viɪkl̩〕n. 車輛　　low〔lo〕adj. 低的
　　　morale〔mə'ræl〕n. 鬥志；士氣

33. (**A**) What task has the speaker pledged to do?
      A. Find and fix the problem.
      B. Initiate new programs.
      C. Purchase safety devices.
      D. Donate time and money.

   * task〔tæsk〕n. 任務
     pledge〔plɛdʒ〕v. 保證   fix〔fɪks〕v. 修理；解決
     initiate〔ɪ'nɪʃɪˌet〕v. 開始
     purchase〔'pɝtʃəs〕v. 購買
     device〔dɪ'vaɪs〕n. 設備；裝置
     donate〔'donet〕v. 捐贈

Questions 34-35 are based on the following advice.

> Tom, I suggest that you work out in the morning before work, rather than in the afternoon on your way home. First thing in the morning, your body is fresh and rested. A vigorous workout will stimulate you and increase your metabolism. The exercise will boost your energy levels all day long. Most fitness experts and physicians, strongly recommend exercising early in the day and doing it on an empty stomach. Your biorhythm is at its best in the morning.

Vocabulary

advice〔əd'vaɪs〕n. 建議；忠告

suggest〔sə'dʒɛst〕v. 建議　　**work out** 運動

rather than 而不是　　**first thing** 首先

fresh〔frɛʃ〕adj. 精力充沛的

rested〔'rɛstɪd〕adj. 精力充沛的；充分休息的

vigorous〔'vɪgərəs〕adj. 精力充沛的

workout〔'wɜk,aut〕n. 運動

stimulate〔'stɪmjə,let〕v. 刺激　　increase〔ɪn'kris〕v. 增加

metabolism〔mɛ'tæbḷ,ɪzəm〕n. 新陳代謝

boost〔bust〕v. 促進；增加　　energy〔'ɛnədʒɪ〕n. 活力；能量

level〔'lɛvḷ〕n. 水準　　**all day long** 一整天

fitness〔'fɪtnɪs〕n. 健康　　expert〔'ɛkspɜt〕n. 專家

physician〔fə'zɪʃən〕n. 醫師

strongly〔'strɔŋlɪ〕adv. 強烈地

recommend〔,rɛkə'mɛnd〕v. 推薦；建議

empty〔'ɛmptɪ〕adj. 空的　　stomach〔'stʌmək〕n. 胃

biorhythm〔,baɪo'rɪðəm〕n. 生物週期

at *one's* **best** 處於最佳的狀態

34. (**C**) What should Tom do?

    A. Jog after breakfast.

    B. "Pump iron" every afternoon.

    C. Exercise before breakfast.

    D. Practice for a marathon.

    * jog〔dʒɑg〕v. 慢跑　　**pump iron** 舉重

    marathon〔'mærə,θɑn〕n. 馬拉松

35. (**D**) What is one benefit of a workout?

    A. Increased heart rate.

    B. Lower blood pressure.

    C. A dark complexion.

    D. Increased feeling of energy.

* benefit ('bɛnəfɪt) *n.* 好處

   increase (ɪn'kris) *v.* 增加   ***heart rate*** 心率

   lower ('loɚ) *v.* 降低   blood (blʌd) *n.* 血液

   pressure ('prɛʃɚ) *n.* 壓力

   blood pressure 血壓

   dark (dɑrk) *adj.* 暗沉的

   complexion (kəm'plɛkʃən) *n.* 氣色

Questions 36-38 refer to the following announcement.

To all Tampa residents…Due to a recent infestation of mosquitoes and cockroaches, our City Health Department officials have implemented an insect extermination and eradication program. The spraying of all lawns, parks and forested areas will occur every weekend for the next month. Please try to avoid being outside from 5 a.m. to 7 a.m. Thank you for your cooperation. Clean neighborhoods and a safe environment are everyone's responsibility.

Vocabulary

Tampa (ˈtæmpə) *n.* 坦帕市 (位於美國佛羅里達州)
resident (ˈrɛzədənt) *n.* 居民　　**due to** 由於
recent (ˈrisn̩t) *adj.* 最近的
infestation (ˌɪnfɛsˈteʃən) *n.* (動物) 侵擾
mosquito (məˈskito) *n.* 蚊子　　cockroach (ˈkɑkˌrotʃ) *n.* 蟑螂
department (dɪˈpɑrtmənt) *n.* 部門
implement (ˈɪmpləˌmɛnt) *v.* 實施　　insect (ˈɪnsɛkt) *n.* 昆蟲
extermination (ɪkˌstɝməˈneʃən) *n.* 消滅
eradication (ɪˌrædɪˈkeʃən) *n.* 根除
spray (spre) *v.* 噴灑　　lawn (lɔn) *n.* 草地
forested (ˈfɔrəstɪd) *adj.* 樹木叢生的　　occur (əˈkɝ) *v.* 發生
avoid (əˈvɔɪd) *v.* 避免
cooperation (koˌɑpəˈreʃən) *n.* 合作
environment (ɪnˈvaɪrənmənt) *n.* 環境
responsibility (rɪˌspɑnsəˈbɪlətɪ) *n.* 責任

36. (**C**) Who is this message addressed to?
    A. To all senior citizens.
    B. To the government officials.
    C. The citizens of Tampa.
    D. To the Health Administration.

    * message (ˈmɛsɪdʒ) *n.* 信息
      address (əˈdrɛs) *v.* 提出
      senior (ˈsinjɚ) *adj.* 年長的　　citizen (ˈsɪtəzn̩) *n.* 公民
      government (ˈgʌvɚnmənt) *n.* 政府
      administration (ədˌmɪnəˈstreʃən) *n.* 行政機關

37. (**B**) What's the main message of the announcement?
    A. Insects are a threat.
    B. Parks will be sprayed, so avoid the danger.
    C. Mosquitoes spread disease.
    D. Pitch in and help us out.

    * threat〔θrɛt〕n. 威脅　　disease〔dɪ'ziz〕n. 疾病
    pitch in 開始做　　**help out** 幫助

38. (**D**) When will the areas be most dangerous?
    A. At dusk.　　　　　　B. Around midday.
    C. From dawn to dusk.　D. From 5 a.m. to 7 a.m.

    * dusk〔dʌsk〕n. 黃昏　　midday〔'mɪd,de〕n. 中午
    dawn〔dɔn〕n. 黎明

Questions 39-40 are based on the following talk.

Peter, hurry up! We're going to be late for the meeting. If we're not punctual, we'll make a bad impression on our visiting clients. I don't want to aggravate the boss in any way. So forget about flirting with that girl over there and follow me! If we don't hustle, we're going to be in big trouble.

📺 Vocabulary

punctual〔'pʌŋktʃʊəl〕adj. 準時的
impression〔ɪm'prɛʃən〕n. 印象
visiting〔'vɪzɪtɪŋ〕adj. 參觀的　　client〔'klaɪənt〕n. 客戶

aggravate〔'ægrə,vet〕v. 激怒　　boss〔bɔs〕n. 老闆

in any way 不管怎樣　　flirt〔flɜt〕v. 調情

hustle〔'hʌsḷ〕v. 趕緊　　***be in trouble*** 處於困境中

39. (**A**) Why do they have to hurry?

    A. A meeting is starting soon.

    B. Their boss is waiting for them.

    C. They want to miss a client.

    D. Their girlfriends are waiting.

40. (**C**) What does Peter want to do?

    A. Sprint fast to the meeting.

    B. Buy a few things.

    C. Chat with a girl.

    D. "Hustle" some clients.

    * sprint〔sprɪnt〕v. 奮力地跑　　chat〔tʃæt〕v. 聊天

Questions 41-43 are based on the following instructions.

Welcome to the "24-7" Laundromat. We are open around the clock, seven days a week. Please read these instructions before operating the washing machines and the dryers. All machines are coin-operated; only quarters can be put into the slots. If you need change, put your dollar bills into the money changer machine on the back wall. Please don't put anything in the machines other than clothes, laundry detergent and fabric softener. That means no shoes, blankets, pillows, belts or any flammable materials. Also, please clean out the lint screens after using the dryers. We have video cameras throughout the facility for your safety. Thank you for your cooperation and patronage......the management.

📺 Vocabulary

instructions〔ɪn'strʌkʃənz〕 n. pl. 說明

laundromat〔'lɔndrə,mæt〕 n. 自助洗衣店（= *launderette*）

open〔'opən〕 adj. 營業的

around the clock 二十四小時連續不斷地

operate〔'ɑpə,ret〕 v. 操作　　***washing machine*** 洗衣機

dryer〔'draɪə〕 n. 烘衣機

coin-operated〔'kɔɪn'ɑpə,retɪd〕 adj. 投入硬幣即發生作用的

quarter〔'kwɔrtə〕 n.（美國、加拿大的）25 分硬幣

slot〔slɑt〕 n. 投幣口　　change〔tʃendʒ〕 n. 零錢

bill〔bɪl〕 n. 紙鈔　　***money changer machine*** 兌幣機

other than 除了　　laundry〔'lɔndrɪ〕 n. 送洗的衣物

detergent〔dɪ'tɝdʒənt〕 n. 洗潔劑

fabric〔'fæbrɪk〕 n. 布料　　softener〔'sɔfənə〕 n. 柔軟劑

blanket〔'blæŋkɪt〕 n. 毛毯　　pillow〔'pɪlo〕 n. 枕頭

belt〔bɛlt〕 n. 皮帶　　flammable〔'flæməbḷ〕 adj. 易燃的

material〔mə'tɪrɪəl〕 n. 物質　　***clean out*** 清理

lint〔lɪnt〕 n. 線頭　　screen〔skrin〕 n. 過濾器

video camera 錄影機　　throughout〔θru'aʊt〕*prep.* 遍佈

facility〔fə'sɪlətɪ〕*n.* 場所　　safety〔'seftɪ〕*n.* 安全

patronage〔'pætrənɪdʒ〕*n.* 惠顧

management〔'mænɪdʒmənt〕*n.* 管理部門

41. (**A**) What are the laundromat operating hours?

　　A. All day, every day.

　　B. From noon till midnight.

　　C. 24 days a month, 7 hours a day.

　　D. Every day from 9 a.m. to 7 p.m.

　　* noon〔nun〕*n.* 正午

　　　midnight〔'mɪd,naɪt〕*n.* 午夜

42. (**C**) What can't you put in the machines?

　　A. Shirts and pants.

　　B. Hats and gloves.

　　C. Blankets and pillows.

　　D. Put quarters in only.

　　* shirt〔ʃɜt〕*n.* 襯衫　　pants〔pænts〕*n. pl.* 長褲

　　　hat〔hæt〕*n.* 帽子　　gloves〔glʌvz〕*n. pl.* 手套

43. (**D**) What must you do to operate the machines?

　　A. Put in some lint.

　　B. Flatten out your dollar bills.

　　C. Put in powder detergent.

　　D. Put quarters in only.

　　* *flatten out* 弄平　　powder〔'paʊdɚ〕*n.* 粉末

Questions 44-45 are based on the following talk.

OK, Eagles, this is it, this is the big moment we've been training, practicing, working hard and sweating for in the last three months. We have made it to the championship game and for some of you, the seniors, this will be the last time you will ever play in a competition like this. You guys don't need a pep talk from me. You know how much you deserve to win. Every one of you knows that we can beat these guys. We've already faced your opponent the Tigers twice this season and both times we've won by more than twenty points. Tonight they are hungry, determined and desperate to pull off a big upset. But we won't let them win. All we have to do is play smart ball, execute the basic fundamentals, pass, dribble, take good shots and play tough defense. Let's go win this game!

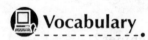 **Vocabulary**

eagle (ˈigl̩) *n.* 老鷹　　big (bɪg) *adj.* 重要的

moment (ˈmomənt) *n.* 時刻

sweat (swɛt) *v.* 流汗　　*make it* 成功

championship (ˈtʃæmpɪənˌʃɪp) *n.* 冠軍 (頭銜)

senior (ˈsinjə) *n.* 前輩　　competition (ˌkɑmpəˈtɪʃən) *n.* 比賽

pep talk 鼓勵性演說   deserve〔dɪˈzɝv〕*v.* 應得

beat〔bit〕*v.* 打敗   face〔fes〕*v.* 面對

opponent〔əˈponənt〕*n.* 對手   season〔ˈsizn̩〕*n.* 球季

point〔pɔint〕*n.* 分數   determined〔dɪˈtɝmɪnd〕*adj.* 堅決的

desperate〔ˈdɛspərɪt〕*adj.* 拼命的   *pull off* 贏得

upset〔ˈʌpˌsɛt〕*n.* 逆轉   smart〔smɑrt〕*adj.* 出色的

execute〔ˈɛksɪˌkjut〕*v.* 實行   basic〔ˈbesɪk〕*adj.* 基本的

fundamental〔ˌfʌndəˈmɛntl̩〕*n.* 基本的原則

pass〔pæs〕*v.* 傳球   dribble〔ˈdrɪbl̩〕*v.* 運球

shot〔ʃɑt〕*n.* 投球   tough〔tʌf〕*adj.* 很棒的；堅固的

defense〔dɪˈfɛns〕*n.* 防禦

44. (**B**) Which team is favored to win?

A. The Tigers.

B. The Eagles.

C. Basketball team.

D. The championship team.

* favor〔ˈfevɚ〕*v.* 有利於

45. (**D**) Who is probably giving this talk?

A. A sports reporter.

B. A team parent.

C. The referee.

D. The team coach.

* give〔ɡɪv〕*v.* 發表   talk〔tɔk〕*n.* 講話

sports reporter 體育記者

parent〔ˈpɛrənt〕*n.* 母公司；創始機構

referee〔ˌrɛfəˈri〕*n.* 裁判   coach〔kotʃ〕*n.* 教練

中高級閱讀測驗詳解 ③

PART A : Sentence Completion

1. (**D**) The most <u>plausible</u> explanation for the recession would seem to be that people had lost confidence in the economy.

不景氣最<u>合理的</u>解釋，似乎是人們對經濟已失去信心。

(A) pictorial〔pɪkˋtorɪəl〕adj. 圖畫的；有插圖的

(B) productive〔prəˋdʌktɪv〕adj. 有生產力的；多產的

(C) prescriptive〔prɪˋskrɪptɪv〕adj. 規定的；命令的

(D) **plausible**〔ˋplɔzəb!〕adj. 合理的；有道理的

* explanation〔͵ɛkspləˋneʃən〕n. 解釋

recession〔rɪˋsɛʃən〕n. 不景氣

confidence〔ˋkɑnfədəns〕n. 信心

economy〔ɪˋkɑnəmɪ〕n. 經濟

2. (**A**) He was an <u>introvert</u> by nature; he preferred reading a book at home alone to going out with friends.

他天生就是個<u>內向的人</u>；他寧可一個人在家讀書，也不願跟朋友出去。

(A) **introvert**〔ˋɪntrə͵vɝt〕n. 內向的人

cf. extrovert n. 外向的人

(B) egoist〔ˋigoɪst〕n. 利己主義者

(C) adversary〔ˋædvɚ͵sɛrɪ〕n. 對手；競爭者

(D) exhibition〔͵ɛksəˋbɪʃən〕n. 展覽會；展示

* **by nature** 天生　　**prefer** A **to** B 寧願 A 也不願 B

3. (**B**) Some children display an <u>unquenchable</u> curiosity about every new thing they encounter.

有些兒童碰到每樣新事物，都會展現出<u>無法滿足的</u>好奇心。

(A) inherent〔ɪnˈhɪrənt〕*adj.* 與生俱來的；固有的

(B) ***unquenchable***〔ʌnˈkwɛntʃəbḷ〕*adj.* 無法滿足的；不能消除的　quench *v.* 熄滅

(C) insensitive〔ɪnˈsɛnsətɪv〕*adj.* 不敏感的；遲鈍的

(D) uninvited〔ˌʌnɪnˈvaɪtɪd〕*adj.* 不請自來的；多管閒事的

* display〔dɪˈsple〕*v.* 展現
curiosity〔ˌkjʊrɪˈɑsətɪ〕*n.* 好奇
encounter〔ɪnˈkaʊntɚ〕*v.* 碰到；遭遇

4. (**B**) As the plane descended gradually, we were able to enjoy the <u>panoramic</u> view of the city.

當飛機逐漸下降時，我們得以欣賞到本城的<u>全景</u>。

(A) paralyzed〔ˈpærəˌlaɪzd〕*adj.* 麻痺的

(B) ***panoramic***〔ˌpænəˈræmɪk〕*adj.* 全景的

(C) patronizing〔ˈpetrənˌaɪzɪŋ〕*adj.* 擺出恩賜態度的

(D) paralleled〔ˈpærəˌlɛld〕*adj.* 平行的

* descend〔dɪˈsɛnd〕*v.* 下降
gradually〔ˈgrædʒʊəlɪ〕*adv.* 逐漸地

5. (**B**) Students learning about how life began on Earth may be presented with the <u>perplexing</u> question, "Which came first, the chicken or the egg?"

學習地球生物起源的學生，都會碰到一個<u>令人困惑的</u>問題：
「哪一個先生，是雞還是蛋？」

(A) pressing〔'prɛsɪŋ〕adj. 緊急的

(B) **perplexing**〔pə'plɛksɪŋ〕adj. 令人困惑的（= *confusing*）

(C) peripheral〔pə'rɪfərəl〕adj. 周遭的　n. （電腦）周邊設備

(D) penetrating〔'pɛnə,tretɪŋ〕adj. 貫穿的；有洞察力的

* present〔prɪ'zɛnt〕v. 提出（問題等）

6. (**D**) Although research has shown that asparagus does contain many important nutrients, it is not, as it was once regarded, a panacea.

雖然研究已顯示，蘆筍的確含有許多重要的營養素，它卻非如以往所認定是個萬靈丹。

(A) delicacy〔'dɛləkəsɪ〕n. 優雅；纖細；精密；美味

(B) organism〔'ɔrgən,ɪzm̩〕n. 有機體；生物

(C) resonance〔'rɛzənəns〕n. 回響；共鳴

(D) **panacea**〔,pænə'siə〕n. 萬靈丹（= *cure-all*）；萬全對策

* asparagus〔ə'spærəgəs〕n. 蘆筍

　contain〔kən'ten〕v. 含有

　nutrient〔'njutrɪənt〕n. 營養素　　regard〔rɪ'gɑrd〕v. 認為

7. (**A**) If there is smoke in a room, you should crawl out of the room slowly. Don't panic.

房間裡如果有煙的話，你應該緩緩地爬出去。別慌張。

(A) **crawl**〔krɔl〕v. 爬

(B) crutch〔krʌtʃ〕v. 以枴杖支撐

(C) cruise〔kruz〕v. 巡航；漫遊

(D) cringe〔krɪndʒ〕v. 畏縮；奉承

* panic〔'pænɪk〕v. 慌張

8. (**C**) The children in the neighborhood have an exclusive club that <u>leaves out</u> everyone over eight.

附近的孩子組成一個排他性的社團，所有八歲以上的小孩都<u>排除在外</u>（不能參加）。

(A) root out 到處搜東西

(B) sneer at 嘲笑；輕蔑　　　sneer〔snɪr〕 *v.* 嘲笑

(C) ***leave out*** 排除在外；遺漏（= *omit*）

(D) hang around 閒蕩；無所事事（= *hang about*）

* neighborhood〔'nebə,hud〕 *n.* 附近；鄰近地區

exclusive〔ɪk'sklusɪv〕 *adj.* 排他性的

9. (**C**) Most people believed that Mr. Smith committed the crime but <u>got away</u> with a plea of insanity.

大部份的人都相信史密斯先生犯了罪，只是用精神異常當藉口，藉以<u>脫罪</u>。

(A) come down with～ 因～而病倒（= *fall sick with*～）

(B) put up with 忍耐（= *tolerate* = *endure*）

(C) ***get away with***～ 逃脫懲罰

(D) pass away 死亡（比 die *文雅、委婉的說法*）

* commit〔kə'mɪt〕 *v.* 犯（罪、過錯等）

crime〔kraɪm〕 *n.* 罪　　plea〔pli〕 *n.* 藉口

insanity〔ɪn'sænətɪ〕 *n.* 精神異常

10. (**D**) The man who was seen hanging around the area <u>prior to</u> the shooting was considered to be the prime suspect in the murder case.

在槍擊發生<u>之前</u>，被人看到在本區附近閒逛的人，被視為是這件謀殺案的主嫌。

(A) beforehand 事先（此字為副詞，故其後不能接名詞）

(B) other than 除～之外（＝except）

(C) no sooner～than… 一～就…（是連接詞，要連接兩個子句）

(D) *prior to* 在～之前（＝before）（to 是介系詞）

* *hang around* 閒逛　　shooting（'ʃutɪŋ）n. 槍擊
  prime（praɪm）adj. 主要的
  suspect（'sʌspɛkt）n. 嫌疑犯　　*murder case* 謀殺案件

11. (D) "Are you coming to Dr. Kennedy's lecture tonight?"

"No, I'm sorry I <u>won't be</u> able to attend."

「今晚甘迺迪博士的演講你會參加嗎？」「不會，恐怕我將<u>無法參加</u>。」

(A) will not have been 為未來完成式，表示在未來某時間點之前，已完成的動作，不適用於此句。

(B) can't be 則因 be able to 就是 can 的意思，句意重複，故不能選此答案。

(C) am not to 改成 am not to be，其後才能接 able to。

* lecture（'lɛktʃɚ）n. 演講　　attend（ə'tɛnd）v. 參加

12. (B) <u>Much to my surprise</u>, this shabby eatery provides excellent food.

令我很訝異的是，這家破舊的小吃店竟然提供絕佳的食物。

* to *one's* ＋（驚、喜、滿意等）情緒「令人感到很～」，要用 much 或 very much 來修飾此片語，不能用 very 來加強語氣。
  shabby（'ʃæbɪ）adj. 破舊的
  eatery（'itərɪ）n. 小吃店　　provide（prə'vaɪd）v. 提供
  excellent（'ɛkslənt）adj. 極好的

13. (**D**) He didn't care <u>about</u> his schoolwork so he flunked again.

他不<u>在乎</u>課業，所以他又考不及格了。

* ***care about~*** 在乎~

(A) care for「喜歡；想要」句意不合；(B)、(C) 無此片語。

schoolwork (ˈskulˌwɝk) *n.* 課業

flunk (flʌŋk) *v.* 不及格；當掉

14. (**A**) Come <u>what</u> may, we will never give up our project.

不管發生<u>什麼事</u>，我們永不放棄這個計畫。

* 「原形動詞＋what＋助動詞」表示「讓步」，所以本題的
Come what may 就等於 No matter what may come。

give up 放棄

project (ˈprɑdʒɛkt) *n.* 計畫

15. (**C**) We don't think she is as attractive as her younger sister, <u>is she</u>?

我們認為她沒有她妹妹漂亮，<u>她有嗎</u>？

* 英文句尾的附加問句，要以主要思想為基準，而主要思想
不一定是主要子句。如本題，We don't think she is as
attractive as her younger sister.「我們不認為她跟妹妹
一樣漂亮。」其實就是在說「<u>她沒有她妹妹漂亮</u>。」因此，
附加問句用 is she「她有嗎」，而非 do we 來問。

attractive (əˈtræktɪv) *adj.* 漂亮的；吸引人的

📋 **PART B : Cloze**

Questions 16-23

Ancient science, or natural philosophy, as it was called, saw no conflict between scientific knowledge and religious faith.
16   17

However, conflict between scientists and religious leaders arose
18

in the medieval age, the age of theological inquiry.

　　古代的科學，也就是所謂的自然哲學，認為科學知識與宗教信仰並不衝突。然而，在中世紀這個研究神學的時代，科學家和宗教領袖之間，卻發生了衝突。

> ancient〔ˈenʃənt〕adj. 古代的　　or〔ɔr〕conj. 也就是
> **natural philosophy** 自然哲學；物理學
> conflict〔ˈkɑnflɪkt〕n. 衝突
> religious〔rɪˈlɪdʒəs〕adj. 宗教的
> medieval〔ˌmidɪˈivḷ〕adj. 中世紀的　　age〔edʒ〕n. 時代
> theological〔ˌθɪəˈlɑdʒɪkḷ〕adj. 神學的
> inquiry〔ɪnˈkwaɪrɪ〕n. 研究；探究

16. (**B**) 依句意，選 (B) **no**「沒有」。

17. (**C**) 科學知識與宗教「信仰」並不衝突，選 (C) **faith**〔feθ〕n. 信仰。
　　而 (A) believe「相信」是動詞，在此不合；(B) trust「信任」，
　　(D) thought「思想」，則不合句意。

18. (**C**) 依句意為過去式，選 (C) **arose**「發生」。
　　arise〔əˈraɪz〕v. 發生【三態變化為：arise-arose-arisen】

The relationship between Christianity and science became increasingly adversarial as scientific researchers developed new
    19
ways of seeing the natural world — ways that contradicted
                                                    20
Christian teachings. Such beliefs as creation and geocentrism (the theory that the earth is the center of the universe) were increasingly open to rational doubt, which in turn threatened to undermine the
    21   22
authority and power of the Church leaders. Galileo, the Italian scientist who advanced the notion of a heliocentric (sun-centered) universe, stands as the traditional symbol of the conflict of this age.
                          23

　　基督教和科學之間的關係變得越來越敵對，因為科學研究人員發展出看待自然界的新方法 —— 這些方法和基督教的教義是互相矛盾的。像是創世紀與地球中心說（也就是地球為宇宙中心的理論）這樣的想法，越來越受到大家的合理懷疑，並轉而損害宗教領袖的權威與權力。義大利科學家伽利略推動太陽為宇宙中心的觀念，也就成為這個時代的衝突的傳統象徵。

Christianity〔ˌkrɪstʃɪˈænətɪ〕n. 基督教
adversarial〔ˌædvəˈsɛrɪəl〕adj. 敵對的
researcher〔rɪˈsɜtʃə〕n. 研究人員
the natural world 自然界
Christian〔ˈkrɪstʃən〕adj. 基督教的
teachings〔ˈtitʃɪŋz〕n. pl. 教訓；教義；學說
belief〔bɪˈlif〕n. 信仰；想法
creation〔krɪˈeʃən〕n.（神的）創造物；天地萬物
geocentrism〔ˌdʒioˈsɛntrɪzm〕n. 地球中心說
theory〔ˈθiərɪ〕n. 理論　　universe〔ˈjunəˌvɜs〕n. 宇宙

increasingly〔ɪn'krisɪŋlɪ〕adv. 越來越

rational〔'ræʃənḷ〕adj. 理性的；合理的　　*in turn* 轉而

threaten〔'θrɛtṇ〕v. 威脅到；危及

authority〔ə'θɔrətɪ〕n. 權威　　church〔tʃɜtʃ〕adj. 教會的

Galileo〔,gælə'lio〕n. 伽利略【1564-1642，義大利天文、物理學家】

advance〔əd'væns〕v. 推動；使前進

notion〔'noʃən〕n. 觀念

heliocentric〔,hilɪo'sɛntrɪk〕adj. 以太陽爲中心的

sun-centered〔'sʌn'sɛntəd〕adj. 以太陽爲中心的

symbol〔'sɪmbḷ〕n. 象徵　　conflict〔'kɑnflɪkt〕n. 衝突

19. (**A**)　(A) *increasingly*〔ɪn'krisɪŋlɪ〕adv. 越來越

(B) additionally〔ə'dɪʃənḷɪ〕adv. 附加地；此外

(C) absolutely〔'æbsə,lutlɪ〕adv. 絕對地

(D) relatively〔'rɛlətɪvlɪ〕adv. 相對地

20. (**B**)　依句意，這些方法「和」基督教的教義是「互相矛盾」的，故選 (B)
contradict〔,kɑntrə'dɪkt〕v. 與…矛盾。而 (A) commemorate
〔kə'mɛmə,ret〕v. 紀念，(C) apologize〔ə'pɑlə,dʒaɪz〕v. 道歉，
(D) prevail〔prɪ'vel〕v. 盛行；普及，均不合句意。

21. (**C**)　(A) be committed to　致力於

(B) be prone to　易於；傾向於

(C) *be open to*　遭受

(D) be inclined to　易於；傾向於

22. (**D**)　依句意，可能會「損害」宗教領袖的權威與權力，故選 (D)
undermine〔,ʌndə'maɪn〕v. 損害。而 (A) underlie〔,ʌndə'laɪ〕v.
成爲…的基礎，(B) 了解，(C) undersell〔,ʌndə'sɛl〕v. 售價比…
低，均不合句意。

23. (**B**) 依句意，選 (B) *stand*「處於（…狀態）；作爲」。而 (A) 坐，(C)
lie「躺；位於」，(D) crouch〔krautʃ〕v. 蹲伏，均不合句意。

Questions 24-30

Despite all one can say about it, however, the nature and value
24
of art are still not widely understood by the general public. In a
society preoccupied with material success, like the one we are in,
25
art does not appear to be very useful, since it does not produce
such obvious benefits as those of medicine or engineering. Even
those artists (including performers) who are widely known and
accepted are usually admired more for their commercial success
than for their artistic talents, having shown that they can compete
26
in the business world.

然而，不管怎麼說，一般大衆還是不了解藝術的本質與價值。在一
心只想追求物質成功的社會，就像我們所處的社會，藝術似乎不是很有
用，因爲它無法提供像醫學或工程學一樣明顯的好處。即使是那些廣爲
人知與接受的藝術家（包括表演者），通常都是因爲他們在商業上的成
功，表示在商場上具有競爭力，而獲得讚賞，而不是因爲藝術才能。

nature〔'netʃə〕n. 本質　　***the general public*** 一般大衆
be preoccupied with 專心於　　material〔mə'tɪrɪəl〕adj. 物質的
appear〔ə'pɪr〕v. 似乎　　obvious〔'abvɪəs〕adj. 明顯的
benefit〔'bɛnəfɪt〕n. 利益　　engineering〔ˌɛndʒə'nɪrɪŋ〕n. 工程學
performer〔pə'fɔrmə〕n. 表演者
admire〔əd'maɪr〕v. 欽佩；讚賞
commercial〔kə'mɝʃəl〕adj. 商業的
talent〔'tælənt〕n. 才能　　compete〔kəm'pit〕v. 競爭

24. (**B**) 依句意，選 (B) *despite*「儘管」。而 (A) regard〔rɪˋgɑrd〕
    v. 認為，(C) 須改成 in spite of「儘管」，(D) 須改成 in regard
    to「關於」，用法與句意均不合。

25. (**B**) 依句意，選 (B) *like the one we are in*「就像我們所處的社會」。

26. (**B**) 本句是由形容詞子句 which has shown…省略關代 which，且
    將 has 改成 having 簡化而來的分詞片語，故選 (B) *having
    shown*。　　show〔ʃo〕*v.* 顯示

Generally, careers in the arts are considered highly risky because
they seldom offer financial security. Such attitudes about art have
led to a situation in which children are systematically (although
not necessarily intentionally) discouraged from developing their
talents. By the time adulthood is reached, the average American
has suppressed all artistic inclinations. <u>Far too many</u> adults are
                                                    27
thus cut off from or are only partly aware of one of man's primary
ways of knowing his world and understanding himself.

通常和藝術有關的職業，都被認為是非常冒險的，因為它們很少提供財務
上的保障。這種對藝術的心態，使情況變成是，孩子會被有計劃地（雖然
未必是有意地）勸阻，不要發展他們的才能。一般美國人到了成年時，都
已經壓抑住所有對藝術的喜好了。有太多成年人因而無法接觸到，或是只
察覺到部分人類認識這個世界，以及了解自己的主要方法之一。

generally〔ˋdʒɛnərəlɪ〕*adv.* 通常　　career〔kəˋrɪr〕*n.* 事業
highly〔ˋhaɪlɪ〕*adv.* 高度地；非常　　risky〔ˋrɪskɪ〕*adj.* 冒險的
financial〔faɪˋnænʃəl〕*adj.* 財務的
security〔sɪˋkjurətɪ〕*n.* 安全；保障　　*lead to* 導致；造成
systematically〔ˌsɪstəˋmætɪkḷɪ〕*adv.* 有系統地；有計劃地

not necessarily 未必　　intentionally〔ɪnˈtɛnʃənḷɪ〕*adv.* 故意地
discourage〔dɪsˈkɝɪdʒ〕*v.* 使打消念頭
adulthood〔əˈdʌlthʊd〕*n.* 成年（時期）　　*reach adulthood* 成年
average〔ˈævərɪdʒ〕*adj.* 一般的　　suppress〔səˈprɛs〕*v.* 壓抑
inclination〔͵ɪnkləˈneʃən〕*n.* 傾向；喜愛　　*cut off* 切斷
be aware of 知道；察覺到　　primary〔ˈpraɪ͵mɛrɪ〕*adj.* 主要的

27. (**D**) 依句意，選 (D) *Far too many*「太多」。　　*far too* 極為
　　　　而 (A) 沒有 many more 的說法，(B) 沒有 far many 的說法，
　　　　因為 far 用於修飾比較級，(C) far more「更多」，後面無比
　　　　較級連接詞 than，故用法均不合。

Still, it is difficult to defend art on the basis of <u>its immediate</u>
28
<u>utility</u>. Art ultimately must be valued because of its capacity to
improve the quality of life: by increasing our sensitivity to <u>others</u>
<u>and our surroundings</u>, by sharpening our perceptions, by reshaping
　　29
our values or by instilling the idea that moral and societal concerns
<u>take precedence over</u> material well-being.
　　30

　　儘管如此，還是很難以立即的實用性為藝術辯解。藝術最終還是必須
被重視，因為它能改善生活品質：使我們的知覺更加敏銳，重塑我們的價
值觀，或灌輸我們道德與社會所關心的事優於物質福祉的觀念，因而讓我
們對別人以及週遭的環境更加敏感。

　　　　still〔stɪl〕*adv.* 儘管如此　　defend〔dɪˈfɛnd〕*v.* 為…辯解
　　　　on the basis of 以…為基礎　　ultimately〔ˈʌltəmɪtlɪ〕*adv.* 最後
　　　　value〔ˈvælju〕*v.* 重視　*n.* 價值；(*pl.*) 價值觀
　　　　capacity〔kəˈpæsətɪ〕*n.* 能力
　　　　improve〔ɪmˈpruv〕*v.* 改善　　*quality of life* 生活品質

sensitivity〔͵sɛnsə'tɪvətɪ〕 *n.* 敏感

  sharpen〔'ʃɑrpən〕 *v.* 使敏銳

  perception〔pə'sɛpʃən〕 *n.* 知覺

  reshape〔ri'ʃep〕 *v.* 重塑 instill〔ɪn'stɪl〕 *v.* 灌輸

  moral〔'mɔrəl〕 *adj.* 道德的

  societal〔sə'saɪətḷ〕 *adj.* 社會的

  concern〔kən's3n〕 *n.* 關心的事

  well-being〔'wɛl'biɪŋ〕 *n.* 福利；幸福

28. (**A**) 依句意，選 (A) *its immediate utility*「它立即的效用」，utility
   〔ju'tɪlətɪ〕 *n.* 效用。而 (B) being utilized「被利用」，(C) its
   utilitarian immediacy「它功利主義的立即性」，(D) some
   immediate usage「一些立即的用法」，均不合句意。
   utilize〔'jutḷ͵aɪz〕 *v.* 利用
   utilitarian〔͵jutɪlə'tɛrɪən〕 *adj.* 功利主義的
   immediacy〔'ɪmidɪəsɪ〕 *n.* 即時性
   usage〔'jusɪdʒ〕 *n.* 用法

29. (**D**) 依句意，選 (D) *others and our surroundings*「別人以及我
   們週遭的環境」。

30. (**A**) 依句意，選 (A) *take precedence over*「比…優先；在…之上」。
   precedence〔prɪ'sidns〕 *n.* 優先權
   而 (B) precedent〔prɪ'sidnt〕 *adj.* 在…之前的，其後須接 to，
   (C)(D) precede〔prɪ'sid〕 *v.* 在…之前；帶領，爲及物動詞，
   其後不可接 over，用法均不合。

📂 PART C：Reading

Questions 31-34

Data collection aids the smooth functioning of government, business, and research. Personal data is used for tax assessment, job selection, credit rating, and many other purposes. Aggregate data is useful for planning and formulating social policies. The general availability of data supports freedom of speech and freedom of the press.

資料的收集，有助於使政府及企業順利運作，並且讓研究順利進行。個人的資料被用來做稅額的估算、工作的選擇、信用的評比，以及很多其他的用途。整體的資料則有助於用來規劃社會政策。取得一般資料，可促進言論以及新聞自由。

> data (ˈdetə) n. 資料【可當複數或單數用】
> aid (ed) v. 幫助；促進
> smooth (smuθ) adj. 順利的　　function (ˈfʌŋkʃən) v. 運作
> tax (tæks) n. 稅　　assessment (əˈsɛsmənt) n. 核定；評估
> credit (ˈkrɛkɪt) n. 信用　　rating (ˈretɪŋ) n. 評估
> purpose (ˈpɝpəs) n. 目的；用途
> aggregate (ˈægrɪˌget) adj. 集合的；總計的
> formulate (ˈfɔrmjəˌlet) v. 規劃　　policy (ˈpɑləsɪ) n. 政策
> general (ˈdʒɛnərəl) adj. 大體的；總括的；全面的
> availability (əˌveləˈbɪlətɪ) n. 可用；可得到
> *the press* 出版物；新聞；雜誌

Conversely, the gathering of data can erode personal privacy. Data can be used for blackmail, especially large-scale political blackmail by governments or police with too much power.

Harassment of individuals by law enforcement agencies and monopolistic corporations (including utility companies) can also occur. Errors in data collection can lead to many unfair practices, such as denial of employment or denial of credit. Outdated or incomplete data can lead to personal trauma. Retention of information for long periods can result in excessive punishment of a person for a misdemeanor long since atoned for.

　　相反地，資料的收集可能會侵犯個人隱私。資料可能會被用來勒索，尤其是被擁有過多權力的政府或警方，拿來做大規模的政治勒索。可能也會發生個人被執法機關和獨占的公司（包括公用事業公司）騷擾的情況。資料收集時所發生的錯誤，也可能會造成許多不公平的做法，像是不予雇用，或是不給信用貸款。過時或不完整的資料，可能會造成個人的精神創傷。長時間保留資料，可能會對很久以前就已經爲自己不當的行爲贖過罪的人，造成過度的懲罰。

conversely〔kən'vɜslɪ〕adv. 相反地

erode〔ɪ'rod〕v. 腐蝕；侵犯　　privacy〔'praɪvəsɪ〕n. 隱私權

blackmail〔'blæk,mel〕n. v. 敲詐；勒索

large-scale〔'lardʒ'skel〕adj. 大規模的

harassment〔hə'ræsmənt〕n. 騷擾

individual〔,ɪndə'vɪdʒʊəl〕n. 個人

enforcement〔ɪn'forsmənt〕n. 執行

agency〔'edʒənsɪ〕n. 政府機構

monopolistic〔mə,napə'lɪstɪk〕adj. 獨占的；壟斷的

corporation〔,kɔrpə'reʃən〕n. 公司

utility〔ju'tɪlətɪ〕n. 公共事業（水、電、瓦斯、石油等）

error〔'ɛrɚ〕n. 錯誤　　unfair〔ʌn'fɛr〕adj. 不公平的

practice〔'præktɪs〕n. 做法　　denial〔dɪ'naɪl〕n. 拒絕；不給

employment〔ɪm'plɔɪmənt〕n. 僱用；工作

credit〔'krɛkɪt〕n. 信用貸款

outdated〔aʊt'detɪd〕adj. 過時的

incomplete〔ˌɪnkəm'plit〕adj. 不完整的

trauma〔'trɔmə〕n. 精神創傷

retention〔rɪ'tɛnʃən〕n. 保留   *result in* 導致

excessive〔ɪk'sɛsɪv〕adj. 過度的

misdemeanor〔ˌmɪsdɪ'minɚ〕n. 行為不檢；輕罪

long since 很久以前   atone〔ə'ton〕v. 補償；贖罪

31. (**C**) 根據本文，作者

(A) 贊成資料的收集。

(B) 不贊成資料的收集。

(C) 擔心收集來的資料的可能用途。

(D) 對於無法避免隱私權被侵犯，感到無可奈何。

* favorable〔'fevərəbḷ〕adj. 贊成的

unfavorable〔ʌn'fevərəbḷ〕adj. 不贊成的

fearful〔'fɪrfəl〕adj. 擔心的

be resigned to 對…無可奈何的

inevitability〔ɪnˌɛvətə'bɪlətɪ〕n. 不可避免；必然

intrusion〔ɪn'truʒən〕n. 侵入；干涉

32. (**D**) 資料會促進言論和新聞自由的理由是

(A) 人們需要自由地討論資料。

(B) 我們擁有越多資料，就越能自由地討論它。

(C) 它配合自由的企業體系。

(D) 它讓大眾能取得資料。

* *fit into* 配合   enterprise〔'ɛntɚˌpraɪz〕n. 企業

available〔ə'veləbḷ〕adj. 可獲得的

33. (**A**) 本文暗示

  (A) 有些政府會勒索人民。

  (B) 有信用問題的人，都是資料收集不公平的受害者。

  (C) 資料收集應該被廢除。

  (D) 精神受創的受害者應該獲得補償。

  * imply〔ɪmˈplaɪ〕v. 暗示　citizen〔ˈsɪtəzṇ〕n. 公民
    victim〔ˈvɪktɪm〕n. 受害者　abolish〔əˈbɑlɪʃ〕v. 廢除
    compensate〔ˈkɑmpənˌset〕v. 彌補；補償

34. (**B**) 當資料被保留過久，可能會導致

  (A) 新聞審查制度。　　　(B) 對個人造成過度的懲罰。

  (C) 政府的干涉。　　　　(D) 失業。

  * retain〔rɪˈten〕v. 保留
    censorship〔ˈsɛnsɚˌʃɪp〕n. 審查
    press censorship 新聞審查制度
    deserve〔dɪˈzɜv〕v. 應得
    interference〔ˌɪntɚˈfɪrəns〕n. 干涉
    unemployment〔ˌʌnɪmˈplɔɪmənt〕n. 失業

Questions 35-39

The process of perceiving other people is rarely translated (to ourselves or others) into cold, objective terms. "She was 5 feet 8 inches tall, had fair hair, and wore a colored skirt." More often, we try to get inside the other person to <u>pinpoint</u> his or her attitudes, emotions, motivations, abilities, ideas and characters. Furthermore, we sometimes behave as if we can accomplish this difficult job very quickly — perhaps with a two-second glance.

　　觀察別人的過程，很少能（對自己或別人）轉為冷靜又客觀的言詞。「她身高五呎八吋，金髮，並穿著有顏色的裙子。」我們常想要深入了解一個人，明確指出他或她的態度、情緒、動機、能力、想法，以及人格。此外，我們有時表現得好像能非常快地完成這個困難的工作——也許只要看個兩秒鐘。

process〔'prɑsɛs〕 n. 過程　　　　perceive〔pəˈsiv〕 v. 察覺
rarely〔'rɛrlɪ〕 adv. 很少　　　　translate〔trænsˈlet〕 v. 轉換；更改
cold〔kold〕 adj. 冷靜的　　　　objective〔əbˈdʒɛktɪv〕 adj. 客觀的
term〔tɜm〕 n. 名詞；用語　　　*fair hair*　金髮
colored〔'kʌləd〕 adj. 彩色的　　　*more often*　常常
pinpoint〔'pɪnˌpɔɪnt〕 v. 明確指出　　emotion〔ɪˈmoʃən〕 n. 情緒
motivation〔ˌmotəˈveʃən〕 n. 動機
character〔'kærɪktə〕 n. 性格
behave〔bɪˈhev〕 v. 表現；行為舉止
accomplish〔əˈkɑmplɪʃ〕 v. 完成　　glance〔glæns〕 n. 看一眼

　　We try to obtain information about others in many ways. Experts suggest several methods for reducing uncertainties about others: watching, without being noticed, a person interacting with others, particularly with others who are known to you so you can compare the observed person's behavior with the known others' behavior. Try to observe a person in a situation where social behavior is relatively unrestrained or where a wide variety of behavioral responses are called for. Deliberately structure the physical or social environment so as to observe the person's responses to specific stimuli. Ask people who have had or have frequent contact with the person about him or her. And use various strategies in face-to-face interaction to uncover information about another person — questions, self-disclosures, and so on.

我們會試著用很多方式，來獲得與別人有關的資訊。專家建議好幾個方法，可以減少我們對別人的不確定感：要不被注意地觀察一個人，看他跟別人，尤其是跟你認識的人的互動，如此你便可以比較你所觀察的人，和你所熟知的人的行為。試著在較不須克制社交行為的場合，或是需要各種行為反應的場合中，觀察一個人。要刻意營造實質的或社交的環境，以便觀察一個人對某些特定刺激的反應。去跟他經常接觸的人打聽他的為人。並且在面對面接觸時，運用各種策略，來挖掘關於對方的資訊——問問題、自我揭露等等。

obtain〔əbˋten〕v. 獲得　　reduce〔rɪˋdjus〕v. 減少；降低

uncertainty〔ʌnˋsɝtṇtɪ〕n. 不確定性

notice〔ˋnotɪs〕v. 注意　　interact〔͵ɪntəˋækt〕v. 互動

particularly〔pəˋtɪkjələˇlɪ〕adv. 尤其；特別是

known〔non〕adj. 已知的　　compare〔kəmˋpɛr〕v. 比較

observe〔əbˋzɝv〕v. 觀察　　behavior〔bɪˋhevjə〕n. 行為

social〔ˋsoʃəl〕adj. 社交的　　relatively〔ˋrɛlətɪvlɪ〕adv. 比較上

unrestrained〔͵ʌnrɪˋstrend〕adj. 未受抑制的；不受控制的

a wide variety of 很多各式各樣的

behavioral〔bɪˋhevjərəl〕adj. 行為的；與行為有關的

response〔rɪˋspɑns〕n. 回應；反應　　*call for* 需要；要求

deliberately〔dɪˋlɪbərɪtlɪ〕adv. 故意地

structure〔ˋstrʌktʃə〕v. 建立；安排

physical〔ˋfɪzɪkḷ〕adj. 實質的

specific〔spɪˋsɪfɪk〕adj. 特定的

stimuli〔ˋstɪmjə͵laɪ〕n. pl. 刺激物；刺激【單數是 stimulus】

contact〔ˋkɑntækt〕n. 接觸　　various〔ˋvɛrɪəs〕adj. 各種的

strategy〔ˋstrætədʒɪ〕n. 策略

face-to-face〔ˋfestəˋfes〕adj. 面對面的

interaction〔͵ɪntəˋækʃən〕n. 互動　　uncover〔ʌnˋkʌvə〕v. 揭發

self-disclosure〔͵sɛlfdɪsˋkloʒə〕n. 自我揭露

and so on 等等

Getting to know someone is a never-ending task, largely because people are constantly changing and the methods we use to obtain information are often imprecise. You may have known someone for ten years and still know very little about him. If we accept the idea that we won't ever fully know another person, it enables us to deal more easily with those things that get in the way of accurate knowledge such as secrets and deceptions. It will also keep us from being too surprised or shocked by seemingly inconsistent behavior. Ironically, those things that keep us from knowing another person too well, (e.g. secrets and deceptions) may be just as important to the development of a satisfying relationship as those things that enable us to obtain accurate knowledge about a person (e.g. disclosures and truthful statements).

要了解一個人，是一項永無止境的工作，主要是因為人會不停地改變，而且我們用來獲得資訊的方法，常常不準確。你可能認識一個人十年，仍然對他了解得不多。如果我們能接受，不可能完全了解別人的這種想法，那麼就能讓我們更容易應付，那些阻礙我們準確地了解一個人的事情，像是秘密和欺騙。這樣也會使我們對於那些看似矛盾的行為，不會太驚訝或震驚。諷刺的是，那些使我們無法清楚了解一個人的事物（例如秘密和欺騙），可能和那些能使我們準確認識一個人，因而發展出令人滿意的關係的那些事物（例如傾吐秘密和真實的陳述）一樣重要。

get to 得以　never-ending〔'nɛvə'ɛndɪŋ〕*adj.* 永無止境的
task〔tæsk〕*n.* 任務；工作
largely〔'lɑrdʒlɪ〕*adv.* 主要地
constantly〔'kɑnstəntlɪ〕*adv.* 不斷地
imprecise〔,ɪmprɪ'saɪs〕*adj.* 不精確的　*not ever* 絕不
enable〔ɪn'ebl̩〕*v.* 使能夠　*deal with* 應付；處理

get in the way of 阻礙　　accurate〔'ækjərɪt〕*adj.* 準確的

knowledge〔'nɑlɪdʒ〕*n.* 知識；認識

deception〔dɪ'sɛpʃən〕*n.* 欺騙

keep *sb.* ***from*** 使某人無法…　　shocked〔ʃɑkt〕*adj.* 震驚的

seemingly〔'simɪŋlɪ〕*adv.* 看來

inconsistent〔,ɪnkən'sɪstənt〕*adj.* 矛盾的；不一致的

ironically〔aɪ'rɑnɪklɪ〕*adv.* 諷刺地

satisfying〔'sætɪs,faɪɪŋ〕*adj.* 令人滿意的　　***e.g.*** 例如

disclosure〔dɪs'kloʒɚ〕*n.* 揭發的事物；透露的話

truthful〔'truθfəl〕*adj.* 誠實的；眞實的

statement〔'stetmənt〕*n.* 陳述；說明

35. (**D**) 第一段的 "pinpoint" 基本上是指

　　(A) 欣賞。　　(B) 獲得。　　(C) 詮釋。　　(D) 確認。

　　* appreciate〔ə'priʃɪ,et〕*v.* 欣賞；感激

　　　interpret〔ɪn'tɜprɪt〕*v.* 詮釋

　　　identify〔aɪ'dɛntə,faɪ〕*v.* 確認

36. (**B**) 我們從第一段可得知什麼？

　　(A) 用冷靜客觀的名詞形容一個人比較恰當。

　　(B) 要了解一個人的困難程度通常都被低估了。

　　(C) 不應該以貌取人。

　　(D) 我們評估別人的個性時，通常是客觀的。

　　* describe〔dɪ'skraɪb〕*v.* 描述；形容

　　　underestimate〔'ʌndɚ'ɛstə,met〕*v.* 低估

　　　judge〔dʒʌdʒ〕*v.* 判斷　　assess〔ə'sɛs〕*v.* 評估

　　　personality〔,pɜsn̩'ælətɪ〕*n.* 個性

37. (**A**) 從專家給的建議我們可以推論，

(A) 人們不會在任何場合都表現出眞實的自我。

(B) 在大部分的情況下，我們都應該避免直接跟所要觀察的人接觸。

(C) 要了解一個人，最好的方法就是做比較。

(D) 面對面的互動，是了解關於一個人的資訊的最好策略。

* reveal〔rɪ'vil〕v. 透露　　case〔kes〕n. 情況

comparison〔kəm'pærəsn〕n. 比較

38. (**C**) 根據作者的看法，在發展個人關係時，秘密和欺騙

(A) 是個人的事情，應該要認眞處理。

(B) 是應該被除去的障礙。

(C) 和透露秘密及眞實陳述同樣重要。

(D) 是人們要小心防範的事情。

* *in one's opinion* 依某人之見；某人認爲

matter〔'mætɚ〕n. 事情

seriously〔'sɪrɪəslɪ〕adv. 嚴肅地；認眞地

barrier〔'bærɪɚ〕n. 障礙　　*do away with* 廢除

significant〔sɪg'nɪfəkənt〕adj. 重要的

guard against 小心防範

39. (**D**) 作者寫本文的目的，是要

(A) 對於社交場合適當的行爲提供建議。

(B) 提供獲得關於別人的資訊的方法。

(C) 讀者注意人們的負面性格。

(D) 討論認識一個人的不同層面。

* advice〔əd'vaɪs〕n. 勸告；建議

appropriate〔ə'proprɪɪt〕adj. 適當的

conduct〔'kɑndʌkt〕n. 行爲

call one's attention to 要某人注意

negative〔'nɛgətɪv〕adj. 負面的　　aspect〔'æspɛkt〕n. 方面

Questions 40-43

A revolution in our understanding of Earth is reaching its
climax as evidence accumulates that the continents of today are
not venerable landmasses but amalgams of other lands repeatedly
broken up, juggled, rotated, scattered far and wide, then crunched
together into new configurations like ice swept along the shore of
a swift-flowing stream.

當證據不斷累積，告訴我們現在的五大洲，並不是脆弱的古老陸塊，
而是不斷地破裂、挪移、旋轉，四處散落，然後再集體壓碎成新的外形，就
像沿著湍急的河岸被帶走的冰一樣，我們對地球認知的革命也達到顛峰。

revolution〔ˌrɛvəˈluʃən〕n. 革命；大改革　Earth〔ɝθ〕n. 地球
climax〔ˈklaɪmæks〕n. 高峰　evidence〔ˈɛvədəns〕n. 證據
accumulate〔əˈkjumjəˌlet〕v. 累積
continent〔ˈkɑntənənt〕n. 洲；大陸
vulnerable〔ˈvʌlnərəbļ〕adj. 易受傷害的；脆弱的
landmass〔ˈlændˌmæs〕n. 大塊陸地
amalgam〔əˈmælgəm〕n. 混合物
repeatedly〔rɪˈpitɪdlɪ〕adv. 反覆地　*break up* 破裂
juggle〔ˈdʒʌgļ〕v. 變戲法；挪移　rotate〔ˈrotet〕v. 旋轉
scatter〔ˈskætɚ〕v. 分散　*far and wide* 到處
crunch〔krʌntʃ〕v. 壓碎
configuration〔kənˌfɪgjəˈreʃən〕n. 地形
sweep〔swip〕v. 橫掃；沖走　shore〔ʃor〕n. 海岸
swift〔swɪft〕adj. 快速的　stream〔strim〕n. 溪流；河流

After considerable modification this became the now largely
accepted concept of "plate tectonics," explaining much of what
is observed regarding our dynamic planet. Some oceans, such

as the Atlantic, are being split apart, their opposing coasts carried away from one another at one or two inches per year as lava wells up along the line of separation to form new seafloor.　Other oceans, such as the Pacific, are shrinking as seafloor descends under their fringing coastlines or offshore arcs of islands.

　　在經過相當大的修正後，就變成現在大家普遍認可的「板塊構造學」的概念，能替我們為多變的地球所做的觀察，提供相當多的解釋。有些海洋會被分開來，像是大西洋，其相對的兩岸，每年都會再拉開一兩英吋，因為沿著分界線湧出的岩漿，形成了新的海底。其他的海洋則在縮小，像是太平洋，因為其海岸線邊緣，或近海島弧下方的海底下陷。

considerable〔 kən'sɪdərəb!〕*adj.* 相當大的

modification〔,mɑdəfə'keʃən〕*n.* 修正

largely〔'lɑrdʒlɪ〕*adv.* 大多；普遍地

accepted〔 æk'sɛptɪd〕*adj.* 為一般所認可的

concept〔'kɑnsɛpt〕*n.* 概念　　plate〔 plet〕*n.* 板塊

tectonics〔 tɛk'tɑnɪks〕*n.* 構造學

observe〔 əb'zɜv〕*v.* 觀察　　regarding〔 rɪ'gɑrdɪŋ〕*prep.* 關於

dynamic〔 daɪ'næmɪk〕*adj.* 充滿活力的；動態的

planet〔'plænɪt〕*n.* 行星　　***the Atlantic*** 大西洋

split〔 splɪt〕*v.* 使分裂　　opposing〔 ə'pozɪŋ〕*adj.* 相對的

coast〔 kost〕*n.* 海岸　　per〔 pɚ〕*prep.* 每

lava〔'lɑvə , 'lævə〕*n.* 岩漿

well〔 wɛl〕*v.* 湧出；湧上來＜*up*＞

separation〔,sɛpə'reʃən〕*n.* 分離

seafloor〔'si,flor〕*n.* 海底　　***the Pacific*** 太平洋

shrink〔 ʃrɪŋk〕*v.* 縮小　　descend〔 dɪ'sɛnd〕*v.* 下降

fringe〔 frɪndʒ〕*v.* 成為…的邊緣

coastline〔'kost,laɪn〕*n.* 海岸線

offshore〔'ɔf,ʃor〕*adj.* 在近海的　　arc〔 ɑrk〕*n.* 弧；弧形

The earth's crust, in this view, is divided into several immense plates that make up the continents and seafloors, and all float on a hot, plastic, subterranean "mantle." What causes these plates to jostle each other, splitting apart or sliding under one another at their edges, is still a mystery to geologists: it may be friction from circulating rock in the earth's mantle, or it may be an effect produced by gravity.

　　就這個觀點看來，地殼被分成好幾個組成五大洲及海底的廣大陸塊，並且全都在一個炙熱、有可塑性的地幔上漂浮。是什麼使這些陸塊互相碰撞、分離，或在彼此的邊緣底下滑動，對地質學家而言，仍然是個謎：可能是在地幔中流動的岩石的摩擦，或是重力造成的影響。

crust〔krʌst〕n. 地殼

view〔vju〕n. 看法；見解　　**be divided into** 被分成

immense〔ɪˈmɛns〕adj. 廣大的

make up 組成　　float〔flot〕v. 漂浮

plastic〔ˈplæstɪk〕adj. 有可塑性的

subterranean〔ˌsʌbtəˈrenɪən〕adj. 地下的

mantle〔ˈmæntl̩〕n. 地幔【地殼與地球外核心間之地層，約在地下 35～2900 公里的部分】

jostle〔ˈdʒɑsl̩〕v. 推；撞；擠　　slide〔slaɪd〕v. 滑

edge〔ɛdʒ〕n. 邊緣　　mystery〔ˈmɪstrɪ〕n. 謎

geologist〔dʒiˈɑlədʒɪst〕n. 地質學家

friction〔ˈfrɪkʃən〕n. 摩擦

circulating〔ˈsɝkjəˌletɪŋ〕adj. 循環的；流動的

effect〔ɪˈfɛkt〕n. 影響

gravity〔ˈɡrævətɪ〕n. 重力；地心引力

40. (**D**) 本文作者的主要目的是什麼？

    (A) 要消除關於地球自轉的誤解。

    (B) 要稱讚地質學家的探測與發現。

    (C) 要將大西洋與太平洋做比較與對照。

    (D) <u>要解釋陸塊地質學的理論。</u>

    * dispel〔dɪ'spɛl〕*v.* 消除；解除

      misconception〔‚mɪskən'sɛpʃən〕*n.* 誤解；錯誤的觀念

      rotation〔ro'teʃən〕*n.* 自轉

      exploration〔‚ɛksplə'reʃən〕*n.* 探勘；探險

      contrast〔kən'træst〕*v.* 使對比；對照

41. (**D**) 作者暗示，人們以前認爲五大洲是

    (A) 冰凍的石塊。   (B) 旋轉的石塊。

    (C) 岩漿變硬的外殼。   (D) <u>不會動的陸塊。</u>

    * ***used to V.*** 以前⋯   chunk〔tʃʌŋk〕*n.* 厚塊

      mass〔mæs〕*n.* 一團   ***mass of rock*** 石塊

      hardened〔'hɑrdn̩d〕*adj.* 硬化的

      crust〔krʌst〕*n.* 東西的硬表層

      immobile〔ɪ'mobl̩〕*adj.* 不能移動的；固定的；靜止的

      body〔'bɑdɪ〕*n.* 一團

42. (**C**) 第一段的 "swept" 這個字可以用 ＿＿＿＿＿ 取代。

    (A) 贏得   (B) 清除   (C) <u>攜帶</u>   (D) 除去

    * replace〔rɪ'ples〕*v.* 取代

43. (**B**) 根據本文，太平洋是以下列何種方式改變？

    (A) 變得較溫暖。   (B) <u>變小。</u>

    (C) 被分開。   (D) 被岩漿填滿。

    * grow〔gro〕*v.* 變得

Questions 44-47

Most of us are taught to think linearly; that is, our thinking goes in straight lines. A causes B causes C causes D; we are taught to look for cause and effect. The natural world is not so simple; it is a huge system of systems. A fundamental principle of environmental thinking is that biospheric elements circulate in systems. For example, environmental scientists talk about the carbon cycle or the nitrogen cycle or the water cycle as they admonish us to think systematically. Systematic thinkers focus on wholes rather than on parts. Within wholes they concern themselves with relationships more than objects, with processes more than structures.

我們大部分的人，都被教導要做直線性的思考；也就是說，我們的思考是直線進行的。A 導致 B 導致 C 導致 D；我們被教導，要尋找因果關係。自然界並非如此簡單：它是一個巨大的系統中的系統。環境思考的基本原則，就是生物圈的要素，是以系統的方式在循環。例如，當環境科學家告誡我們，要做系統性的思考時，他們會談到碳循環、氮循環，或是水循環。做系統性思考的人，會專注於整體，而非部分。在整體當中，他們關心的是相互的關連，而非物體本身，他們關心過程，而非結構。

linearly (ˈlɪnɪəlɪ) adv. 直線地　　***that is*** 也就是
cause (kɔz) v. 導致；造成　n. 原因
cause and effect 原因和結果；因果
huge (hjudʒ) adj. 巨大的
fundamental (ˌfʌndəˈmɛntḷ) adj. 基本的
principle (ˈprɪnsəpḷ) n. 原則
biospheric (ˌbaɪəˈsfɛrɪk) adj. 生物圈的；生物範圍的

element（'ɛləmənt）n. 要素；成分

circulate（'sɜkjə,let）v. 循環

carbon（'karbən）n. 碳　　cycle（'saɪkḷ）n. 循環

nitrogen（'naɪtrədʒən）n. 氮

admonish（əd'manɪʃ）v. 告誡；勸告

systematically（,sɪstə'mætɪkḷɪ）adv. 系統地

focus on 集中於　　whole（hol）n. 全體；整體

rather than 而不是　　*concern oneself with* 關心

more than 不只是　　object（'abdʒɪkt）n. 物體

process（'prasɛs）n. 過程

structure（'strʌktʃɚ）n. 結構；構造

For example, a gallon of gasoline contains a lot of carbon. When it's burned in your car, the carbon combines with oxygen to form CO_2. The carbon in oil does not come from plants living now but from plants that lived millions of years ago. So burning millions of gallons of gasoline today quickly releases extraordinary amounts of CO_2 that nature had not figured into the current carbon balance between plants and animals. But now that there aren't enough growing plants to take up the extra CO_2, it's accumulating rapidly.

例如，一加侖的汽油包含很多碳。當它在你的汽車裡被燃燒時，碳會和氧結合，形成二氧化碳。石油裡的碳並不是來自現存的植物，而是來自數百萬年前的植物。所以現在燃燒數百萬加侖的汽油，就會很快地釋放出超乎尋常的二氧化碳的量，可是大自然在計算動植物之間的碳平衡時，並沒有將這些二氧化碳算進去。既然沒有足夠的生長中的植物，來吸收多餘的二氧化碳，它們當然會快速地累積。

gallon〔'gælən〕n. 加侖【容量單位】　　gasoline〔'gæsḷ,in〕n. 汽油
contain〔kən'ten〕v. 包含　　combine〔kəm'baın〕v. 結合
oxygen〔'ɑksədʒən〕n. 氧　　release〔rı'lis〕v. 釋放
extraordinary〔ık'strɔrdṇ,ɛrı〕adj. 異常的；奇怪的
figure〔'fıgjɚ〕v. 計算　　current〔'kɝənt〕adj. 目前的
balance〔'bæləns〕n. 平衡　　**now that** 既然　　**take up** 吸收
extra〔'ɛkstrə〕adj. 額外的　　rapidly〔'ræpıdlı〕adv. 快速地

In fact, we humans further insult the system by cutting down forests to get timber or by clearing land for farming or ranching. Environmentalists, most atmospheric scientists, and some political leaders are warning us that the extra carbon dioxide is adding to the greenhouse effect that warms the planet and probably will change the climate system.

　　事實上，我們人類藉由砍伐森林，以獲得木材，或開墾土地，以利農耕與經營牧場，因而對這個系統造成更進一步的破壞。環保人士、大部分的大氣科學家，以及一些政治領袖，都在警告我們，多餘的二氧化碳會使溫室效應更嚴重，因而讓地球暖化，而且可能會改變氣候系統。

further〔'fɝðɚ〕adv. 更進一步地　　insult〔ın'sʌlt〕v. 損害
timber〔'tımbɚ〕n. 木材　　clear〔klır〕v. 開墾；開闢
farming〔'fɑrmıŋ〕n. 農耕　　ranching〔'ræntʃıŋ〕n. 經營牧場
environmentalist〔,ınvaırən'mɛntḷıst〕n. 環境保護論者
atmospheric〔,ætməs'fɛrık〕adj. 大氣的
carbon dioxide 二氧化碳　　**add to** 增添
greenhouse effect 溫室效應　　warm〔wɔrm〕v. 使溫暖

The point (of this article) is that different parts of a system are so interconnected that we can never do merely one thing. We should always ask, "And then what?"

　　（本文的）重點是，系統中的不同部分，是彼此密切相關的，所以我們不能只做一件事。我們要不斷地自問：「然後呢？」

　　point〔pɔɪnt〕n. 重點
　　interconnected〔ˌɪntəkəˈnɛktɪd〕adj. 彼此相關的

44. (**A**) 環境思考的基本原則是什麼？
　　(A) 生物圈的要素是以系統的方式在循環。
　　(B) 生物圈的要素是以局部的方式在循環。
　　(C) 生物圈的要素是專注於環境。
　　(D) 生物圈的要素是專注於自然界。

45. (**B**) 會做系統性的思考的人都專注於什麼？
　　(A) 局部而非整體。　　　　(B) 整體而非局部。
　　(C) 物體本身而非相互關係。　(D) 結構而非過程。

46. (**A**) 人類如何讓環境受到更進一步的損害？
　　(A) 藉由砍伐森林。
　　(B) 藉由吸收更多的二氧化碳。
　　(C) 藉由讓植物生長。
　　(D) 藉由燃燒數百萬加侖的汽油。
　　* allow〔əˈlau〕v. 讓

47. (**C**) 本文的主旨是什麼？
　　(A) 對我們大家而言，環保是最重要的。
　　(B) 多餘的二氧化碳使溫室效應更嚴重，讓行星暖化。
　　(C) 系統的各個部分都是密切相關的，所以我們不能只做
　　　　一件事。
　　(D) 應該教導人們做直線性的思考。
　　* essential〔əˈsɛnʃəl〕adj. 必要的；非常重要的

Questions 48-50

Memorandum to: Department Managers, Research Division
From : Akira Inoue, Sr. V.P. for Research

The federal government has just announced for the next fiscal year it will accept applications from small unaffiliated businesses for grants to conduct research and initial product development in several frontier technologies, including semiconductors, robotics and micro-robotics, and laser application. Both U.S.-based and non-U.S. firms are eligible for these grants, except that for non-U.S. firms all government-funded activities must be carried out in the U.S. See the attached circular for other restrictions.

We plan to apply for funding for some of our on-going projects. As a non-U.S. firm, we will have to submit documentation on what work we are carrying out, where it is being carried out, and by whom.

As a first step, could you please review your activities and submit to Ms. Lee by April 10 a list of projects. We will then decide which projects stand the best chance of being funded and proceed accordingly.

傳閱文件　　TO：部門主管及研究部門
From：研究部資深副總 Akira Inoue

聯邦政府剛剛已經宣布，在下一個會計年度，將接受來自小型非附屬企業申請補助金，以進行一些尖端科技的研究，及初期產品的研發，其中包括半導體、機器人學、微機器人學，以及雷射應用。不論是設立於美國的公司，或是非美國的公司，都符合申請這些補助金的資格，只是非美國的公司，其所有政府補助的活動，都必須在美國境內進行。詳見所附上的傳閱文件，以了解其他的限制。

我們打算用正在進行的一些計畫，去申請補助金。我們是非美國的公司，所以必須提出一些證明文件，說明我們從事什麼樣的工作，會在哪裡執行，以及負責人是誰。

第一步能不能請你們檢視自己的活動，並在四月十日之前，將計畫的一覽表交給李女士。然後我們會決定，哪些計畫最有機會獲得贊助，然後就照著進行。

---

* memorandum〔ˌmɛmə'rændəm〕 *n.* 備忘錄；（公司內部）傳閱的文件
department〔dɪ'pɑrtmənt〕 *n.* 部門
research〔'risɜtʃ〕 *n.* 研究　　division〔də'vɪʒən〕 *n.* 部門
Sr. V. P. 資深副總（= *Senior Vice President*）
federal〔'fɛdərəl〕 *adj.* 聯邦的　　announce〔ə'nɑʊns〕 *v.* 宣布
fiscal〔'fɪskḷ〕 *adj.* 會計的　　***fiscal year*** 會計年度
application〔ˌæplə'keʃən〕 *n.* 申請；應用
unaffiliated〔ˌʌnə'fɪlɪˌetɪd〕 *adj.* 附屬的　　grant〔grænt〕 *n.* 補助金
conduct〔kən'dʌkt〕 *v.* 進行　　initial〔ɪ'nɪʃəl〕 *adj.* 初期的
development〔dɪ'vɛləpmənt〕 *n.* 開發
frontier〔frʌn'tɪr〕 *adj.* 尖端的
semiconductor〔ˌsɛmɪkən'dʌktɚ〕 *n.* 半導體

robotics (ro'batıks) n. 機器人學　　micro- ('maɪkrə) adj. 微…

laser ('lezə) n. 雷射　　U.S.-based adj. 設立於美國的

firm (fɝm) n. 公司　　eligible ('ɛlɪdʒəbḷ) adj. 合格的

fund (fʌnd) v. 提供資金；贊助　　*carry out* 執行

attached (ə'tætʃd) adj. 附加的　　circular ('sɝkjələ) n. 供傳閱的文件

restriction (rɪ'strɪkʃən) n. 限制　　*apply for* 申請

funding ('fʌndɪŋ) n. 資金　　ongoing ('an,goɪŋ) adj. 進行中的

submit (səb'mɪt) v. 提出；遞交

documentation (,dakjəmɛn'teʃən) n. 文件；證據資料

review (rɪ'vju) v. 檢視　　project ('pradʒɛkt) n. 計畫

stand the best chance of 最有機會　　proceed (prə'sid) v. 進行

accordingly (ə'kɔrdɪŋlɪ) adv. 照著；相應地

48. (**D**) 這個傳閱文件的主旨是什麼？

    (A) 國家安全　　　　　　(B) 會計原則

    (C) 政府規定　　　　　　(D) <u>研究計畫的資金來源</u>

    * security (sɪ'kjʊrətɪ) n. 安全

       practice ('præktɪs) n. 慣例；原則

       regulation (,rɛgjə'leʃən) n. 規定　　source (sors) n. 來源

49. (**B**) 這家公司希望獲得什麼？

    (A) 投資　　　　　　　　(B) <u>政府的援助</u>

    (C) 銀行信用額度　　　　(D) 進口許可

    * investment (ɪn'vɛstmənt) n. 投資

       credit ('krɛdɪt) n. 信用　　import (ɪm'port) n. 輸入；進口

       concession (kən'sɛʃən) n. 許可

50. (**D**) Inoue 先生希望部門經理提供什麼？

    (A) 新計畫的點子　　　　(B) 降低成本

    (C) 人事變動　　　　　　(D) <u>推薦</u>

    * staff (stæf) v. 給…提供職員

       recommendation (,rɛkəmɛn'deʃən) n. 推薦；建議

全民英語能力分級檢定測驗
GENERAL ENGLISH PROFICIENCY TEST
中高級聽力測驗
HIGH-INTERMEDIATE LISTENING COMPREHENSION TEST

This listening comprehension test will test your ability to understand spoken English. In this test, each conversation, short talk and question will be spoken JUST ONE TIME. They will not be written out for you. There are three parts to this test. Special instructions will be given to you at the beginning of each part.

Part A

In part A, you will hear 15 questions. After you hear a question, read the four choices in your test book and decide which one is the best answer to the question you have heard.

Example:

<u>You will hear</u>: Mary, can you tell me what time it is?

<u>You will read</u>: A. About two hours ago.
                     B. I used to be able to, but not now.
                     C. Sure, it's half past nine.
                     D. Today is October 22.

The best answer to the question "Mary, can you tell me what time it is?" is C: "Sure, it's half past nine." Therefore, you should choose answer C.

1. A. The investors are arriving today.
   B. The government is very supportive.
   C. The owner is noble.
   D. They say he ran out of funds.

2. A. Maybe after I complete my education.
   B. It's beyond my control.
   C. I plan to depart next week.
   D. Any return on that investment will be meager.

3. A. Nobody sells pawns anymore.
   B. Yes, but extremely far away.
   C. There's only a few blocks away.
   D. I used to work in a pawn shop.

4. A. Last year I fell while skiing.
   B. Yes, I was in a head-on collision.
   C. It wasn't a work related to mishap.
   D. No, it wasn't by accident.

5. A. That's our new school administrator.
   B. The principal will be here soon.
   C. That's up to the homeroom teacher to decide.
   D. Hallway monitors do security checks.

6. A. It's illegal to make.
   B. Management really frowns on it.
   C. No employee can decide.
   D. I've been trying to quit for years.

7. A. Please don't try too hard.
   B. I hope you'll like my cooking.
   C. That would really be great, thanks.
   D. I'm on my way to the bank.

8. A. I sure did. How did you know it?
   B. They close early on Sunday afternoon.
   C. I went window shopping with friends.
   D. I'll mull over your advice.

9. A. I don't usually try.
   B. I skate a few times a month.
   C. I ski every winter.
   D. As often as possible.

10. A. He regularly maintained the smoke alarms.
    B. He always did, too.
    C. Mr. Jones did a tremendous job.
    D. He was negligent on the job.

Please turn to the next page. ⟹

11. A. I seldom catch a cold.
    B. The temperature is dropping.
    C. No, it's durable.
    D. No, my legs never get cold.

12. A. My schoolwork is so demanding.
    B. Actually it has.
    C. The academic subjects are tough.
    D. I plan to switch majors next semester.

13. A. How much does it cost?
    B. Don't forget to lock the doors.
    C. It'll be no problem at all.
    D. Can you give me a discount?

14. A. I'm as slow as molasses.
    B. I try to be punctual.
    C. It's a bad habit.
    D. I'm not a patient person.

15. A. I greatly admire and respect all teachers.
    B. I'm still attending classes in education.
    C. Yes, I was a teacher once.
    D. I'm a physics major.

Part B

In part B, you will hear 15 conversations between a man and a woman. After each conversation, you will hear a question about the conversation. After you hear the question, read the four choices in your test book and choose the best answer to the question you have heard.

Example:

You will hear: (Man)   May I see your driver's license?
(Woman) Yes, officer. Here it is. Was I speeding?
(Man)   Yes, ma'am. You were doing sixty in a forty-five-mile-an-hour zone.
(Woman) No way! I don't believe you.
(Man)   Well, it is true and here is your ticket.

Question: Why does the man ask for the woman's driver's license?

You will read: A. She was going too fast.
B. To check its limitations.
C. To check her age.
D. She entered a restricted zone.

The best answer to the question "Why does the man ask for the woman's driver's license?" is A: "She was going too fast." Therefore, you should choose answer A.

Please turn to the next page. ⇨

16. A. She devised a memory acronym.
    B. She studied philosophy.
    C. She has a photographic memory.
    D. She lived in Greece before.

17. A. An insect made a noise.
    B. An insect bit them.
    C. The neighbors are noisy.
    D. They both heard a noise.

18. A. They're silly as birds.
    B. They have a lot in common.
    C. Spelling is difficult.
    D. Spelling is strange.

19. A. He was very late.
    B. He got the wrong time.
    C. He lost his job.
    D. He went to the wrong place.

20. A. He's lonely.
    B. He's looking for romance.
    C. He likes the woman he's talking to.
    D. He enjoys being admired.

21. A. Her middle finger is sore.
    B. She feels pressure in her hand.
    C. She has a wart on her finger.
    D. She's got a terrible headache.

22. A. Computer books.
    B. History books.
    C. Politically related books.
    D. Business related books.

23. A. On Tuesday.
    B. On Thursday.
    C. After the weekend.
    D. On Friday.

24. A. A little surprised.
    B. It was a peaceful way to die.
    C. Shocked that it happened.
    D. Close to God.

25. A. Jenny will lose lots of weight.
    B. Jenny's tonsils will be removed.
    C. She'll get to eat ice cream.
    D. She'll be sick for a long time.

26. A. Nobody knows.
    B. It's a secret.
    C. It's a surprise.
    D. An old friend of the man's.

27. A. Not at all.
    B. Yes, a little bit.
    C. Yes, she's my ex-girlfriend.
    D. He ridicules her.

28. A. He wants her to be more polite.
    B. He wants them to work together.
    C. He wants to be called Mr. Johnson.
    D. He wants a more informal relationship.

29. A. Taking a special medicine.
    B. Using pillows on your head.
    C. Having an operation.
    D. Sleeping on a flat surface.

30. A. The electrical system is faulty.
    B. The power cell isn't working.
    C. The key is broken.
    D. The car is too old.

Please turn to the next page. ⇨

Part C

In part C, you will hear several short talks. After each talk, you will hear 2 to 3 questions about the talk. After you hear each question, read the four choices in your test book and choose the best answer to the question you have heard.

Example:

<u>You will hear:</u>

Thank you for coming to this, the first in a series of seminars on the use of computers in the classroom. As the brochure informed you, there will be a total of five seminars given in this room every Monday morning from 6:00 to 7:30. Our goal will be to show you, the teachers of our schoolchildren, how the changing technology of today can be applied to the unchanging lessons of yesterday to make your students' learning experience more interesting and relevant to the world they live in. By the end of the last seminar, you will not be computer literate, but you will be able to make sense of the hundreds of complex words and technical terms related to the field and be aware of the programs available for use in the classroom.

Question number 1: What is the subject of this seminar series?

You will read: A. Self-improvement.
 B. Using computers to teach.
 C. Technology.
 D. Study habits of today's students.

The best answer to the question "What is the subject of this seminar series?" is B: "Using computers to teach." Therefore, you should choose answer B.

Now listen to another question based on the same talk.

You will hear:

 Question number 2: What does the speaker say participants will be able to do after attending the seminars?

You will read: A. Understand today's students.
 B. Understand computer terminology.
 C. Motivate students.
 D. Deal more confidently with people.

The best answer to the question "What does the speaker say participants will be able to do after attending the seminars?" is B: "Understand computer terminology." Therefore, you should choose answer B.

Please turn to the next page. ▯⟩

31. A. Health and medical insurance.
    B. Fire and flood insurance.
    C. Car insurance.
    D. Stocks and bonds.

32. A. A subscription.
    B. An insurance guide.
    C. A coverage manual.
    D. A booklet and a video tape.

33. A. Less stress.
    B. Be healthier.
    C. Lower blood pressure.
    D. No emergencies.

34. A. Sales director.
    B. Quality control agency.
    C. Marketing analyst.
    D. Personnel manager.

35. A. They want to hire him.
    B. They were impressed.
    C. He might be too old.
    D. It wasn't accurate.

36. A. Fifteen years.
    B. A minimum of three.
    C. A maximum of twenty.
    D. Five years.

37. A. At the dentist office.
    B. At the optician.
    C. In a hospital.
    D. At a skin clinic.

38. A. His son was late.
    B. The game went into overtime.
    C. His plane was late.
    D. He got stuck in a traffic jam.

39. A. In 24 hours.
    B. Around 7 a.m.
    C. After 24 hours.
    D. After midnight.

40. A. Help the elderly.
    B. Stock up on supplies.
    C. Drive on the roads.
    D. Secure all windows.

Please turn to the next page. ▯⟹

41. A. Fifty five.
    B. Forty five.
    C. 54 years old.
    D. 44 years old.

42. A. Star Wars.
    B. E.T.
    C. Indiana Jones.
    D. Titanic.

43. A. technical innovations.
    B. black and white
       movies.
    C. creating studios.
    D. martial arts movies.

44. A. More students are
       looking for jobs.
    B. There is a world
       recession.
    C. Jobs went overseas.
    D. Major companies
       went bankrupt.

45. A. Very badly.
    B. No progress at all.
    C. It's rising and falling.
    D. It's very healthy and
       strong.

-The End-

中高級閱讀測驗

HIGH-INTERMEDIATE

READING COMPREHENSION TEST

This test has three parts, with 50 multiple-choice questions (each with four choices) in total. Special directions will be provided for each part. You will have 50 minutes to complete this test.

Part A: Sentence Completion

This part of the test has 15 incomplete sentences. Beneath each sentence, you will see four words or phrases, marked A, B, C and D. You are to choose the word or phrase that best completes the sentences. Then on your answer sheet, find the number of the question and mark your answer.

1. She worked hard at her desk around the clock because she felt sure that the results would _____ her efforts.
   A. justify
   B. testify
   C. rectify
   D. verify

Please turn to the next page. ▯⟹

2. Henry is extremely _____. He associates with people who are part of "the upper classes" and with high social status.
   A. alert
   B. solitary
   C. restless
   D. snobbish

3. The history of the exploration of Antarctica _____ many tales of perseverance and suffering.
   A. undermines
   B. monopolizes
   C. accelerates
   D. recounts

4. At the _____ of her career, she was one of the best known journalists in the U.S.
   A. outset
   B. completion
   C. zenith
   D. provision

5. Ornette Coleman was _____ influential in introducing elements of Black folk music into Jazz.
   A. appropriately
   B. enormously
   C. diversifiedly
   D. uniquely

6. The suspect is being held for arraignment without
   _____.

    A. bail

    B. conviction

    C. jury

    D. detainment

7. People with _____ personalities find it difficult to
   make friends.

    A. outgoing

    B. excessive

    C. spectacular

    D. introverted

8. Very few scientists can _____ with completely new
   answers to the world's problems.

    A. come up

    B. come round

    C. come to

    D. come in

Please turn to the next page. ⟹

9. _____ the fact that his initial experiments had failed, Professor White persisted in his research.

    A. Due to

    B. In spite of

    C. In view of

    D. As to

10. I used to be able to play well, but I'm _____ now.

    A. out of date

    B. out of practice

    C. out of touch

    D. out of place

11. _____, all machines are combinations of simpler machines such as the lever and the pulley.

    A. How complex is not a matter

    B. The matter is complex

    C. It doesn't matter if the complexity

    D. No matter how complex

12. _____ of gift-giving, bartering, buying and selling goes on among the native Indians here.

    A. A great deal

    B. A great many

    C. Much greater

    D. Many

13. It is a widely held theory _____ the ancestral
    prototype of this flowering plant was a woody plant,
    perhaps a small tree.
    A. where
    B. until
    C. while
    D. that

14. Throughout history, the moon has inspired not only song
    and dance _____.
    A. and also poetry and prose
    B. but poetry also prose
    C. together with poetry and prose
    D. but poetry and prose as well

15. _____ that modern corn may be a hybrid of other wild
    species that no longer exist.
    A. Now is thought
    B. Thinking
    C. It is thought
    D. The thought

Please turn to the next page. ⬛⇨

Part B: Cloze

This part of the test has two passages. Each passage contains seven or eight missing words or phrases. There is a total of 15 missing words or phrases. Beneath each passage, you will see seven or eight items with four choices, marked A, B, C and D. You are to choose the best answer for each missing word or phrase in the two passages. Then, on your answer sheet, find the number of the question and mark your answer.

Questions 16-22

Almost all universities in the United States have some form of student government — (16) , students are allowed — even encouraged — to participate in the free election of students to represent them on a Student Council. Last week my roommate Jack said that he was going to (17) student president. I was surprised because, to tell the truth, I don't think Jack would make a good president. Of course, I didn't tell him that. After all, I wanted to stay on (18) terms with him. And so I (19) and said that he would make a good president. Then he told me that he wanted me to be his campaign manager. I said, "No, no, a thousand times no!" Since I am his closest friend, it (20) that he was dismayed by my refusal. He was disappointed and, although he didn't say so, I think he was also angry. Later, when he told me that

his girlfriend said that she would be his manager, I felt a little
___(21)___ . I told myself that perhaps I ___(22)___ . After all,
you never can tell, maybe some day I'll need him to help me.

16. A. on the other hand
    B. that is to say
    C. generally speaking
    D. to begin with

17. A. elect
    B. be chosen
    C. run for
    D. come by

18. A. speaking
    B. talking
    C. telling
    D. saying

19. A. told the truth
    B. spoke ill
    C. talked big
    D. told a white lie

20. A. is no need to say
    B. is needless saying
    C. is obviously
    D. goes without saying

21. A. shy
    B. shame
    C. shameful
    D. ashamed

22. A. must have agreed
    B. should agree
    C. should have agreed
    D. need not have agreed

Please turn to the next page. ⬛⟹

The key to the industrialization of space is the U.S. space shuttle. ___(23)___ it, astronauts will acquire a workhouse vehicle capable of flying into space and returning many times. ___(24)___ by reusable rockets that can lift a load of 65,000 pounds, the shuttle will carry devices for scientific inquiry, as well as a variety of military hardware. But more significantly, it will ___(25)___ materials and machines into space for industrial purposes unimagined four decades ago when "sputnik" (artificial satellite) was added to the vocabulary. In short, the ___(26)___ importance of the shuttle lies in its ___(27)___ as an economic tool.

What makes the space shuttle unique is that it takes off like a rocket but lands like an airplane. ___(28)___, when it has accomplished its ___(29)___, it can be ready for another trip in about two weeks.

The space shuttle, the world's first true spaceship, is a magnificent step ___(30)___ making the impossible possible for the benefit and survival of man.

23. A. In
    B. On
    C. By
    D. With

24. A. Served
    B. Powered
    C. Forced
    D. Reinforced

25. A. supply
    B. introduce
    C. deliver
    D. transfer

26. A. general
    B. essential
    C. prevailing
    D. ultimate

27. A. promise
    B. prosperity
    C. popularity
    D. priority

28. A. Thus
    B. Whereas
    C. Nevertheless
    D. Yet

29. A. venture
    B. mission
    C. commission
    D. responsibility

30. A. for
    B. by
    C. in
    D. through

Please turn to the next page. ⏵

Part C: Reading

In this part of the test, you will read several passages. Each passage is followed by several questions. There is a total of 20 questions. You are to choose the best answer, A, B, C or D, to each question on the basis of what is stated or implied in the passage. Then on your answer sheet, find the number of the question and mark your answer.

Questions 31-33

A noted anthropologist states that humans are basically adapted to life in more primitive environments, with relatively simple technologies. These were environments which called for a closer and more limited relation to the world, which was basically composed of small groups of people, short time periods, and things that were near-at-hand. In these settings, humans learned early to become emotionally attached to their own kin and group and to regard others as "outsiders" toward whom they learned to feel indifferent and hostile. Though humans today still adhere to relatively ancient behavioral forms, these are more suited for survival in sparsely populated environments, in the anthropologist's view, the modern technical world is relatively new, and new customs are vitally needed to meet problems it has created. According to him, the new customs that are so vitally needed today are those which would promote understanding among groups, which would reduce economic and political inequalities among them, and which would solve conflicts among them by non-military means. (以下各題選出一項與上面內容不一致的答案)

31. A. In primitive days, man's interest was primarily directed to things that took place within the boundary of his environment.

   B. In primitive days, man used to think of the world in terms of his limited relation to it.

   C. Since early days, man had been accustomed to thinking of the world as something beyond his own kin and group.

   D. Human beings are able to make themselves suited for life in more primitive environments.

32. A. As the ancient environments were sparsely populated, humans had only to care for their own kin and group.

   B. In primitive days, humans lived in relatively small groups, which were separated from one another.

   C. Even today, man's behavior is still influenced by the forms of primitive days.

   D. The anthropologist maintains that the biggest obstacle to the development of the world has been man's conflicts created by non-military means.

Please turn to the next page. ⟹

33. A. The anthropologist maintains that man has to change
        his traditional behavioral forms, which are suited for
        primitive environments rather than modern ones.
    B. In primitive days, man's knowledge of technology
        was rather poor.
    C. New customs are vitally needed to promote peace and
        understanding among groups.
    D. In sparsely populated ancient environments, humans
        were very much in need of helping one another,
        whether they were their own kin and group or not.

Questions 34-38

   Aimlessness has hardly been typical of the postwar Japan
whose productivity and social harmony are the envy of the
United States and Europe. But increasingly the Japanese are
seeing a decline of the traditional work-moral values. Twenty
years ago young people were hardworking and saw their jobs
as their primary reason for being, but now Japan has largely
fulfilled its economic needs, and young people don't know
where they should go next.

   The coming of age of the postwar baby boom and an entry
of women into the male-dominated job market have limited the
opportunities of teenagers who are already questioning the
heavy personal sacrifices involved in climbing Japan's rigid
social ladder to good schools and jobs. In a recent survey, it
was found that only 24.5 percent of Japanese students were
fully satisfied with school life, compared with 67.2 percent of

students in the United States. In addition, far more Japanese workers expressed dissatisfaction with their jobs than did their counterparts in the 10 other countries surveyed.

While often praised by foreigners for its emphasis on the basics, Japanese education tends to stress test taking and mechanical learning over creativity and self-expression. "Those things that do not show up in the test scores — personality, ability, courage or humanity — are completely ignored," says Toshiki Kaifu, chairman of the ruling Liberal Democratic Party's education committee. "Frustration against this kind of things leads kids to drop out and run wild." Last year Japan experienced 2,125 incidents of school violence, including 929 assaults on teachers. Amid the outcry, many conservative leaders are seeking a return to the prewar emphasis on moral education. Last year Mitsuo Setoyama, who was the education minister, raised eyebrows when he argued that liberal reforms introduced by the American occupation authorities after World War II had weakened the "Japanese morality of respect for parents."

But that may have more to do with Japanese life styles. "In Japan," says educator Yoko Muro, "it's never a question of whether you enjoy your job and your life, but only how much you can endure." With economic growth has come centralization, fully 76 percent of Japan's 119 million citizens live in cities where community and the extended family have been abandoned in favor of isolated, two-generation households.

Please turn to the next page. ▮⟶

Urban Japanese have long endured lengthy commutes (travels to and from work) and crowded living conditions, but as the old group and family values weaken, the discomfort is beginning to tell. In the past decade, the Japanese divorce rate, while still well below that of the United States, has increased by more than 50 percent, and suicides have increased by nearly one-quarter.

34. In the Westerners' eyes, postwar Japan was
    A. under aimless development. B. a positive example.
    C. a rival to the West.   D. on the decline.

35. The underlined word "counterparts" means
    A. many associates.   B. corresponding people.
    C. biggest rivals.   D. enthusiastic supporters.

36. What may chiefly be responsible for the moral decline of Japanese society?
    A. Women's participation in social activities is limited.
    B. More workers are dissatisfied with their jobs.
    C. Excessive emphasis has been placed on the basics.
    D. The life style has been influenced by Western values.

37. Which of the following is true according to the author?
    A. Japanese education is praised for helping the young climb the social ladder.
    B. Japanese education is characterized by mechanical learning as well as creativity.
    C. More stress should be placed on the cultivation of creativity.
    D. Dropping out leads to frustration against test taking.

38. The change in Japanese life style is revealed in the fact that
    A. the young are less tolerant of discomforts in life.
    B. the divorce rate in Japan exceeds that in the U.S.
    C. the Japanese endure more than ever before.
    D. the Japanese appreciate their present life.

Questions 39-42

Science, in practice, depends far less on the experiments it prepares than on the preparedness of the minds of the men who watch the experiments: Sir Isaac Newton supposedly discovered gravity through the fall of an apple. Apples had been falling in many places for centuries and thousands of people had seen them fall. But Newton for years had been curious about the cause of the orbital motion of the moon and planets. What kept them in place? Why didn't they fall out of the sky? The fact that the apple fell down toward the earth and not up into the tree answered the question he had been asking himself about those larger fruits of the heavens, the moon and the planets.

How many men would have considered the possibility of an apple falling up into the tree? Newton did because he was not trying to predict anything. He was just wondering. His mind was ready for the unpredictable. Unpredictability is part of the essential nature of research. If you don't have unpredictable things, you don't have research. Scientists tend to forget this when writing their cut-and-dried reports for the technical journals, but history is filled with examples of it.

Please turn to the next page. ⬅⟹

In talking to some scientists, particularly younger ones, you might gather the impression that they find the "scientific method", a substitute for imaginative thought. I've attended research conferences where a scientist has been asked what he thinks about the advisability of continuing a certain experiment. The scientist has frowned, looked at the graphs, and said "the data are still inconclusive." "We know that," the men from the budget office have said. "But what do you think? Is it worthwhile going on? What do you think we might expect?" The scientist has been shocked at having even been asked to speculate.

What this amounts to, of course, is that the scientist has become the victim of his own writings. He has put forward unquestioned claims so consistently that he not only believes them himself, but has convinced industrial and business management that they are true. If experiments are planned and carried out according to plan as faithfully as the reports in the science journals indicate, then it is perfectly logical for management to expect research to produce results measurable in dollars and cents. It is entirely reasonable for auditors to believe that scientists can keep one eye on the cash register while the other eye is on the microscope. If regularity and conformity to a standard pattern are as desirable to the scientist as the writing of his papers would appear to reflect, the management won't be blamed for discriminating against the "oddballs" among researchers in favor of more conventional thinkers who "work well with the team."

39. The author wants to prove with the example of Isaac Newton that
    A. inquiring minds are more important than scientific experiments.
    B. science advances when fruitful researches are conducted.
    C. scientists seldom forget the essential nature of research.
    D. unpredictability weighs less than prediction in scientific research.

40. The author asserts that scientists
    A. shouldn't replace "scientific method" with imaginative thought.
    B. shouldn't neglect to speculate on unpredictable things.
    C. should write more concise reports for technical journals.
    D. should be confident about their research findings.

41. It seems that some young scientists
    A. have a keen interest in prediction.
    B. often speculate on the future.
    C. think highly of creative thinking.
    D. stick to "scientific method."

42. The author implies that the results of scientific research
    A. may not be as profitable as they are expected.
    B. can be measured in dollars and cents.
    C. rely on conformity to a standard pattern.
    D. are mostly underestimated by management.

Please turn to the next page. ⊏⟩

Questions 43-47

British Columbia is the third largest Canadian province, both in area and population. It is nearly one and half times as large as Texas, and extends 800 miles (1,280 km) north from the United States border. It includes Canada's entire west coast and the islands just off the coast.

Most of British Columbia is mountainous, with long, rugged ranges running north and south. Even the coastal islands are the remains of a mountain range that existed thousands of years ago. During the last Ice Age, this range was scoured by glaciers until most of it was beneath the sea. Its peaks now show as islands scattered along the coast.

The southwestern coastal region has a humid mild marine climate. Sea winds that blow inland from the west are warmed by a current of warm water that flows through the Pacific Ocean. As a result, winter temperatures average above freezing and summers are mild. These warm western winds also carry moisture from the ocean.

The winds from the Pacific meet the mountain barriers of the coastal ranges and the Rocky Mountains. As they rise to cross the mountains, the winds are cooled, and their moisture begins to fall as rain. On some of the western slopes almost 200 inches (500 cm) of rain falls each year.

More than half of British Columbia is <u>heavily</u> forested. On mountain slopes that receive plentiful rainfall, huge Douglas firs rise in towering columns. These forest giants often grow to be as much as 300 feet (90 m) tall, with diameters up to 10 feet (3 m). More lumber is produced from these trees than from any other kind of trees in North America. Hemlock, red cedar, and balsam fir are among the other trees found in British Columbia.

43. With which aspect of British Columbia is the passage primarily concerned?

A. Its people. B. Its culture.

C. Its geography. D. Its history.

44. In which part of British Columbia can a mild climate be found?

A. In the southwest.

B. Inland from the coast.

C. In the north.

D. On the entire west coast.

45. The underlined word "heavily" can be replaced by

A. weightily. B. densely.

C. sluggishly. D. seriously.

Please turn to the next page. ▯⟹

46. Which of the following is NOT mentioned as a tree found in British Columbia?
    A. Hemlock   B. Cedar
    C. Fir   D. Pine

47. Where in the passage does the author mention the effect the mountains have on winds?
    A. Lines 4-5   B. Lines 8-10
    C. Lines 12-13   D. Lines 19-21

Questions 48-50

Acquaint Millions of People with Your Products Fast, Promoting on Cable With CABLE Promotions!

Cable television promotion is fast becoming one of the most widespread and effective mediums for advertising in the world. With an ability to access an international viewership of over 120 million households in North America, Europe, and Asia, Cable Promotions is the world's retail outlet of the air. Cable viewers are affluent, consuming and often impulsive buyers and cable television advertising has far fewer regulations than regular broadcast television.

If you have a product that you want to promote, consider today's technology and the potential it holds for increasing sales. Phone Cable Promotions today at 555-6000. Let us tell you how we can help you double, triple, or even quadruple your sales.

48. What does Cable Promotions say about the cable market?
    A. It is fast growing.
    B. It can send to specific locations.
    C. There are a few licenses still available.
    D. Viewers in cable households are younger than in regular television households.

49. What is an advantage of cable television advertising over regular broadcast television?
    A. It is less regulated.
    B. It accesses more households.
    C. It is available around the clock.
    D. It requires less lead time to arrange.

50. What does the Cable Promotions say it can do for advertisers?
    A. Increase sales by more than 100%.
    B. Put them in touch with retail outlets.
    C. Increase profits by reducing costs.
    D. Put them ahead of the competition.

中高級聽力測驗詳解 ④

PART A

1. (**D**) Why did the owner cancel the project?
   A. The investors are arriving today.
   B. The government is very supportive.
   C. The owner is noble.
   D. They say he ran out of funds.

   * owner ('onɚ) n. 老闆　　cancel ('kænsl̩) v. 取消
     project ('prɑdʒɛkt) n. 計劃　　investor (ɪn'vɛstɚ) n. 投資者
     arrive (ə'raɪv) v. 抵達　　government ('gʌvɚnmənt) n. 政府
     supportive (sə'pɔrtɪv) adj. 支持的
     noble ('nobl̩) adj. 高貴的　　***run out of*** 用完
     fund (fʌnd) n. 資金

2. (**A**) When do you expect to return?
   A. Maybe after I complete my education.
   B. It's beyond my control.
   C. I plan to depart next week.
   D. Any return on that investment will be meager.

   * expect (ɪk'spɛkt) v. 預計
     return (rɪ'tɝn) v. 返回　n. 收益
     complete (kəm'plit) v. 完成
     education (,ɛdʒʊ'keʃən) n. 教育
     beyond *one's* ***control*** 某人無法控制
     depart (dɪ'pɑrt) v. 離開
     investment (ɪn'vɛstmənt) n. 投資
     meager ('migɚ) adj. 不足的

3. (**C**) Is there a pawn shop in the vicinity?

    A. Nobody sells pawns anymore.

    B. Yes, but extremely far away.

    C. There's only a few blocks away.

    D. I used to work in a pawn shop.

    * pawn〔pɔn〕*n.* 典當；典當品　　***pawn shop*** 當鋪

    vicinity〔və'sɪnətɪ〕*n.* 鄰近地區

    sell〔sɛl〕*v.* 賣；出售

    anymore〔'ɛnɪ,mor〕*adv.* (不)再

    extremely〔ɪk'strimlɪ〕*adv.* 非常地

    far away 遙遠的　　block〔blɑk〕*n.* 街區

    used to + *V.* (過去)常常~

4. (**B**) Did you get in an accident?

    A. Last year I fell while skiing.

    B. Yes, I was in a head-on collision.

    C. It wasn't a work related to mishap.

    D. No, it wasn't by accident.

    * ***get in*** 陷入　　accident〔'æksədənt〕*n.* 車禍

    fall〔fɔl〕*v.* 跌倒(動詞三態是：fall-fell-fallen)

    ski〔ski〕*v.* 滑雪

    head-on〔'hɛd'ɑn〕*adj.* 迎面的

    collision〔kə'lɪʒən〕*n.* 碰撞

    work〔wɜk〕*n.* 作品　　***related to*** 和~有關

    mishap〔'mɪs,hæp〕*n.* 事故

    by accident 意外地

5. (**A**) Who's that walking down the hallway?

    A. That's our new school administrator.

    B. The principal will be here soon.

    C. That's up to the homeroom teacher to decide.

    D. Hallway monitors do security checks.

    * hallway ('hɔl,we) n. 走廊
    administrator (əd'mɪnə,stretɚ) n. 行政官員
    principal ('prɪnsəpl̩) n. 校長
    soon (sun) adv. 不久；馬上
    be up to sb. 由~決定   ***homeroom teacher*** 導師
    decide (dɪ'saɪd) v. 決定
    monitor ('mɑnətɚ) n. 監視器
    security (sɪ'kjurətɪ) n. 安全
    check (tʃɛk) n. 檢查

6. (**B**) What's the company policy on cigarette smoking?

    A. It's illegal to make.

    B. Management really frowns on it.

    C. No employee can decide.

    D. I've been trying to quit for years.

    * company ('kʌmpənɪ) n. 公司
    policy ('pɑləsɪ) n. 策略
    cigarette ('sɪgə,rɛt) n. 香煙
    illegal (ɪ'ligl̩) adj. 非法的
    management ('mænɪdʒmənt) n. 管理部門
    frown (fraun) v. 對~不滿 < on >
    employee (,ɛmplɔɪ'i) n. 員工
    quit (kwɪt) v. 戒除

7. (**C**) Let me treat you to a meal.

    A. Please don't try too hard.

    B. I hope you'll like my cooking.

    C. That would really be great, thanks.

    D. I'm on my way to the bank.

    * treat〔trit〕*v.* 請客　　meal〔mil〕*n.* 一餐

      hard〔hɑrd〕*adv.* 努力地

      cooking〔'kʊkɪŋ〕*n.* 烹調；飯菜

      on one's way to 在前往～的途中

8. (**A**) Did you go to the mall last weekend?

    A. I sure did. How did you know it?

    B. They close early on Sunday afternoon.

    C. I went window shopping with friends.

    D. I'll mull over your advice.

    * mall〔mɔl〕*n.* 購物中心

      go window shopping 瀏覽櫥窗

      mull〔mʌl〕*v.* 仔細考慮　　***mull over*** 仔細考慮

      advice〔əd'vaɪs〕*n.* 建議

9. (**D**) How often do you go swimming?

    A. I don't usually try.

    B. I skate a few times a month.

    C. I ski every winter.

    D. As often as possible.

    * skate〔sket〕*v.* 溜冰　　time〔taɪm〕*n.* 次數

      as …as possible 儘可能…

10. (**D**)　Why was Tim Jones fired?

　　A.　He regularly maintained the smoke alarms.

　　B.　He always did, too.

　　C.　Mr. Jones did a tremendous job.

　　D.　He was negligent on the job.

　　* fire﹝faɪr﹞ v. 解僱

　　　regularly﹝'rɛgjələ‧lɪ﹞ adv. 定期地

　　　maintain﹝men'ten﹞ v. 保養；維修

　　　smoke﹝smok﹞ n. 煙霧

　　　alarm﹝ə'lɑrm﹞ n. 警報器

　　　smoke alarm 煙霧警報器

　　　tremendous﹝trɪ'mɛndəs﹞ adj. 很棒的

　　　negligent﹝'nɛglədʒənt﹞ adj. 粗心的；疏忽的

11. (**D**)　Isn't it too cold for shorts?

　　A.　I seldom catch a cold.

　　B.　The temperature is dropping.

　　C.　No, it's durable.

　　D.　No, my legs never get cold.

　　* shorts﹝ʃorts﹞ n. pl. 短褲

　　　seldom﹝'sɛldəm﹞ adv. 很少

　　　catch a cold 感冒

　　　temperature﹝'tɛmprətʃɚ﹞ n. 溫度

　　　drop﹝drɑp﹞ v. 下降

　　　durable﹝'djurəbl̩﹞ adj. 耐用的

　　　leg﹝lɛg﹞ n. 腿

12. (**B**) Has your grade point average steadily improved?

    A. My schoolwork is so demanding.

    B. Actually it has.

    C. The academic subjects are tough.

    D. I plan to switch majors next semester.

    * grade〔gred〕*n.* 分數　　average〔'ævərɪdʒ〕*n.* 平均
    grade point average（學生各科成績的）平均積點分
    steadily〔'stɛdəlɪ〕*adv.* 穩定地
    improve〔ɪm'pruv〕*v.* 進步
    schoolwork〔'skul,wɜk〕*n.* 學校作業
    demanding〔dɪ'mændɪŋ〕*adj.* 讓人感到吃力的
    actually〔'æktʃʊəlɪ〕*adv.* 實際上
    academic〔,ækə'dɛmɪk〕*adj.* 人文學科的（指英語，歷史、
    經濟學）
    subject〔'sʌbdʒɪkt〕*n.* 科目
    academic subjects 文科科目　　tough〔tʌf〕*adj.* 困難的
    switch〔swɪtʃ〕*v.* 變更　　major〔'medʒə〕*n.* 主修
    semester〔sə'mɛstə〕*n.* 學期

13. (**C**) Can I leave my car parked here today?

    A. How much does it cost?

    B. Don't forget to lock the doors.

    C. It'll be no problem at all.

    D. Can you give me a discount?

    * leave〔liv〕*v.* 使～處於某種狀態
    park〔pɑrk〕*v.* 停車
    lock〔lɑk〕*v.* 上鎖　　***no problem*** 沒問題
    at all 一點也（不）　　discount〔'dɪskaʊnt〕*n.* 折扣

14. (**A**) How come you're always late?
  A. I'm as slow as molasses.
  B. I try to be punctual.
  C. It's a bad habit.
  D. I'm not a patient person.

  * ***How come ···?*** 爲什麼···？（接直述句）
  slow〔slo〕*adj.* 緩慢的
  molasses〔məˈlæsɪz〕*n.* 糖蜜
  as slow as molasses 慢得像蝸牛；極端緩慢
  punctual〔ˈpʌŋktʃʊəl〕*adj.* 準時的
  habit〔ˈhæbɪt〕*n.* 習慣
  patient〔ˈpeʃənt〕*adj.* 有耐心的

15. (**C**) Have you ever taught a class before?
  A. I greatly admire and respect all teachers.
  B. I'm still attending classes in education.
  C. Yes, I was a teacher once.
  D. I'm a physics major.

  * teach〔titʃ〕*v.* 教導（三態變化爲：teach-taught-taught）
  greatly〔ˈgretlɪ〕*adv.* 非常地
  admire〔ədˈmaɪr〕*v.* 欽佩
  respect〔rɪˈspɛkt〕*v.* 尊敬
  attend〔əˈtɛnd〕*v.* 上（學）
  once〔wʌns〕*adv.* 曾經
  physics〔ˈfɪzɪks〕*n.* 物理學
  major〔ˈmedʒə〕*n.* 主修學生

PART B.

16. (**A**) M: Who are the three greatest philosophers?

W: That's easy, SPA. S-P-A, it's a memory acronym.

M: What do the letters stand for?

W: Socrates, Plato and Aristotle.

M: Cool memory trick. I'm impressed.

Question: How did she know the answer?

A. She devised a memory acronym.

B. She studied philosophy.

C. She has a photographic memory.

D. She lived in Greece before.

* philosopher (fə'lɑsəfə) n. 哲學家

  memory ('mɛmərɪ) n. 記憶

  acronym ('ækrənɪm) n. 首字母縮略詞；頭字語 (由一複合詞
  　各字的頭一個字母或幾個字母連結而成的字)

  letter ('lɛtə) n. 字母　　***stand for*** 代表

  Socrates ('sɑkrə,tiz) n. 蘇格拉底 (古希臘哲學家)

  Plato ('pleto) n. 柏拉圖 (古希臘哲學家)

  Aristotle ('ærə,stɑtl) n. 亞里斯多德 (古希臘哲學家)

  trick (trɪk) n. 竅門

  impressed (ɪm'prɛst) adj. 印象深刻的

  devise (də'vaɪz) v. 發明

  philosophy (fə'lɑsəfɪ) n. 哲學；哲理

  photographic (,fotə'græfɪk) adj. 極精確的

  Greece (gris) n. 希臘

17. (**D**) W：Did you hear that?

M：Shhhh, listen! Yes, I did!

W：What do you think it was?

M：It sounded like a mouse scurrying across the attic!

W：How about a giant cockroach?!

Question：What happened?

A. An insect made a noise.

B. An insect bit them.

C. The neighbors are noisy.

D. They both heard a noise.

* shh〔ʃ〕 interj. 【命令對方安靜】噓！
  sound like 聽起來像　　mouse〔maʊs〕 n. 鼠
  scurry〔'skɜɪ〕 v. 匆忙地跑　　attic〔'ætɪk〕 n. 閣樓
  giant〔'dʒaɪənt〕 adj. 巨大的
  cockroach〔'kɑk,rotʃ〕 n. 蟑螂
  insect〔'ɪnsɛkt〕 n. 昆蟲　　***make a noise*** 製造噪音
  bite〔baɪt〕 v. 咬（動詞三態是：bite-bit-bitten）
  neighbor〔'nebɚ〕 n. 鄰居　　noisy〔'nɔɪzɪ〕 adj. 吵鬧的

18. (**B**) M：How do you spell weird?

W：Do you mean weird as in strange?

M：Yes, that weird, I always forget its spelling.

W：Me too, now isn't that unusual.

M：I guess we're birds of a feather!

Question：What does the man mean?

A. They're silly as birds.

B. They have a lot in common.

C. Spelling is difficult.

D. Spelling is strange.

* weird〔wɪrd〕*adj.* 奇怪的

strange〔strendʒ〕*adj.* 奇怪的

unusual〔ʌn'juʒʊəl〕*adj.* 不平常的

birds of a feather 同類的人

silly〔'sɪlɪ〕*adj.* 愚笨的　　***in common*** 共同的

difficult〔'dɪfə,kʌlt〕*adj.* 困難的

19. (**D**) W：How was the meeting?

M：I don't know, nobody showed up at the conference room.

W：That's because the meeting is in the conference hall.

M：You mean the big auditorium? Oh no, I goofed up.

W：You should pay more attention to details next time.

Question：What happened to the man?

A. He was very late.

B. He got the wrong time.

C. He lost his job.

D. He went to the wrong place.

* meeting〔'mitɪŋ〕*n.* 會議　　***show up*** 出現

conference〔'kɑnfərəns〕*n.* 會議

conference room 會議室　　***conference hall*** 會議廳

auditorium〔,ɔdə'torɪəm〕*n.* 禮堂；會堂

goof〔guf〕*v.* 出差錯　　***goof up*** 搞砸

pay attention to 注意　　detail〔'ditel〕*n.* 細節

20. (**C**)　M：I just received a mystery letter.

W：What did it say?

M：Lots of romantic and mushy stuff.

W：I guess you have a secret admirer.

M：I wish it were you.

Question：What is the man really saying?

A.　He's lonely.

B.　He's looking for romance.

C.　He likes the woman he's talking to.

D.　He enjoys being admired.

* receive (rɪ'siv) v. 收到
 mystery ('mɪstərɪ) adj. 神祕的
 romantic (ro'mæntɪk) adj. 浪漫的
 mushy ('mʌʃɪ) adj. 談情說愛的；肉麻的
 stuff (stʌf) n. 事情　　guess (gɛs) v. 猜測
 secret ('sikrɪt) adj. 祕密的
 admirer (əd'maɪrɚ) n. 愛慕者
 lonely ('lonlɪ) adj. 寂寞的　　*look for* 尋找
 romance (ro'məns) n. 浪漫
 admire (əd'maɪr) v. 讚賞

21. (**A**)　W：I have a huge blister on my middle finger.

M：What from?

W：From pressing too hard on my pen when I
　　take notes.

M：It's time to get a laptop computer.

W：You're right.　I can type notes in class.

Question: What is ailing the woman?

A. Her middle finger is sore.

B. She feels pressure in her hand.

C. She has a wart on her finger.

D. She's got a terrible headache.

* blister ('blɪstə) n. 水泡　　*middle finger* 中指
press (prɛs) v. 壓　　hard (hɑrd) adv. 用力地
take notes 做筆記　　laptop ('læptɑp) n. 筆記型電腦
type (taɪp) v. 打字　　ail (el) v. 使痛苦
sore (sor) adj. 疼痛的　　pressure ('prɛʃə) n. 壓力
wart (wɔrt) n. 腫瘤　　headache ('hɛd,ek) n. 頭痛

22. (**D**) M: Where are the books on accounting and economics?

W: They are down that aisle over there, next to the wall.

M: Thanks, I appreciate your help.

Question: What does the man want?

A. Computer books.

B. History books.

C. Politically related books.

D. Business related books.

* accounting (ə'kaʊntɪŋ) n. 會計
economics (,ikə'nɑmɪks) n. 經濟學
aisle (aɪl) n. 走道　　appreciate (ə'priʃɪ,et) v. 感激
history ('hɪstrɪ) n. 歷史
politically (pə'lɪtɪkl̩ɪ) adj. 政治上
related (rɪ'letɪd) adj. 相關的

23. (**C**) W：Do you have any more questions?

M：Yes, when will I be notified about your decision?

W：We'll get back to you on Monday.

M：That's it for me, no more questions. Thank you so much.

W：It's been a real pleasure.

Question：When will he find out if he got the job?

A. On Tuesday. B. On Thursday.

C. After the weekend. D. On Friday.

* notify〔ˈnotə͵faɪ〕*v.* 通知 decision〔dɪˈsɪʒən〕*n.* 決定
pleasure〔ˈplɛʒɚ〕*n.* 快樂的事 ***find out*** 知道

24. (**B**) M：How did she pass away?

W：She died peacefully in her sleep.

M：That's a blessing in a way.

W：I agree, she was almost 100. She was pretty healthy until last year.

M：God bless her. Let's hope she's in a better place.

Question：How do they feel about the lady's death?

A. A little surprised. B. It was a peaceful way to die.

C. Shocked that it happened.

D. Close to God.

* ***pass away*** 去世 die〔daɪ〕*v.* 死亡
peacefully〔ˈpisfəlɪ〕*adv.* 平靜地
blessing〔ˈblɛsɪŋ〕*n.* 祝福 ***in a way*** 在某種程度上
healthy〔ˈhɛlθɪ〕*adj.* 健康的 bless〔blɛs〕*v.* 賜福
shocked〔ʃɑkt〕*adj.* 震驚的 ***close to*** 接近

25. (**B**) W : Jenny is going to have an operation.

M : I'm sorry to hear that. What's the matter?

W : She's having her tonsils taken out.

M : That's not major surgery, is it?

W : Actually, it's an extremely simple procedure.

Question : What is going to happen?

A. Jenny will lose lots of weight.

B. Jenny's tonsils will be removed.

C. She'll get to eat ice cream.

D. She'll be sick for a long time.

* operation〔͵ɑpəˊreʃən〕*n.* 手術

What's the matter? 發生了什麼事？

tonsil〔ˊtɑnslｌ〕*n.* 扁桃腺

take out 取出　　major〔ˊmedʒɚ〕*adj.* 重大的

surgery〔ˊsɝdʒɪrɪ〕*n.*（外科）手術

simple〔ˊsɪmplｌ〕*adj.* 簡單的

procedure〔prəˊsidʒɚ〕*n.* 步驟

lose weight 減輕體重

remove〔rɪˊmuv〕*v.* 去除

26. (**D**) M : Who's coming to dinner?

W : It's a secret. Don't make me tell!

M : Please don't make me guess. We don't have time.

W : It's an old friend of yours. He or she wants to
surprise you.

M : Now, I'm really curious!

Question：Who's coming to dinner?

A. Nobody knows.　　B. It's a secret.

C. It's a surprise.　　D. An old friend of the man's.

* secret〔'sikrɪt〕n. 祕密　　guess〔gɛs〕v. 猜
surprise〔sə'praɪz〕v. 使驚訝　n. 驚喜
curious〔'kjʊrɪəs〕adj. 好奇的

27.（ **A** ）W：The city mayor is a joke.

M：Why do you say that?

W：He's all talk and no action.

M：I disagree, I think he tries hard.

W：Don't be misled.　The media just loves him too much.

Question：Does the woman like the mayor?

A. Not at all.　　　B. Yes, a little bit.

C. Yes, she's my ex-girlfriend.

D. He ridicules her.

* mayor〔'meɚ〕n. 市長　　joke〔dʒok〕n. 笑柄
action〔'ækʃən〕n. 行動　　disagree〔,dɪsə'gri〕v. 不同意
mislead〔mɪs'lid〕v. 誤導（動詞三態是：mislead-misled-
misled）　　media〔'midɪə〕n. 媒體（medium 的複數）
ex-girlfriend〔'ɛks'gɝlfrɛnd〕n. 前女友
ridicule〔'rɪdɪ,kjul〕v. 嘲笑

28.（ **D** ）M：Please check this inventory for any errors.

W：Yes, sir, anything else?

M：Yes, don't be so formal.　We're colleagues.　You're
part of our team.

W：OK, Mr. Johnson, I understand.

M：There you go again. No formalities, please, just call me Edward.

Question：What does the man want?

A. He wants her to be more polite.

B. He wants them to work together.

C. He wants to be called Mr. Johnson.

D. He wants a more informal relationship.

* inventory ('ɪnvən,tɔrɪ) *n.* 存貨清單

error ('ɛrɚ) *n.* 錯誤　　formal ('fɔrml̩) *adj.* 正式的

colleague ('kɑlig) *n.* 同事

There you go again. 你又來了。

formality (fɔr'mælətɪ) *n.* 禮節；繁文縟節

polite (pə'laɪt) *adj.* 有禮貌的

informal (ɪn'fɔrml̩) *adj.* 不正式的

relationship (rɪ'leʃən,ʃɪp) *n.* 關係

29. (**A**) W：My husband snores like a hippo. What can I do?

M：Have you tried medications?

W：Do you want me to poison him? Just kidding.

M：I heard there was a new drug that can loosen the throat.

W：Is a tight throat the reason why people snore?

Question：What is a possible snoring remedy?

A. Taking a special medicine.

B. Using pillows on your head.

C. Having an operation.

D. Sleeping on a flat surface.

* snore ﹝ snor ﹞ v. 打呼
  hippo ﹝'hɪpo ﹞ n. 河馬 (= hippopotamus)
  medication ﹝ ˏmɛdɪ'keʃən ﹞ n. 藥物治療
  poison ﹝'pɔɪzn̩ ﹞ v. 毒死　　drug ﹝ drʌg ﹞ n. 藥
  loosen ﹝'lusn̩ ﹞ v. 放鬆　　throat ﹝ θrot ﹞ n. 喉嚨
  tight ﹝ taɪt ﹞ adj. 緊的　　remedy ﹝'rɛmədɪ ﹞ n. 治療
  pillow ﹝'pɪlo ﹞ n. 枕頭　　flat ﹝ flæt ﹞ adj. 平的
  surface ﹝'sɝfɪs ﹞ n. 表面

30. (**B**)　M：Need a hand? I used to be a mechanic.

W：Oh, thank God, you're a life saver.

M：Try turning the key again, I think your battery is dead.

W：OK, here goes. What's that clicking noise?

M：It's definitely a dead battery.

Question：Why won't her car start?

A. The electrical system is faulty.

B. The power cell isn't working.

C. The key is broken.

D. The car is too old.

* mechanic ﹝ mə'kænɪk ﹞ n. 機械工
  life saver 救命恩人　　battery ﹝'bætərɪ ﹞ n. 電池
  dead ﹝ dɛd ﹞ adj. (電池) 沒電的　　click ﹝ klɪk ﹞ v. 發出喀嚓聲
  definitely ﹝'dɛfənɪtlɪ ﹞ adv. 肯定地
  electrical ﹝ ɪ'lɛktrɪkl̩ ﹞ adj. 電的
  system ﹝'sɪstəm ﹞ n. 系統　　faulty ﹝'fɔltɪ ﹞ adj. 有缺陷的
  cell ﹝ sɛl ﹞ n. 電池　　work ﹝ wɝk ﹞ v. 運作
  broken ﹝'brokən ﹞ adj. 折斷的

PART C

Questions 31-33 refer to the following advertisement.

Are you fully prepared for any unexpected accident? Are your financial savings enough to cover any unforeseen medical emergency? If not, give Red Shield Medical Insurance Company a call and we'll make sure you're prepared. We'll cover and protect you and your loved ones from any misfortune, and we'll do it at extremely low and reasonable rates. We offer health, medical, life and accident insurance. Call us now for an information booklet and we'll send you a free video tape as well. We have many plans and many policies that will interest you. Buy that "peace of mind" today and relax. We'll take care of you.

Vocabulary

prepared (prɪˈpɛrd) adj. 準備好的
unexpected (ˌʌnɪkˈspɛktɪd) adj. 意想不到的
financial (faɪˈnænʃəl) adj. 財務的
saving (ˈsevɪŋ) n. 存款   cover (ˈkʌvɚ) v. (錢)足夠付~
unforeseen (ˌʌnforˈsin) adj. 預料不到的；意外的
medical (ˈmɛdɪkḷ) adj. 醫療的
emergency (ɪˈmɝdʒənsɪ) n. 緊急情況

give ~ a call 打電話給~　　　shield〔ʃild〕n. 盾

insurance〔ɪnˈʃʊrəns〕n. 保險　　make sure 確定

protect〔prəˈtɛkt〕v. 保護

misfortune〔mɪsˈfɔrtʃən〕n. 不幸

reasonable〔ˈriznəbḷ〕adj. 合理的　　rate〔ret〕n. 費用

information〔ˌɪnfəˈmeʃən〕n. 資料

booklet〔ˈbʊklɪt〕n. 小冊子　　free〔fri〕adj. 免費的

video tape 錄影帶　　as well 同時

policy〔ˈpɑləsɪ〕n. 保險單　　interest〔ˈɪntrɪst〕v. 使感興趣

peace〔pis〕n. 安心　　mind〔maɪnd〕n. 心

relax〔rɪˈlæks〕v. 放輕鬆　　take care of 照顧

31. (**A**)　What is the company selling?

　　A.　Health and medical insurance.

　　B.　Fire and flood insurance.

　　C.　Car insurance.

　　D.　Stocks and bonds.

　　* flood〔flʌd〕n. 水災　　stock〔stɑk〕n. 股票
　　　bond〔bɑnd〕n. 公債

32. (**D**)　What will they send you for free?

　　A.　A subscription.

　　B.　An insurance guide.

　　C.　A coverage manual.

　　D.　A booklet and a video tape.

　　* for free 免費　　subscription〔səbˈskrɪpʃən〕n. 訂購契約
　　　guide〔gaɪd〕n. 指南　　coverage〔ˈkʌvərɪdʒ〕n. 保險項目
　　　manual〔ˈmænjʊəl〕n. 手冊

33. (**A**) What is a benefit of having a policy?
   A. Less stress.
   B. Be healthier.
   C. Lower blood pressure.
   D. No emergencies.

   * benefit ('bɛnəfɪt) *n.* 好處   stress (strɛs) *n.* 壓力
   blood pressure 血壓

Questions 34-36 are based on the following letter.

Dear Mr. Lee,

   We received your application for the position of marketing analyst and after having given it careful consideration, it is with regret that we must inform you that we cannot offer you employment at this time.

   Although we were impressed by your résumé, we are looking for someone with a minimum of five years direct experience in marketing for this position.

   We will keep your résumé on file in case a position opens up for which you are qualified. Please keep us informed of any change in your employment status. Thank you for your interest in our company.

🖥 Vocabulary

application〔͵æplə'keʃən〕*n.* 申請

position〔pə'zɪʃən〕*n.* 職位

marketing〔'mɑrkɪtɪŋ〕*n.* 行銷   analyst〔'ænḷɪst〕*n.* 分析師

consideration〔kən͵sɪdə'reʃən〕*n.* 考慮

regret〔rɪ'grɛt〕*n.* 遺憾

inform〔ɪn'fɔrm〕*v.* 通知   offer〔'ɔfɚ〕*v.* 提供

employment〔ɪm'plɔɪmənt〕*n.* 雇用;工作

resume〔͵rɛzju'me〕*n.* 履歷

minimum〔'mɪnəməm〕*n.* 最小量

direct〔də'rɛkt〕*adj.* 直接的

experience〔ɪk'spɪrɪəns〕*n.* 經驗   *on file* 存檔

in case 假使   qualify〔'kwɑlə͵faɪ〕*v.* 使合格

informed〔ɪn'fɔrmd〕*adj.* 消息靈通的

status〔'stetəs〕*n.* 狀況

34. (**C**) What position was applied for?

    A. Sales director.

    B. Quality control agency.

    C. Marketing analyst.

    D. Personnel manager.

    * *apply for* 申請   sales〔selz〕*adj.* 銷售的

    director〔də'rɛktɚ〕*n.* 主管

    quality〔'kwɑlətɪ〕*n.* 品質   control〔kən'trol〕*n.* 控制

    agency〔'edʒənsɪ〕*n.* 局;處

    personnel〔͵pɝsṇ'ɛl〕*n.* 人事部門

    manager〔'mænɪdʒɚ〕*n.* 經理

35. (**B**) How did they feel about Mr. Lee's résumé?

    A. They want to hire him.

    B. They were impressed.

    C. He might be too old.

    D. It wasn't accurate.

    * hire〔haɪr〕*v.* 雇用

      impressed〔ɪm'prɛst〕*adj.* 印象深刻的

      accurate〔'ækjərɪt〕*adj.* 精確的

36. (**D**) How much experience did they want a person to have?

    A. Fifteen years.

    B. A minimum of three.

    C. A maximum of twenty.

    D. Five years.

    * maximum〔'mæksəməm〕*n.* 最大量

Questions 37-38 refer to the following talk.

    Morning, Mr. Jones, please take a seat. Dr. Jenkins will be about 15 minutes late. He just called from the airport. His flight was delayed this morning and he told me to go ahead and start cleaning your teeth. Dr. Jenkins flew across the state yesterday to see his son's basketball game. His boy is a star player in his university team. Dr. Jenkins is a big sports fan. OK, please open up.

💻 Vocabulary

take a seat 坐下　　delay〔dɪ'le〕v. 延誤

go ahead 開始　　*fly across* 飛越

state〔stet〕n. 國土　　star〔stɑr〕adj. 優秀的

university〔,junə'vɝsətɪ〕n. 大學　　team〔tim〕n. 隊伍

a big sports fan 忠實球迷　　*open up* 打開

37. (**A**)　Where are they?

A.　At the dentist office.

B.　At the optician.

C.　In a hospital.

D.　At a skin clinic.

* dentist〔'dɛntɪst〕n. 牙醫

optician〔ɑp'tɪʃən〕n. 眼鏡商

clinic〔'klɪnɪk〕n. 診所

38. (**C**)　Why was the doctor late?

A.　His son was late.

B.　The game went into overtime.

C.　His plane was late.

D.　He got stuck in a traffic jam.

* *go into* 進入

overtime〔'ovɚ,taɪm〕n.（比賽中賽成和局後的）延長時間

get stuck 受困　　*traffic jam* 交通阻塞

Questions 39-40 refer to the following report.

> This is the WKBW weather. We have an emergency storm warning in effect for the next 24 hours. Typhoon Terry is expected to hit land at about 1 a.m. this evening. Winds are estimated at over 70 miles per hour. All coastal residents are advised to evacuate if possible. If not, please board up your windows and stock up on extra water, flashlights and food supplies. If you know people living alone, especially senior citizens, please help them out. This is a big one, folks, please stay off the roads and be extra cautious. Stay tuned for more typhoon updates every half an hour.

🖥 Vocabulary

report〔rɪˈport〕 *n.* 報導

weather〔ˈwɛðɚ〕 *n.* 氣象

emergency〔ɪˈmɝdʒənsɪ〕 *adj.* 緊急的

storm〔storm〕 *n.* 暴風雨

warning〔ˈwɔrnɪŋ〕 *n.* 警告　　***in effect*** 有效的

typhoon〔taɪˈfun〕 *n.* 颱風

be expected to 預定　　hit〔hɪt〕 *v.* 侵襲

land〔 lænd 〕 *n.* 陸地

estimate〔ˈɛstə,met 〕 *v.* 估計

mile〔 maɪl 〕 *n.* 哩   per〔 pɝ 〕 *prep.* 每

coastal〔ˈkostl̩ 〕 *adj.* 海岸的

resident〔ˈrɛzədənt 〕 *n.* 居民

advise〔 ədˈvaɪz 〕 *v.* 建議

evacuate〔 ɪˈvækju,et 〕 *v.* 從～離去

board up 封死   ***stock up*** 囤積 < *on* >

extra〔ˈɛkstrə 〕 *adj.* 額外的   *adv.* 特別地

flashlight〔ˈflæʃ,laɪt 〕 *n.* 手電筒

supplies〔 səˈplaɪz 〕 *n. pl.* 補給品

alone〔 əˈlon 〕 *adv.* 單獨地

especially〔 əˈspɛʃəlɪ 〕 *adv.* 特別地

senior〔ˈsinjɚ 〕 *adj.* 年長的

citizen〔ˈsɪtəzn̩ 〕 *n.* 居民

help out 幫助   folks〔 foks 〕 *n. pl.* 各位

off〔 ɔf 〕 *prep.* 離開   cautious〔ˈkɔʃəs 〕 *adj.* 小心的

tuned〔 tjund 〕 *adj.* 調好（收音機）頻道的

update〔ˈʌp,det 〕 *n.* 最新資訊

39. (**D**) When is the typhoon expected?

    A. In 24 hours.

    B. Around 7 a.m.

    C. After 24 hours.

    D. After midnight.

* around〔 əˈraʊnd 〕 *adv.* 大約

  midnight〔ˈmɪd,naɪt 〕 *n.* 午夜

40. (**C**) What should people NOT do?
     A. Help the elderly.
     B. Stock up on supplies.
     C. Drive on the roads.
     D. Secure all windows.

     * elderly (ˈɛldəlɪ) *n.* 老人
      secure (sɪˈkjur) *v.* 關好 (門窗)

Questions 41-43 refer to the following article.

Steven Spielberg, the motion-picture director is a Hollywood icon, whose name is synonymous with successful, and high quality entertainment. He has directed such brilliant movies as Star Wars, E.T., Jaws, and Indiana Jones movies. His direction and creativity almost guarantee that his films will be exceptional. But, very few people realize that his true expertise lies in the technical innovations he has pioneered. Spielberg has worked very hard to develop realistic and creative movies. He is a 55-year-old genius who is already noted as the greatest film maker in history. Our hats are off to this motion-picture giant.

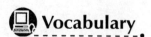 **Vocabulary**

Steven Spielberg 史蒂芬・史匹柏 (美國知名導演)

motion-picture (ˈmoʃənˈpɪktʃə) adj. 電影的

director (dəˈrɛktə) n. 導演

Hollywood (ˈhɑlɪˌwud) n. 好萊塢 (美國洛杉磯市的一區)

icon (ˈaɪkɑn) n. 偶像

synonymous (sɪˈnɑnəməs) adj. 同義的

successful (səkˈsɛsfəl) adj. 成功的

entertainment (ˌɛntəˈtenmənt) n. 娛樂

direct (dəˈrɛkt) v. 導演

brilliant (ˈbrɪljənt) adj. 精彩的

Star Wars 星際大戰 (電影名)

E.T. 外星人 (電影名)　　　***Jaws*** 大白鯊 (電影名)

Indiana Jones 聖戰奇兵

direction (dəˈrɛkʃən) n. 導演

creativity (ˌkrieˈtɪvətɪ) n. 創造力

guarantee (ˌgærənˈti) v. 保證　　film (fɪlm) n. 電影

exceptional (ɪkˈsɛpʃənḷ) adj. 出眾的

realize (ˈriəˌlaɪz) v. 了解

expertise (ˌɛkspəˈtiz) n. 專門技術　　***lie in*** 在於

technical (ˈtɛknɪkḷ) adj. 技術性的

innovation (ˌɪnəˈveʃən) n. 創新

pioneer (ˌpaɪəˈnɪr) v. 率先 (做) ～

develop (dɪˈvɛləp) v. 發展

realistic (ˌriəˈlɪstɪk) adj. 實際的

creative (krɪˈetɪv) adj. 有創意的

genius (ˈdʒinjəs) n. 天才

be noted as 以～（身份）著名

hat〔hæt〕*n.* 帽子　　off〔ɔf〕*adv.* 脫離

Our hats are off to sb. 我們向某人脫帽致敬

giant〔'dʒaɪənt〕*n.* 巨人；傑出人物

41.（ **A** ）How old is Mr. Spielberg?

　　A. Fifty five.

　　B. Forty five.

　　C. 54 years old.

　　D. 44 years old.

42.（ **D** ）Which movie was NOT mentioned?

　　A. Star Wars.

　　B. E.T.

　　C. Indiana Jones.

　　D. Titanic.

　　* mention〔'mɛnʃən〕*v.* 提到

　　　Titanic 鐵達尼號（電影名）

43.（ **A** ）Steven Spielberg is an expert in

　　A. technical innovations.

　　B. black and white movies.

　　C. creating studios.

　　D. martial arts movies.

　　* expert〔'ɛkspɜt〕*n.* 專家

　　　black and white 黑白的　　create〔krɪ'et〕*v.* 創造

　　　studio〔'stjudɪ,o〕*n.* 攝影棚　　*martial arts* 武術

Questions 44-45 *refer to the following government report.*

　　The GIO, which stands for the government
information office, released third quarter employment
statistics today, which cover July through September.
The bad news is that unemployment rose from 5.5 to
5.9 percent during this period. The main reason was
a large increase in labor force applicants. This is
mainly attributed to recent college graduates entering
the work force. On the other hand, the economy is
still going strong as the stock market rose over 200
points in the last two months.

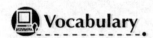 **Vocabulary**

government (ˈgʌvənmənt) *n.* 政府
GIO 行政院新聞局全球資訊網 (= *government information office*)
stand for 代表
release (rɪˈlis) *v.* 發表 (新聞)
quarter (ˈkwɔrtə) *n.* 一季　　***third quarter*** 第三季的
employment (ɪmˈplɔɪmənt) *n.* 就業
statistics (stəˈtɪstɪks) *n. pl.* 統計　　cover (ˈkʌvə) *v.* 涵蓋
unemployment (ˌʌnɪmˈplɔɪmənt) *n.* 失業
rise (raɪz) *v.* 上升　　percent (pəˈsɛnt) *n.* 百分之一
period (ˈpɪrɪəd) *n.* 期間　　main (men) *adj.* 主要的

reason (´rizn̩) *n.* 理由

increase (´ɪnkris) *n.* 增加　(ɪn´kris) *v.* 增加

labor force 勞動力　applicant (´æpləkənt) *n.* 申請人

mainly (´menlɪ) *adv.* 主要地

attribute (ə´trɪbjut) *v.* 歸因於　recent (´risn̩t) *adj.* 近來的

college (´kɑlɪdʒ) *n.* 大學　graduate (´grædʒuɪt) *n.* 畢業生

enter (´ɛntɚ) *v.* 進入；加入　**the work force** （總）勞動力

on the other hand 另一方面　economy (ɪ´kɑnəmɪ) *n.* 經濟

strong (strɔŋ) *adj.* 行情看漲的

stock market 股市　point (pɔɪnt) *n.* 點

44. (**A**) Why did unemployment increase?

　　A. More students are looking for jobs.

　　B. There is a world recession.

　　C. Jobs went overseas.

　　D. Major companies went bankrupt.

　　* recession (rɪ´sɛʃən) *n.* 不景氣

　　　overseas (´ovɚ´siz) *adv.* 到海外

　　　major (´medʒɚ) *adj.* 較大的；較重要的

　　　bankrupt (´bæŋkrʌpt) *adj.* 破產的

45. (**D**) How is the economy doing?

　　A. Very badly.

　　B. No progress at all.

　　C. It's rising and falling.

　　D. It's very healthy and strong.

　　* progress (´prɑgrɛs) *n.* 進步　fall (fɔl) *v.* 下降

中高級閱讀測驗詳解 ④

PART A：Sentence Completion

1. (**A**) She worked hard at her desk around the clock because she felt sure that the results would <u>justify</u> her efforts.

她不分晝夜在辦公桌前工作，因為她確信成果會<u>證明</u>她的努力沒有白費。

(A) **justify** (ˈdʒʌstəˌfaɪ) v. 證明～為正當的

(B) testify (ˈtɛstəˌfaɪ) v. 作證；表示 (= *show*)

(C) rectify (ˈrɛktəˌfaɪ) v. 修正；矯正 (= *correct*)

(D) verify (ˈvɛrəˌfaɪ) v. 確認 (= *make sure*)

* **around the clock** 不分晝夜；日以繼夜

result (rɪˈzʌlt) n. (事情的)結果；收場

effort (ˈɛfət) n. 努力

2. (**D**) Henry is extremely <u>snobbish</u>. He associates with people who are part of "the upper classes" and with high social status.

亨利很<u>勢利眼</u>。他只跟「上流社會」、社會地位高的人來往。

(A) alert (əˈlɝt) adj. 機警的

(B) solitary (ˈsɑləˌtɛrɪ) adj. 單獨的 (= *alone*)；孤立的

(C) restless (ˈrɛstlɪs) adj. 無休止的；急躁的

(D) **snobbish** (ˈsnɑbɪʃ) adj. 勢利眼的

* extremely (ɪkˈstrimlɪ) adv. 極；非常

associate with ～ 跟～來往

the upper class 上流社會   **social status** 社會地位

3. (**D**) The history of the exploration of Antarctica <u>recounts</u> many tales of perseverance and suffering.

南極洲的探險史，<u>描述</u>許多毅力和受苦受難的故事。

(A) undermine〔͵ʌndɚ'maɪn〕 v. 挖地基；破壞

(B) monopolize〔mə'nɑpl͵aɪz〕 v. 壟斷；占爲己有

(C) accelerate〔æk'sɛlə͵ret〕 v. 加速（↔ decelerate 減速）

(D) **recount**〔rɪ'kaʊnt〕 v. 描述（= describe）；細說

* exploration〔͵ɛksplə'reʃən〕 n. 探險

Antarctica〔ænt'ɑrktɪkə〕 n. 南極洲　　tale〔tel〕 n. 故事

perseverance〔͵pɝsə'vɪrəns〕 n. 毅力

suffering〔'sʌfərɪŋ〕 n. 受苦受難

4. (**C**) At the <u>zenith</u> of her career, she was one of the best known journalists in the U.S.

在她事業的<u>巔峰</u>時，她是美國最知名的記者之一。

(A) outset〔'aʊt͵sɛt〕 n. 一開始

(B) completion〔kəm'pliʃən〕 n. 完成　　complete v.

(C) **zenith**〔'zinɪθ〕 n. 頂點；巔峰（= top）

at the zenith of～ 在～巔峰（= at the top of～）

(D) provision〔prə'vɪʒən〕 n. 準備（= preparation）

* career〔kə'rɪr〕 n. 事業　　journalist〔'dʒɝnl͵ɪst〕 n. 記者

5. (**B**) Ornette Coleman was <u>enormously</u> influential in introducing elements of Black folk music into Jazz.

把黑人民俗音樂的基本要素引進到爵士樂裡面，歐尼柯文有<u>極大</u>的影響力。

(A) appropriately〔ə'proprɪ,etlɪ〕*adv.* 適當地 (= *properly*)

(B) *enormously*〔ɪ'nɔrməslɪ〕*adv.* 極大地 (= *tremendously*)

(C) diversifiedly〔daɪ'vɝsə,faɪdlɪ〕*adv.* 多變化地

(D) uniquely〔ju'niklɪ〕*adv.* 獨特地；特有地

* influential〔,ɪnflu'ɛnʃəl〕*adj.* 有影響力的

introduce〔,ɪntrə'djus〕*v.* 引進

element〔'ɛləmənt〕*n.* 要素   *folk music* 民俗音樂

Jazz〔dʒæz〕*n.* 爵士樂

6. (**A**) The suspect is being held for arraignment without <u>bail</u>.

嫌疑犯被留下來等候傳訊，不得<u>保釋</u>。

(A) *bail*〔bel〕*n.* 保釋；保釋金

(B) conviction〔kən'vɪkʃən〕*n.* 堅信；信念

(C) jury〔'dʒurɪ〕*n.* 陪審團（集合名詞，字尾不加複數的 s）

(D) detainment〔dɪ'tenmənt〕*n.* 拘留；扣押

* suspect〔'sʌspɛkt〕*n.* 嫌疑犯   hold〔hold〕*v.* 拘留；扣留

arraignment〔ə'renmənt〕*n.* （被告）傳訊

7. (**D**) People with <u>introverted</u> personalities find it difficult to

make friends. 個性<u>內向</u>者，很難交到朋友。

(A) outgoing〔'aut,goɪŋ〕*adj.* （個性）外向的；離去的

(B) excessive〔ɪk'sɛsɪv〕*adj.* 過度的

(C) spectacular〔spɛk'tækjələ˞〕*adj.* 壯觀的

(D) *introverted*〔,ɪntrə'vɝtɪd〕*adj.* 內向的

(↔ *extroverted* 外向的)

* personality〔,pɝsn̩'ælətɪ〕*n.* 個性   *make friends* 交朋友

8. (**A**) Very few scientists can <u>come up</u> with completely new answers to the world's problems.

世上的各種問題，幾乎沒有科學家可以<u>想到</u>全新的解決之道。

(A) ***come up with*** （人）想到（想法、解答）

(B) come round 甦醒 (= *come around* = *come to*)；
順道過來

(C) come to 甦醒

(D) come in 進來；到達；得獎

* completely 〔kəm'plitlɪ〕 *adv.* 完全地

9. (**B**) <u>In spite of</u> the fact that his initial experiments had failed, Professor White persisted in his research.

<u>儘管</u>懷特教授起初的實驗都失敗了，他還是堅持繼續研究下去。

(A) due to 由於 (= *owing to* = *because of* = *in view of*)

(B) ***in spite of*** 儘管 (= *despite*)

(C) in view of 由於

(D) as to 至於 (= *as for*)

* initial 〔ɪ'nɪʃəl〕 *adj.* 起初的
experiment 〔ɪk'spɛrəmənt〕 *n.* 實驗
persist 〔pɚ'sɪst〕 *v.* 堅持　　research 〔'risɝtʃ〕 *n.* 研究

10. (**B**) I used to be able to play well, but I'm <u>out of practice</u> now.

我以前球打得相當好，但是現在已經<u>疏於練習</u>。

(A) out of date 過時的 (= *outdated*) (↔ up-to-date 現代的)

(B) ***out of practice*** 缺乏練習 (↔ *in practice* 經常練習)

(C) out of touch 失去聯絡 (↔ *in touch* 保持聯絡)

(D) out of place 不適當的 (↔ *in place* 適當的)

* ***used to*** 以前

11. (**D**) No matter how complex, all machines are combinations of simpler machines such as the lever and the pulley.

無論有多複雜，所有機器都是簡單機械如槓桿和滑輪的組合。

* 此空格是副詞子句 *No matter how complex machines are*，
省略掉重覆的主詞 (machines) 與動詞 (are)簡化而來。其他
(A) (B) (C) 答案，均缺乏連接詞，不能連接前後兩個子句。
no matter 無論 (為連接詞)
complex 〔kəm'plɛks 〕 *adj.* 複雜的
combination 〔͵kɑmbə'neʃən 〕 *n.* 組合
lever 〔'lɛvɚ 〕 *n.* 槓桿　　　pulley 〔'pulɪ 〕 *n.* 滑輪

12. (**A**) A great deal of gift-giving, bartering, buying and selling goes on among the native Indians here.

在這裡的本土印地安人當中，還有很多的送禮、以物易物與買賣活動在進行著。

(A) *a great deal of* + 不可數名詞 「很多的」
(B) a great many + 可數名詞 「很多的」
(C) much greater 「更偉大的」
(D) many + 可數名詞 「許多的」

* barter 〔'bɑrtɚ 〕 *v.* 交換；以物易物　　　*go on* 進行
native 〔'netɪv 〕 *adj.* 本土的

13. (**D**) It is a widely held theory that the ancestral prototype of this flowering plant was a woody plant, perhaps a small tree.

人們普遍相信的理論是，這種開花植物的原始雛形，是一種木本植物，或許是一種小樹。

* 本句中的 It 是形式主詞，代替其後的真正主詞 that the ancestral....small tree。此真正主詞是一個名詞子句，故選
(D) *that*，做連接詞，來引導此名詞子句。

widely (ˈwaɪdlɪ) *adv.* 普遍地

hold (hold) *v.* 認為；相信

theory (ˈθiərɪ) *n.* 理論

ancestral (ænˈsɛstrəl) *adj.* 祖先的；原始的

prototype (ˈprotəˌtaɪp) *n.* 雛形

flowering (ˈflaʊərɪŋ) *adj.* 開花的

woody (ˈwʊdɪ) *adj.* 木本的

14. (**D**) Throughout history, the moon has inspired not only song and dance <u>but poetry and prose as well</u>.

綜觀歷史，月亮啓發的不止是歌舞（的產生），<u>還有詩及散文</u>。

* 此空格考的是 ***not only*** A ***but also*** B 「不只有 A 還有 B」的變化形。因為 also「也」，與 as well「也」同意，故選答案 (D) ***not only*** A ***but*** B ***as well***。

inspire (ɪnˈspaɪr) *v.* 啓發；導致產生

poetry (ˈpoɪtrɪ) *n.* 詩（集合名詞）   prose (proz) *n.* 散文

15. (**C**) <u>It is thought</u> that modern corn may be a hybrid of other wild species that no longer exist.

<u>人們認為</u>現代的玉米，可能是其他已絕種的野生品種的混種。

* 名詞子句 that modern....exist 之前，本句的主、動詞皆尚未出現，故判斷選答案 (C) ***It is thought***，便有主詞也有動詞。本句中的 It 是形式主詞，名詞子句 that modern....exist 才是眞正主詞。答案 (A) Now is thought，固然 Now 可當名詞，但句子意義不通，故不能選。

hybrid (ˈhaɪbrɪd) *n.* 混種   wild (waɪld) *adj.* 野生的

species (ˈspiʃɪz) *n.* （生物）種   ***no longer*** 不再

📑 PART B : **Cloze**

Questions 16-22

Almost all universities in the United States have some form of student government—that is to say, students are allowed—even

<u>　　　　　</u>
16

encouraged—to participate in the free election of students to represent them on a Student Council.

幾乎所有美國的大學都有某種形式的學生會——也就是說，學生被允許——甚至是被鼓勵——要參與自由選舉，選出他們學生會的代表。

university〔͵junə'vɝsətɪ〕*n.* 大學
form〔fɔrm〕*n.* 形式　　　***student government*** 學生會
allow〔ə'laʊ〕*v.* 允許　　encourage〔ɪn'kɝɪdʒ〕*v.* 鼓勵
participate〔par'tɪsə͵pet〕*v.* 參與< *in* >
election〔ɪ'lɛkʃən〕*n.* 選舉
represent〔͵rɛprɪ'zɛnt〕*v.* 代表
council〔'kaʊnsḷ〕*n.* 會議；議會　　***Student Council*** 學生會

16. (**B**) 依句意，選 (B) ***that is to say*** 「也就是說」。而 (A) on the other hand 「另一方面」，(C) generally speaking 「一般說來」，(D) to begin with 「首先」，均不合句意。

Last week my roommate Jack said that he was going to <u>run for</u>

<u>　　　　　</u>
17

student president. I was surprised because, to tell the truth, I don't think Jack would make a good president. Of course, I didn't tell him that.

上星期，我的室友傑克說他想競選學生會長。我很驚訝，因為老實說，
我認為傑克不會成為一個好的會長。我當然沒告訴他那樣。

> roommate〔'rum,met〕*n.* 室友　　president〔'prɛzədənt〕*n.* 主席
> ***to tell the truth*** 老實說　　make〔mek〕*v.* 成為

17. (**C**) 依句意，選 (C) ***run for***「競選」。而 (A) elect「選舉」，
　　　(B) be chosen「被選擇」，(D) come by「經過；得到」，均
　　　不合句意。

After all, I wanted to stay on <u>speaking</u> terms with him.　And so
　　　　　　　　　　　　　　18
I <u>told a white lie</u> and said that he would make a good president.
　　19
Then he told me that he wanted me to be his campaign manager.
I said, "No, no, a thousand times no!"

畢竟我還想跟他維持見面寒喧的交情，所以我說了一個善意的謊言，說
他會成為一個好的會長。然後他告訴我說，他希望我當他的競選總幹事。
我說：「不，不行，絕對不行！」

> ***after all*** 畢竟　　terms〔tɝmz〕*n.* 關係；交情
> campaign〔kæm'pen〕*n.* 運動；競選活動
> manager〔'mænɪdʒɚ〕*n.* 經理；幹事　　time〔taɪm〕*n.* 次

18. (**A**) ***on speaking terms***　（碰面）有寒喧的交情

19. (**D**) 依句意，選 (D) ***told a white lie***「說善意的謊言」。而 (A) 說實
　　　話，(B) speak ill「說壞話」，(C) talk big「吹牛」，均不合。

Since I am his closest friend, it <u>goes without saying</u> that he was
　　　　　　　　　　　　　　　　　20
dismayed by my refusal.　He was disappointed and, although he
didn't say so, I think he was also angry.

因為我是他最好的朋友，所以他當然會對我的拒絕感到吃驚。他很失望，而且雖然他沒說，但我覺得他也很生氣。

> close〔klos〕*adj.* 親密的　　dismay〔dɪsˈme〕*v.* 使吃驚
> refusal〔rɪˈfjuzḷ〕*n.* 拒絕
> disappointed〔ˌdɪsəˈpɔɪntɪd〕*adj.* 失望的

20. (**D**) 依句意，選 (D) *it goes without saying that*… 「不用說…」
　　　　　(= *needless to say*)。而 (C) is obviously 須改為 is obvious 「是明顯的」才能選。

Later, when he told me that his girlfriend said that she would be his manager, I felt a little <u>ashamed</u>. I told myself that perhaps I <u>should</u>
　　　　　　　　　　　　　　　　　　21
<u>have agreed</u>. After all, you never can tell, maybe some day I'll need
　22
him to help me.

後來，當他告訴我他的女朋友會當他的總幹事時，我覺得有點羞愧。我告訴自己，或許我早該同意的。畢竟，誰也不知道，也許將來有一天，我會需要他的幫助。

> later〔ˈletɚ〕*adv.* 後來　　tell〔tɛl〕*v.* 知道
> *some day* 將來有一天

21. (**D**) (A) shy〔ʃaɪ〕*adj.* 害羞的
　　　　　(B) shame〔ʃem〕*n.* 羞恥
　　　　　(C) shameful〔ˈʃemfəl〕*adj.* 可恥的
　　　　　(D) *ashamed*〔əˈʃemd〕*adj.* 感到羞恥的

22. (**C**) 與過去事實相反的假設，主要子句須用 should / would / could / might + have + p.p.，故選 (C) *should have agreed*「早該同意」。

Questions 23-30

The key to the industrialization of space is the U.S. space shuttle. <u>With</u> it, astronauts will acquire a workhouse vehicle
　　　　　　　23
capable of flying into space and returning many times.

太空工業化的關鍵就是美國的太空梭。有了太空梭,太空人就能取得工作場所的交通工具,能夠飛進太空及重返地球很多次。

> key〔ki〕*n.* 關鍵
> industrialization〔ɪn͵dʌstrɪələ'zeʃən〕*n.* 工業化
> space〔spes〕*n.* 太空　　***space shuttle***　太空梭
> astronaut〔'æstrə͵nɔt〕*n.* 太空人　　acquire〔ə'kwaɪr〕*v.* 獲得
> workhouse〔'wɝk͵haʊs〕*n.* 工作室
> vehicle〔'viɪkl̩〕*n.* 交通工具　　***be capable of***　能夠

23. (**D**) 依句意,選 (D) ***With*** 「有」(= *Having*)。

<u>Powered</u> by reusable rockets that can lift a load of 65,000 pounds,
　　24
the shuttle will carry devices for scientific inquiry, as well as a variety of military hardware.

太空梭是用可載重六萬五千磅且可重複使用的火箭來驅動,它會攜帶用來進行科學研究的裝置以及各種軍事裝備。

> reusable〔ri'juzəbl̩〕*adj.* 可重複使用的
> rocket〔'rɑkɪt〕*n.* 火箭　　lift〔lɪft〕*v.* 運送
> load〔lod〕*n.* 重擔;負擔　　device〔dɪ'vaɪs〕*n.* 裝置
> inquiry〔ɪn'kwaɪrɪ〕*n.* 調查;探究
> ***as well as***　以及　　***a variety of***　各式各樣的
> military〔'mɪlə͵tɛrɪ〕*adj.* 軍事的
> hardware〔'hɑrd͵wɛr〕*n.* 武器;軍事裝備

24. (**B**) 依句意，選 (B) **Powered**。　　power〔'pauə〕 *v.* 驅動
　　　　 而 (A) serve「服務」，(C) force〔fors〕*v.* 強迫，(D) reinforce
　　　　〔,riin'fors〕*v.* 加強，均不合句意。

But more significantly, it will <u>deliver</u> materials and machines into

　　　　　　　　　　　　　　　25

space for industrial purposes unimagined four decades ago when

"sputnik" (artificial satellite) was added to the vocabulary. In short,

the <u>ultimate</u> importance of the shuttle lies in its <u>promise</u> as an

　　26　　　　　　　　　　　　　　　　　　　　　　27

economic tool.

但是更重要的是，它能運送工業用的材料及機器進入太空，這是在四十年
前所無法想像的，當時「人造衛星」這個詞剛加入字彙中。總之，太空梭
最重要的地方就在於，它有可能成為經濟的工具。

　　　　　significantly〔sɪg'nɪfəkəntlɪ〕*adv.* 重要地
　　　　　purpose〔'pɝpəs〕*n.* 目的；用途
　　　　　unimagined〔,ʌnɪ'mædʒɪnd〕*adj.* 想像不到的
　　　　　decade〔'dɛked〕*n.* 十年
　　　　　sputnik〔'spʌtnɪk〕*n.*（蘇聯的）人造衛星「史普尼克」；人造衛星
　　　　　artificial〔,ɑrtə'fɪʃəl〕*adj.* 人造的
　　　　　satellite〔'sætḷˌaɪt〕*n.* 衛星；人造衛星
　　　　　be added to 被加入　　vocabulary〔vo'kæbjəˌlɛrɪ〕*n.* 字彙
　　　　　in short 簡言之；總之　　***lie in*** 在於
　　　　　economic〔,ikə'namɪk〕*adj.* 經濟的

25. (**C**) 依句意，選 (C) ***deliver***〔dɪ'lɪvə〕*v.* 遞送；送交。而 (A) supply
　　　　　「供給」，(B) introduce「介紹；引進」，(D) transfer
　　　　　〔træns'fɝ〕*v.* 轉移，均不合句意。

26. (**D**) 依句意，選 (D) **ultimate** (ˊʌltəmɪt) *adj.* 最終的；最大的；根本的。而 (A) general「一般的」，(B) essential「必要的」，(C) prevailing (prɪˊvelɪŋ) *adj.* 流行的，均不合句意。

27. (**A**) (A) **promise** (ˊprɑmɪs) *n.* 可能性；前途；希望
     (B) prosperity (prɑsˊpɛrətɪ) *n.* 繁榮
     (C) popularity (ˌpɑpjəˊlærətɪ) *n.* 受歡迎
     (D) priority (praɪˊɔrətɪ) *n.* 優先權

What makes the space shuttle unique is that it takes off like a rocket but lands like an airplane. <u>Thus</u>, when it has accomplished
28
its <u>mission</u>, it can be ready for another trip in about two weeks.
29

　　太空梭的特色在於，它能像火箭一樣起飛，像飛機一樣降落。因此，當它完成任務時，在兩週之內就能準備好進行另一趟任務。

     unique (juˊnik) *adj.* 獨特的
     take off 起飛　　land (lænd) *v.* 降落
     accomplish (əˊkɑmplɪʃ) *v.* 完成

28. (**A**) 依句意，選 (A) **Thus** (ðʌs) *adv.* 因此。而 (B) whereas「然而」，(C) nevertheless「然而」，(D) yet「但是」，均不合句意。

29. (**B**) (A) venture (ˊvɛntʃə) *n.* 冒險（行動）
     (B) **mission** (ˊmɪʃən) *n.* 任務
     (C) commission (kəˊmɪʃən) *n.* 委託；佣金
     (D) responsibility (rɪˌspɑnsəˊbɪlətɪ) *n.* 責任

The space shuttle, the world's first true spaceship, is a magnificent step <u>in</u> making the impossible possible for the benefit
30
and survival of man.

太空梭是人類第一艘眞正的太空船，在爲了人類的利益與生存，而把不可能變成可能這方面，跨出了了不起的一步。

> spaceship〔'spes,ʃɪp〕n. 太空船
> magnificent〔mæg'nɪfəsṇt〕adj. 了不起的
> benefit〔'bɛnəfɪt〕n. 利益
> survival〔sə'vaɪvḷ〕n. 生存　　man〔mæn〕n. 人類

30. (**C**) 表「在…方面」，介系詞用 ***in***，選 (C)。

PART C : Reading

Questions 31-33

A noted anthropologist states that humans are basically adapted to life in more primitive environments, with relatively simple technologies. These were environments which called for a closer and more limited relation to the world, which was basically composed of small groups of people, short time periods, and things that were near-at-hand.

有位著名的人類學家說，人類基本上會用比較簡單的科技，來適應比較原始的生活。這樣的環境是需要和世界有更親密且有限的關係，這樣的關係基本上是由較小的族群、較短的時間，以及在手邊的事物所組成。

noted（'notɪd）*adj.* 著名的

anthropologist（ˌænθrə'pɑlədʒɪst）*n.* 人類學家

state（stet）*v.* 敘述；說明

basically（'besɪklɪ）*adv.* 基本上

be adapted to 適應　　primitive（'prɪmətɪv）*adj.* 原始的

relatively（'rɛlətɪvlɪ）*adv.* 相對地；相當地

technology（tɛk'nɑlədʒɪ）*n.* 科技；技術

call for 需要　　limited（'lɪmɪtɪd）*adj.* 有限的

relation（rɪ'leʃən）*n.* 關係　　***the world*** 世界；世人

be composed of 由…組成

period（'pɪrɪəd）*n.* 期間；時期

near-at-hand *adj.* 在手邊的

In these settings, humans learned early to become emotionally attached to their own kin and group and to regard others as "outsiders" toward whom they learned to feel indifferent and hostile.

在這樣的環境中，人們學會在感情上依賴自己的親戚與族群，而將別人視為「外人」，並且學會對他們漠不關心，或是有敵意。

setting（'sɛtɪŋ）*n.* 環境；背景

emotionally（ɪ'moʃənlɪ）*adv.* 在情感上

be attached to 依附；依賴　　kin（kɪn）*n.* 親戚

regard A ***as*** B 認為 A 是 B

outsider（aut'saɪdə）*n.* 外人

toward（tord）*prep.* 對於

indifferent（ɪn'dɪfərənt）*adj.* 漠不關心的

hostile（'hɑstɪl）*adj.* 有敵意的

Though humans today still adhere to relatively ancient behavioral forms, these are more suited for survival in sparsely populated environments, in the anthropologist's view, the modern technical world is relatively new, and new customs are vitally needed to meet problems it has created.

雖然現在的人類仍然堅守相當古老的行爲模式，但這樣的行爲模式比較適合在人口稀疏的環境中求生存，根據人類學家的看法，現代的科技世界是相當新的，所以極需要新的習俗，來應付它所產生的問題。

today〔 tə'de 〕adv. 現在　　**adhere to** 遵守；堅持
ancient〔'enʃənt 〕adj. 古代的
behavioral〔 bɪ'hevjərəl 〕adj. 行爲的
form〔 fɔrm 〕n. 形式　　**behavioral form** 行爲模式
be suited for 適合　　survival〔 sə'vaɪvl 〕n. 生存
sparsely〔'spɑrslɪ 〕adv. 稀疏地
populate〔'pɑpjə‚let 〕v. 使居住於
sparsely populated 人口稀疏的
　　(↔ *densely populated* 人口密集的)
in one's view 根據某人的看法
technical〔'tɛnɪkḷ 〕adj. 科技的
vitally〔'vaɪtḷɪ 〕adv. 極端地　　meet〔 mit 〕v. 應付；處理
create〔 krɪ'et 〕v. 製造；產生

According to him, the new customs that are so vitally needed today are those which would promote understanding among groups, which would reduce economic and political inequalities among them, and which would solve conflicts among them by non-military means.

根據他的說法，現在極需要的新習俗，要能促進群體之間的了解，減少彼此經濟及政治上的不平等，並以非軍事的方法解決彼此之間的衝突。

promote〔prə'mot〕v. 促進

reduce〔rɪ'djus〕v. 減少

economic〔͵ikə'namɪk〕adj. 經濟的

political〔pə'lɪtɪk!〕adj. 政治的

inequality〔͵ɪnɪ'kwɑlətɪ〕n. 不平等

solve〔sɑlv〕v. 解決　　conflict〔'kɑnflɪkt〕n. 衝突

non-military〔'nɑn'mɪlə͵tɛrɪ〕adj. 非軍事的

means〔minz〕n. 方法；手段

（以下各題選出一項與上面內容**不一致**的答案）

31. (**C**) (A) 在原始時代，人類主要是對發生在其環境界限內的事物感興趣。

(B) 在原始時代，人類看待世界，常常是以和世界之間有限的關係來思考。

(C) 自古以來，人類就習慣於把世界看成是超越其親戚和族群以外的事。

(D) 人類能夠讓自己習慣比較原始的環境。

* interest〔'ɪntrɪst〕n. 興趣

primarily〔'praɪ͵mɛrəlɪ〕adv. 主要地

be directed to 朝向；專注於　　**take place** 發生

within〔wɪð'ɪn〕prep. 在…之內

boundary〔'baundərɪ〕n. 界限；範圍

be accustomed to 習慣於

32. (**D**) (A) 由於古代的環境人口稀疏，所以人們只需要照顧自己的親戚和族群。

     (B) 在古代，人們生活在相當小的族群中，而且族群之間是互相分離的。

     (C) 即使在現在，人類的行爲仍然受到古代行爲模式的影響。

     (D) <u>人類學家認爲，世界發展的最大阻礙，就是非軍事手段所造成的人類衝突。</u>

    * ***care for*** 照顧   separate〔'sɛpəˌret〕v. 使分開

        maintain〔men'ten〕v. 主張；堅持

        obstacle〔'ɑbstəkl̩〕n. 阻礙

33. (**D**) (A) 人類學家認爲，人類必須改變傳統的行爲模式，因爲那是適合原始的環境，不適合現代的環境。

     (B) 在遠古時代，人類的科技知識相當貧乏。

     (C) 我們極需要新的習俗，以促進族群之間的和平與了解。

     (D) <u>在古代人口稀疏的環境中，人類非常需要互相幫助，無論彼此是不是親戚或同一族群。</u>

    * ***rather than*** 而不是   rather〔'ræðɚ〕adv. 相當地

      be in need of 需要

Questions 34-38

Aimlessness has hardly been typical of the postwar Japan whose productivity and social harmony are the envy of the United States and Europe. But increasingly the Japanese are seeing a decline of the traditional work-moral values.

漫無目標幾乎不是戰後的日本的特色，它的生產力和社會的和諧是美國與歐洲羨慕的對象。但是日本已經逐漸經歷到傳統工作道德價值觀的衰退。

aimlessness〔'emlısnıs〕*n.* 無目標

hardly〔'hardlı〕*adv.* 幾乎不　　***be typical of*** 是…的特點

postwar〔'post'wɔr〕*adj.* 戰後的

productivity〔,prədʌk'tıvətı〕*n.* 生產力

harmony〔'harmənı〕*n.* 和諧　　envy〔'ɛnvı〕*n.* 羨慕的對象

increasingly〔ın'krisıŋlı〕*adv.* 越來越

see〔si〕*v.* 經歷過；遭遇到　　decline〔dı'klaın〕*n.* 衰退

traditional〔trə'dıʃənḷ〕*adj.* 傳統的

work-moral values 工作道德價值觀

Twenty years ago young people were hardworking and saw their jobs as their primary reason for being, but now Japan has largely fulfilled its economic needs, and young people don't know where they should go next.

二十年前的年輕人，非常努力工作，把工作視為生存的主要理由，但是日本現在已經滿足了其大部分的經濟需求，所以年輕人不知道接下來該何去何從。

hardworking〔'hard'wɜkıŋ〕*adj.* 努力工作的；勤勉的

primary〔'praı,mɛrı〕*adj.* 主要的

being〔'biıŋ〕*n.* 存在　　largely〔'lardʒlı〕*adv.* 主要地；大多

fulfill〔fʊl'fıl〕*v.* 滿足（需求）

The coming of age of the postwar baby boom and an entry of women into the male-dominated job market have limited the opportunities of teenagers who are already questioning the heavy personal sacrifices involved in climbing Japan's rigid social ladder to good schools and jobs.

在戰後嬰兒潮出生的人長大成年，以及女性進入由男性主導的就業市場，這些都限制了青少年的機會，所以他們已經開始質疑，爲了爬上嚴格的社會位階，以進入好的學校或工作，所做的重大個人的犧牲。

> ***coming of age*** 成年
> ***baby boom*** 嬰兒潮【出生率急遽上升的時期，如第二次世界大戰後】
> entry (ˈɛntrɪ) *n.* 進入
> male-dominated (ˈmelˈdomə͵netɪd) *adj.* 由男性主導的
> ***job market*** 就業市場　　teenager (ˈtin͵edʒɚ) *n.* 青少年
> question (ˈkwɛstʃən) *v.* 質疑　　heavy (ˈhɛvɪ) *adj.* 大量的
> sacrifice (ˈsækrə͵faɪs) *n.* 犧牲　　***be involved in*** 與…有關
> rigid (ˈrɪdʒɪd) *adj.* 嚴格的
> ***social ladder*** 立身成功的途徑
> ***climb the social ladder*** 爬升社會位階

In a recent survey, it was found that only 24.5 percent of Japanese students were fully satisfied with school life, compared with 67.2 percent of students in the United States. In addition, far more Japanese workers expressed dissatisfaction with their jobs than did their <u>counterparts</u> in the 10 other countries surveyed.

最近的一項調查發現，和美國學生的百分之六十七點二相比，日本學生只有百分之二十四點五的人，對於學校生活完全滿意。此外，日本的員工對於工作不滿意的程度，也比其他十個受調查的國家的員工高出許多。

> recent (ˈrisn̩t) *adj.* 最近的　　survey (səˈve) *n. v.* 調查
> ***compared with*** 和…相比　　***in addition*** 此外
> express (ɪkˈsprɛs) *v.* 表達
> dissatisfaction (͵dɪssætɪsˈfækʃən) *n.* 不滿
> counterpart (ˈkaʊntɚ͵pɑrt) *n.* 同類的人、事、物

While often praised by foreigners for its emphasis on the basics, Japanese education tends to stress test taking and mechanical learning over creativity and self-expression.

雖然外國人常稱讚日本教育著重基礎原理，但是日本教育傾向於重視考試及機械式的學習，甚於創意與自我表現。

while〔hwaɪl〕*conj.* 雖然　　foreigner〔'fɔrɪnɚ〕*n.* 外國人
emphasis〔'ɛmfəsɪs〕*n.* 強調；重視
basics〔'besɪks〕*n. pl.* 基礎；原理　　***tend to*** 易於；傾向於
stress〔strɛs〕*v.* 強調；重視　　***test taking*** 參加考試
mechanical〔mə'kænɪkl̩〕*adj.* 機械式的
creativity〔ˌkrie'tɪvətɪ〕*n.* 創意
self-expression〔ˌsɛlfɪk'sprɛʃən〕*n.* 自我表現

"Those things that do not show up in the test scores — personality, ability, courage or humanity — are completely ignored," says Toshiki Kaifu, chairman of the ruling Liberal Democratic Party's education committee. "Frustration against this kind of things leads kids to drop out and run wild."

「考試成績顯現不出來的那些東西──個性、能力、勇氣，與人性──則完全被忽略，」自民黨這個執政黨的教育委員會會長 Toshiki Kaifu 說。「對這類事情的失望，使得孩子輟學或是放縱自己。」

show up 出現　　score〔skor〕*n.* 分數；成績
personality〔ˌpɝsn̩'ælətɪ〕*n.* 個性
humanity〔hju'mænətɪ〕*n.* 人性；慈悲　ignore〔ɪg'nor〕*v.* 忽視
chairman〔'tʃɛrmən〕*n.* 主席；會長　ruling〔'rulɪŋ〕*adj.* 執政的
the Liberal Democratic Party 自民黨
committee〔kə'mɪtɪ〕*n.* 委員會
frustration〔frʌs'treʃən〕*n.* 挫折；失望　***lead sb. to V.*** 使某人…
drop out 輟學　　***run wild*** 放縱

Last year Japan experienced 2,125 incidents of school violence, including 929 assaults on teachers. Amid the outcry, many conservative leaders are seeking a return to the prewar emphasis on moral education.

去年日本有兩千一百二十五件校園暴力事件，其中包括九百二十九件是攻擊老師。在大家的抗議聲中，許多保守的領袖，尋求回復戰前對於道德教育的重視。

experience (ɪk'spɪrɪəns) v. 經歷
incident ('ɪnsədənt) n. 事件   violence ('vaɪələns) n. 暴力
assault (ə'sɔlt) n. 攻擊   amid (ə'mɪd) prep. 在…中
outcry ('aut,kraɪ) n. (大眾的) 抗議
conservative (kən'sɜvətɪv) adj. 保守的   seek (sik) v. 尋求
return (rɪ'tɜn) n. 回歸；恢復   prewar (pri'wɔr) adj. 戰前的
moral ('mɔrəl) adj. 道德的

Last year Mitsuo Setoyama, who was the education minister, raised eyebrows when he argued that liberal reforms introduced by the American occupation authorities after World War II had weakened the "Japanese morality of respect for parents."

去年，當時的教育部長 Mitsuo Setoyama 使人們大吃一驚，他堅稱在第二次世界大戰之後，由美國占領軍當局所引進的自由主義改革，削弱了「日本尊重父母的道德觀」。

minister ('mɪnɪstə) n. 部長
eyebrows ('aɪ,brau) n. 眉毛   *raise eyebrows* 使人們大吃一驚
argue ('ɑrgju) v. 爭論；主張   liberal ('lɪbərəl) adj. 自由主義的
reform (rɪ'fɔrm) n. 改革   introduce (,ɪntrə'djus) v. 引進
occupation (,ɑkjə'peʃən) n. 占領軍
authorities (ə'θɔrətɪz) n. pl. 當局   weaken ('wikən) v. 削弱
morality (mɔ'rælətɪ) n. 道德

But that may have more to do with Japanese life styles. "In Japan," says educator Yoko Muro, "it's never a question of whether you enjoy your job and your life, but only how much you can endure."

但是那可能和日本的生活方式比較有關聯。「在日本，」教育家 Yoko Muro 說，「這絕對不是你是否喜歡你的工作和生活的問題，而是你能忍受多少。」

have more to do with 和…比較有關聯 ***life style*** 生活方式
educator〔'ɛdʒʊ͵ketɚ〕*n.* 教育家 endure〔ɪn'djʊr〕*v.* 忍受

With economic growth has come centralization, fully 76 percent of Japan's 119 million citizens live in cities where community and the extended family have been abandoned in favor of isolated, two-generation households.

經濟成長已到達集中化，日本的一億一千九百萬人口中，整整有百分之七十六的人，住在都市中，在都市裡人們已經放棄大家庭，寧可選擇較孤立的兩代家庭。

economic〔͵ikə'nɑmɪk〕*adj.* 經濟的
come〔kʌm〕*v.* 到達；幾乎
centralization〔͵sɛntrəlaɪ'zeʃən〕*n.* 集中（化）
community〔kə'mjunətɪ〕*n.* 社區 ***extended family*** 大家庭
abandon〔ə'bændən〕*v.* 拋棄 ***in favor of*** 贊成；寧可選擇
isolated〔'aɪsl͵etɪd〕*adj.* 孤立的
generation〔͵dʒɛnə'reʃən〕*n.* 世代
household〔'haʊs͵hold〕*n.* 家族

Urban Japanese have long endured lengthy commutes (travels to and from work) and crowded living conditions, but as the old group and family values weaken, the discomfort is beginning to tell.

住在都市的日本人,長久以來忍受長時間的通勤路程(也就是上下班的路程),以及擁擠的生活環境,但是隨著團體與家庭的古老價值觀日漸薄弱,這種不滿就開始產生作用了。

urban〔ˋɝbən〕 adj. 都市的

lengthy〔ˋlɛŋθɪ〕 adj. 長久的;漫長的

commute〔kəˋmjut〕 n. 上下班交通路程

crowded〔ˋkraʊdɪd〕 adj. 擁擠的   values〔ˋvæljuz〕 n. pl. 價值觀

discomfort〔dɪsˋkʌmfət〕 n. 不舒服   tell〔tɛl〕 v. 發生作用

In the past decade, the Japanese divorce rate, while still well below that of the United States, has increased by more than 50 percent, and suicides have increased by nearly one-quarter.

在過去十年,日本的離婚率,雖然遠低於美國,但已經增加百分之五十以上,而自殺人數則增加了將近四分之一。

decade〔ˋdɛked〕 n. 十年   divorce〔dəˋvors〕 n. 離婚

rate〔ret〕 n. 比率   well below 遠低於

suicide〔ˋsuə͵saɪd〕 n. 自殺   one-quarter n. 四分之一

34. (**B**) 在西方人的眼中,戰後的日本是

(A) 處於無目標的發展中。   (B) 一個正面的例子。

(C) 西方國家的對手。   (D) 在衰退中。

* positive〔ˋpɑzətɪv〕 adj. 正面的   rival〔ˋraɪv!〕 n. 對手

35. (**B**) counterparts 這個劃底線的字,意思是

(A) 很多同事。   (B) 相對應的人。

(C) 最大的對手。   (D) 熱情的支持者。

* associate〔əˋsoʃɪɪt〕 n. 同事;夥伴

corresponding〔͵kɔrəˋspɑndɪŋ〕 adj. 相對應的

enthusiastic〔ɪn͵θjuzɪˋæstɪk〕 adj. 狂熱的

36. (**D**) 什麼是造成日本社會道德衰退的主要原因？

    (A) 婦女對社會活動的參與受限。

    (B) 有更多的員工對工作不滿。

    (C) 過度重視基礎原理。

    (D) 生活方式受到西方的價值觀影響。

    * chiefly〔'tʃiflɪ〕*adv.* 主要地

      be responsible for 是…的原因

      excessive〔ɪk'sɛsɪv〕*adj.* 過度的；過多的

      place emphasis on 重視；強調

37. (**C**) 根據作者的說法，下列何者正確？

    (A) 日本的教育受到稱讚，是因爲它幫助年輕人爬上社會位階。

    (B) 日本教育的特色是機械化的學習以及創意。

    (C) 應該更重視培養創意。

    (D) 中途輟學導致對考試的失望。

    * *be characterized by* 特色是   *as well as* 以及

      cultivation〔,kʌltə'veʃən〕*n.* 培養   *lead to* 導致

38. (**A**) 生活方式的改變可由 _____ 這個事實顯現出來。

    (A) 年輕人較不能忍受生活中的不滿

    (B) 日本的離婚率超過美國

    (C) 日本人比以前更能忍耐

    (D) 日本人很珍惜目前的生活

    * reveal〔rɪ'vil〕*v.* 顯示

      tolerant〔'tɑlərənt〕*adj.* 能容忍的

      exceed〔ɪk'sid〕*v.* 超過   *than ever before* 比以前

      appreciate〔ə'priʃɪ,et〕*v.* 欣賞；珍視

Questions 39-42

Science, in practice, depends far less on the experiments it prepares than on the preparedness of the minds of the men who watch the experiments: Sir Isaac Newton supposedly discovered gravity through the fall of an apple.

事實上，科學依賴它所預設的實驗，但更仰賴觀察實驗者的心理準備：據說牛頓就是透過蘋果的掉落，而發現萬有引力。

> ***in practice*** 事實上　　***depend on*** 依賴
> experiment〔 ɪkˈspɛrəmənt〕*n.* 實驗
> prepare〔 prɪˈpɛr〕*v.* 預備；預設
> preparedness〔 prɪˈpɛrdnɪs〕*n.* 心理準備
> Sir Isaac Newton　*n.* 牛頓【1642-1727，英國物理學家，發現萬有
> 　　引力原理，發明微積分】
> supposedly〔 səˈpozɪdlɪ〕*adv.* 據說
> gravity〔ˈɡrævətɪ〕*n.* 重力；萬有引力

Apples had been falling in many places for centuries and thousands of people had seen them fall. But Newton for years had been curious about the cause of the orbital motion of the moon and planets. What kept them in place?

好幾百年來，很多地方都有蘋果掉下來，而且也有好幾千人看到它們掉下來。但是牛頓多年來，就一直對於月球和行星循軌道運行很好奇。是什麼使它們維持在一定的位置？

> century〔ˈsɛntʃərɪ〕*n.* 世紀　　curious〔ˈkjurɪəs〕*adj.* 好奇的
> cause〔 kɔz〕*n.* 原因　　orbital〔ˈɔrbɪtl̩〕*adj.* 軌道的
> motion〔ˈmoʃən〕*n.* 運行　　planet〔ˈplænɪt〕*n.* 行星
> ***in place*** 在一定的位置

Why didn't they fall out of the sky? The fact that the apple fell down toward the earth and not up into the tree answered the question he had been asking himself about those larger fruits of the heavens, the moon and the planets.

為什麼它們不會掉到天空外？蘋果掉向地面而不是飛到樹上這個事實，解答了他長久以來對天空中更大的果實，也就是月球和行星所存的疑問。

> ***fall out of*** 從…掉出去
>
> toward〔tord〕*prep.* 朝著　　***the heavens*** 天空

How many men would have considered the possibility of an apple falling up into the tree? Newton did because he was not trying to predict anything. He was just wondering. His mind was ready for the unpredictable.

有多少人會考慮到，蘋果飛上樹的可能性呢？牛頓就會，因為他不想預設立場。他只是很想知道。他有心理準備，要接受不可預知的事情。

> consider〔kən'sɪdə〕*v.* 考慮到　　predict〔prɪ'dɪkt〕*v.* 預測
> wonder〔'wʌndə〕*v.* 想知道
> unpredictable〔ˌʌnprɪ'dɪktəbḷ〕*adj.* 不可預知的

Unpredictability is part of the essential nature of research. If you don't have unpredictable things, you don't have research. Scientists tend to forget this when writing their cut-and-dried reports for the technical journals, but history is filled with examples of it.

不可預知是研究的重要本質的一部分。如果沒有不可預知的事情，就不會做研究。科學家在為科技期刊寫呆板的報告時，往往會忘記這一點，但是歷史卻充滿了這樣的例子。

unpredictability〔ˌʌnprɪˌdɪktəˋbɪlətɪ〕*n.* 不可預知
essential〔əˋsɛnʃəl〕*adj.* 必要的；非常重要的
nature〔ˋnetʃɚ〕*n.* 本質　　research〔ˋrisɝtʃ〕*n.* 研究
tend to V. 易於；傾向於　　cut-and-dried *adj.* 老套的；呆板的
technical〔ˋtɛknɪkḷ〕*adj.* 學術的；技術的
journal〔ˋdʒɝnḷ〕*n.* 期刊；雜誌　　***be filled with*** 充滿了

In talking to some scientists, particularly younger ones, you might gather the impression that they find the "scientific method", a substitute for imaginative thought. I've attended research conferences where a scientist has been asked what he thinks about the advisability of continuing a certain experiment.

在跟一些科學家談話時，尤其是較年輕的科學家，你可能會有的印象是，他們認為「科學的方法」，可以取代富有想像力的想法。我參加過一些研究會議，有位科學家曾被問到，他覺得繼續做某個實驗是否合理。

gather〔ˋgæðɚ〕*v.* 獲得　　impression〔ɪmˋprɛʃən〕*n.* 印象
substitute〔ˋsʌbstəˌtjut〕*n.* 代替物
imaginative〔ɪˋmædʒəˌnetɪv〕*adj.* 富有想像力的
conference〔ˋkɑnfərəns〕*n.* 會議
advisability〔ədˌvaɪzəˋbɪlətɪ〕*n.* 適當；合理
certain〔ˋsɝtṇ〕*adj.* 某個

The scientist has frowned, looked at the graphs, and said "the data are still inconclusive." "We know that," the men from the budget office have said. "But what do you think? Is it worthwhile going on? What do you think we might expect?" The scientist has been shocked at having even been asked to speculate.

那位科學家皺起眉頭，看著圖表，然後說：「這些資料還沒有結論。」「我們知道，」預算部門的人說。「但是你覺得如何？值得繼續做下去嗎？你

覺得我們可以預期些什麼？」那位科學家甚至對於被要求作出推測感到
很震驚。

> frown〔fraʊn〕v. 皺眉頭
> graph〔græf〕n. 圖表　　data〔ˈdetə〕n. pl. 資料
> inconclusive〔ˌɪnkənˈklusɪv〕adj. 未獲得結論的
> budget〔ˈbʌdʒɪt〕n. 預算
> worthwhile〔ˈwɝθˈhwaɪl〕adj. 值得做的　　**go on** 繼續
> shocked〔ʃɑkt〕adj. 震驚的　　speculate〔ˈspɛkjəˌlet〕v. 推測

What this amounts to, of course, is that the scientist has become
the victim of his own writings.　He has put forward unquestioned
claims so consistently that he not only believes them himself, but has
convinced industrial and business management that they are true.

當然，這就等同於這位科學家已經成為自己著作的受害者。他提出毫
無疑問且前後一致的主張，以致於不僅他自己相信，他還說服工業與商業
的管理階層相信它們是真的。

> **amount to** 等同於　　　victim〔ˈvɪktɪm〕n. 受害者
> writings〔ˈraɪtɪŋz〕n. pl. 著作；作品　　**put forward** 提出
> unquestioned〔ʌnˈkwɛstʃənd〕adj. 毫無疑問的；公認的
> claim〔klem〕n. 宣稱；主張
> consistently〔kənˈsɪstəntlɪ〕adv. 前後一致地
> **not only…but (also)~** 不僅…而且~
> convince〔kənˈvɪns〕v. 使相信
> industrial〔ɪnˈdʌstrɪəl〕adj. 工業的
> management〔ˈmænɪdʒmənt〕n. 管理階層；資方

If experiments are planned and carried out according to plan as
faithfully as the reports in the science journals indicate, then it
is perfectly logical for management to expect research to produce
results measurable in dollars and cents.

如果實驗是完全準確地按照科學期刊上的報告所說的來規劃與執行，那麼管理階層理所當然會期望，研究所獲得的結果，可以用金錢來衡量。

carry out 執行　　faithfully〔'feθfəlɪ〕*adv.* 忠實地；正確地
indicate〔'ɪndə‚ket〕*v.* 指出　　perfectly〔'pɝfɪktlɪ〕*adv.* 完全地
logical〔'lɑdʒɪkḷ〕*adj.* 合邏輯的；合理的
measurable〔'mɛʒərəbḷ〕*adj.* 可測量的

It is entirely reasonable for auditors to believe that scientists can keep one eye on the cash register while the other eye is on the microscope.

稽查人員會相信，科學家能一邊注意收銀機，一邊注意顯微鏡，是很合理的。

entirely〔ɪn'taɪrlɪ〕*adv.* 完全地
reasonable〔'riznəbḷ〕*adj.* 合理的
auditor〔'ɔdɪtɚ〕*n.* 查帳員；稽核員
keep an eye on 留意；監視　　*cash register* 收銀機
microscope〔'maɪkrə‚skop〕*n.* 顯微鏡

If regularity and conformity to a standard pattern are as desirable to the scientist as the writing of his papers would appear to reflect, the management won't be blamed for discriminating against the "oddballs" among researchers in favor of more conventional thinkers who "work well with the team."

如果規律和符合標準的模式是科學家想要的，正如他的論文想反映出的一樣，那麼管理階層歧視「怪傑」，而支持思想傳統，且有團隊精神的研究人員，就不會被責備了。

regularity〔‚rɛgjə'lɛrətɪ〕*n.* 規則；規律
conformity〔kən'fɔrmətɪ〕*n.* 一致
standard〔'stændəd〕*adj.* 標準的　　pattern〔'pætən〕*n.* 模式
desirable〔dɪ'zaɪrəbḷ〕*adj.* 合意的；理想的

paper〔'pepɚ〕*n.* 論文　　appear〔ə'pɪr〕*v.* 看起來；似乎

reflect〔rɪ'flɛkt〕*v.* 反應　　blame〔blem〕*v.* 責備

discriminate〔dɪs'krɪmə,net〕*v.* 歧視

oddball〔'ad,bɔl〕*n.* 怪人　　*in favor of* 贊成；支持

conventional〔kən'vɛnʃənḷ〕*adj.* 傳統的

team〔tim〕*n.* 團隊

39.(**A**) 作者想用牛頓的例子證明

(A) 愛追根究底的想法比科學實驗更重要。

(B) 進行成果豐碩的研究會使科學進步。

(C) 科學家很少忘記研究的重要本質。

(D) 在科學研究中，預測比不可預測性重要。

　* inquiring〔ɪn'kwaɪrɪŋ〕*adj.* 探詢的；愛追根究底的

　　advance〔əd'væns〕*v.* 進步

　　fruitful〔'frutfəl〕*adj.* 成果豐碩的

　　conduct〔kən'dʌkt〕*v.* 進行

　　weigh〔we〕*v.* 有重要性

40.(**B**) 作者堅稱科學家

(A) 不應該用富有想像力的想法取代「科學的方法」。

(B) 不應該忽略推測不可預知的事情。

(C) 應該多寫一些簡明的報告給科技期刊。

(D) 應該對他們的研究結果有信心。

　* assert〔ə'sɝt〕*v.* 堅稱　　replace〔rɪ'ples〕*v.* 取代

　　replace A *with* B 用 B 取代 A

　　concise〔kən'saɪs〕*adj.* 簡明的

　　confident〔'kɑnfədənt〕*adj.* 有信心的

　　findings〔'faɪndɪŋz〕*n. pl.* 研究發現

41. (**D**) 有些年輕的科學家似乎
    (A) 很熱中預測。　　　　　(B) 常會推測未來。
    (C) 非常重視有創造力的思考。　(D) 堅持「科學的方法」。

    * keen〔kin〕*adj.* 強烈的；深厚的
      have a keen interest in 熱中於　　***think highly of*** 重視
      creative〔krɪ'etɪv〕*adj.* 有創造力的　　***stick to*** 堅持；遵守

42. (**A**) 作者暗示，科學研究的結果
    (A) 可能不如一般預期的有利。　(B) 可以用金錢來衡量。
    (C) 依賴與標準模式的一致性。　(D) 大多會被管理階層所低估。

    * imply〔ɪm'plaɪ〕*v.* 暗示
      profitable〔'prɑfɪtəbḷ〕*adj.* 有利的
      rely on 依賴；倚靠；指望　　mostly〔'mostlɪ〕*adv.* 大多
      underestimate〔'ʌndɚ'ɛstə,met〕*v.* 低估

Questions 43-47

British Columbia is the third largest Canadian province, both
in area and population. It is nearly one and half times as large as
Texas, and extends 800 miles (1,280 km) north from the United
States border. It includes Canada's entire west coast and the
islands just off the coast.

英屬哥倫比亞不論是面積或人口，都是加拿大第三大省。它幾乎是
德州的一點五倍大，並自美國邊界往北延伸八百英里（即 1280 公里）。
它包括了加拿大整個西部海岸，以及海岸之外的島嶼。

> ***British Columbia*** 英屬哥倫比亞【加拿大西南部一省，首府維多利亞】
> Canadian〔kə'nedɪən〕*adj.* 加拿大的
> province〔'prɑvɪns〕*n.* 省　　area〔'ɛrɪə〕*n.* 面積
> population〔,pɑpjə'leʃən〕*n.* 人口　　time〔taɪm〕*n.* 倍
> extend〔ɪk'stɛnd〕*v.* 延伸　　border〔'bɔrdɚ〕*n.* 邊界
> coast〔kost〕*n.* 海岸　　off〔ɔf〕*prep.* 離開…

　　Most of British Columbia is mountainous, with long, rugged ranges running north and south.　Even the coastal islands are the remains of a mountain range that existed thousands of years ago.

　　英屬哥倫比亞大部分都是山區，有長而崎嶇的山脈縱貫南北。即使是沿海的島嶼，都是數千年前就存在的山脈的遺跡。

　　　mountainous〔ˈmaʊntn̩əs〕adj. 多山的
　　　rugged〔ˈrʌgɪd〕adj. 崎嶇的；多起伏的　　range〔rendʒ〕n. 山脈
　　　run〔rʌn〕v. 延伸　　coastal〔ˈkostl̩〕adj. 沿海的
　　　remains〔rɪˈmenz〕n. pl. 遺跡；殘餘　　exist〔ɪgˈzɪst〕v. 存在

During the last Ice Age, this range was scoured by glaciers until most of it was beneath the sea.　Its peaks now show as islands scattered along the coast.

在上一個冰河時期，這座山脈受到冰河的沖刷，直到大部分都沉入海中。它的山頂現在就變成散佈在沿岸的島嶼。

　　　last〔læst〕adj. 上一次的；最後的　　*Ice Age* 冰河時代
　　　scour〔skaʊr〕v. 沖刷；侵蝕　　glacier〔ˈgleʃɚ〕n. 冰河
　　　beneath〔bɪˈniθ〕prep. 在…之下　　peak〔pik〕n. 山頂；尖峰
　　　scatter〔ˈskætɚ〕v. 散佈

　　The southwestern coastal region has a humid mild marine climate.　Sea winds that blow inland from the west are warmed by a current of warm water that flows through the Pacific Ocean.

　　西南沿岸地區是潮濕溫和的海洋性氣候。從西方吹向內陸的海風，因流經太平洋的暖流而變得較溫暖。

　　　southwestern〔ˌsaʊθˈwɛstɚn〕adj. 西南的
　　　region〔ˈridʒən〕n. 地區；地帶　　humid〔ˈhjumɪd〕adj. 潮濕的
　　　mild〔maɪld〕adj. 溫和的　　marine〔məˈrin〕adj. 海洋的
　　　climate〔ˈklaɪmɪt〕n. 氣候　　inland〔ˈɪnlənd〕adv. 向內陸
　　　warm〔wɔrm〕v. 使溫暖　　current〔ˈkɝ ənt〕n. 洋流
　　　the Pacific Ocean 太平洋

As a result, winter temperatures average above freezing and summers are mild. These warm western winds also carry moisture from the ocean.

因此，冬天的平均溫度在冰點以上，而夏天則很溫和。這些溫暖的西風也從海洋帶來水氣。

as a result 因此　　average〔ˋævərɪdʒ〕v. 平均為
freezing〔ˋfrizɪŋ〕n. 冰點　　*above freezing* 在冰點以上
carry〔ˋkærɪ〕v. 攜帶　　moisture〔ˋmɔɪstʃɚ〕n. 水氣；濕氣

The winds from the Pacific meet the mountain barriers of the coastal ranges and the Rocky Mountains. As they rise to cross the mountains, the winds are cooled, and their moisture begins to fall as rain. On some of the western slopes almost 200 inches (500 cm) of rain falls each year.

從太平洋吹來的風，會遇到沿岸山脈以及落磯山脈的阻礙。當這些風上升越過山脈時，就會冷卻，水氣就會開始變成雨水落下。在一些西部的山坡，每年降雨量將近 200 英吋（即 500 公分）。

barrier〔ˋbærɪɚ〕n. 障礙；阻礙
the Rocky Mountains 落磯山脈　　rise〔raɪz〕v. 上升；聳立
cool〔kul〕v. 使冷卻　　slope〔slop〕n. 斜坡

More than half of British Columbia is <u>heavily</u> forested. On mountain slopes that receive plentiful rainfall, huge Douglas firs rise in towering columns. These forest giants often grow to be as much as 300 feet (90 m) tall, with diameters up to 10 feet (3 m).

英屬哥倫比亞有一半以上，都是森林茂密的地區。在降雨量豐富的山坡上，巨大的北美黃杉像圓柱般聳立著。這些森林中的大樹常長到 300 英尺（即 90 公尺）高，直徑長達 10 英尺（即 3 公尺）。

heavily〔'hɛvɪlɪ〕*adv.* 濃密地
forest〔'fɔrɪst〕*v.* 植林於 *n.* 森林
plentiful〔'plɛntɪfəl〕*adj.* 豐富的；很多的
rainfall〔'ren,fɔl〕*n.* 降雨；降雨量　　huge〔hjudʒ〕*adj.* 巨大的
fir〔fɝ〕*n.* 樅樹　Douglas fir〔'dʌgləs'fɝ〕*n.* 花旗杉；北美黃杉
towering〔'tauərɪŋ〕*adj.* 高聳的　　column〔'kɑləm〕*n.* 圓柱
giant〔'dʒaɪənt〕*n.* 巨大之物
diameter〔daɪ'æmətɚ〕*n.* 直徑　　***up to*** 高達

More lumber is produced from these trees than from any other kind of trees in North America. Hemlock, red cedar, and balsam fir are among the other trees found in British Columbia.

這些樹所生產的木材，比北美洲任何其他種類的樹要多。其他英屬哥倫比亞常見的樹，還包括鐵杉、紅柏，以及香脂冷杉。

lumber〔'lʌmbɚ〕*n.* 木材　　hemlock〔'hɛmlɑk〕*n.* 鐵杉
cedar〔'sidɚ〕*n.* 柏　　balsam fir〔'bɔlsəm'fɝ〕*n.* 香脂冷杉

43. (**C**) 本文主要是跟英屬哥倫比亞的哪個方面有關？
    (A) 它的人民。　　　　　(B) 它的文化。
    (C) 它的地理。　　　　　(D) 它的歷史。
    * aspect〔'æspɛkt〕*n.* 方面　geography〔dʒi'ɑgrəfɪ〕*n.* 地理

44. (**A**) 英屬哥倫比亞的哪個地區會出現溫和的氣候？
    (A) 西南方。　　　　　　(B) 海岸的內陸。
    (C) 北方。　　　　　　　(D) 在整個西岸。

45. (**B**) 劃底線的 heavily 可以換成
    (A) weightily〔'wetəlɪ〕*adv.* 很重地
    (B) ***densely***〔'dɛnslɪ〕*adv.* 稠密地
    (C) sluggishly〔'slʌgɪʃlɪ〕*adv.* 不景氣地
    (D) seriously〔'sɪrɪəslɪ〕*adv.* 嚴肅地；認眞地

46. (**D**) 下列何者不是本文所提到，會在英屬哥倫比亞發現的樹？

        (A) 鐵杉   (B) 柏樹   (C) 樅樹   (D) <u>松樹</u>

        * pine〔paɪn〕*n.* 松樹

47. (**D**) 作者在本文中的那個部分提到山脈對風的影響？

        (A) 第四到第五行   (B) 第八到第十行

        (C) 第十二到第十三行   (D) <u>第十九到第二十一行</u>

Questions 48-50

Acquaint Millions of People with Your Products Fast, Promoting on Cable With CABLE Promotions!

Cable television promotion is fast becoming one of the most widespread and effective mediums for advertising in the world. With an ability to access an international viewership of over 120 million households in North America, Europe, and Asia, Cable Promotions is the world's retail outlet of the air. Cable viewers are affluent, consuming and often impulsive buyers and cable television advertising has far fewer regulations than regular broadcast television.

If you have a product that you want to promote, consider today's technology and the potential it holds for increasing sales. Phone Cable Promotions today at 555-6000. Let us tell you how we can help you double, triple, or even quadruple your sales.

利用「第四台促銷」，
快速地讓數百萬人熟悉你的產品！

　　第四台促銷正快速地成為全世界最普遍，而且有效的廣告媒介之一。第四台促銷在北美洲、歐洲，和亞洲，擁有超過一億兩千萬戶的觀眾，是全世界的空中零售商店。第四台的觀眾都是有錢、肯消費，而且是衝動型的購買者，還有第四台的廣告法規，遠比一般的廣播電視法規要少很多。

　　如果你有產品要促銷，就要考慮第四台促銷所擁有的，能增加銷售量的現代科技及潛力。今天就打電話給「第四台促銷」，電話是 555-6000。讓我們告訴你，我們會如何幫你把銷售量變成兩倍、三倍，或甚至是四倍。

---

* acquaint〔əˋkwent〕v. 使熟悉　　promote〔prəˋmot〕v. 促銷
  cable〔ˋkebḷ〕n. 有線電視；第四台
  promotion〔prəˋmoʃən〕n. 促銷
  widespread〔ˋwaɪdˋsprɛd〕adj. 普遍的
  effective〔əˋfɛktɪv〕adj. 有效的
  advertising〔ˋædvɚˏtaɪzɪŋ〕n. 廣告　　medium〔ˋmidɪəm〕n. 媒體
  access〔ˋæksɛs〕n. 接近；取得　　viewership〔ˋvjuɚˏʃɪp〕n. 觀眾
  household〔ˋhausˏhold〕n. 家庭　　retail〔ˋritel〕adj. 零售的
  outlet〔ˋautˏlɛt〕n. 零售店　　the air 空中
  viewer〔ˋvjuɚ〕n. 觀眾　　affluent〔ˋæfluənt〕adj. 富裕的
  consuming〔kənˋsjumɪŋ〕adj. 熱烈的
  impulsive〔ɪmˋpʌlsɪv〕adj. 衝動的
  regulation〔ˏrɛgjəˋleʃən〕n. 規定　　regular〔ˋrɛgjəlɚ〕adj. 一般的
  broadcast〔ˋbrɔdˏkæst〕n. 廣播　　potential〔pəˋtɛnʃəl〕n. 潛力
  hold〔hold〕v. 掌握；擁有　　sales〔selz〕n. pl. 銷售額
  phone〔fon〕v. 打電話給　　double〔ˋdʌbḷ〕v. 使加倍
  triple〔ˋtrɪpḷ〕v. 使成為三倍
  quadruple〔kwɑdˋrupḷ〕v. 使變成四倍

48. (**A**) 「第四台促銷」如何描述第四台的市場？

(A) 它成長得很快。

(B) 它可以寄到特定的地點。

(C) 仍然可以取得一些執照。

(D) 第四台的收視戶觀眾比一般收視戶觀眾要年輕。

* specific〔spɪˋsɪfɪk〕*adj.* 特定的

location〔loˋkeʃən〕*n.* 地點　　license〔ˋlaɪsn̩s〕*n.* 執照

available〔əˋveləbḷ〕*adj.* 可獲得的

49. (**A**) 第四台廣告勝過一般廣播電視的優點是什麼？

(A) 它比較不受限制。

(B) 它的收視戶更多。

(C) 它二十四小時都有。

(D) 它從訂貨至交貨所需要的安排時間較短。

* regulate〔ˋrɛgjəˏlet〕*v.* 管制；限制；

access〔ˋæksɛs〕*v.* 接近；取得

around the clock 二十四小時地

lead time 訂貨至交貨所隔之時間

arrange〔əˋrendʒ〕*v.* 安排

50. (**A**) 「第四台促銷」說它能為廣告客戶做什麼？

(A) 增加超過百分之百的銷售量。

(B) 讓他們和零售店接觸。

(C) 藉由降低成本而增加利潤。

(D) 使他們超越競爭對手。

* advertiser〔ˋædvɚˏtaɪzɚ〕*n.* 刊登廣告者；廣告客戶

profit〔ˋprɑfɪt〕*n.* 利潤　　***ahead of*** 超越

competition〔ˏkɑmpəˋtɪʃən〕*n.* 競爭對手